Scorpion

Truth Sister, Volume 3

Phil Gilvin

Published by Phil Gilvin, 2024.

SCORPION

First edition. April 1, 2024.

ISBN: 978-0995780071

Written by Phil Gilvin.

Table of Contents

1 The Slavers

Clara woke, cold. Cold in her feet and hands, cold in her legs, icy cold down her spine. The dream ebbed away, a dream in which there was a pounding in her ears, a dream in which she gasped for breath in the freezing water until she was dragged and bumped and scraped into a boat...

She opened her eyes on near-darkness. There was no boat, but the pounding was still there, and with a groan she put a hand to her head. A gusty wind was rattling the thin, barred windows above her bed and splashing them with rain. Lights flickered. She blinked, and at last she identified the pounding: it wasn't inside her head after all. It was the clatter of spoons on steel pans, the shouts of the slavers. Morning, it must be morning. Hurriedly she pushed herself up, anxious to avoid another beating. Her legs itched, and she knew that if there'd been enough light, she'd have seen a mass of angry bite-marks.

She hauled herself to her feet and began to roll her thin blanket up. It smelt faintly of piss, and somebody else's piss at that, but it had been better than no blanket at all. Then she stood erect by her pallet-bed, and shivered. The grey February dawn was creeping in through the windows and through the open door at the far end, while the roof creaked and groaned in the wind. Straggling across the hall were three lines of beds and three lines of captives, mostly women, a few men. Someone was lighting lanterns. Half a dozen slavers in warm overalls and warm boots were marching up the aisles, hustling the captives out of their beds and encouraging the slow ones with their batons. One slaver, a grey-haired woman with broad shoulders and a bent nose, stalked past Clara's bed, raking her with her gaze. *Don't make trouble*, Clara told herself again.

She clamped her teeth together to quell the shivering. How many hours' sleep had she managed? One? Two? She thought she could feel the nits excavating her scalp.

That dream! She and Jack had been thrown into the Thames just as the Great Flood surged upriver. That had been, what, eighteen months ago? It had been Tori Shavila, one of the elite Republican Security Guards, who'd saved them, who'd pulled them from the water. Clara blinked. Where was Shavila now? Where was Jack? Not that it matters, she thought with a pang. I'll never see either of them again.

There was a skull-piercing whistle and the captives scrambled to form a queue that led out into the yard. As far as Clara could remember from their arrival last night, the toilets were in a separate block. Yes, that was right – she remembered stumbling out of the cattle-truck in the dusk and hurrying to use them. This place, she recalled, was an old community hall, now converted to a holding centre by the addition of bars on the windows and a thick blackthorn hedge around it. Times change, she thought.

Once they were outside, the slavers made them queue through the wind and the pelting rain. The earth smelt marshy. Pace by shivering pace they edged forward, and as Clara reached the toilet block, she heard laughter. She wiped the rain out of her eyes and glanced to her left: the slavers had got the half-dozen male captives to urinate into the thorn hedge – no toilets for them – and were amusing themselves by shoving them forward mid-pee. She gritted her teeth. *Don't cause trouble.* That's what she'd decided. If she was going to be a slave, causing trouble would only make things worse, wouldn't it?

When she got back into the hall, trembling even more in her now-sodden clothes, she saw three of the slavers bent over one of the beds, shaking something.

'She's only gone and died,' said one.

'That's you, Yardley,' said another. 'That whack you gave her last night.'

Clara could hear the whispers running back among the other captives: *someone's dead – they've killed her – don't say nothing.*

Now the forewoman, tall, with hollow cheeks and piercing eyes, came bustling up. She gave the corpse a prod, and swore. 'Stupid bitches!' she growled. 'We paid good money for that,' she added, pointing at the corpse, 'and one of you arseholes has done her in. Whoever it is, I'll stop you a week's pay. Got that? Now,' she added, gesturing at the remaining captives, 'get these going. We're out of here in fifteen. Lose any more, and I'll personally disembowel every single one of yer! You,' she added to one of the slavers, 'go throw the stiff in the pit. And be quick about it.'

Breakfast was stale bread, chucked at them from grubby baskets. While that was happening, one of the slavers flipped the corpse over her shoulder and toted it out of the door. A frail girl standing next to Clara fumbled her roll and dropped it; Clara gave her her own and retrieved the other, dusting it off with a sleeve. As she chewed, she thought again of what she'd done. It kept coming back into her head. She and her Natural, non-Clone parents had been captured by a woman called Hurn, a chieftain in the Dorset badlands. And who should happen to be working for Hurn but Jack Pike?

The roll was gone. Now to drink. A pail of grey water, and a cup they had to share. The slavers kept watch.

Clara and Jack had history – they were, she supposed, friends who just happened to argue a lot. They'd met when the Scrapers had found her sheltering in a barn, and Jack had taught her how to steal. Later he'd tried to kill her, thinking she'd betrayed them, but then he'd stuck with her for three or four months before they lost each other again. A year later, when the Wessex army had broken up Hurn's band, Jack had been taken prisoner. But then Clara had secretly taken his place, and as a result, she was going to be sold as a slave. No regrets, she told herself. No regrets.

As she wiped her lips, the whistle blew again. Time to go. The slavers hustled them out into the yard, where cold rain spat into their faces. Two wooden cattle-trucks, with heavy-set horses harnessed between their shafts, awaited them; but first, the prisoners were counted. Clara watched the slavers' faces. They seemed somehow kinder, more human when they were counting, when they weren't dishing out gratuitous violence. Don't think that, she told herself. It won't help.

She looked up at the grey sky, then at the drowned fields beyond the trucks. Freedom lay there. Then, even as she had that thought, one of the male captives shoved a slaver to the ground and made a break for it. He dodged around the carts and the horses; he got across the road; he reached the overgrown garden of one of the houses. He was still scrambling through the hawthorn hedge when the bullet took him in the head. He hung there for a moment, then subsided slowly into the bushes. Clara felt sick. The slavers had real, loaded firearms. They could only have got those from the Republic, of course, but every one of the captives knew about them. She could only assume the man had been too desperate to care.

Another whistle blew, so Clara didn't see what happened to the second corpse of the morning. The captives began shuffling up the ramps into the trucks, the slavers prodding and pushing them all the time. The frail girl was in front of Clara, and as she passed one of the slavers she stumbled against her. The slaver's response was to swing her baton at the girl's head, making a hollow *thwock* that echoed around the yard. 'Get on the truck!' she screamed as the girl fell, near-senseless, to the ground. 'Little turd!' the slaver yelled. Her baton was raised, ready to strike again, when Clara grabbed it. But even before she could think what to do next, the slaver had slammed her fist into Clara's cheekbone. She felt her jaw jarred to the right as her left eye rolled back and up. Pain exploded all over her head and she, too, tumbled to the ground.

She was dimly aware of hands grabbing her armpits, of being dragged up the ramp into the truck, and of the forewoman yelling at the slaver who'd hit her, something about "damaged goods". Clara was thrown into the far corner of the truck, where one of the other captives, a short dark-skinned woman, grabbed her hand. 'You're gonna have to get up,' she told her, 'if you don't want to get trod on. Hang on to the window.'

Clara nodded, which made her head hurt so much that she nearly threw up. The woman was right, once the truck was loaded it'd be standing-room only: thirty captives in a space that would normally house a couple of cows. The "window" was one of the narrow openings that ran along the side of the truck, at about cow's-nose height. Clara reached up and gripped the edge then, with the woman's help, pulled herself up far enough to be able to lean against the wall. By now the truck had filled with more captives and there was little room to move.

'Okay?' said the woman.

'Sorry,' said Clara. 'Stupid thing to do. Made it worse for everyone.'

The woman shook her head. 'Nah,' she said. 'Things can't get no worse, can they?' She studied Clara's face. 'No blood,' she said, and Clara winced as the woman felt her cheek. 'Not broken,' she said, 'but you're gonna have a nasty bruise. You okay now? I'll go check on the other girl.'

The tailgates were slammed and bolted. Through the window Clara could peer down at the wheels of the second cart. She could see the feet of the captives moving forward as that, too, was loaded. In her own truck, her recent helper had wriggled through the press of bodies to the other side, where it looked as if the frail girl was just recovering her senses. A whip cracked, the horses whinnied, and the truck lurched away.

The road was a bad one, and the cart bumped and swayed from pothole to pothole. In the big towns, the great

SCORPION

Women's Republic of Anglia mostly managed to keep the roads in good repair, but in the countryside they didn't. Clara remembered that even on the way to Briar Farm, her childhood home in Sussex, there'd been bad stretches. Here on the edge of the badlands, no-one had repaired anything for decades. One especially wild lurch made her bang her head again, and for a few minutes it was all she could do to stay upright. She mustn't throw up this early in the day. Yesterday, two people had vomited in the morning and someone had wet themselves in the afternoon, and then someone else had been sick at the smell. The carts were hosed down in the evenings, but by morning the smells still lingered. She held a hand to her mouth. At least here, by the open slots, there was some air. She had to keep going, she told herself. And, she thought, so much for her vow not to make trouble. Although maybe that woman was right: things couldn't get any worse, could they?

She thought of her parents, and of Jack. With any luck they'd be well on their way into Wessex now. In the note she'd left in Jack's pocket, when she'd hidden him behind the straw-bales before taking his place among the prisoners, she'd begged him to make sure her parents got to safety. Away from the fighting and away from the Republic's hatred of Naturals and of men. And he would, he'd see to it. She knew Jack well enough for that.

Why *had* she swapped places with him? She wasn't sure. Was it guilt? Was it the knowledge that he needed a break in life, he needed things to go well for a change? Or was it to prove – to prove what?

2 Meggers

By mid-morning, Clara's head was still throbbing and her left eye was closing under a purple swelling so big that she could see it with her good eye. The nausea, however, was beginning to subside, and she felt able to peer out of the window-slot and feel a thin rain on her face. The carts had passed through the dense timber plantations around Lyndhurst and were now lumbering onto the old motorway at Ower. Luckily the centuries-old bridge still stood, for it was now the only means of crossing the flooded Test valley without a fifty-mile detour. They were properly back in Anglia now, leaving behind the disputed lands of the middle south, of old Dorset and Wiltshire; and, beyond them, Wessex, the country where Jack and her parents were heading.

It was a Wessex army that had defeated Hurn's people and captured Jack, and, after Clara had drugged him and taken his place, it was the Wessexers who'd sold the prisoners for slaves. As yet, there was no open war between Anglia and Wessex, and money still talked, so trade went on. The sixty-odd captives had been handed over to these middle-women, who in turn were shipping them into Anglia then onward to the slave market at Southampton. Most of the prisoners on Clara's cart had been among Hurn's fighters, but there'd been some mixing with other consignments during the handover at Ringwood. And now, maybe because they'd left two corpses behind, there'd been another change. Now there was someone in the cart whom Clara knew from Hurn's camp. It was the girl who'd brought breakfast to Clara and her mother, Sophia, when they were imprisoned. The girl had escorted them to Hurn, and Clara had asked her about Jack. And now here she was, heading for the same fate. And as Clara watched, the girl, broad-shouldered and dark-haired, looked up and caught her eye. A minute later she came squeezing through the press of bodies. Clara frowned. How was she going to explain about Jack?

The girl reached her. 'Hey,' she said. 'You're that Clara, ain't you? You was Hurn's prisoner. They picked you up too, then?'

'Sorry,' said Clara, 'I can't remember–'

'Meggers,' said the girl, holding out a hand. 'Saw yer getting whacked. Nasty bruise you got there.'

Clara blinked. Suddenly she remembered how sore her face was.

'You seen Jack?' said Meggers, peering around.

'No,' said Clara. 'Er, I suppose he must be here somewhere...'

'Coulda taken 'im off somewhere else. What d'you reckon they're going to do wiv us?'

'I'm not sure I care,' said Clara.

'Yeah, I guess,' said Meggers. 'I've heard rumours, though,' she added, nodding towards the women she'd just been standing with. 'Domestics, they say, or labour gangs – y'know, taking down the old cranes – or shit-cleaners. And the men – well, if Jack's gone somewhere else, he'll be better off.'

Yes, thought Clara, he's better off.

'As for me,' Meggers was saying, 'they can't keep me for ever. I'll make a run for it as soon as I can.'

The woman behind Meggers turned. 'Oh yeah? she sneered. 'That's what we're all thinkin', ain't we? But this is the Republic. We'll never get away. They'll see to that. So don't talk none of that shit. You're stuffed, girl. Get used to it.'

Soon the carts reached the east side of the inlet and turned south, on yet another potholed road that made the axles creak. Yes, thought Clara, Jack was better off. But once he'd got Sophia and James into Wessex, and found them somewhere to stay – what then? Surely he wouldn't come looking for her, would he? She chewed her lip and wished that she hadn't had that thought.

They passed under a bridge and down a long, straight road where Clara began to notice more carts, more riders and even a few pedestrians. Her stomach began to clench: soon they'd be at the slave-market. Further along the road, the wagon was forced to a sudden halt, making the prisoners curse as they were pitched forward. Everyone was shivering. Among the press of bodies someone was crying, and a guard thumped on the side of the wagon to shut them up. Peering out, Clara could see why they'd stopped: a marching line of grey-clad figures. 'Soldiers,' she said, shaking her head. 'I thought they'd called truce with Milland.'

Meggers peered out. 'Nah,' she said. 'They'll be off to Wessex.'

Clara sighed. Yes, she knew it. She'd once met a Wessex army officer, Callington, who'd told her that war with Anglia was coming. And when Clara had said what a stupid idea that was, she'd just told Clara that she wouldn't understand.

'We can't afford it,' she said to Meggers. 'We can't afford to fight.'

'Depends on how much money they've got, I s'pose.'

'No,' said Clara, 'I mean – I mean, civilisation's crashing down around us, and all we can do is fight. The floods are getting higher each year, the energy's running out, there's more and more plagues, and all that those stupid, stupid women can do is try to kill each other. The world's ending, and they don't care.'

Meggers looked at her. 'That's scary talk. But you might be right, and all.' She nodded. 'Still, there's one consolation.'

'What?'

'You and me, girl – we're not gonna live long enough to find out.'

Repsegs in rain-capes waved them through the town gates. The wagons pitched and jolted over the uneven road, passing a few dilapidated houses that huddled by the roadside as if sheltering from the rain. Then further on, they came upon a Closed Area, a zone of houses and shops that had been abandoned at the end of the twenty-first century, when the plagues came and the population crashed. Just as in London, there was a notice threatening trespassers with death.

After another mile the wagon slowed again, and eventually halted. Clara could smell salt on the wind.

'What's going on?' said Meggers.

'Traffic,' said Clara. 'We're in the middle of town.'

They looked out on a busy sidewalk, where women pushed and dodged their way along the crowded shopfronts and between the sturdy market-stalls.

Meggers whistled. 'Never been nowhere as big as this before,' she said. 'Where're they all going?'

They lurched twenty yards onward, then halted next to a news stand that sold *The Republican Woman*. Here the vendor had scrawled a couple of placards that read "Wessex Atrocities", and "Gen Clark Daughter Missing".

The woman next to Meggers shook her head. 'Who cares if the fucker's daughter's missing?' she growled. 'What's it to us?'

'Who's Gen Clark?' said Clara.

The woman swore again. 'Gen-er-al Clark, stupid. Chair of the bloody military council. The boss. Top bitch, ain't she? I tell ya, if I was her daughter, I'd go missing too.'

But Clara had spotted another placard, made grubby by the collisions of muddy boots and by splashes of rain. "Naturals to be Unbarred", it said.

She nudged Meggers. 'Look,' she said. 'They're going to make Naturals legal again!'

Meggers laughed. 'Like, big deal. Clones is all weird anyway.'

Clara looked at her. Of course, she supposed, if you'd grown up outside Anglia, like Meggers had, you wouldn't know much about cloning. But if you were a girl who for fifteen years had thought herself a Clone, and then discovered that your parents had really mated, and that you were natural-born, you'd know a lot more. Since then, Clara had discovered that the cloning labs were failing, despite the Republic's desperate efforts to maintain them. And now the government were more or less admitting it.

Further down the wagon, something flew in through the window. At the same time, Clara became aware of jeering. On the sidewalk, a bunch of young girls had spotted the carts and were yelling and laughing at the prisoners. 'Trash! Trash!' they were shouting. One of them held a bucket, from which the others were grabbing handfuls of something and flinging it through the window-slots. By the disgusted cries coming from the captives, whatever they were throwing was unsavoury. Rotten food, thought Clara, and for a moment she thought she could smell rancid fish. But then she was hit in the face by a gobbet of excrement. Cursing, she scooped some off and tried to throw it back at the jeering girls, but then they started throwing stones. It was only when the slavers jumped down from the wagon and threatened them that they dispersed. As the cart rolled away, Clara wiped her face and neck with her hand. She scraped the excrement onto the side of the wagon, but the stench was everywhere, and her hands stank, and her clothes stank. She kicked the wall in frustration.

It was only as her anger subsided that she realised the other prisoners had gone quiet. Giving her face a final wipe with her sleeve, she turned to Meggers.

'What's happened?' she asked.

Meggers was peering out of the window-slot. 'We're here,' she said, her voice quivering.

SCORPION

Looking out, Clara could see a large, rusted sign with red lettering: *Labour Exchange*. The Republic never changes, she thought. Never call a thing by its real name. This is the slave market.

'D'you think she was right?' asked Meggers, and Clara saw that she was fidgeting with her sleeve and breathing hard. 'That woman, earlier. She said we'd never get away.'

Before she knew what she was doing, Clara had reached out and put a hand on Meggers' arm. A proper Truth Sister, a true daughter of the clone-infested Republic, would never have done something so impure as to voluntarily touch someone. So, she thought, here's one in the eye for the Republic. They haven't won, because I'm free.

She looked out at the sign, its words like blood in the grey drizzle. I'm free of all the lies, she told herself. But it'd be good to be really free, free like Mother and Father. And Jack. Briefly, she wondered what he thought of her now. Not stuck-up any more, maybe. Heroic? Stupid? But she pushed the thought away. If I do get out, she thought, if I ever get free, I'll try and stop the war. If everyone rises up, maybe we can overthrow the government...

But then she sneered at herself. She knew it could never be. The government were too strong. And as the wagon rolled forward and the great steel gates clanged shut behind them, she had to grab the edge of the window. Her legs were giving way.

3 The Labour Exchange

There was a murmur among the prisoners as the wagon rolled down the short road and onto a broad concrete apron. No-one was crying now, but all the faces that Clara could see were pale and tense. Meggers was hugging herself and muttering. Back in the depths of the wagon there was a scuffle, and Clara heard voices saying 'Stop!' and 'Leave her alone!'

Surely there's no point in fighting now, she thought. Looking out, she could see that the Labour Exchange was an open area about two hundred yards square, surrounded by tall wire fences. Just ahead, three more wagons queued in front of an inner enclosure where women in glistening rain-capes were supervising the unloading.

Meggers banged a fist on the wall. 'Why are we waiting?' she moaned. 'Why can't we just get on with it?'

But they did have to wait, for another half-hour, while the wind blew and the rain splashed in through the window-slots. Then the wagon rumbled forward for the last time. The bolts were drawn, then the slavers flung the doors open and urged the prisoners out, thumping on the sides of the wagon and shouting abuse. As Clara climbed down, her legs stiff and her back sore, she overheard the chief slaver arguing with one of the marketeers about the two prisoners who'd been "lost". The people who they'd murdered.

The captives were driven along a narrow, caged walkway before emerging into a circular enclosure, where the rainwater stood in wide puddles and mud collected at the drain covers. The cries and squeals from the women behind gave Clara just a second's warning before she was almost knocked off her feet by a powerful jet of water. She yelled and tried to dodge the jet, but then she noticed that the two women who plied the hoses were laughing and picking out anyone who tried to run. They'd had hosings-down before, but never with anything at this pressure, and some of the captives lost their footing and slithered to the floor. Clara decided to make the best of it – after all, she did need to clean the excrement off – so she stood where she was and made a show of washing herself. Her tunic and trousers, too, she pretended to clean, and when the jet played on her again, it passed quickly. She saw that Meggers was following her example.

The hoses stopped and the laughter subsided, until the only sounds came from the busy drains and the shivering prisoners. The slavers drove them on again. Clara saw the frail girl slumped on the ground in a pool of water. She reached her before the slavers could, and helped her up. 'Keep moving,' she told her. The girl nodded, her brown eyes huge in a skeletal face.

Finally, they were counted into a large brick-walled pen. A school-teachery woman with a Labour Exchange badge and a clipboard was taking some paperwork from an overalled slaver.

'Make the most of these,' the overalled one was saying, pointing at the paperwork. 'I heard the army's coming in next week. That might cut the routes off.'

The other looked at her over the top of her glasses. 'Why?' she said.

'Why? 'cause they reckon there's gonna be war. Sort out Wessex.'

Their own slaver now came up and handed over her paperwork. By now Clara had been moved further down the pen, past a short tower where two guards toted rifles. At the far end was a platform, five feet above the ground, with a low brick shelter built on top, looking for all the world like the stage in a theatre. Under its tiled roof a brazier glowed, and although they couldn't reach it, the prisoners huddled forward, watching as the smoke rolled out from under the roof and blew away on the wind. Overhead, gulls wailed.

Next, three women in blue caps and overalls came into the pen and, waving heavy batons, separated the men – there were only five left – into one corner. This done, they marched them out through a second gate.

'Sex slaves,' said Meggers. 'They'll go to pervy rich women.'

'Pervy?' asked Clara.

'Sex mad, like. Mind you,' she sneered, 'who'd be interested in men? What do they see in 'em?'

'Well,' said Clara, thinking of her parents, 'isn't that the way it used to be? Women and men, mating?'

'Whatever. But men, they're second rate, ain't they? Come and gone in a minute.' She looked at Clara. 'You ever been attracted to a man?'

'Oh!' said Clara. And she thought, and thought, and realised the nearest she'd come to being attracted to anyone was when Bella had once kissed her. Bella, and her paintings of men... Last she'd heard, Bella had gone back to her mother's place, in Kent. She hoped she was still okay. Out loud she said, 'No. I've never really thought about it. How about you?'

Meggers shook her head. 'No. There've been some women, though. But I never – it was just in my head, like.' She put a hand to her face. 'Won't get much chance now,' she added, stifling a sob.

Clara patted her shoulder.

'I hope we get picked together,' sniffed Meggers. 'I mean,' she added quickly, 'it'd be good to know someone.'

Clara didn't know what to say to that.

And now the prisoners waited. The wind blew colder, and their sodden clothes didn't dry out because the rain returned in squalls. There was a smell of mud and clogged drains. Hugging herself, Clara tried to imagine sitting by a roaring fire, with her clothes drying on the fireguard while she snuggled into a blanket with a mug of Sussex cocoa in her hands. But the sounds of her companions' groans, and of their chattering teeth, drove the image away. Then, from away to her right, she heard the metallic clang of gates. A moment later, marching onto the platform came a dozen women dressed in raincoats and thick boots. One or two went to warm themselves at the brazier while the rest stood above the pit and surveyed the prisoners.

'The buyers,' somebody said.

Following them came a tall woman in a dripping cape, a scarlet coat and a broad-brimmed hat. She shook out the cape and joined the others as they looked down on the captives. Clara saw that her cheeks were as red as the coat, and she wore – even in January – a yellow flower in her lapel.

A leather coin-bag hung from one shoulder and she carried a silver-tipped cane.

She looked across the prisoners' heads. 'Haba!' she called in a strong, high voice. Clara turned to see that the clipboard woman had entered the pit, together with four of the blue-overalled muscle-women. *Security*, read their badges. 'Coastforce want one,' the auctioneer went on. 'They've lost another.'

The woman nodded and wrote something on her clipboard, bending over it to keep the rain off.

'Well, here we are,' cried the auctioneer, turning to the buyers. 'Lay-dies! Feast your eyes on today's special bargains! Unrivalled anywhere in Anglia! High-est quality,' she intoned, 'brought to you exclusively by... the Labour Exchange!' She waved her cane across the pit. 'Look well, ladies. Any questions, just ask. We got strong ones, we got docile ones, we got hardworking ones.' Clara wondered how the auctioneer knew this, then realised she was probably making it up.

The auctioneer beckoned to the first of the buyers, who handed her a slip of paper. 'Roight!' cried the auctioneer. 'Road gang! Six of 'em! Well, take yer pick, friend,' she went on, gesturing at the shivering prisoners. 'Good few strong ones here. Once you've fed 'em up a bit, anyway,' she added, and spat.

The buyer came down the steps and the security women – whom Clara saw had knives in their belts as well as batons in their hands – forced a path for her through the huddle of prisoners. The auctioneer followed, one hand gripping her lapel. 'Ah, yes, nice one there, Ma'am,' she simpered. 'Good muscles on that one...'

One by one the buyers inspected the prisoners, feeling their arms, checking their teeth and staring into their faces, to a running commentary from the auctioneer. When they finally selected a slave, they called the security women, who marched her out through the gate. Prisoners who looked muscular were selected for the road gang, agile-looking ones for the scaffolders (four of these), stocky ones for the sea defences (nine). After picking, there was always a delay while the buyer haggled with the auctioneer ('I'm robbing myself here, my friend.' 'A good slave like that's hard to come by these days.' 'My costs are going up, ain't they, with the army coming in?')

As their numbers dwindled, Clara looked around at her fellow prisoners. Mostly they seemed cold and despondent. A few, including Meggers, looked genuinely scared. The frail girl stood nearby, but her head was bowed so low that Clara couldn't see her face.

'Chemical works,' said the next buyer. 'Have you got any men?'

'Nah girl,' said the auctioneer, 'you're too late. What d'you want men for?'

'Ain't they cheaper?' said the buyer.

Clara felt Meggers shifting behind her. 'Don't go to the chem works,' she muttered.

Clara turned. 'Why?' she asked.

'You die,' said Meggers, 'but you die slow.'

Meanwhile the auctioneer was shaking her head. 'Men ain't cheap no more, friend. We got special customers.'

The buyer rolled her eyes. 'Oh, special bloody customers, is it? Don't they know some of us have got proper work to do?'

'And what's wrong with these here girls?' said the auctioneer. 'Nice and strong – well, some of 'em are. Here,' she said, pointing at Clara. Look at this one.'

With a lurching in the pit of her stomach Clara turned to Meggers. A slow death, she thought. Is this it? Is this where my story ends? She'd grabbed Meggers' hand, and she'd actually felt a guard's hand on her shoulder, when she heard the auctioneer saying, 'We'll have some more men in tomorrow.'

'Why didn't ya say so?' said the buyer. 'You keep 'em for me, hey?' She waved a wad of notes. 'Savvy?'

The auctioneer chuckled; the guard gave an exasperated gasp and released Clara. She found herself hugging Meggers out of relief.

The next buyer wanted ten slaves for a building site, and now Clara and Meggers really were separated. As they took Meggers away she looked into Clara's eyes, and they nodded to each other. Clara watched as she disappeared through the gate. Her own face was wet with rain, so she wasn't sure if she was crying or not, crying for someone she hardly knew. She shivered. There were only a few prisoners left now, standing alone in the chill wind.

There was a commotion on the platform as a stocky woman with cropped blonde hair came hurrying up, panting. Clara watched as the woman took off her cape and strode to the edge of the pit, surveying the few slaves left.

But then another buyer walked up to Clara and poked at her arms, her legs, her neck. 'Hmm,' she said, 'good bit of muscle there...'

'Ah yes, Ma'am,' said the auctioneer, noticing. 'She'll make a good domestic, all right.'

Domestic service, thought Clara. I'll be working in someone's house. Surely there'll be a way to escape. They'll have to open the door sometimes.

'Let's see her face,' said the buyer, pushing Clara's chin up. 'Here, where'd she get the bruise?'

'Hey, I wouldn't touch that one!' the voice came from her right, and Clara recognised the slave-mistress who'd brought them in that morning. She was leaning on the fence, her rain-hood up and a damp cigarette glowing feebly in her hand. She gestured at Clara. 'Trouble-maker, she is. That's where she got the bruise.'

The auctioneer turned and stomped over to the slaver, wagging a finger and swearing. Clara and the buyer looked at each other as they watched them argue. 'Well!' said the buyer, and turned away.

Looking around, Clara saw that the next batch of slaves were at the gates, waiting to be brought in. While she'd been distracted, more of her own batch had gone. Now only she, the frail girl, and an older, thick-set woman remained. The older one was being inspected by the blond-headed woman who'd just arrived. The prisoner eyed her insolently.

'Crudger!' The auctioneer had finished her argument with the slaver. She came hurrying up. A security guard slouched after her. 'Who let you in?'

SCORPION

The blond woman turned. 'Coastforce privileges, love. This one'll do,' she added, gesturing with her thumb.

But the prisoner turned pale. 'Coastforce?' she said. 'What, going on the sea?'

'What's it to you?' sneered Crudger. 'You're a bloody slave, ain'tcha?'

'But,' wailed the woman, 'I'll never get out! It'll kill me!'

'If you don't shut yer mouth,' said Crudger, '*I'll* kill yer, so help me.' She turned to the auctioneer while thrusting a hand into her breast-pocket. 'How much, then?'

'Now listen here,' said the auctioneer. 'You can't come in here and just–'

The prisoner swore. 'I'm not goin' on no suicide boat!' She shoved the auctioneer backwards so that she stumbled into Crudger, before turning and sprinting towards the back of the pen.

Crudger and the auctioneer disentangled themselves, looked at each other and shook their heads. Clara wondered why they weren't trying to stop the prisoner, but as the woman reached the gates there was a *crack* that made Clara jump. Blood spurted from the woman's head and her lifeless body hit the ground, skidding to a halt in a puddle. There was raucous laughter from the onlookers, as one of the sentries lowered her rifle. Clara turned away.

The auctioneer extracted a flask from one of her pockets and took a swig. Then she turned to Crudger. 'They all know about Coastforce,' she said, poking a finger into the other's chest. 'You need to keep your mouth shut about it, see?'

'Well what do I say, then?' said Crudger.

'Don't say nothing,' said the auctioneer. 'Obviously.'

'Still need a skivvy. What have you got left?'

The auctioneer frowned. 'Here, you can take that one,' she said, pointing at the frail girl. Across the pen, two security women were dragging the corpse away.

Crudger looked up to heaven, stamped out her cigarette and grabbed the frail girl's arm. The girl looked like she might dissolve into the rain before she ever made it to any boat. Before Clara could think better of it, she stepped up to Crudger and said, 'Take me.'

'Eh?' said Crudger. 'What's that?'

Behind them, the domestics buyer was staring open-mouthed.

'Take me,' said Clara. 'It's a boat, isn't it?' Then she frowned. Was it really herself, talking like this? To the auctioneer she added, nodding at the frail girl, '*She's* got no bruises. She can be a domestic.'

They stood there in the rain for another five seconds before anyone spoke. Then Crudger said, her voice rasping, 'Fair enough. Come on, then.' She shoved a wad of notes at the auctioneer, who shook her head and fished a receipt out of her pocket. Then, while Crudger turned away to inspect it, she took Clara by the arm and said in a low voice, 'You'll never see the light of day again. You know that?'

Clara had no time to answer before Crudger marched her away. As they passed the frail girl, Clara gave her a nod. Her eyes were still wide.

4 Coastforce

Crudger waved her docket at the security guards, then led Clara down through loading-yard and out into the rainy street, where a second woman was waiting. She was dressed in a grey-green, hooded cape just like Crudger's, and carried a short stick in her hand.

'Wilson,' said Crudger, nodding. 'All right?'

'This all you could get?' said Wilson, looking Clara up and down. Her voice sounded rough, as if she'd been coughing.

They set off along a straight tarmac road that led down to the gunmetal-grey waters of the Solent. Clara noticed a bunch of snowdrops beneath a stunted roadside tree. Spring will still come, she thought, no matter what happens to me.

'You should've seen what else was left,' Crudger was saying as she pushed Clara ahead. 'And,' she added, 'another one tried to run.' She spat on the pavement. 'Got a fag?'

Wilson shrugged. She was of middle height, and her face was pale and blotchy. She had an old scar that drew up the corner of her left eye, and as far as Clara could make out under the hood, the sides of her head were shaved, leaving a rug of thick black hair on top. 'Shot?' she asked.

Crudger nodded.

'Slaves, hey?' said Wilson, handing Crudger a cigarette. 'If they wanna get killed, that's their look-out.' She looked Clara up and down. 'So, what we got here then?'

Crudger glanced back. 'Oh, yeah,' she said with a chuckle. 'We got ourselves a volunteer.'

'A volunteer?' repeated Wilson.

'Said she'd rather come with us than be a skivvy in someone's house.'

'I d-didn't,' said Clara, shivering. 'I just–'

But Wilson was laughing. 'Ha-hah!' she said. 'A volunteer! That's the funniest thing I've heard in weeks!'

Clara squared her shoulders and walked on. She wouldn't play; she wouldn't give them the satisfaction. They could laugh all they liked.

But then she cried out. A spasm shot down her right leg like a burning wire and she staggered, barely keeping her footing. Wilson was chortling again, and waving her stick.

'I *know* you've got a shock-stick,' said Clara between her teeth. 'I've seen them before. I know what they do.'

'Well then,' said Wilson, waving it in her face, 'you'll know that you've got to behave yourself. This ain't no picnic, girl. Volunteering, hey? By the Teacher, you're gonna learn, and learn fast.'

'Hey,' said Crudger, giving Wilson a shove. 'Don't be stupid. Captain'll have us flogged if we don't get her back in one piece. Can't you keep that bloody stick to yourself? Hey?'

'Was only a nip,' said Wilson sullenly. 'Look,' she added, showing the stick, 'it's on min.'

'I don't care,' said Crudger. 'No sodding more, okay?'

At the bottom of the road they turned left towards the waterside. *Millbrook Dock*, read a sign. By now the rain had thinned into a fine, drifting haze that spattered down the pavements. The sky was lead.

Clara blinked rain from her eyes. 'So, what's Coastforce?' she asked Crudger, who was hurrying along a few paces in front.

Crudger half-turned. 'No questions,' she said. 'You're a slave, all right?'

'I just–'

She wagged a finger. 'Enough lip, or I'll let her–' she gestured at Wilson '–play with her stick again.'

Clara glanced behind. Wilson was concentrating on lighting another cigarette, and hadn't overheard. Clara knew there was no hope of making a run for it; the shock-stick was still there at Wilson's side, and she herself was too weak to get far. And, in another minute, they reached some broad gates where security guards waved them through and onto the dockside. There was even less hope now.

Crudger led the way to an iron ladder that descended the face of the dock. She peered over, then beckoned to Clara. 'Follow me down,' she snapped. 'And go careful.' Behind her, Wilson stamped a boot onto the end of her cigarette and, grinning, waved the shock-stick again. As Clara descended the ladder she saw a small rowing-boat, crewed by two women in rain capes and peaked caps. One of them helped Clara off the last rung and into the boat, but as she did so, Clara felt her legs go limp. She collapsed onto one of the thwarts.

'I never touched her!' said Wilson.

'All right, I saw,' said Crudger. 'Hey,' she added to Clara. 'When did ya last eat?'

Clara struggled into a sitting position, and found she was shivering uncontrollably. 'This morning,' she managed.

'*Scorpion*,' Wilson was saying to one of the boatwomen, 'middle of the channel'.

The boatwomen plunged their oars into the water and the boat sprang away from the harbourside. Clara felt her empty stomach rising and falling inside her, even as the boat rode up and down on the swell. She held onto the gunwale. Peering over the side she could see, just a few feet beneath the surface, shadowy rectangles of brick and concrete: the remains of cranes and warehouses and offices, swallowed by the rising seas years ago and now left to decay. No ships could venture this close to the dockside, no matter how shallow their draught. Hence the boat.

Passing further out, they came to the anchorages. They navigated between several timber-built ketches then two naval patrol ships: grey steelhulls, streaked with rust but still maintained and armed with the last of Anglia's resources. Then, as they rounded the stern of the second ship, Clara saw, over the shoulder of the front oarswoman, a low, round-backed shape some sixty yards long. No-one said anything, but Clara knew this must be where they were heading. It was a ship unlike any she'd ever seen before, in life or in books. It was painted a deep matt black, so that it seemed to swallow the little light that fell on it. The prow speared forward into the water, and two electric lamps protruded like great insect eyes; it was broad in the beam and its sides curved inward as they rose above the waves. Forward of the central well stood a low wheelhouse with sloping windows, while from the stern a strange, forward-curved funnel rose, making the whole vessel look like something alert and intent.

SCORPION

As they pulled alongside, Crudger stood up and reached for the boarding-rope. 'Welcome to the *Scorpion*,' she said with the faintest of smiles. Wilson chuckled.

The oarswomen held the boat steady as Crudger climbed onto the rungs that led up from the water, and hauled herself up. 'Now you,' growled Wilson.

Clara staggered as she got to her feet, but managed to grab the rope. Concentrating hard, she planted first one foot then the other on the slippery rungs while the waters sucked and churned beneath. Twice she had to stop; twice Wilson yelled at her. Her legs were trembling and her arms were burning. The hull curved forward and away from her, until at last Clara felt like she was reaching the top. Then a pit seemed to open before her. After the mountain she'd just climbed, she was surprised that the drop to the deck was only six feet. But she could hold on no longer, and with a cry she fell heavily onto the ironwork. She rolled onto her back, groaning. Above her the grey clouds frowned. To her right she could see a gun, an artillery weapon with a barrel as thick as her arm, mounted on a gimbal and painted black, like the rest of the ship. An electric searchlight had been fitted next to the gun.

Then Crudger's head came into view. 'Drink this,' she said, helping Clara to sit up and offering her a small flask. Clara took a swig; the fluid burned her throat and she broke into a choking cough. 'Do you good,' said Crudger, offering her hand. 'Take another?'

Clara pulled herself up. 'N-no thanks,' she stammered. But then she grabbed the flask and put it to her lips again. It burnt, but it burnt right down into her stomach and she didn't care if it killed her or cured her, and this was the end anyway...

Crudger snatched it back. 'Hey! You gotta stay sober. Least, till you've seen the cap'n.'

Clara propped herself against a bulkhead, panting.

'Bit more colour in you, anyhow,' said Crudger, pocketing the flask. Behind her, Clara saw that Wilson had now reached the deck and was talking to a tall, grinning woman with long black hair who toted a short rifle. Once or twice in making a point she waved the gun up and down.

'See this?' Crudger was saying, nodding at the ship's incurved hull. 'The *Scorpion* can take the heavy seas better than anything else in the Channel.'

'I still don't know what you do,' croaked Clara.

'I'll take you to Cap'n Suggs,' said Crudger. 'She'll tell ya.'

This is it then, thought Clara. I'm on my own. She tried not to think of Meggers, of the frail girl, of the prisoners who'd tried to escape. They were all in the past now. So were her parents, so was Jack. Everything was.

'This way,' said Crudger, beckoning. As she followed towards the stern, Clara noticed that Wilson was no longer with them. No need for a guard now. Above them, black smoke eddied from the stubby funnel. They passed down a short companionway that led to a steel door with a circular window, where Crudger knocked three times. A moment later Clara found herself in a low cabin. Its steel floor was covered with rust-blistered green paint, and in front of her a row of thick portholes let in some daylight. An oil lamp hung from a bracket over a broad table strewn with papers and charts.

'Got this one, Captain,' said Crudger.

A tall, muscular woman with a mass of grey hair was bending over the table, wielding a pair of compasses. She wore a thick sea-smock and heavy boots, and almost filled the room on her own. She straightened herself, looking Clara up and down. 'Looks a bit scrawny,' she said in a deep, gruff voice.

'Bit of muscle on her, Ma'am,' said Crudger. 'Seems all right.'

The captain took a step towards Clara and braced her legs against the pitching of the ship. 'Where did you get the bruise?' she asked, peering at Clara's swollen eye.

'The slavers,' said Clara. 'Uh, Captain,' she added. Better not upset her, she thought.

The captain raised her eyebrows. 'Go on.'

'They were beating up another girl,' said Clara. 'Just for being ill.'

The captain shook her head. 'So, like a fool, you tried to stop 'em.' She wagged a finger. 'Misplaced loyalty,' she said. 'I like spirit, but I don't like stupidity.'

Clara waited. Then the captain grasped her upper arms and squeezed them tightly, all the time staring down into her face and exhaling tobacco fumes. Clara couldn't return her gaze, and looked away.

'She's shivering,' the captain said to Crudger. 'Get her something.'

Crudger rummaged in a cupboard and pulled out a thick, checked shirt, which she threw to Clara. It was far too big, and she had to drag it over her sodden tunic, but immediately she felt warmer.

'Suggs is the name,' the captain went on. 'Been a seawoman all my life. There's no-one who knows the Channel better, and there's no ship better than the *Scorpion*.'

'And,' said Clara, 'what *is* it? What's the *Scorpion*?'

'It's not for you to ask questions,' snapped the captain. 'As it's your first time, I'll let it go, but,' she said with a leer, 'just remember that we've cut people's tongues out before. Understood?'

Clara nodded.

The captain chuckled. 'I'll answer your question, because you'll need to know anyway – we're Coastforce. Keeping the Women's Republic safe. We're not Navy, we got a contract. Republic pays us, we do it our way. See?

'Now listen, and listen good. You belong to me now, but that don't mean I won't treat you fair. First thing: no escaping, no trying to escape, no even thinking about escaping. There's always a guard in the boiler room – an' I bet Wilson's shown you her shock-stick?'

'I know what shock-sticks are,' said Clara.

'And there's an armed watch posted at the top of the companion. We call her Twitcher, 'cause her trigger-finger's twitchy, see? You come up there without leave, you get shot. Second thing: you work. You work when you're told – Crudger here's the forewoman, and there's Vina, first mate. Do what they tell you, when they tell you. If you slack, if you disobey orders, then you're over the side – and in the Channel, you know what that'll mean.

'Third, you never, ever use this,' she said, thudding a thick finger onto Clara's skull. 'Misplaced loyalty like that,' she added, pointing at her bruise, 'gets you in trouble. Got it?'

Clara nodded again.

'Do all that,' the captain continued, 'and you'll get fed. Slaves you might be, but you're no good to me dead. You get rations twice a day, six hours sleep, grog when we've got it. The guards are under orders not to use their shock-sticks unless they have to. And if they have to – see above. All right?'

'Yes, Captain,' said Clara. At least, she told herself, it's not going to be mindless brutality all the way. At least I've got a chance of surviving. But she couldn't stop the churning in her stomach.

The captain turned back to her charts. 'Give her bread,' she told Crudger. 'Then,' she added to Clara, 'you're working. Go.'

'Come on,' said Crudger.

5 In the Pit

Five minutes later Clara found herself on deck, holding a heavy pair of boots. Crudger led her forward to where Twitcher – all knees and elbows and staring eyes – sat fingering her gun. She gave Clara a leer. Facing her, steel steps led down into a dark pit, from which rose a current of hot air. Clara heard a low roaring and felt the deck throbbing beneath her feet.

'Down there,' said Crudger, thrusting a small, hard roll of bread into her hand. Clara looked up through the rain at the rolling clouds. Would this be the last time she saw the open sky? No, she told herself, it won't. I'll survive. That's what I've got to do. Just stay alive.

Then, remembering how hungry she was, she raised the roll to her mouth, imagining how good it would feel to have some food inside her.

But Crudger wasn't going to let her get away with it. 'I said, *down*!' she growled, and gave Clara a shove, toppling her forward. She managed to find one of the steel steps with her foot, but it was slippery with rain, and before she could react, the rest of the steps hurtled up out of the dark. As she landed, their rough edges bit deep into her ribs and thighs. Bread gone, boots gone, dim light, a gust of heat. She rolled down the last steps and hit her head on the floor. She tried to sit up, but the world was spinning and she lay back down with a groan. The steel rumbled under her back and she could smell coal, grease and hot metal.

I could give up now, she told herself. I could just lie here, while people fight and fight and starve and die and the lights go out across the world. And if they throw me over the side, it'll be like rocking in a cradle, up and down, up and down. But then, she thought, it'll be cold. I wouldn't like the cold...and dimly, she remembered she'd just been telling herself to survive. Hadn't she?

As her eyes got used to the gloom – or perhaps because her double vision was clearing – she became aware of the grey daylight that struggled through the three small portholes above her. And there was a different glow, too, flickering and dim, on her left. It came from a square slab of thick glass that glowed orange. And from a ceiling-hook above, a dim oil lamp swung in time with the swell.

Now there were shapes in the gloom. People, two of them. Someone's voice. A hand under her left arm, another under her right.

'You are all right?' a male voice, a dark face just above hers. Black hair, lank and sweaty, glistening in the lamplight. Dark eyes, too, each with a deep-down spark. There was a second man: short, grey beard, wiry arms, close-fitting grey cap. Two men. No women.

'I don't know,' murmured Clara, putting a hand to her head and flinching as she touched a fresh bruise. 'Where am I?'

The man with the cap was peering at her. 'She hit her head,' he said. 'You wait, Miss. Wait for your head.'

The taller one bent to pick something up then, dusting it off, handed it to Clara. His beard was dark and matted, like his hair. 'Eat,' he said.

SCORPION

Food! Clara grabbed the bread and the only thing that stopped her squashing it all into her mouth at once was that her jaws wouldn't open any further. She chewed, she swallowed, and it was almost like she was coming to life again; she chewed some more and found there was coal-grit on the bread. She spat. Then she gagged.

The second man brought her a water-bottle. 'Here,' he said. 'Do not eat so quick.'

Clara nodded her thanks while she slurped. Some of the water ran down her chin. Now, as she finished the rest of the roll, she had a moment to study her companions. By the dim light she could just tell that although their faces were black, that wasn't their skin colour. She looked at the last of her bread, she looked at her hands, her clothes. All black.

'Is dust,' said the tall one. 'Dust of the coal. Is our job here, to put coal in fire.' He pointed behind Clara.

She turned. Furnaces, then. The amber glow she'd seen was coming from an inspection port at eye level. Heat was beating from behind the closed hatches, and all around them the air shimmered. Wonderingly, she realised she didn't feel cold any more. And now she could hear the sounds more clearly: a roaring, like a winter fire magnified a hundred times, and under it, a throbbing, a sound so deep it made her bones vibrate.

'Will she survive, do you think?' said the short one. Clara could see that under the coal-dust, his face was lined and creased with age.

Clara's mouth was still full. 'Mm course I'll bloody s'vighv. You'd look like this if you'd...well, itsh a long shtory...'

The tall one was grinning. Clara could see his teeth, which stood out because they were still white. When he stroked his beard, Clara noticed his thumb was curled back. '*Sí*, I think she will. How do you call yourself?'

'Carga,' said Clara, swallowing.

'Cara?'

She took another swig of water. 'Clara.'

'Clara,' repeated the tall one. He placed his hand on his chest. 'I Xavi,' he said. 'This,' he added, nodding at his companion, 'Hashim.'

The older man bowed. Then the stairs clanged as Crudger and Wilson hurried down. Wilson had her shock-stick.

'Right,' said Crudger. 'Get them bloody fires stoked up. Got to be out of here in half an hour.' She turned to peer at a set of gauges mounted on a bulkhead. 'Come on!' she cried, waving an arm. 'Get moving.'

A shovel was pressed into Clara's hands. 'Use this,' said Xavi. 'Do same as me, yes?' He pointed down at her feet. 'Put your boots. Is important.'

The other man, Hashim, brought Clara a dripping rag. 'Wear this on your face,' he said.

Clara hardly had time to look puzzled before Xavi took it. 'Like this,' he said, passing it over Clara's mouth and nose and tying it roughly behind. She felt her head jerking, felt Xavi's fingers on her neck. While Xavi fetched another rag for himself, Clara saw Hashim retreating into the back of the chamber. She hadn't paid it any attention before, but now she saw there was an irregular heap of something dark, something that glinted dully: coal, tons of it. Hashim clambered to the top of the heap and, wielding his shovel, started pushing down little avalanches that trickled to her feet. All the while, the ship rolled.

Gingerly, for her bruised thigh was stiffening, Clara bent and swapped her shoes for the boots she'd been given. They were worn and dirty, but the soles were strong and the toecaps were, reassuringly, made of steel. While she watched, Xavi donned a thick mitten and then used a long, forked implement to turn the handle on one of the furnace-hatches. Clara blinked in the blast of heat.

'Shovel this coal,' said Xavi, pointing, 'in here. Go fast. You watch,' he finished, as he opened the second hatch.

Clara stood and began to shovel, at the same time trying to follow him. His movements were smooth and strong, and she guessed that there must be big muscles under that shirt. I can keep pace, she told herself. I've worked at a smithy. I can stand the heat. But then she chewed her lip. Yes, she thought, I may have worked at the forge right through that baking summer with temperatures in the forties; but then there were rests, there was some breeze, there was the cool of night. Here, there'll be no escape.

Crudger, meanwhile, had finished inspecting the gauges. She glanced at Clara and Xavi. 'Keep that up,' she ordered, then disappeared up the companionway. Wilson grinned before settling herself on a tall stool near the foot of the steps. She lit a cigarette and sat watching, her shock-stick dangling at her side.

But Clara soon began to tire. She saw that Xavi was filling his shovel then twisting around in one fluid movement to fling the coal down the chute, and she tried to imitate him. But her back and her ribs ached, her limbs trembled and sweat ran in her eyes. She felt stifled under her mask. No-one spoke.

For ten minutes, maybe fifteen, Clara matched Xavi's pace, but eventually the pain and the stiffness and the heat became too much. She stopped and leant, panting, on her shovel. Instantly she was aware of Wilson climbing down from her stool and reaching for the shock-stick.

'No!' said Xavi, holding up a hand. Turning to Clara he said, 'You work. You must work. Otherwise is punishment.'

'Yeah,' sneered Wilson. 'Otherwise it's toasted nose,' she went on, waving the shock-stick inches from Clara's face.

Cursing inwardly, Clara turned back to the coal-heap and resumed shovelling. She wasn't sure whom she hated more – Wilson, with her cruel grin and menacing smugness, or Xavi, for siding with her. Bloody *man*.

Wilson had resumed her seat. After watching them for a minute, she drew out a battered news-sheet and held it up to the lamplight.

'Ten minutes, is all,' said Xavi, so quietly that at first Clara thought she'd imagined it. 'They keep us work, yes, until we reach open sea. Please, you try?'

She was aware of his eyes upon her. She gave a brief nod and carried on shovelling. Her hands were sore and her limbs felt like logs, but deep down she knew there'd be trouble if she stopped. Ten minutes, Xavi had said. She hoped he was right.

SCORPION

There were no clocks in the ship's belly. Hashim kept sending coal skittering down the heap, Clara and Xavi kept shovelling, and the ship kept rolling and pitching. To Clara it felt like an hour had passed before she heard footsteps on the stairs. Crudger made straight for the pressure gauges, tapping each one in turn.

'Sixty,' she muttered, making a tick on a chart. 'Hundred and five... eighty-seven...' She nodded and turned to Xavi. 'All right,' she said. 'Ease off. Just keep these pressures up,' she added, waving her pencil at the gauges.

Meanwhile, Wilson had got off her stool. Crudger turned to her. 'Half an hour,' she said. 'Make sure you're back.'

Wilson scowled but nodded, and started up the companionway. 'Hey, Twitcher,' she shouted up the steps. 'Wilson. Coming up.'

There was an indistinct reply from above, and Wilson carried on her way.

While Crudger took over the stool, Xavi turned to Clara. 'She call up, she does not get shot,' he said. 'We try, we are shot.'

Clara nodded. 'Do we rest now?' she asked.

Xavi pulled a face and shook his head. 'No, no. We no rest. But we no work so fast.'

They returned to feeding the furnaces, but now the pace was slower and Clara could get her breath back.

'So,' she said, 'your name's Zavvy?'

He nodded. 'You spell with equis.'

'A kiss?'

Hashim had descended from the coal-heap and was helping himself to water. He chuckled. 'He is foreign,' he said. 'He speaks bad English.'

Xavi grinned. 'Hey! My English is very good, old man. Is just your ears, they are full with dust.'

Hashim chuckled again and ambled off towards a door at the side of the coal-heap.

'Where's he going?' asked Clara.

'Is toilet,' said Xavi. 'It stinks. We have to clean, but not enough soap, so it stinks.' Then bending down, he began to write in the dust on the floor. 'But here, important thing. Is how you write my name.'

'Oh!' said Clara. 'With an "ex".'

'*Sí*, equis. And you call yourself Clara, yes?'

'Yes. Clara Perdue.'

'Ah,' said Xavi thoughtfully. 'You are lost.'

'Eh?' said Clara. 'What do you mean, lost?'

'Perdida. Is lost. In Francia they say Perdue. Means same.'

'Really?' said Clara, frowning.

'Is true. You no learn at school?'

Then Crudger, still perched on the stool, looked up from her clipboard. 'Work!' she snarled.

Clara grabbed her shovel and bent to fill it again. Lost, am I? She thought. Well, I can't argue with that.

6 Heat

They toiled through the long afternoon, well past the time when the daylight faded from the portholes. Hashim showed Clara how to send the coal down from the top of the heap so that there was always a supply for stoking, and she took a turn there.

Shifting the coal was back-breaking, but at least she could go at her own pace. Later, when she returned to stoking and had to work as fast as Xavi, she felt her muscles cramping. Her heavy shirt was too long, and it stuck to her back. When she wiped her face with a sleeve, she knew she was just spreading the grime. Wilson returned, and Clara noticed that with Crudger gone it was Xavi who kept an eye on the pressure gauges, leaving Wilson to brood and squint at her news-sheet.

'Do you work for them?' she said to Xavi.

'What?' he said. He'd rolled his sleeves up and his forearms rippled as he shovelled.

'They let you watch the gauges, don't they? How come? Are you trying to join them?'

'I? Join them?' Xavi snapped, glaring. 'You do not know,' he said, shaking his head. 'You do not understand.' With a glance at Wilson, he went to tap on one of the gauges, bracing his legs as the deck swayed.

He's just doing that to annoy me, Clara told herself. But he's a man, what do you expect?

Xavi turned back to the coal-heap. 'Come,' he said, 'we must work.' Then he added, 'I no check gauges, ship gets problems.'

'You could refuse,' said Clara.

Just then Crudger came hurrying down the steps. As she did so, there was a loud metallic creak from the hull, and the ship rolled heavily to one side. The pipes rattled, and Crudger swore as she grabbed the handrail. Coal slithered down the heap.

'What's happening?' gasped Clara. She'd heard about ships breaking up in heavy seas. If that happened, she'd be truly lost.

Crudger laughed. 'Don't worry, girl. *Scorpion*'ll take it all. She's built for high seas like this. We got the shape from the Vikings, apparently. It's one thing that men got right, at least.'

'Who is Vikings?' said Xavi.

'Uh,' said Clara, 'ancient history. They came from the north, I think.'

'Yeah,' said Crudger, 'she's right. Men from the north who came to rape and pillage. Nothing changes, hey, *boy*?' she added, leering at Xavi. She looked at the gauges, wrote on her board and turned to the steps. 'Wilson,' she said, 'make 'em work. Cap'n says we might make a run later.' Then, shouting a warning to Twitcher and her gun, she disappeared.

'What does she mean, a run?' asked Clara.

'You heard,' growled Wilson, waving her stick. 'Work!'

'Come,' said Xavi, and Clara thought he might be frowning. 'We clear fire. Rake, move coals. Small clear now, big clear when we come to port.' He took a long-handled implement with splayed-out prongs at one end. 'This is called "clow".'

'Clow?'

Hashim was already working on the second furnace. 'Claw,' he said, gesturing with his hand.

'*Sí*,' said Xavi, 'clow. Use this way, yes?' and he reached it into the furnace. The amber light glinted on his skin. 'You see? Bring out cinders, and ashes.'

Clara tried. The heat was so intense that she could hardly bear to keep her eyes open, and she was sure she could smell singeing hair. She reached as far in as she could bear, and pulled. Red-hot ashes and clinker spilled out.

'Careful!' said Xavi, pulling her away by the arm. 'Watch to your boots.'

He was right. Clara could feel her feet getting hot.

'You burn boot, they do not give you more,' said Xavi. Clara thought his eyes had their own glow.

They fed the fire. Still the ship creaked, and still the boilers roared and throbbed. Clara's throat began to feel sore. She realised she'd been having to shout to make herself heard.

Xavi watched her working. 'Is good. You do what they say, you survive.'

Clara thought she'd better say something. 'And you?' she asked. 'How long have you survived?'

'I am here since autumn.' He glanced over his shoulder at Wilson, who had put her paper down and was eyeing them keenly. 'Shh,' Xavi went on, pressing a finger to his lips. 'Now we work.'

It got still hotter. The ship pitched and rolled so much that even Xavi spilt some of the coal as he tried to shovel it down the furnace's maw. Clara began to feel as if the work would never end. Would she die here? Her face was sore, her dark trousers were hot to the touch, and her legs felt like they were being boiled; her sweat-soaked shirt dragged and clung, and under it her torso felt slick and sticky. It was her neck where she felt the heat the most, and she kept rubbing at it. Then she noticed that Xavi and Hashim had peeled back their shirts and were stripped to the waist. For a moment she watched them. Both were muscular, in a skinny sort of way: muscles bunching, flexing, relaxing. She bent to shovel some more; her shirt stuck again.

That's it, she thought, I've had enough. She saw that Wilson still had her shirt on, but then Wilson wasn't doing any work. She remembered what the Academy had told her about men, that they were all violent thugs, ready to rape you or kill you; and now here she was, working with two of them. But against that, Wilson was still there with her shock-stick. It'd be OK, Clara told herself. Undoing the buttons, she struggled out of her own shirt, the thick cloth sucking on her slimy skin, and threw it down. Straight away she could feel the heat beating on her bare midriff and arms, but she felt freer. She filled a shovel and flung coal down the chute. Another, and another.

But then Hashim was there, his white beard standing out in the gloom. He stood before her, stooped, his hands clasped before him. 'No,' he said, indicating her chest. 'You must cover. Please. It is not right.'

Clara frowned. 'What's the matter?' she snapped. 'You've got *your* shirt off.'

Xavi came up, too, and Clara felt he was staring. She saw him swallow. Yes, he was definitely staring at her. Then he raised his eyes to hers. 'Please,' he said, 'you cover.' He bent and picked up her shirt.

'I'm wearing a bra, aren't I?' snarled Clara. 'What kind of animals are you–'

She broke off, because now Wilson had arrived, too. 'Do it,' she snapped, waving her shock-stick. 'Shirt back on, or else.' The stick crackled in the air.

Clara snatched the shirt from Xavi and, scowling at all three of them, wriggled it back on. It seemed even heavier, stickier and smellier than before. She left it unbuttoned and went back to shovelling.

It was only a few minutes later that Crudger came down the companionway, this time followed by Captain Suggs. As they reached the deck the ship gave an especially large pitch, and Crudger staggered. The captain simply swayed along with the ship, as if she were part of it. She looked around, nodding. 'This one all right?' she said, nodding at Clara. She was asking Crudger, not Wilson. Which, Clara thought, was probably a good thing.

'Seems okay,' replied Crudger.

Suggs nodded. 'She's still on her feet, at least,' she said with a chuckle. 'Like I said,' she added to Clara, 'do well, and

I'll treat you fair. Do badly, and you know what'll happen. I run a good ship here, and a good operation. And nobody,' she said, waving a finger, 'spoils it.'

Clara watched her go. This is the world we're in, she told herself. We're all struggling, and some people like the captain there – well, they're making a go of it. She felt a sneaking respect for that solid, competent sailor.

As for the two men – that business with her shirt! How dare they? And how could Wilson just back them up like that? She sighed and shovelled some more. You're a slave, she told herself. You'll never be free. Considered in that light, being stuck with two mad men didn't make things much worse, did it? It was just another thing to put up with, like the heat and the endless work.

Xavi tapped her on the shoulder. 'Is nearly night,' he said. 'You go take rest. Six hours. Then they bring food. I wake you.'

'Where...?'

He gave a quick grin and pointed. 'You make bed in coal. Is okay, we try not shovel you in flames.'

Clara shook her head and looked up to heaven. But as soon as Xavi had said the word "rest", two things had happened. First, Clara's limbs had instantly become heavy. She could hardly drag herself away. And the second was, to her horror, she'd wanted to hug him.

I never hug anyone, she told herself as she arranged some coal into a dish-shape to stop herself rolling off, least of all a know-it-all man, who doesn't think I can do the same as him, and who stares at me like that. She lay down, and the coal prodded and pushed at her back. She'd never sleep here, surely?

It seemed no more than five minutes later when Xavi woke her. 'Hey!' he said, shaking her by the shoulder. Coal dug into her back.

'Go 'way,' she mumbled.

'Okay,' he said, clambering off the coal-heap. 'So, we eat your food.'

Clara scrambled from her makeshift bed, jumped to her feet and hurried after him. On an iron ledge attached to the furnace stood two enamel bowls – Hashim had already taken his and was tucking in with a wooden spoon – and three small pewter cups.

'Careful,' said Xavi. 'Furnace is still hot.'

Clara blinked. A cool current of air came down the companionway, making the boiler-room feel a little fresher. Under her feet the deck still heaved and rolled.

She took up her bowl, narrowly avoiding burning her fingers on the ironwork. Xavi and Hashim were standing nearby, gobbling their food down, while beyond them, Wilson had been relieved by an owl-faced woman who was reading a tattered book by the light of an electric torch.

Clara sniffed at the bowl. Her stomach lurched. Fish? It smelt like fish. Well, they were at sea, weren't they? Of course it'd be fish. She felt sick.

'Eat,' said Xavi. 'Keep you strong. Later they bring bread.'

Hashim nodded. 'He is right. You must eat.'

Clara looked back at the bowl. By the dim light she couldn't see what was in there, but maybe that was for the best. She took a deep breath, then began to eat. Salt. Pepper. And yes, fish, oily and sour, and crunching bones...something rubbery...she kept eating. Spoonful by spoonful, she forced it down. She had nearly finished...

She retched, dropped the bowl, and retched again.

'Come, take this,' said Xavi, pressing one of the cups into her hand. 'Quick – drink!'

She took a deep draught, only to find it wasn't water. It was grog, and it burnt her throat and stomach and set her coughing. Xavi chuckled while Hashim thumped her on the back.

'You – you bastards,' she croaked.

'Is only food we get,' said Xavi. 'Small piece of bread at midday, and this. Is tasting bad, but if you complain, you get no other. This helps,' he said, grinning and holding up his cup. 'You finish. Helps stop you to be sick.'

Now that it was Xavi's turn to sleep, Clara found herself tending the furnaces with Hashim. His face was swarthy, his white beard covered his chin but not his upper lip, and his cap clung close to his forehead. Sometimes he winced as he moved, and he never quite managed to stand straight.

'We are on patrol speed,' he told her. 'We feed the furnaces, but slowly. This is the best time of the day.'

'It smells like rain,' said Clara, glancing up the companionway.

SCORPION

He nodded. 'Yes, it often rains at sea.' Peering at her through the gloom, he added, 'It would be nice to breathe the good air, eh? They tell me that the night guard often falls asleep,' he went on, looking up the stairs. 'But if she wakes up, she shoots the first thing she sees.'

'I wasn't even going to try,' said Clara.

She noticed the owl-faced guard watching them. '*How* fast do we have to work?' she asked Hashim.

'Fast enough,' he said, handing Clara her shovel.

7 The First Run

The night hours dragged by. Clara and Hashim worked fitfully, and a bleary-eyed deckhand came to check the gauges every hour or so, but otherwise all was quiet. The *Scorpion* rolled and pitched, the wind blew, and a fine rain squalled down the companionway. Clara was silent, unsure what to say. She was still annoyed with Hashim, for one thing; and for another, he seemed too weary for conversation. At one point he broke into a fit of coughing, and she had to fetch him some water. At length Xavi appeared, rubbing his eyes with his cuff, and told Hashim to take some rest.

'It is early,' said Hashim, straightening his back. 'You have another hour. Go back. Sleep some more.'

Xavi put a hand on Hashim's shoulder. 'I am refreshed,' he said. 'Go. Rest.'

Hashim nodded, and patted Xavi's hand. 'You are good to an old man,' he said.

Clara watched as Hashim retired to the back of the boiler-room. Then she caught Xavi's eye.

He raised a hand. 'We speak later,' he said.

They went back to feeding the furnaces, but when Xavi checked the gauges, he found that the pressure was stable. The throbbing of the engines was less noticeable. 'We watch,' he said. 'Maybe one shovel for every minute, yes?'

Clara noticed that Hashim had knelt down in a corner, sometimes lifting his upper body, sometimes bowing.

'Is he all right?' asked Clara.

'*Sí*, yes. He is okay.' As Xavi spoke, Hashim finished his bowing, climbed onto the coal-heap and began to arrange the coal into a bed.

'No beds for slaves,' said Xavi. 'When I get out, I will go find a soft, soft bed and sleep for a month.'

Clara glanced at where Hashim had now lain down. 'What was he just doing? Why did he bend down like that?'

Xavi stepped closer, and Clara tried to focus on his face while they swayed in time to the movement of the ship.

He lowered his voice. 'He pray. He is – how you say – *religioso*.'

Clara nodded, keeping her eyes on his. 'I met a priest once,' she said. 'I had to watch as she was executed.'

He raised his eyebrows. 'You have had *aventuras*, is true?'

There were sparks in those eyes, Clara thought. She could feel the warmth from his body. She had to lower her gaze. 'Er, yeah...'

'Hashim,' said Xavi. 'He is old man. Is ill, dying. All his family are killed. Many years past, his father was teacher in, how you say? Mosque? Guards came and closed it. They took strong people for slaves. He has worked in mines, in forests. He say he has been on *Scorpion* two years.'

Clara tugged at her collar. 'And why did he say I had to put this shirt back on? It's stifling.'

Now Xavi looked away. '*Pues*, Hashim, his religion. To him, is important that women are covered. I think it is so that any man who looks does not have bad thoughts.'

Bad thoughts. Instantly Clara pictured Tesley, the tall, fair-haired man she'd known when she was travelling with the Scrapers, when they were burgling their way across the

Thames Valley. Tesley had saved her life, but then later he'd tried to rape her. Luckily for Clara, someone had interrupted him; but even now she could feel his breath on her neck, hear his poisonous words in her ear. Tesley had had *bad thoughts*, hadn't he? But Tesley was a man, so what did she expect? Never trust men, that's what the Women's Republic was all about.

And yet...and yet, there was something about Xavi, this strange foreigner who smelt of sweat and coal. She shook herself. This was nonsense.

Out loud she said, 'And what about you, Xavi? Are you *religioso*?'

'No, I–'

'Because *you* wanted me to put my shirt back on, too.'

He shook his head. 'No.'

'You did.'

'I – I do not want to say.'

'Please. You have to tell me. We – we're probably going to be stuck with each other for a long time. I need to trust you.'

Xavi swallowed. 'All right,' he stammered. 'You – you are beautiful woman. You sweat much, your – how you say, bra? – is wet.' He gestured down his own front. 'I see – I see everything...' Quickly, he turned away and took his shovel. 'Come,' he said loudly, 'we fix fire.'

Clara stood dumbstruck. Part of her was ready to say, well that's your problem, you typical man, I've got a right to do what I want, haven't I? But another part of her knew she couldn't say that. She couldn't say it, because he'd called her a beautiful woman, and she'd never even been called a woman, let alone a beautiful one, before. Her throat felt tight.

Words, though, she told herself, they're just words. Take no notice. He's flattering me, he's smarmy, just like Tesley was. But then, she wondered, why would he do that? We're slaves, there's nothing he can do to me here, is there? Not when we're guarded all the time. She remembered the look on his face earlier as he turned away, a look as if he were pleading. Was he – could he have been – embarrassed? And, she thought, if he really had been like Tesley, he'd have sided with me, and let me leave my shirt off, then he could have ogled me all he wanted. I don't get it. How does all this work?

'Hey.' Xavi held out her shovel. 'We work.'

'Right,' said Clara. Just now, she could think of nothing else to say.

Luckily, Xavi had decided that talking was the best thing to do. 'Sometimes,' he said, glancing at her for perhaps too long, 'we work much at night. Ship stops, one hour, maybe two. Other times we sail in open sea – make speed, hit things.'

Clara paused. '*Hit* things? What do you mean?'

Now she thought he was pretending to concentrate on the shovelling, even though they were supposed to be going slower. '*No lo sé*. I do not know. Maybe is, how you say, rubbish. Fall from ships...'

Clara resumed her shovelling. There was something he wasn't telling her. Well, that might stop her from thinking about those eyes of his. He's a liar, a deceiver. A man. She worked on, blinking the tears from her eyes and feeling the shirt clinging to her back, and the dust in her pores, and her life slipping away into black nothingness in this hole, in this pit in the company of a religious maniac, a liar, and a guard with a shock-stick.

She looked up to find Xavi standing before her.

He reached out and tugged at her sleeve. 'We can change,' he said.

Clara frowned. 'What?'

'Your *camisa*. Is too big for you. Mine, she is smaller. You take mine, I take yours.'

She frowned still more. 'Oh, now you want me to take my shirt off?'

He shrugged. 'You said you no like to wear,' he said slowly. 'Is okay,' he added, turning away, 'you keep.'

Clara thought fast. He only wants to swap, she thought. He hasn't changed his mind, he just... is he being kind?

'Wait,' she said. 'All right. Uh, thank you.'

Xavi nodded. 'Is better.'

She watched as he removed his own shirt, his smooth chest glistening in the amber light. He held it out and cocked his head to one side.

'Oh!' she said. 'Yes. Right.' She took his shirt and, turning her back, slipped out of her own. Again, she felt the heat from the furnaces on her skin. She threw her shirt to Xavi then struggled into his. She sniffed at it: like her own, it smelt strongly of coal. What had she expected?

She couldn't help staring as Xavi wriggled into her shirt. It did fit him better, she thought.

He didn't fasten it, but came up to her. 'You can tie,' he said, pointing at the ends of the shirt she was now wearing.

'What?'

He looked her in the eyes. 'Is okay if I show?'

She swallowed, and nodded.

Gently, he took the ends of her shirt. She found herself swaying with him, in time to the ship's movements. Looking down, she saw that he was tying the ends of the shirt together, so that it sat a little higher over her waist. The air could get to her midriff and she felt a little freer. His fingers brushed against her skin.

'Thank you,' she whispered, looking into those eyes again.

He just nodded and turned back to his work.

Clara realised her heart was beating faster. Cursing, she grabbed her shovel.

Somehow she'd got back on rest break. This time it was Hashim who woke her, prodding his knuckles into her shoulder.

'Whasser time?' Clara mumbled.

Hashim's face was in shadow. 'You must come,' he said. 'Orders.'

'Haven't had my hours,' muttered Clara as she forced her aching back into movement. Scrambling to her feet, she sensed a bustle in the boiler-room. Crudger had just clattered down the companionway and was talking rapidly to Xavi, who was feeding one of the furnaces. Shouts came from the deck above. Even Wilson had stirred from her post and was calling a question up to a crewmate. Under Clara's feet the floor trembled and the engines boomed. The ironwork groaned as the ship beat its way through the waves.

She noticed that Hashim was back at his accustomed task of pushing coal down the heap. The heap was diminishing, and briefly she wondered how they'd get more. Would they go back to port? Would that mean a chance to escape?

Xavi motioned her to join him. 'We make big fire,' he said. 'Must work now.'

Clara nodded and began shovelling. She looked down at her shirt, tied by Xavi's hands. The furnaces roared. Crudger ran up the steps and down again, and called something through a speaking-tube.

'What's happening?' Clara asked.

'Is a run,' said Xavi. He was wearing a facecloth again, and sweat was rolling down his face. His chest glistened.

'A run?'

'Ship make speed. You see.'

Clara soaked a facecloth for herself. As she tied it, she staggered forward and back, because under her feet the deck was rolling more than ever. She and Xavi found it difficult to work, and once she spilt a shovelful of coal as the deck dropped away beneath them and the ship's screws screamed. Behind Clara on the coal-heap, Hashim slithered and slipped as he strove to keep the coal rolling down.

Clara began to feel sick. 'Why are we going so fast?' she panted.

An order – Clara couldn't make out the words – was called down to Crudger. The engines roared again.

Then there was a shock and, from somewhere under the hull, a loud *clang*. Clara was pitched forward, and instinctively she held out the shovel to keep herself away from the scorching furnace. As she recoiled, she lost her balance and toppled back. Xavi was on the floor too, and coal was spilling all around them.

'What is it?' Clara cried, struggling to her feet. 'Have we hit a rock?'

'Work!' shouted Crudger.

The ship surged forward again, then turned rapidly to starboard. Another shock came, smaller this time. Wilson swore, but from the deck above came a cheer. 'Good one!' someone cried.

Now the engines eased hard back and the roaring dwindled.

'Keep at it,' said Crudger.

There was a thumping on the hull, as if something was dragging. Clara heard the crackle of a shock-stick and then, to her horror, a scream. She stopped shovelling and stood open-mouthed. Another scream came, and laughter from the crew above.

'What's happening?' Clara gasped.

Xavi shook his head at her, then waved a hand as if to say no, I'll tell you later.

'Ease off,' Crudger told them, then hurried up the steps.

The ship rode quietly on the swell. A gull cried. Xavi dropped his shovel and went to get a drink.

Clara followed. 'Are we on a warship?' she asked. 'The captain said it was some kind of patrol boat. Something about a contract. She didn't say we were in the navy.'

Xavi glugged his water back and turned away.

'What's going on?' said Clara. 'I didn't think we'd be fighting. Hey!' she said, grabbing his arm. 'I'm talking to you.'

He turned, and Clara was surprised to see pale tears on his dusty cheeks.

'What is it?' she said. 'What's going on?'

'Oi!' came a voice. 'Too many questions!'

Clara spun. Crudger had reappeared. She marched up to Clara, wagging a finger. Wilson was following, shock-stick in hand.

'What did the captain tell you?' growled Crudger. 'About using *this*?' And she poked her finger into Clara's forehead.

Clara swallowed, but said nothing.

'Any more lip, girl, any more trying to be a smartarse, and I'll let Wilson loose. And believe me, when she gets going with that thing, I can't stop her. Ain't that right, Wilson?'

Wilson chuckled. 'Yeah,' she said, leering. 'I can do you,' she said, making the electrode crackle in front of Clara's face, 'or I can do *him*!' Suddenly she swung the shock-stick down in the direction of Xavi's genitals. She didn't make contact, but he still recoiled, stumbled over some coal and landed on his back. Wilson guffawed.

'You've been working all right so far, new girl,' said Crudger. 'Don't spoil it. And if the shock-stick don't teach yer, there's always the sudden swimming lesson.' She jerked a thumb in the direction of the deck.

The speaking-tube sounded. Crudger answered it, then turning to Wilson she said, 'They're bringing up the proofs. Keep an eye on this one.'

'With pleasure,' said Wilson.

8 Keeping the Republic Safe

The *Scorpion* resumed patrol speed. In the corner of the boiler room Hashim prayed again, but it seemed to Clara there was a new desperation in his bowing and his rising. When she turned to Xavi, he insisted she finish her rest break. 'Is your turn,' he said, but he wouldn't catch her eye.

Clara was too exhausted to argue. She threw herself down on the coal but, despite her weariness, sleep wouldn't come. What had just happened? She'd heard screams, but there'd been no fighting, no gunfire, so it wasn't some kind of battle. And it had been over too quickly. She tried to make sense of it all: the ship's frantic speed, those impacts, the thuds on the side of the ship, the shock-sticks and the screams. What was the *Scorpion* up to?

And then there was Xavi. He knew what was going on, she was sure of it. But he'd been crying, hadn't he? So, he wasn't just being a dishonest liar of a man. Whatever it was, it was something he couldn't face talking about.

She frowned. Xavi seemed kind and thoughtful, in a way that reminded her of James, her father. He'd given up some of his rest for Hashim, and then, seeing how annoyed Clara had been with her shirt, he'd sorted something out for her. But there was something else, wasn't there? His touch as he'd tied the shirt for her, the heat radiating from his body, those sparks in his eyes... She swallowed. There was a stirring in her stomach that wasn't seasickness.

She was dreaming, dreaming about the dead bodies that she and Sophia had found floating in Keyhaven lagoon, the night that the smuggler, Khan, had helped them escape from Wight. Dead faces, bloated flesh, ragged shirts, and limbs that tangled around their oars... someone was shaking her again...

It was Hashim, and as Clara stirred, she registered that he was breathing harder than ever and clutching a fist to his chest. 'Come,' he gasped.

She struggled to her feet, and again there was noise and bustle from the deck above. 'Is it another run?' she asked. As before, the *Scorpion* was pounding through the water, lurching over the waves, while the great beast of an engine roared and howled in its cage beneath.

Hashim nodded and coughed. 'Yes,' he said, and scrambled onto what remained of the coal-heap.

Soaking her face-cloth again, Clara hurried to help Xavi. Crudger was there, too, reporting the gauge readings down the speaking-tube. The owl-faced woman was there, holding onto the stair-rail, her jaws clamped shut. Above, the row of portholes showed dim and grey. Day was coming.

Now Crudger was shouting something at them, but Clara didn't need to listen. Whatever it was, it meant work. She grabbed her shovel. Xavi nodded briefly at her before returning to his work. She thrust her shovel into the heap – her back was stiff – she turned and flung coal into the flames – her back hurt. The hurt grew worse with every thrust and twist, and the furnace heat beat upon her face and hands. Dust filled the air.

SCORPION

'Range five hundred,' somebody yelled down the speaking-tube. Clara could hear it even above the roar of the furnaces. She braced herself. The guard was hanging desperately on to the stair-rail, but she still held her shock-stick.

Light flickered from the deck: the searchlight was swinging out to sea. Now came an impact, abrupt and sickening. This time Clara was ready and she flung herself to her left, away from the furnace-doors, as the *Scorpion* juddered and the engine screamed. The guard had fallen and rolled under the staircase. Clara tried to listen. This time she heard no screams, but – what was it? A splintering, cracking sound. Bangs and scrapes came from deep under the hull.

There was no let-up. Crudger signalled for them to continue stoking, and the *Scorpion* turned in a wide circle. This time the impacts were smaller, mere bumps among the waves, and Clara could make out cheers from the deck.

At last, the engine throttled back to a murmur, and Crudger told Xavi to choke the furnaces. As the noise subsided Clara could hear voices. Not just the crew's voices, but others, raised in anger, in pleading. She could make out no words. Then, a rifle-shot rang out.

She slumped among the coals. They were killing people out there, weren't they? And she was helping them. She was a murderer! So was Xavi, so was Hashim. Beside her, Xavi had dropped to his knees, face in hands.

Something dripped from Clara's chin. Her tears had run under the facecloth.

'All right,' Crudger called. 'Less of that, back to work now. It's low steam,' she added. 'Got to refuel.'

Clara hauled herself to her feet. She couldn't stop them, could she? They'd kill her if she tried. And yet, she couldn't stand by and do nothing...

Hashim came to relieve Xavi. She saw him place a gentle hand on the young man's back and send him off to rest. Xavi's head was bowed.

For a while, Clara and Hashim worked in silence. She decided she'd try to do more than her fair share of work, from time to time adding an extra shovelful for him. He looked crumpled.

Food came, a small chunk of bread each. Hashim took Xavi's portion to him, then returned and bowed his head. His lips moved.

'Are you praying?' asked Clara.

Hashim looked at her for a moment, then nodded. 'Be mindful of time,' he said, peering at her. 'Use your anger,' he went on, 'to create, not to destroy.'

'What about you?' Clara asked. 'Are *you* angry?'

'Of course,' Hashim said, nodding. He coughed and spat, then cleared his throat. 'But there is nothing we can do. Nothing.'

Clara added a shovelful of coal. 'Can *you* tell me what we're doing?' she asked. 'When there's a run, what do we hit? Xavi doesn't want to talk about it.'

Hashim took a bite from his bread. 'Have you asked him?'

'No. But he cries.'

'You see well,' said Hashim. 'And you are right, you do need to know. What did the captain tell you?'

Clara shrugged. 'Just something about keeping the Republic safe.'

Hashim shook his head. 'Many people try to come to Britain,' he said. '*He*,' he added, gesturing at where Xavi slept among the coal, 'will tell you his tale. But everywhere there is war, and everywhere there are people starving.'

'So...what are you saying?'

'They try to come to Britain. They cross the Channel in any boat they can.'

'They cross the Channel? With these winds?'

'What else can they do?' Hashim was saying. 'If they stay, they starve or get killed.'

'Even in France?'

'Ask Xavi. He knows.' Now Hashim bent to add coal to the furnace.

Clara frowned. At school she'd learned that, long ago, people had been able to sail the Channel, even in small boats, for most of the year. Some people rowed it, and some even swam across. But since searise and climate change, the Channel had become the lair of storms and heavy seas, all year round. In the equinoctial gales, even the largest diesel ships would be driven onto rocks or sent miles off course.

'So,' she said, 'people try to cross in little boats...?'

Hashim nodded. 'Even rowing boats. Men, women, children.' He passed a hand down his face, and Clara could see his lip trembling. 'They are desperate. Most of them drown.'

She knew now. That was why she'd dreamed about the bodies in the Keyhaven lagoon. Those people had been trying to reach Britain. 'And any that get this far,' she said, 'the *Scorpion* runs them down? We run down little rowing boats? *That's* how we're keeping the Republic safe?'

Hashim nodded. 'It is one of the ways, yes.'

'That's barbaric. It's murder.'

'We can do nothing,' he reminded her, wagging a finger. 'Do not blame yourself.'

'But–'

He held up a hand. 'If you stop work, they will kill you. Then they can get someone else. I have seen it.'

'You've seen it?'

'There was a woman, before Xavi came. She said – she said she would not work any more. She ran up those stairs, and Twitcher shot her. They threw her body in the sea.'

'And you?' Clara asked, peering into Hashim's face. Now she was looking for it, she could see his pain and his sorrow. 'How do you survive?'

But Hashim broke into another fit of coughing, and as Clara fetched him water, Crudger appeared down the steps. Clara could see her eying Hashim.

'He's all right,' Clara told her. 'It's just the coal-dust.'

Hashim swallowed, and fought to get his breath back. 'You must never forget the people we kill,' he whispered to Clara. 'You must keep them in your heart,' he said, pressing his own chest. 'Remember them, *there*.'

'Why didn't you tell me about running the boats down?' demanded Clara. It was shift-change and she and Xavi had just watched Hashim stagger off to his coal-bed, wheezing.

'He has not prayed,' said Xavi.

'What?'

Xavi blinked. 'Hashim. Always he prays.'

'He's tired,' said Clara.

'No. Is *enfermo*. Sick.'

Clara peered after Hashim. 'Are you worried about him?' she asked. But she knew the answer, because she was worried herself.

Xavi shook himself. 'You say about the boats?'

Clara found it was hard to be angry. 'Did you think I wouldn't find out?' she said.

'Is clear, no. Is just–' he sighed. 'There is too much of sadness. And you,' he added, 'I think you have had sadness.' Those eyes were on her again.

Clara fought back tears. 'Of course I have,' she snapped. 'I'm a bloody slave.'

'You're dead right!' came Crudger's voice, as she skipped down the companionway. 'And your job now, *slaves*, is to clear out the furnaces. Start with number two, okay? You,' she said, pointing at Xavi. 'You know how.'

Xavi nodded.

'Wilson,' said Crudger. 'Go on your break. These two'll be all right for bit. Twitcher's on duty up there. But if they haven't finished by the time you get back – shock 'em.'

Wilson grinned. 'Aye, aye,' she said, and spat at Clara's feet. Then, waving her stick, she followed Crudger up the stairs.

9 Xavi's Story

If Clara had thought the work was hot before, she now realised she'd been wrong. Before, they could lunge forward, throw the coal, then step back. Now they had to get in close, with the claw and another long-handled rake, and stay working there until the heat drove them back. She and Xavi worked fast, speaking little. They took it in turns to scrape out the glowing cinders and still-hot ashes, while the other shovelled them into a wide iron bucket. To keep the heat off her skin Clara kept her shirt fastened and her sleeves rolled down, and she had to re-soak her facecloth every couple of minutes. The sweat was rolling down her back, but on her face and front it was simply evaporating. Eventually, after some twenty minutes, the furnace was empty. Following the briefest of rests, they cleared the other furnace, then stood back, panting.

Clara looked at Xavi. His coal-dust face was streaked with sweat, and he'd undone his shirt. Clara did the same with hers, but was careful to leave it hanging "modestly". Even her old Academy teachers would have approved, she thought.

'Xavi,' she said as she filled a cup with water, 'tell me. How did you come to Anglia?'

'No, no,' he said, shaking his head. 'You will not like. And is all past now. All gone.'

She put a hand on his arm. Slicked, grimy, muscled. 'Please?'

He glanced at the companionway. 'Okay,' he said with a sigh. 'But then you tell me of you, yes?'

Clara nodded.

Xavi swallowed some water then wiped his face with a sleeve. 'We live in Sevilla. Is in Spain. Was very beautiful but Guadalquivir, the river, sometimes he dries and sometimes he cause many floods. My father was *abogado*, how you say, lawyer? But always the government changes the laws. So, is hard. Then people come from Africa, much people. Some fight, then people from our town kill some Africans. Father he tell them stop but then our home is attacked, with bricks. And then there is flood again.

'My father, he have family in Talavera, further north. So we go there – my father, my mother, brother and sister. On the road we see many *muertos*, dead people, thin like bones. Some have been beaten, or shot. But we walk and walk, and we arrive to the house of my aunt, and then is okay. Is okay for a few years.'

A family, thought Clara. All Naturals. I must ask him what it was like to have a brother and a sister...

'Then,' Xavi went on, 'crops go bad and famines come, and when I am finishing school, bad disease comes. Many people cough and bleed. There is more fighting and no food, so we go north again. My mother thinks Santander is good, because by the sea they catch many fishes. But again there is much war. *Mi hermano* Enrique, he goes to join fighting. Mama is very sad then. And Santander has armies fighting, so we take boat up to France, like many people, until fighting finish. But the seas are big.' He looked away for a moment, and when he swung his gaze back to Clara, his eyes were glistening. '*Mi madre*, she disappear.'

It was still desperately hot in the boiler-room. Clara felt her shirt – that Xavi had once worn – clinging to her again. 'Overboard?' she asked.

He shrugged. 'I do not know. I do not see her fall. She is just – just gone.'

Now there were white streaks on his dirty face, and once more Clara felt an urge to hug him. He lost his mother, she thought. She'd known loss herself, of course, but at least she'd got Sophia back for a while. And there was Jack – he'd lost his parents, hadn't he? So much loss.

'Peace,' said Xavi. 'Peace is what we should have. Just to let people live. But I do not think is easy.' Then he put a hand to his eyes and began to cry. 'All fighting must stop.' His shoulders shook. 'We should not kill people.'

Clara took his hand. 'Shh,' she said. 'I'm so sorry.' Then, on an impulse, she peeled off her shirt. 'I'm sorry it's a bit smelly,' she said, then, gently, she used it to wipe his face.

He shuddered. 'No. No – do not–'

There was a clatter on the stairs, and as Clara struggled back into her shirt Crudger appeared, a dripping oilskin around her shoulders.

She eyed them suspiciously. 'Right,' she said, glancing around, 'I hope you bloody well got them furnaces cleared, you pair of shitheads. And where's that arsehole Wilson?'

Clara caught Xavi's eye, and found herself blushing.

'Hmm,' said Crudger, inspecting the furnace. 'Looks okay, I suppose. Now, I got a treat for yer. You're going up on deck!'

'What?' said Clara.

'I *know*!' said Crudger. 'Soul o' generosity, that's what I am. Twitcher's expecting yer, it's okay. She prob'ly won't shoot.'

Cautiously, Clara followed Xavi up the steps. She resisted the desire to take his hand again. No shots rang out, but what did meet them was a swirling, persistent rain that soaked them in an instant. After so long in the heat and the dry, the wind was like an icy knife. But it was fresh, and it was free.

Clara tried to take in her surroundings – the crew in oilskins; the artillery gun and the searchlight; the smoking funnel; the heave and swell of the sea; the gulls; the foam-topped breakers on the mountainous grey waves; the dark, low-frowning clouds. The world still existed, then, thought Clara. It did, but it was carrying on without them.

'This,' said Crudger, raising her voice against the wind and pointing to a heap of splintered wood. 'Take it down. You're to use it for fuel.'

Clara found the planks were stout and unexpectedly heavy, broken though they were. A few had clearly been sawn through to shorten them.

'Is this from the boats?' she asked Xavi as they negotiated the stairs.

'*Si*,' he said. 'They keep boat name, or keep something to show their kills. Rest we burn.'

Hashim relieved Clara. As she lay herself down on the coal, she frowned. What was going on? Was she actually beginning to feel something for Xavi? She thought back to Bella, and her pictures of men. What would Bella have made of him? She lay back, trying to imagine being close to him once more, trying to remember his touch on her waist. But sleep took her.

When she woke, it was Xavi's turn for rest. She tried to catch his eye as they passed, but his head was down and his shoulders bent. She sighed. Did he feel anything for her? Maybe not.

For this shift the work was steady, and the rolling of the ship no worse than usual. But Hashim spent most of the six hours coughing, holding his chest and leaning on his shovel. Again and again Clara had to help him to some water. Time dragged. By the time Hashim staggered back to his bed and Xavi re-joined Clara, they'd been stood down to patrol speed. Still Wilson was watching them as a cat watches a mouse, and Clara decided she'd try to act normally: she'd have to be content with hearing Xavi's voice. She asked him how his remaining family had reached France.

'Francia has no war,' he answered, 'but people are scared and do not trust. Also they have little food. So always, we have to move on. Polices arrest me twice, and I am beaten. We reach San Malo, *mi padre* he finds house. He pay much money. But one day, I go too near docks and some women take me. They throw me in here.'

'The *Scorpion* goes to France? As well as Anglia?'

Xavi shrugged. 'Is what happen.' He shook his head. 'I will get back,' he added. 'I swear it.'

They looked up as Crudger appeared on the companionway once more. 'Right! Pay attention,' she said.

'In a few hours, we're in port to refuel.' She gestured at the coal-heap. 'But don't even think about making a break for it. Twitcher's got toothache, and that makes her jumpy, see? Anyhow, we'll be in the anchorage, so you'd have half a mile to swim.'

'Well, thanks,' said Clara.

'Just trying to brighten your day,' said Crudger, skipping up the steps.

Wilson, slouching by her stool, spat on the floor. 'And we ain't even staying long enough to go ashore,' she grunted.

'I wake Hashim,' said Xavi. He edged around the remaining coal to where the old man had made his bed.

Clara peered up the steps, out to the rectangle of sky, a lighter grey today. A gull flew high overhead, its cry scratching the air.

'Clara!' Xavi's voice, low and urgent. He beckoned from the gloomy depths of the boiler room.

Clara hurried over. Wilson had heard, too, and followed warily.

'He does not wake,' Xavi said, straightening up and pointing to the shape among the coal.

Clara crept forward. Hashim lay curled in a foetal position, knees drawn up; but his head was turned upward and his mouth hung open. Clara touched his hand and then recoiled. He was cold.

'Dead?' said Wilson.

Clara knew it, of course she did. Living people didn't go cold like that. She'd handled corpses before, a long time ago: a stranger, steaming in the sun on a mudbank after a gunfight on Vauxhall Bridge; poor old Matty, shot dead by the Repsegs as the Scrapers fled across the fields; a dead farmer, in a house on Wight. And now there was Hashim. Even though she'd only known the old man for a few days, she'd begun to respect him, even to grow fond of him. But now he was gone.

Xavi had been feeling for a pulse. Now he slowly shook his head. 'He is passed,' he said.

Wilson swore. 'Stay here,' she growled. Then, calling up to Twitcher, she hurried up the companionway, leaving them alone in the dimness.

'Poor Hashim,' said Clara. 'Look, he's still covered in dust. He couldn't even die in his own bed.' And for a moment she imagined him surrounded by his family – maybe it had been a big one, maybe there were grandchildren. Dying contented at home, if anyone ever did that nowadays. She'd read that Naturals used to have big families, so big they were almost like tribes...and she was a Natural herself, she thought, though she'd never had so much as a sister of her own. Her parents hadn't dared.

A sob broke in on her thoughts. Xavi had been staring down at Hashim's shrunken corpse; but now he'd bowed his head and covered his face with his hands. Clara touched his arm, and, next moment, found him weeping on her shoulder. She could feel the convulsions as he cried, while beneath their feet the deck still swayed and the engines still throbbed.

There was a noise on the stairs. Clara and Xavi sprang apart.

'What a fucking mess,' growled Crudger.

Wilson had followed her down. She stood a little way behind, playing with her shock-stick. 'Be back in port soon,' she said.

'No Labour Exchange till tomorrow,' said Crudger. 'Can't afford to stay over.'

'We could always go and grab another one,' said Wilson, nodding at Clara and Xavi.

Crudger stroked her chin. 'Grab one?' she said. 'That's not a bad idea. You wanna be careful, Wilson,' she added. 'I might start thinkin' you got brains.' Then she turned back to Clara and Xavi. 'Pick that up,' she snapped, pointing at the corpse, 'and follow me.'

Clara and Xavi looked at each other.

'I *said*,' went on Crudger, 'get the stiff, and follow me. Wilson'll be behind yer,' she added.

With another glance at each other, they climbed onto the coal-heap and stood over Hashim's body. Crudger waited for them at the foot of the steps.

'We go up,' said Xavi. 'I take his arms. You, his feet?'

Clara nodded.

Gently, Xavi slipped his hands under Hashim's armpits and lifted him a short way while Clara grabbed his legs. She'd heard how dead bodies stiffened after death, but that hadn't happened so far. He couldn't have been dead very long. Now she had to concentrate as, together, she and Xavi first manoeuvred the corpse off the coal then, bracing their feet against the ship's pitching, staggered towards the companionway. Clara wondered if the old man had woken, if he'd known he was dying, or if he'd just slipped away in his sleep. She was grateful that his head had lolled forward now, because it meant she couldn't see his face properly.

Behind them, Wilson sniggered. Clara clamped her jaws together – even though she wanted to turn and punch the guard, she knew she couldn't do anything, she couldn't say anything. If only there was a way of fighting back.

Crudger had warned the sentry, and now she stood waiting for them at the top of the steps. The sky was grey, the breeze was strong and the air salty. As the ship rolled, Xavi and Clara staggered from one side of the companionway to the other. Once, Hashim's leg slipped from Clara's grip and got tangled in the railings; and when they reached the deck Xavi toppled over backwards, the corpse falling on top of him. As Clara crouched, panting, at the top of the steps, black coal-drips fell from her face.

'Right,' cried Crudger. 'Over the side, then.'

Clara tried to tell herself she'd expected this. People who died at sea were fed to the waves. And for this death-ship, that drowned people for a living, what did one more corpse matter?

Xavi was staring at the high gunwales and the iron ladder that rose vertically from the deck. 'How to get him up there?' he said.

'Aha,' said Crudger. 'The easy way, right?'

'Fling?' said Wilson.

Crudger grinned and nodded. 'Fling,' she said. 'You two,' she added to Xavi and Clara, 'take the legs.'

'We're going to *throw* him?' asked Clara.

'An' if you do a good job,' said Crudger, poking her in the chest, 'he'll clear it in one and you won't have to do it again.

Plus,' she added, prodding the body with her foot, 'he gets to keep a nice corpse.'

Then, grabbing Wilson's shock stick, she motioned Wilson and Twitcher to take Hashim's arms.

'Got it then, you two?' Crudger asked Clara and Xavi.

Clara couldn't believe what she was having to do. Xavi caught her eye, and with a nod to each other, they took their positions. He was right, there was no other way. They had no choice. And to respect Hashim's memory, they had to do it properly.

'Right,' said Crudger. 'Keep hold till I say. Now swing–'

Clara was aware that the other crewwomen had gathered to watch.

'One–' said Crudger. The body swung forward and back.

'Two–' Hashim's hat fell onto the deck.

'Three – wait for it!' went on Crudger. 'One more swing...now!' she cried.

They let go. The corpse flew high in the air, its clothes flapping – and cleared the bulkhead. But they hadn't got enough distance, and it landed with a thud on the curved hull before bouncing off into the sea.

Clara had been half-expecting the watching crew to jeer and laugh, but to her surprise there was just one ironic cheer. Most of them turned away without another glance. One or two even shook their heads. Maybe they were sick of death, too.

As Wilson forced them back down to the boiler room, Clara vomited. Then she was made to clear it up.

10 Riss

The seas grew heavier. Clara and Xavi worked in silence, hardly sharing a glance. With Hashim gone there was more work, and Clara was glad of it. She didn't want time to think, time to remember, time to picture Hashim's corpse flying through the air.

Then, as the last of the light faded from the portholes, the pitching and rolling eased. They heard the engine throttling back, the roar sinking to a low growl. They heard gull-cries, shouted orders, a ship's horn, a bustle on deck. The clatter and rattle of a chain, the *ploosh* of something heavy hitting the water.

'We reach port,' murmured Xavi.

The owl-faced woman, whose turn it was to oversee them, slouched off her stool. 'Going up top,' she announced, her voice heavy and rasping.

'Where are we?' asked Clara.

The woman shrugged. 'Southampton, I guess,' she said. 'Makes no odds, if we can't go ashore.' She started for the steps. 'Twitchy!' she called.

In answer there was a loud bang. A piece of coal leapt up from the heap and skittered across the floor.

'Oi!' called the woman. 'I'm not bloody laughing, Twitchy!' she added, as she toiled up the stairs.

Xavi sat down and gestured at the coal-heap, now only a few inches deep and covering less than half of the floor. 'They bring more soon.'

Clara dropped beside him and put an arm around his shoulders.

'I am tired,' said Xavi. 'Very tired. Always there is dying. Many people at home, they die. *Mi madre*, she die.' He waved an arm towards the sea. 'These people that we, how you say, run down.'

'And now Hashim,' said Clara, watching his face.

'*Sí*, and now Hashim. He was a good man...'

'He said we must not forget,' said Clara. 'We must always remember them.'

Xavi shook his head. 'Soon I have no-one. Soon I have no thing, *nada*.'

'Xavi,' said Clara, squeezing him, 'you've got me.'

He gave a quick sigh, then took her hand. 'Yes,' he said, looking over his shoulder at her. 'Is good. While we have each other.'

Clara nestled her head into his shoulder.

But Xavi sat up. 'Listen!' he said.

Through the *Scorpion*'s thick hull, they could hear an unfamiliar, higher-pitched hum. The ship lurched. Iron clattered and screeched.

'Is coal,' Xavi said, pulling her up. 'Quick, come.'

Clara got to her feet and hurried after him.

'There will be much dust,' he explained as they reached the toilet cubicle. 'This door, it keeps dust back.' He closed it behind them, and Clara's nostrils filled with the lingering smells: the faeces, the urine and the bleach. A little daylight filtered through a tiny, salt-stained porthole. The clattering on the hull became louder.

'Is that why they've left us alone down here?' asked Clara.

Xavi nodded. 'Dust is very small, it stay in air long time. Hashim showed me how to hide...' He wiped his eyes on his shirt.

They were standing very close. Clara held his arm and peered into his eyes. 'I'm so sorry,' she whispered.

Now he met her gaze. 'I am very sad,' he said. 'I think maybe I do not get back to my family. Is too difficult. And if I do arrive to San Malo, maybe they not there. Maybe they move on, or maybe they – maybe they killed already.' He sniffed. 'Peace,' he said. 'We need peace so much.'

Clara couldn't stand to see him like this. Besides, she thought, I need him to be strong, because otherwise it'll get to me too. She shook his arm. 'No,' she said. 'We *will* escape. We *will* get away. And – and I'll help you get to France.'

He bent his head. She looked up at him, and it was like a thousand butterflies had filled her chest. 'Will you – will you kiss me?' she said.

'Okay,' he whispered, and in the darkness they leaned into each other. Uncertainly, clumsily, Clara touched her lips to his, and they felt soft and warm. But they tasted of coal...

A deep clang echoed through the hull. 'Look out below!' yelled someone. 'Coal a-comin'!'

With booms and thuds and a great roar, tons of coal came cascading down a chute from the deck above, reverberating so loudly that they had to cover their ears. Outside the cubicle, the coal rolled and scattered and shifted, and there was a hissing as the thicker dust settled.

'We have to go,' said Xavi, holding Clara to him. 'They come soon, make us work.' He kissed the top of her head.

Clara thought of all the years at the Academy, all the lessons where they'd been taught that men were evil. There'd even been posters, hadn't there? *Save us from evil men*, they'd read. But they were wrong. 'I'll come with you, Xavi,' she whispered, thrilling at the feel of his body against hers. 'I promise.' She forced away the thought that they'd never get out of the *Scorpion* alive. Donning their facecloths, they opened the door on a haze of black dust that swirled and glinted in the dim light. Despite the cloth, Clara could taste a metallic bitterness on her lips. She found she was bowing her head and blinking, to keep her eyes clear. But there was no respite. As Xavi had predicted, it was only a few minutes before Crudger came halfway down the steps and peered through the haze.

'Okay, you two – get stoking! I want full pressure in an hour. Got it?'

'Yes,' called Xavi, and began to cough.

Clara frowned. She remembered James saying something, one long-ago evening as they watched a reclamation gang trudging past: *the dust gets you in the end*. It was probably the dust that had killed Hashim. Was it going to kill Xavi too? Would it even kill her? She chewed her lip.

They stood near the companionway, close enough to taste the fresh air while keeping out of Twitcher's line of sight. Then they re-soaked their cloths and set to work. As the furnaces heated up, new currents lifted the dust back into the air so that it collected in their ears, on their hair, in the creases of their skin. The flames roared. Somebody started the engine and the deck began to throb again.

Then, just as Xavi checked the gauges for the third time, they heard shouts and screams from the deck above. They stopped shovelling. There were crackles as the shock-stick was used.

'Ow! Ow!' a woman's voice, a strong one. 'Let me go! What're you doing? D'you know who I am? Get your filthy—'

Someone – Clara didn't think it was either Crudger or Wilson – was yelling at her to shut up. There was another crack, then a thud on the deck, and something wearing a maroon shirt and dark corduroy trousers tumbled down the steps. It bounced and rolled, then came to a halt and began thrashing about.

'Bastards!' it said.

A young, dark-skinned woman with blue-dyed hair glared up at them. She was plump in a muscular way, with arms that looked like they could hurt someone. Which, thought Clara, was probably what she'd been doing, and what had earned her the shocks.

Clara and Xavi stepped forward help the girl to her feet, but she swore at them.

'Get off me!' she screamed. Then she staggered and sat down heavily on the coal. 'Bashtards. Bashtards, you're all – aww...' she trailed off, and lay back, swearing. 'Mindin' my own business...'

Clara tried again. 'Are you okay?' she said, raising her voice above the engine-noise. 'That was a bad fall you had.'

The girl heaved herself up. 'Pish off,' she spat, then ran at the steps again. 'You can't keep me here!' She yelled. 'Don't you know who I am? Lemme out!'

Xavi caught her as she reached the bottom step and pulled her back just as Twitcher's gun went off, the bullet splintering the coal. The girl fell on top of Xavi and started trying to hit him. Clara pushed her off, ready to punch her if she tried it again, but the girl just rolled onto her side and said, 'Aww, leave me alone. Wanna sleep.'

'Is she . . ?' said Clara, looking down. 'Is she what I think she is?'

'*Sí*,' said Xavi, getting back to his feet. 'She is *borracha*. Drunked.'

'Oi!' came Crudger's voice. 'You two! If you can't shut her up, you're *all* in for a tickle! Got it?'

Xavi looked down at the sleeping girl, then at Clara, and grinned. 'Is no problem,' he called back.

'So what are *you*, ship's captain or something?' It was an hour later, and the girl was squeezing her foot into one of the boots that Wilson had thrown at her. They'd managed to wake her at last, then Crudger had come down to the boiler room to make them work harder.

'Don't be ridiculous,' said Clara. 'I'm only saying, if you don't do as they say–'

'As *you* say,' snapped the girl. 'And what's he doing here?' she asked, pointing at Xavi. 'They let men in, then?'

Xavi, who'd been laying coals in one of the furnaces, straightened up. 'We are slaves. Like you.'

SCORPION

'And they'll throw you over the side if you don't work,' put in Clara.

'Or they shoot you,' said Xavi, holding out a shovel.

The girl snatched it. 'Well, how can you stand it?' she said.

'Come,' said Xavi. 'You get coal on shovel. Like this, yes?' He demonstrated. 'Then you put in furnace, like this. You understand?'

'Of course I understand,' said the girl. 'I'm not stupid.'

'Neither are we,' snapped Clara. If she wasn't careful, this girl would get them all into trouble.

'How are you called?' said Xavi.

'What's it to you?' said the girl.

'If you've got a name,' said Clara, 'we can use that, instead of calling you "stupid idiot".'

'Hey, Clara,' said Xavi. 'Is enough.'

'Yeah,' said the girl, 'listen to what dago-features says. And call me stupid again,' she went on, waving the shovel, 'and I'll rearrange your ugly face!'

Xavi stepped right up to her. 'I said to you,' he growled, glaring down at her, 'how are you called?'

She stared back. 'Riss,' she said, between her teeth.

'*Bueno*!' said Xavi, nodding. 'I call myself Xavi. This, Clara. Now we work, and we work together, yes?'

'Piss off,' said Riss.

Xavi shrugged. 'Is no problem. You make no difference. You are too weak. No muscles.'

Clara climbed the newly-replenished heap and began pushing the coal down. At the furnaces, Xavi's ruse had worked: Riss's blue-tinted curls were bobbing up and down as she bent, turned and threw; bent, turned and threw. Clara felt proud of Xavi, and the way he'd dealt with that silly girl. But then she wished she hadn't been so tetchy herself. I hope Xavi doesn't get to like her, she thought.

For an hour they worked steadily, while Wilson watched from her stool. The pressure built in the boilers, the pistons hissed, the engine groaned. The *Scorpion* rolled and pitched as it emerged from the channel into the open sea.

As she sent the coal down the heap, Clara had to admit – with a prick of jealously – that Riss was strong. She was keeping pace with Xavi, grunting as she dug then flinging the coal down the furnace-chute as if it were chaff. Clara was wondering how long they'd have to keep up the pace when Crudger appeared on the companionway and ordered them to step down to cruising.

Clara's throat was dry and raw. She slithered down the heap and made for the water-stoup.

'So,' said Riss, breathing hard, 'we're slaves, are we?'

'That's right,' said Clara, turning.

'Here for ever, are we?' Riss threw her shovel down.

'Pick it up, girl.'

Riss turned to find Wilson's shock-stick in front of her face. The guard had quietly come up behind her. 'I said, pick it up,' said Wilson, slowly.

Keeping her eyes on the stick, Riss bent and retrieved the shovel.

'You wanna listen to these two,' sneered Wilson. 'You belong to Coastforce now.'

'Coastforce?' said Riss, frowning. '*This* is Coastforce?'

'An' the only way out of here,' Wilson went on, 'is the way old Hashim went. Over the side. Geddit?' And she turned away.

'Fuck this,' said Riss. Planting her hands squarely on Wilson's back, she shoved her head-first into the coal-heap. The shock-stick went flying, and Riss ran for the steps.

'No!' cried Clara. 'Stop!'

There was an explosion from above. Riss cried out and tumbled back off the steps. Meanwhile Wilson had leapt to her feet and when Riss, clutching her shoulder, struggled to her knees, she began yelling at her.

'Try it out on me, would yer?' she screamed, and pointed the stick at Riss. 'Bitch! I'll shock yer! I'll shock yer!'

'Wilson, no!' cried Clara. 'You'll kill her if you do that! Look at her arm – she's been shot.'

Even by the dim candle-light Clara could see the dark stain on Riss's overall and the glistening sheen on her fingers. The girl was whimpering.

Xavi read Clara's glance and hung back. With Wilson in this mood, they were already pushing their luck.

'Bloody well serves her right!' Wilson was shouting. 'She's got what was coming to her, ain't she?'

'That's right,' said Clara. 'She got what she deserved.'

'Fuck off,' said Riss.

Wilson gave her a kick, and waved the stick again.

'Go on, then,' said Clara to Wilson, 'do what you like. But what will the captain say if you kill her?'

'What's going on?' Crudger came hurrying down the companionway. She took one look at Riss, then swore. 'Wilson!' she growled. 'What the hell are you doing?'

'She made a run for it!' squealed Wilson. 'Ask *them*,' she added, pointing at Clara and Xavi. 'They saw her!'

'She needs help,' put in Clara. 'She's bleeding. We need to stop it at once.'

Crudger went to the foot of the steps. 'Twitcher, you nutter!' she called. 'Send a medikit down, for pity's sake!'

11 Crossing Over

Rain and spray whirled down through the open hatch, out of the grey dawn. The wind howled and the *Scorpion* rolled more than ever in the heavy seas.

Xavi was holding on to the bulkhead as he tried to examine the gauges. 'The sea, he is big today,' he said. 'Hmm... we need make more steam.'

'Won't be a minute,' said Clara, frowning at the fresh bandage that she was tying around Riss's upper arm. It had taken half an hour the previous evening to stanch the bleeding, and the dressing that she and Crudger had improvised had been rough and cumbersome.

'Does that feel okay?' Clara asked.

'Uh, a bit tighter?' said Riss. Having been ill most of the night, she'd managed to take some food this morning and Clara thought she looked a little more comfortable.

'Like this?'

'Ow!'

'Sorry,' said Clara, chewing her lip. She hadn't admitted it, but she'd never bandaged anyone before. 'Is it sore?'

Riss nodded. 'Bloody hurts,' she said. 'Could've been worse, though,' she added with a sigh. 'Could've been dead.'

'Is that all right now?' said Clara, releasing Riss's arm.

Riss grimaced. 'Yeah. Thanks.' She flexed her fingers. 'So,' she said, 'what about you? How did they get you?'

Clara chose her words carefully. 'Oh,' she said, 'I got caught up in some fighting in Dorset.'

'Ah,' said Riss. 'The badlands.'

'Yes. They sold me as a slave. Are you all right to do some work now?'

Riss scrambled to her feet and shook herself. 'Guess so. There was fighting, then?'

Clara saw no harm in telling her. 'The Wessexers came in,' she said. 'Said they were trying to clean the place up.'

'There'll be more soon,' said Riss. 'Fighting, I mean.'

Clara looked at her. 'With Wessex? What do you know?'

'Oh, only as much as you,' said Riss, looking away. 'What you read in *The Republican Woman* – you know?'

'It's suicide,' Clara said. She waved a hand. 'The world's ending, and all they can do is fight.'

Riss frowned. 'Yeah. I agree.'

'Hey,' called Xavi. 'Wilson, she will be back soon.'

'Sorry,' said Clara, and gave Xavi what she hoped was a smile. Turning to Riss she said, 'you'd better go on the coal.'

'Yeah,' said Riss. 'I think I know what to do.'

Clara picked up her shovel. 'Anyhow,' she said. 'What about you? How did they get you?'

Riss started scrambling up the heap. 'What d'you think?' she snapped. 'I bloody well volunteered.'

Clara had now joined Xavi. They exchanged glances.

'Just fancied a change, didn't I?' added Riss.

Night fell, and for two hours the *Scorpion* struggled through the increasingly heavy seas. Twice Riss, atop the coal heap, stumbled and fell, and once she vomited again. Clara had to admire the way she picked herself up and carried on.

Whenever the hatch opened, they could hear, even over the roar of the furnaces, the thumping of the wind. And that was loud enough, for Crudger seemed to spend half the time running up and down the companionway and yelling at them to feed the furnaces faster. Clara's face ran with sweat, and by the amber light she could see steam rising from her clothes. Riss kept up a train of swearing.

Wilson clung to the bulkhead, her shock-stick dangling forgotten at her side. 'What's goin' on?' she demanded, as Crudger descended the stairs for the nineteenth time.

'Orders,' snapped Crudger. 'We're crossin' over.'

Crossing over what? wondered Clara. To the other side? Death?

'Never!' said Wilson. 'Won't the Frenchies be after us?'

'We'll get 'em when they've left French waters,' said Crudger grimly. 'Captain's had word – there's a dozen of the bleeders this time.'

Clara caught Xavi's eye. She knew what he'd be thinking: if they were headed for France, and if he could escape, and if he could make it ashore, then maybe he could find his family. And, Clara told herself, she'd go with him. She'd go with him, wouldn't she, through all those improbable chances, through all of those ifs and maybes.

They ploughed on. The seas grew heavier still; waves broke over the incurving hull and water splashed down the companionway. The coal began to shift. Riss struggled to stay where she was, while Crudger, heading back up the companionway again, lost her footing and only managed to hold herself up by the handrail. Then the ship heeled sickeningly over until the deck was nearly vertical, the screws screaming as they left the water. With a clatter, the coal shifted over to the port side, and Clara lost her footing, barely missing the hot furnace door as it swung. Riss and Wilson both yelled.

This is it, thought Clara. The ship's going over, we're going to sink. Xavi – where was Xavi? She wanted to hold him, hold him one last time before the water got them. She couldn't see him through the dust...her stomach lurched and it felt as if the ship was dropping through space, falling, falling for an age. Then, by some miracle, the *Scorpion* began to right itself. It tilted back the right way, slowly at first, then quicker, until it passed through the horizontal and halfway up again, the coal rolling back as it did so.

With a groan, Wilson got to her knees and hauled herself onto the companionway steps. Dust swirled. Riss scrambled down the coal heap, her overalls torn and her bandage hanging off. 'Thought we were going there,' she said, and there was a quiver in her voice.

Clara grabbed her by the shoulders. 'Xavi!' she spluttered. 'Where is he?'

Riss scanned the room. 'He's got to be under the coal,' she said. 'Where was he standing?'

'There, by the other furnace,' wailed Clara. 'Xavi! Xavi!'

They found the shovels and started digging away at the coal in the corner nearest the furnace. Nothing, nothing, minutes of nothing. Coal flew, the deck pitched, and still nothing. Then Clara happened to glance further back along the heap. There was an arm, and it was moving.

'Oh!' she cried, her voice breaking. Flinging the shovel down, she scrambled over the coal. Riss followed, and they dug with their hands, hefting the coal out of the way to expose first the rest of Xavi's arm, then his shoulder, then his face; and to Clara's joy, he coughed and spluttered and spat. He was alive.

Then, to their surprise, Crudger joined in, grabbing more coal and chucking it down the heap. Behind them Wilson was sitting on the steps and clinging to the handrail with one hand. Together the three of them heaved Xavi free, to a yelp of pain.

'*Uf*!' he cried. '*Mi tobillo*! This,' he added, pointing at his left ankle. 'Is – *ai*! – I think it breaks.'

In her relief Clara couldn't resist hugging him, but he winced and held her off. 'Is much pain,' he groaned.

Clara fussed and floundered. She felt like she was jabbering, but all the while her heart was soaring. She'd nearly lost him, and now she'd got him back.

In a quarter of an hour, the waves began to subside. The going was still rough, the *Scorpion* hiccupping its way among the troughs and crests, but they had no more scares.

Crudger ordered Clara and Riss to stoke while she herself strapped up Xavi's ankle. 'It'll have to do,' she told him, pointing at the makeshift splint. 'It ain't pretty, but it'll hold it straight. Keep it on for a few days at least.'

The engines changed tone, and Clara felt the swing of the deck beneath her feet. Crudger noticed it too. 'Got to go,' she said, slapping Xavi on the boot and making him cry out. Then she hurried up the steps.

France, thought Clara. They'd made it across the Channel, and now they must be nearing the French coast. Was that why the sea was calmer? But one look at Xavi – pale, even under the coal dust, and hunched in pain – told her that the list of maybes had just got longer. *Too* long.

She returned to shovelling just as Crudger called down the steps. 'Sighted 'em!' she yelled to Wilson. 'Keep them two working!'

'What's happening?' asked Riss.

'I think we're going to ram a refugee boat,' said Clara.

Riss paused in her work then, glancing quickly at Wilson, said, 'What d'you mean?'

'Coastforce,' said Clara, 'keeps the Republic safe by running down little boats full of people who are trying to get to Anglia.'

Now Riss did stop. 'That's all?' she said. 'That's what Coastforce do? So what happens to the people?'

'They drown,' said Clara, 'and if they don't drown, they get shot.'

Riss swore, then stood with her mouth open, her gaze far away. 'As if things weren't bad enough. She's just making it worse.'

There wasn't the time to ask who she meant. 'You'd better work,' said Clara, nudging her and nodding at Wilson. Behind her, Xavi was holding his head in his hands.

There was a commotion on the deck above. There were shouts, and the squeal of equipment being moved. Clara thought she saw the flicker of a searchlight. The engines pounded, the *Scorpion* leapt over the waves – and then came the first shock, just like the ones before: the splintering of wood, the cries, the thuds on the hull. But this time the ship forged onward – no turning back to finish off the survivors, no collecting any trophies – as its speed built again. Another impact. Riss swore, and Xavi whimpered. Wilson was called up to the main deck. A third shivering, grinding shock.

Clara tried to keep working, she really tried. The tears rolled down her cheeks; she squeezed her eyes shut and tried to block out the wails, the splintering wood, the booming on the hull. But then the ship turned, and there was gunfire; and then a deafening concussion that made Clara yelp and cover her ears.

She felt her arm clutched. 'What is it?' said Riss, her voice trembling.

'Is gun.' Xavi had limped over to join them. He reached for Clara's shoulder, and she felt his hand warm through her shirt as she took his weight. 'They have big gun. Use for bigger boats.'

The gun fired again, and the *Scorpion* recoiled. This time Clara slipped from Xavi's grip and ran to the portholes, where she scrambled up the coal heap. She could see out: some two hundred yards off, between the steel-grey waves and the lowering clouds, a boat – as big as some she'd seen on the Thames – was burning. Figures, silhouetted against the sickly yellow flames, were leaping into the water. From the deck above, rifles were being fired. Clara cried, she yelled, she beat her fists against the hull; she paid no heed to Xavi or Riss.

Then something struck her thigh. There was a searing, shivering pain and she felt her spine arch, her legs stiffen and all the muscles in her body cramp. She couldn't cry out –

her mouth wouldn't work – and she couldn't stop herself falling backwards and hitting her head on the ironwork. She couldn't move.

Xavi's arms were around her. Wilson was yelling something. Xavi laid her gently down and backed away. Dimly, she realised she'd been shocked. Wilson's stick must have been on full power, and now she was paralysed – apart from the twitching, and the pain. She lay in the dust, staring at the black ceiling while Xavi and Riss stoked the fires of hell. Bodies, bodies, bodies. Death, death, death.

12 The Ferrywoman

Jack Pike was weary. His feet were weary, his arms were weary, his legs could barely support him. He'd been fighting for so long, fighting all alone, and now he felt like he'd had enough. Still his feet managed to carry him onwards, down the dirty road that, according to the woman he'd met a few miles back, would take him to the ferry at Bewley. At last, as the early winter dusk approached, he saw lights. He turned up his collar against the spits of rain flung by the rising wind, and hurried on.

He passed three houses set back from the road, then a terrace of four untidy dwellings jostled together. Those were all in darkness, but further on he came upon an inn with lights in the windows and horse droppings in the forecourt. The *Teacher's Pet*, read the sign. At least there were other people still in the world, he thought. Wincing, he rolled the rucksack off his shoulders and, turning his back to the wind, pulled out a map. By the last of the daylight, he could see that if he'd reached the inn, he must be less than a mile from the ferry.

He continued down the hill towards the water. There were more houses now, and a few already had their lamps lit. It'd be good to get across tonight, he told himself, so I can make an early start in the morning. But twice he stumbled, and he couldn't be sure if it was because it was too dark to see properly, or because his legs were giving out. Then he saw, emerging from the gloom and snaking across his path, a broad, dark band that shifted and slurped and glinted as the wind whipped over its busy surface. There was a cold smell of decayed leaves, of moss and wet stone. Jack noticed that the current had covered the doorstep of an abandoned house and was licking the cracked window-frames of the one beyond. Drowning, that's what this place is, he thought. Like the world. Like me, really. He shivered.

Opposite, where the old roadway slid into the river, he found the ferry: a lone rowing-boat, chained and padlocked to a post. No oars. Above it hung a faded sign, and Jack spent a precious match to read it, cupping his hand against the wind. *Crossing 1 Bd*, it read. *Apply Teacher's Pet Inn*.

He dropped the match in the river and sighed. He recalled the cold of rivers, a cold like the Thames near Abingdon where he'd watched his friends die and where he'd tried to kill Clara, or further downstream where they'd nearly gone over a weir. He smiled at that memory: when they gained the bank they'd laughed and thrown water over each other. But then he remembered the same river, when all of London was flooded and they were rescued from the surging waters by a renegade Repseg.

He shook his head, but it didn't clear. Maybe I can steal the boat, he thought. Or maybe I should just turn around, go back to Sophia and James and tell them I was too late. At least those two are sorted now, he told himself, at least they're safe. I did what Clara wanted.

Making his way back up the lonely village was harder than coming down. Once again, he found himself remembering that grey morning – how long ago was it? Ten days? More? – when he'd woken, achingly cold in a straw-littered yard, to find a note from Clara telling him what that stupid, stupid girl had done.

He swore. Never a thought for her poor parents, hey? No. It was always about Clara, wasn't it? Always about her and her bloody guilt. *She* hadn't had to deal with her parents' grief, had she? *She* hadn't had to watch as her mother sank to her knees and gave a wail, a wail like Jack never wanted to hear again, one that echoed back from the blockhouses and the stone walls, and rang in his ears even now. Clara hadn't had to watch her father limping to and fro on that crutch of his, the rage in his face and the fear on his brow. No, she'd left all that to Jack.

And she'd left it to him to coax her parents into the cart and get away westward, to the safety of Wessex. That's what her note had said. And he'd done it, just to show her – because, he knew, she thought he wasn't up to it. He'd loaded some of Hurn the Chieftain's possessions onto the cart and sold them in the next town, so that they had some money. He'd had to restrain Sophia again when, two days out, she tried to turn back. Then to Exeter, the military checkpoints, the paperwork, the trek north to the commune. Then seeing Clara's parents installed in their cabin. A day's rest, and then back east again. Back east, after Clara.

By the time he got back to the *Teacher's Pet* – it looked like an old schoolhouse – it was properly dark. A lantern swung from the old lych-gate, and Jack realised that somebody had been out to light it in the twenty minutes since he'd passed it on the way down. So that was encouraging.

Dodging the horse droppings and fighting the wind, Jack reached the arched doorway. He set his jaw: no matter how many new places he went to, no matter how much practice he'd had, it was always hard, making himself talk, making himself explain what he wanted. No choice, though, hey?

There was no point in knocking when the wind was this loud, so he turned the handle and pushed the door open. Another cowled lantern hung in the vestibule, and by its light he heaved the outer door shut. The inner door opened onto a small bar-room where dim candles flickered in niches and upon tables. Grey glasses hung over the stained wooden bar, and in the middle of the room a pipe led upwards from a small iron stove. A lone woman sat in a high-backed settle, her face hidden in shadow. The wind rattled the shutters.

'Hello?' he said.

The woman grunted and her head jerked, but she didn't wake.

'Hello?' Jack repeated. Still nobody came. He noticed a second room to his right, its door wide open, where a small fire smoked and a pair of leather-booted legs stretched out towards the hearth. He was just thinking he might as well warm himself there, when there was a thumping on the staircase and down came a short, round woman with dark hair and dark eyes, wiping her hands on a striped apron.

'Ooh! Hello, dear,' she said. 'What's this? A feller? Out on the roads at this time of night?'

Jack was used to this by now. Everywhere he'd stopped, from Honiton to Wareham, people had been surprised –

some insolently – to find a young male travelling alone. But he had his story ready.

'I'm on an errand for my mistress,' he said, reaching into his tunic pocket. 'I need to get to Southampton. Is the ferrywoman here?' He held out the letter that Sophia had given him.

'No need for that, dear,' said the landlady, looking him up and down. 'I'll believe you. But I expect there's some as wouldn't, hey?'

Jack didn't know what to say to that.

'I'm afraid she won't go tonight,' the landlady went on, nodding towards the side room. 'She's finished for the day. Not for any money,' she added, noticing Jack reaching into his pocket again.

Jack sighed and rubbed at his burgeoning beard. 'You got men's rooms then?' he asked. 'And I could do with a bit of food, if you've got any?'

'Of course, dear. They're out past the stables,' she said, pointing down a short corridor. 'We do get the occasional man coming through, see, and so long as they're respectable like your good self – well, it's business, isn't it?' She went to the foot of the stairs. 'Jinny!' she called. 'Jinny'll take you to your room. Then you can come back in the warm and have a bit of bacon. That sound all right?'

Jinny turned out to be a skinny girl of about nine, with cropped black hair and a slouching gait. She held the lantern low and said little as they trudged across the yard, where Jack wrapped his cloak tightly around him and tried to avoid the puddles. The stable doors were all closed against the weather, but Jack could smell the horses within.

'That your mam?' asked Jack. 'The landlady?'

Jinny shrugged. 'O' course,' she said. 'In here,' she added, pushing a door open to reveal a bare-floored room with low pallet bed, a washstand and not much else. 'All right?'

'If it's dry, and out of the wind, I'll sleep anywhere,' said Jack. Then, chucking his backpack into the room, he followed Jinny back indoors. Before long, he was tucking into a plate of bacon and potatoes, wiggling his toes in the warmth from the stove. The woman who'd been asleep on the settle had left, so Jack had the place to himself apart from the ferrywoman – whose boot he could still see through the doorway – and the landlady.

'That all right for you?' she asked as Jack pushed his clean plate away. 'That'll be four boudicks, with your room and breakfast. You've no horse, have you? We got some coffee for the morning.'

Jack pulled out his purse. 'Sounds great,' he said. 'Um, could I talk to the ferrywoman, please?'

The landlady took the coins and grinned. 'Hey, Forty!' she called. 'Customer! First thing in the morning!'

The leg jerked and was drawn back. Somebody groaned. The landlady raised her eyebrows and nodded to Jack. 'See if you can get any sense out of her,' she said.

Grabbing the remains of his pint, Jack made his way into the side-room. The fire might have been small, but it felt unexpectedly warm in there. On a bench to his right the ferrywoman was pulling herself up out of a slouch, leaning heavily on the broad wooden table. She was clad from neck to foot in thick, close-fitting brown leather, with generous padding at the joints. Her face was lean and her long grey hair was tied in a rough ponytail. 'Whatcher want?' she demanded, peering up at him with watery eyes.

Jack eyed the half-dozen empty whisky glasses scattered across the table. 'You gonna be sober by morning?'

'Not if I can help it,' the woman mumbled. 'Show me your money...'

The landlady had lingered. 'She'll be all right,' she said. 'Won't ya, Forty? Always has been, anyhow,' she added in a lower voice to Jack. 'She just likes a bit of a drink at night. Trying to forget something, I reckon.'

'Aren't we all?' said Jack. The landlady raised her eyebrows again.

Forty grabbed the table and eased herself to her feet before subsiding onto a stool and bending towards the fire. 'I feel the cold, all right?' she said. Jack looked again at her face. It seemed vaguely familiar, but in this world of Clones and Geemos, he thought to himself, that meant nothing. Then he realised that she was staring back at him.

'Get me a drink?' Forty said.

Jack glanced at the landlady, who nodded.

'All right,' he said. 'But we're starting at first light.'

'Ha!' said Forty, and turned back to the fire.

Jack went to the bar and came back with the whisky. Then he pulled up another chair and sat opposite her. 'It's too late to cross tonight, then?' he asked.

Forty took the glass and held it up to the light. 'Looks like an ordinary river, doesn't it? It's bad enough in the daylight – you've got to know where the ruins are. Walls, chimneys. And if the river's low...' She shook her head. 'Too dangerous. All the sunken buildings. Dead boats.'

Jack took another draught of his ale. 'Everything's changed, hasn't it?' he mused.

Forty was peering at him. 'Here,' she said, in that careful way that told Jack she was making an effort not to slur her words, 'do I know you?'

Having had the same idea himself, Jack frowned. But he said, 'I need to go to Southampton.'

Forty downed her whisky in one, blinked, and shook her head. 'You'll make for Fawley, then take the steam ferry? Hmm...straight after breakfast, then.' She stood and, remarkably steadily, made her way across the bar-room.

At the foot of the stairs she paused. 'Are you sure we haven't met?' she asked. 'Where did you come in from?'

'Exeter,' said Jack. Any other answer, he decided, was too complicated to explain at this time of night.

Forty pulled a face. 'Can't have done, then.' She shrugged, then trudged up the creaking stairs.

Later, Jack sat on his thin mattress. He could turn back now, couldn't he? Trying to find Clara was hopeless: all he knew was that she'd been taken to the slave market at Southampton – and that was over a week ago. She'd be long gone by now. But it always had been hopeless, hadn't it? Sophia and James had said he could go back to them whenever he wanted. It was tempting, but then he saw again their anguished faces, and their grief. They'd never blamed Jack – at least, they'd never said anything – and if he came back without Clara, they'd understand. But could he bear to face them?

SCORPION

He shook his head. It was like being a little boy again, needing someone to guide him. Everything was okay when he was little, wasn't it? Life had been hard, but at least he'd had a mam and dad. He tried to remember their faces, back across the years, but there was a hole where they should have been.

The shutters rattled and the rain pattered. Jack swore. Things would have been so much simpler if he'd never found Clara in that barn, if she hadn't turned up at Hurn's camp, if she'd stayed out of Jack's life. But then he imagined her being a slave...what were they doing to her? His throat tightened. Where was she? Was she even alive?

13 Small Boats

In the belly of the whale, three days had passed. Now night was coming again. After Wilson had shocked her, it had been a whole day before Clara had been able to work again, and even then, she'd spent the whole shift in a daze. She could remember little of it: she thought she'd heard Xavi and Riss chatting and even laughing, and she'd wanted to stop them because Xavi was hers, no-one else's, and she loved him. Then, as they'd crossed the Channel northward, there'd been a storm, the thunder assaulting their ears, the ship heaving and Clara, still feeling fragile, vomiting. They'd covered the vomit in coal and shovelled it into the furnace. And one night as Clara slept, the engines had eased to a stop. Half-awake, she'd been aware of the sound of small boats, but this time they weren't being ridden down. Instead, it sounded as if they were being lowered from the *Scorpion* into the water.

Now, at last, she was beginning to think straight. Her left arm ached and her left foot still tingled, but despite a residual weakness, she could work without dropping the shovel. The weather was quieter, the sea was steadier and the breezes more moderate. There'd been a gleam of sunshine as the sun set far in the west; but now, in the dark, the rain had returned and rivulets of rainwater ran down the steps, creating black puddles in the coal. An occasional waft of cooler air reached down into the boiler-room. The owl-faced guard was on duty, but in the gloom she wasn't even trying to read. Clara had just relieved Riss, whose bullet-wound was still bandaged.

'Thank fuck for that,' said Riss, and trudged off to her bed.

Xavi handed Clara a cup of water. 'How are you?' he said.

Glancing at the guard, Clara gently placed her hands on his chest. 'What is it?' she said. 'You look like you've been thinking.'

Xavi gave a brief chuckle. 'You do not answer my question,' he said, handing her a shovel.

'I'm okay,' she said. 'My arm still hurts, but I can use it.'

'Is good,' he said, touching her shoulder. 'Next time they shock you, I kill them. Okay?'

'Then I'd better make sure there isn't a next time.'

'So, they are lucky.'

'Now,' said Clara, bending to fill her shovel, 'you answer my question.'

Xavi moved a step closer. She could smell his sweat. 'They do things different now,' he said in a low voice. 'When first I come, we no ride down little boats. It was like this. At night we stop, boats go, boats come back.'

'They're sending out rowing boats?'

'Like night before last. Boats go away, but slow. And *Scorpion* lights, they all go out. When boats come back, we make small steam and travel slow. Sometimes we go west, sometimes south. You can see by light in portholes.'

'South again? To France?'

He shook his head. 'No. Then we come back north. I do not know what they are doing. Mostly is west.'

SCORPION

As he stooped to throw some coal into the furnace, Clara saw that he was still limping. 'Does it hurt?' she asked.

He nodded. 'Sometimes much. The brace, it helps. I hope it arranges soon.' He gave her a brief smile. 'So, why we go west?'

Clara emptied her own shovel and bent to refill it. 'It must be Wessex,' she said, frowning. 'We're off the Wessex coast.' And now she wondered about her parents, and about Jack, and how far away they were.

'What is Wessicks?' Xavi was saying.

'Anglia is East, where London is. Wessex is west. There's talk of war with Wessex.'

'You are not one country, your Britain?'

'No,' said Clara. 'Not for nearly a hundred years. At school,' she went on, wondering if *anything* they'd taught her at the Academy was true, 'they said it was on account of all the pandemics in the last century. The government collapsed...'

'Is same in Spain,' said Xavi.

They lapsed into silence, feeding the furnaces little by little. Xavi checked the gauges. After a while he said, 'Why they use little boats?'

'How do you mean?'

'Little boats are quiet. They use, how you say, rows?'

'Oars. But they're called rowing boats. Rowing is what you do.'

'*Sí*. They cannot go far, so we must be close to land. How far you think we are from shore?'

'I don't know. We can't be too close, I suppose – what, d'you think we could escape?'

'How is water? Water is cold, I think.'

'And we'd get shot.'

They worked some more. 'Little boats are out now,' said Xavi.

'They've gone out?'

'Yes, before you wake. But they no come back yet—'

'Hey!' the guard had left her stool, and was advancing on them. 'None of that, right?'

Xavi scowled. 'We no touch. We just talk.'

'What're you saying then?'

Xavi looked at Clara. 'I – I tell her what I do for her when we get out.'

The guard chuckled. 'Bloody man,' she said. 'Just like they say. You're a typical bloody sex pest. And anyway,' she jeered, 'you'll never get out. *Never*, see?' And she sauntered back to her stool, laughing.

'I want to do something for *you*,' Clara told Xavi, 'when we get out.' She felt she couldn't keep her hands off him for much longer.

But Xavi's smile was a sad one. 'Yes,' was all he said.

A few minutes later, Crudger and Wilson appeared.

'Make a bit more steam,' said Crudger, tapping one of the gauges. 'We're moving. Soon.'

No sooner had she and guard disappeared up the companionway, than Clara and Xavi heard bumps on the hull, the squeal of metal as the derricks were swung out, and voices shouting instructions.

'Get working,' snarled Wilson.

They obeyed. Clara had tried to ignore the shock-stick, but now she could hardly look at it without her limbs feeling weak. They built up the heat in the boilers, the pressure began to rise, and soon the engine changed its pitch. She heard Captain Suggs shouting orders; then she must have paused at the head of the companionway, because Clara could hear clearly.

'Any trouble?' the captain was asking.

Another voice – Clara thought it might be Vina, the first mate – replied. 'No. We saw some lights come up, but we was way out of harbour by then. They might've seen Scorpion's light, but they wouldn't-a-seen our boats.'

Soon afterwards, all the lights were extinguished and they were left in the dark with just the furnace fire for light.

Many miles away, Jack was dreaming of cold ferry-boats and black rivers, of the surging Thames and of being hauled out of the Great Flood by Clara. Which was odd, he told his dream self, because he'd been unconscious when he'd been rescued. When he came to his senses he'd been lying on some concrete steps. But, hadn't somebody else had been with Clara in the motor-launch...yes, it was that Repseg who'd turned nice and released them...he couldn't move...there was a light...

Jinny was shaking him. 'Breakfast,' she snapped when he finally peeled his eyes open. 'Ten minutes.'

With a groan, Jack rolled off the bed and shuffled to the washstand, where he splashed cold water over his face and neck. Then, hugging his cloak about him, he crossed the lantern-lit yard. In the east, an indistinct glow loomed through the mist. As he reached the door he wondered if

Forty the ferrywoman would even be awake yet. How long till she could get him across the river? He wanted to make Southampton today, if he could. Besides, he told himself, once across, it'll be harder for me to turn back.

In the bar-room the stove was lit, although it hadn't yet driven away the night's cold. Forty was slouched at the bar, nursing a coffee, her greying hair splayed about her shoulders. 'Good,' she said. 'Glad you didn't keep me waiting. I'm a busy woman.'

'First I need breakfast,' said Jack with a scowl. He helped himself to a coffee. 'And how are you busy, anyway? The landlady says you don't get much business.'

Forty said nothing, but downed her coffee and, while she tied her hair back, turned her grey eyes on him. Her gaze made Jack uncomfortable, so he looked away until Jinny brought his porridge.

'Why are you going to Southampton?' asked Forty. They'd left the inn and were pounding down the misty street towards the ferry, trying to ward off the muscle-wrenching cold. There was a firmness, an authority to her voice that Jack found odd in a down-at-heel, odd-jobbing woman who spent her life skulking in a backwater like this. Despite that, he noticed that Forty, still dressed in the same padded leathers, was breathing hard.

'Why d'you ask?' he said.

Forty switched the oars that she was carrying from one shoulder to the other. 'It's a rough place.'

Jack didn't see any reason why he shouldn't tell her. 'I need to get to the slave market.'

She turned her head, and again Jack felt that she was studying him. 'You don't look like a slaver,' she said. 'More like a slavee.'

'Very funny,' said Jack. 'Someone I know got taken – they were going to sell her.'

They reached the jetty. Forty pulled out a large key, thrust it into the padlock and loosed the chain. Then she hauled the boat onto the remains of the sloping roadway.

'So she's gone for a slave?' she said. 'Really, I'd give it up. It's a bad place. She could've been taken anywhere. And even if you do find her, what will you do? She'll be someone's property, you know that?'

Jack eyed the boat. This was it, wasn't it? The first time he'd been in a boat since the Great Flood. He licked his lips. 'But I promised, see. I promised Clara's parents I'd find her. I've got to try, at least.'

'Wait a minute,' said Forty. 'What did you say?'

'I promised her parents–'

'Her parents? So she's a Natural. And her name's Clara, right?'

'What about it?' said Jack.

Forty frowned. 'Here,' she said, thrusting the chain into Jack's hand and dropping the oars into the boat. 'Keep hold of that. Wait here.'

'But–'

'No, I mean it,' she said, turning. 'Wait.' She hurried up the road and disappeared into the mist.

14 Across the River

The river sucked and gurgled, dawn edged further into day, and Jack stood holding the end of the chain. He realised his mouth was still open. 'What's got into her?' he said aloud. Did Forty have a problem with Naturals? Surely not, here at the edge of the clone-loving Republic: west of here, lots of people were Naturals. Maybe Forty was a bit mad? That was likely, Jack supposed. All that drink must pickle your brain in the end.

Minutes passed. Jack had just picked up an oar, wondering if he could manage to paddle the boat across those twenty yards of swift water, when he heard footsteps. Emerging from the mist came a grumpy-looking Jinny, followed by Forty with a bulging pack over her shoulder.

'I'm coming with you,' Forty announced as they reached him. 'Jinny's here to bring the boat back.' Jack saw that Jinny had folded her arms tightly across her chest and was doing her best to look annoyed.

'Come again?' said Jack.

'How well do you know the slave market?' said Forty. 'Do you know the right people to ask?'

'No, but–'

'Asking the wrong people could get you killed,' said Forty, looking him in the eye. 'I can help. Promise.'

Jack thought. He could use a bit of help, certainly. But what use would a mere ferrywoman be? Out loud he said, 'Get me across first.'

Forty frowned. 'All right,' she said at last, 'get in. You too, Jinny.' She held the boat while first Jinny stepped in, then Jack. Then she climbed in at the stern and shoved off hard against the bank.

Jack gripped the gunwales, his knuckles white. He supposed he'd have to get used to the water again soon, and there were probably worse ways. All the same, he wished the boat didn't wallow so much. The current was strong, and Forty struggled to keep them heading slantwise across the quick-flowing stream. Cold water flicked from her blades. *I used to be able to paddle a boat*, Jack told himself. Behind him, he was aware of Forty leaning first one way, then the other, peering down into the water. Once or twice the keel bumped against something. This was no broad and stately river. It was little more than a shallow ford where sunken obstacles hid like trolls under a bridge.

It only took five minutes, although to Jack it seemed like half an hour. Once at the far side, Forty splashed into the shallows and fastened the chain to a post. She held the boat while the others stepped out. Jack's boots filled with water.

'Now,' he said to Forty. 'What's going on?'

Forty grinned. 'Am I coming with you, or not?'

'All right,' said Jack with a grimace. 'So long as you're a help.'

Shaking his head, Jack dug in his pockets. 'Here,' he said to Jinny, slapping a coin into her palm. 'That okay? Will you be all right getting back across?'

She looked up to heaven. 'O' course.' She stuffed the coin in her pocket then undid the chain. 'Hey, Forty,' she added. 'Mum says, you're a nutter.'

'Tell her I love her, too,' Forty replied with a chuckle. Then she unslung her rucksack and began rummaging in it.

Jack watched Jinny go. He told himself it was only right to see her safely across, because after all she was only a small girl, and he'd hate to see her drown. He told himself it was nothing to do with his own fears. But he needn't have worried. If anything, she seemed to have an easier time than Forty as she guided the boat back to the western bank.

'She's fine, isn't she?' came Forty's voice.

Jack turned, to see her tucking the last of her hair under an official-looking cap. He stared, then pointed.

'You!' he said with a gasp. 'Y-you're that Repseg – the one at the flood!' The cheekbones were the same, the eyes the same grey; and now that the hair was hidden under a Repseg cap, she looked just like the woman who'd pulled them out of the Great Flood. But Clones, Geemos – they were all alike. How could he be sure?

Forty grinned at Jack's expression. Pulling off the cap, she shook her hair loose and re-tied it behind her shoulders. 'Yep,' she said. 'I used to be Sergeant Tori F Shavila of the Republican Security Guard. The F stands for Fortis, you see. Hence the "Forty".'

Jack began to recover himself. 'It's really you?' he managed to say.

Forty, or Shavila, nodded. 'So,' she said. 'It *is* Clara, isn't it? What's she got herself into this time?'

'Yeah,' said Jack. He swallowed. 'She – she took somebody else's place, and they took her away to be a slave.'

'*Your* place,' said Shavila. 'You're Jack, aren't you? I didn't recognise you at first, with the beard.'

Jack put a hand up to his chin. A proper beard, was it? Out loud he said, 'But your job? What about the ferry?'

'Jinny can run the ferry by herself,' said Shavila, 'for all the custom they get.' She gestured towards where the girl had disappeared into the thinning mist. 'You saw how good she is. Besides, I was getting fed up, stuck here. It'll be good to have one last mission. It should be fun – as I remember, you and Clara are pretty good at making it up as you go along.'

'Fun?' said Jack. 'Fun? For pity's sake, you mad Repseg!'

Shavila laughed.

'Wait,' said Jack. 'You're not a Repseg any more, are yer?'

'Not at the moment. I can be again, if I want.' Shavila stowed the cap back in her rucksack. 'Like I say, *that* might be useful if you need to find things out, down at the slave market...'

Jack nodded. 'You're sure, then? You'll help me find out what's happened to Clara?'

'I'll help you to find her, if you like.'

'You will? Why?'

'Like I say,' said Shavila. 'I was getting bored.'

'The landlady was right,' said Jack. 'You are mad.' He thought for a minute. 'Hey, what do I call you?' he asked. 'I can hardly call you "Sergeant", can I?'

'Call me Tori,' she said. 'Then it'll be like we're friends.'

'All right,' said Jack. 'Tori. You know it'll be dangerous?'

Shavila grimaced. 'Everything's dangerous now. Anything we ever do, it's a risk. Right?'

They turned and walked along in silence for a while. As they climbed out of the valley the mist dispersed, leaving mere shreds in the damp fields. Above them, white clouds ran on a westerly breeze.

It was late morning. They'd been two hours on the road from Bewley, the winds had fallen light and an unseasonable sun was grinning on them, when Jack grimaced and held his nose. 'Phwaugh!' he groaned. 'What's that smell? It's like, I dunno, sewage, with a ton of vinegar and – urgh, what is it? It gets right up yer nose...'

Shavila pointed to their left. 'It's behind these trees,' she said. 'Twentieth-century oil refinery. When searise came, it kept getting flooded. Then, when it was abandoned, all the waste leached into the ground. Even today it sometimes spills into the estuary.'

Still holding his nose, Jack turned off the road. The tough, tussocky undergrowth had a dark tinge to it, and his boots squelched in the spongy leaf-mould.

'You've been in there, then?' said Jack.

'I've looked through the fence,' panted Shavila, who was following a few yards behind. 'See for yourself.'

First the trees gave way to blackened, spindly bushes with cunning thorns that stabbed through Jack's clothing. Then the bushes themselves dwindled to a tough, twisted scrub, likewise black, which stopped in front of a tall steel paling that curved away to left and right. Jack peered through.

'That stench!' he said, through his teeth.

Shavila came up with him. 'Don't stay too long,' she said, gasping. 'It'll give you a headache.'

'It's huge,' said Jack, staring. Thirty yards beyond the first fence was another, taller one, with a sharp spike topping each pale. Between the fences was a deep ditch, full of smashed bricks and crumbling concrete, covered with a film of mud, and beyond that, a vast area of broken ground. He could see miles of pipework, low steel buildings, and huge cylinders hundreds of feet high, all rusting. The ground was black as far as his eyes could see, and the sad wind moaned among the steel.

'It's all of a square mile,' said Shavila. 'Men got through a lot of oil in those days.'

Jack couldn't imagine it. In his fifteen years he'd only seen a handful of motor vehicles, all government-run. He'd seen some diesel-engined boats, too. But how many vans, how many ships, how many of those – what did Clara call them? Aeroplanes? – would this place feed? Hundreds? Thousands?

'There's no green anywhere,' said Shavila. 'Not even a weed.'

Jack realised he had his mouth open. He shut it, and tried not to gag. 'Haven't they reclaimed the steel then?'

'It's too dangerous. The mud's toxic, and even after all these years the vapour's flammable. If they tried using torches, they could blow themselves up. And in the summer, when you get temperatures in the forties – it can go up in flames again.'

'This ditch, then...'

'It's a firebreak.'

Jack sighed. 'Come on,' he said. 'Get me out of here.'

SCORPION

They pushed on. The road descended as it bent to the right, and the air began to smell sweeter. Jack had to slow his pace for Shavila to keep up. The ex-Repseg was breathing heavily again.

'So, er, Tori,' he said. The name still felt strange on his tongue. 'What did you do, after the London Flood? After you pulled us out of the river?'

'Wow,' said Shavila. 'That was a while ago.'

'You gave us the key for the lock-up. Then you went off in your motor-launch.'

'Oh, yes,' said Shavila. 'Let's see. I spent a while pulling people out of the river, or getting them off the bridge footings. But soon, all I could find was corpses. After that I was – well, I was still a bit shaken. And I'd shaved my head, so I needed to give the hair time to grow back.'

'Which didn't take long, you being a Repseg.'

Shavila pulled a face. 'That's me. Super Geemo genes. At least, it *was* me...anyhow, I took a few days out. Pretended to be on duty, but really I was just wandering around, looking at the devastation and helping the odd person who needed it. Eventually, I reported back in. Old habits, I suppose. The army had come in, and were clearing the place. They were doing a lot of work around the Underground tunnels. Mater Hedera's obsession, that was – she thought the Underground were the ones behind all the trouble, all the riots...'

'Old Hedera died, then? Clara told me what happened.'

'After the mob broke in at Somerset House, I left her to them. Later, I heard a rumour that she'd survived, but I didn't believe it. She was old and frail, and that mob was ugly. Here, we go left for the ferry.'

They turned down a leafy lane where tough grass grew long between the cart-ruts. 'Was it you that told everyone she'd deliberately caused the flood?' asked Jack. 'The news got about pretty quick. Clara and me, we heard it the next day, before we even got out of London.'

Shavila shook her head. 'No, not me. You two never said anything?'

"course not. No-one would've believed us if we had.'

'It could have been Medea Carrow. She'd been up there with Hedera. Did a runner when the mob came. But someone else must have been in on the plan. I don't think Hedera could have organised it on her own. Besides...'

'Besides what?'

'If you wanted to get rid of Hedera, and if you knew she was about to make a huge mistake, would you stop her?'

'Who do you mean? The army? They're the ones who took over...'

'And, once she'd made that mistake, you could make sure people knew about it.'

Jack nodded. 'Sounds plausible. You've got pretty good at thinking, haven't you?'

'I do it all the time,' said Shavila with a shrug. 'Now that I'm not taking orders.'

15 The Auctioneer Has a Laugh

They came to a clearing where the road sloped down to a square wooden jetty at the water's edge. Beyond the jetty, a bank of brown reeds led to the mile-wide expanse of Southampton Water, and Jack could see white-topped waves glinting in the sunlight. Two women were slouching on a bench nearby, one with a full rucksack, the other with her feet resting on a laden hand-trolley. A sign fixed to a tall post read, *Foot ferry to Southampton. Pedestrians and riders only. No carts. Riders please dismount. 5 Bd per person, 7 Bd per horse*. Below this, another board had been added. *Sailings only if weather permits. At your own risk.*

'So,' said Jack, they take five boudicks off you, they might not sail at all, and even when they do, it's not safe.'

Shavila chuckled. 'And there's no boat yet,' she said, sitting down on a low wall. 'We're going to have to wait.' She undid her hair and let it flutter in the wind.

Jack sat beside her and watched the reed-buntings as they jostled among the swaying stalks. 'I still get nightmares,' he said. 'Used to be all right on the water, until – until that time you saved me.'

Shavila glanced at him. 'And you're not all right now?'

'Well, I nearly died, didn't I?' Jack looked down at his hands. 'I got the wobbles back there in Bewley. Gotta face it, though. Gotta get out on the water again.'

Shavila nodded. 'It's only half an hour up to Southampton. You'll be okay. Unless you want to walk, and take the rest of the day about it.'

They stood up. A broad, flat-bottomed boat was being poled through the reeds. Five passengers crouched on the thwarts, clutching bags and sacks. As the punt slid up to the jetty they began to scramble to their feet. '*That's* the ferry?' said Jack, swallowing.

'If it is,' said Shavila, 'I'm walking with you.'

It wasn't. The punt took Jack, Shavila and the other passengers a quarter of a mile through the reeds, across the mud-flats and out to the ferry itself, a short diesel-engined vessel with a squat wheelhouse. The ferrywoman moored the punt at a floating stage, then helped the passengers to board. A ramp at the ferry's stern showed where horses could get on. Jack thought it looked very risky.

He headed for the starboard rail and gripped it tightly. Shavila joined him, and Jack found that her arm felt warm against his. He glanced at her. How was it, he thought, that he'd never really thought of her as a woman before, more as a machine. He just wished she didn't smell so sweaty.

'You'll be all right,' she told him, noticing his white knuckles. The engine grumbled into life and the ferry began to turn out into the main channel, rocking on the swell. Spray smacked their faces.

Jack gave a long exhale and nodded. To take his mind off the water he said, 'So, anyhow – you were telling me what happened in London.'

Shavila ran a hand through her greying hair. 'Like I say,' she said, 'eventually I reported in. Everything was confused, and it seemed like nobody knew that I'd been with Hedera, so I just joined the others and pretended I'd been following orders.' She sighed. 'I only lasted a few days. We were helping the army to round up people who, they claimed, had led the riots. I wasn't sure I believed it. Before the flood I'd have followed my orders quite happily – I'd probably have enjoyed it – but then, afterwards, something in my head had flipped, Jack. I was sickened.'

'So what did you do?'

'Clara had asked me about Guards who'd retired. I thought I'd check it out. I had access to records...'

Jack stared out over the grey waters. 'I hope she's okay,' he said.

'Clara?' said Shavila. 'Maybe we'll find out soon.'

'Yeah, I guess.'

'Are you in love with her?'

'What?' Jack felt himself reddening. 'No, no. Nothing like that. We're friends, though. That is, I *think* we're friends...' He looked away.

'I'm sorry,' said Shavila. 'It's just that I've no idea what "love" is. I mean, we – that's us Guards – we know it exists, and all that. We learnt about it in training. I just wondered what it feels like.'

Jack pulled a face. 'Oh,' he said, and thought for a minute. 'Well,' he went on, 'I wouldn't use me and Clara as a good example.'

A stout, blue-painted fishing-boat overtook them, swaying across the swell and spewing diesel-fumes. There were two Repsegs on the deck, and Shavila began to raise a hand in acknowledgement, but stopped herself. 'Whoops,' she said to Jack. 'That was a mistake. Old habits, hey?'

Jack held on as the ferry wallowed in the fishing-boat's wake. 'What are they doing? I mean, why are there Repsegs on a fishing-boat?'

Shavila pointed across the channel, now narrowing as the Itchen peeled off towards the north-east. 'See that big white sign?'

Jack peered. 'Something Pound?'

'Here.' Shavila extracted a pair of binoculars from her rucksack.

Jack took them. '*Marine Guard Pound*?' he read. 'What's that, then?'

'It's where they confiscate boats. Fishing without a licence, that sort of thing. You pay two hundred boudicks, you get your boat back.' Shavila frowned. 'I wish I hadn't waved at those Guards.'

'What, the Repsegs on the boat? Why? You're a civvy now, ain't ya?'

'Yes,' said Shavila. 'I suppose.'

They tied up at another floating stage, then another punt carried them over the old submerged docks into Southampton. Jack noticed this punt was wallowing more than the first had. Looking back, he saw that grey clouds were building in the west, and that out in the channel the waves were dancing. The ferrywoman eased the punt directly to a mooring on the High Street, where a bored queue of travellers waited for the return trip.

SCORPION

Jack blew out his cheeks as he stepped off the punt. Then he bent forward and put his hands on his knees to stop them trembling. He was aware of Shavila standing beside him.

'You all right?' she asked.

He glanced up. 'Yeah,' he said, breathing hard. 'Made it.'

'Well done,' she said.

'It was easier on the ferry. Further away from the water, you know? But that thing...!' He pointed at the punt, which was now filling with passengers for the return trip. 'Come on,' he went on, straightening. 'Let's get started.' He looked around, then went up to the passenger at the end of the queue. 'How far to the slave market?' he asked.

The woman scowled. 'No slave markets round here,' she growled, and spat at his feet. '*Boy*,' she added with a leer.

Jack felt Shavila's hand under his elbow, guiding him away. The passenger stared after them, and only turned when the ferrywoman nudged her.

'They don't use those words,' whispered Shavila. 'Excuse me,' she called to an elderly, straight-backed woman who was hurrying by. 'Are we far from the labour exchange?'

The woman looked her up and down. 'Near three miles. That way,' she said, pointing behind them. 'He looks fit enough,' she said, nodding at Jack. 'Might fetch a decent price.'

'Thanks,' said Shavila, hauling Jack away.

'Wait,' said Jack. 'She thinks you're selling me?'

Shavila chuckled. 'I'm a woman, you're a junior male, I'm asking the way to the labour exchange. Logical deduction.'

'And what's with being all mealy-mouthed about it? Why call it a "labour exchange" when it's a slave market? It *is* a slave market, right?' Then he stopped. 'Wait a minute,' he said. 'You're *not* planning to sell me, are yer?'

Again Shavila chuckled. 'What, with me being an old Repseg? One of the baddies? Well, you can stay here if you want. I'm going to find Clara.' She turned and strode off.

Further down the street, Jack spotted two Repsegs. He thought they'd been watching them, but he didn't want to make it worse by staring back, and he hurried to catch up with Shavila.

'You want to find Clara too?' he panted as he came up with her. 'Why?'

For an answer, Shavila held up a tress of her long hair. 'I'm free,' she said. 'I owe her, I guess.'

They passed along a road where the pungent smells told them they were near the fish market, then along a thoroughfare with dejected shops and dirty pavements. Jack stopped to peer at one of the posters offering a reward for information about General Clark's missing daughter. 'Clark's the top one, ain't she?' he asked Shavila. 'In the military council?'

Shavila nodded. 'There's others in there – Admiral Ndogu, I think, from the navy – but Clark's the real power. I heard she was credited with the truce with Milland. Now come on, we haven't got all day.' Jack took another look at the face staring out from the poster, then once again hurried to catch up.

It took them nearly an hour to find the labour exchange with its red-painted sign. The route hadn't been clear, so they'd taken a couple of wrong turns, and Jack had insisted they stop to buy something to eat and drink. Shavila had shrugged, but when she got the food she'd eaten it greedily. Now they stood opposite the gates, which for the time being were closed. A couple of guards paced up and down in front.

'D'you think they'd let a Repseg in?' said Shavila. 'With a prisoner?'

Jack sighed. 'Here we go,' he said.

They skirted around the site, turning through several residential streets until Shavila found what she was looking for: some dense shrubs, crowded at the edge of a Closed Area. Making sure no-one was watching, she pushed her way between the bushes.

Jack followed. 'What now?' he asked.

For an answer, Shavila pulled a grey tunic out of her backpack and held it up.

'Repseg gear?' said Jack.

'I'll find out more if I'm wearing this,' said Shavila, and began to put it on. Jack had been expecting her to strip off her leather clothes, but instead she slipped the jacket over them. Trousers followed; finally she tucked her hair firmly under the cap. She looked every inch the Repseg, and for a fleeting moment Jack wondered if she was really still one of them, after all.

'You're going to have to tie my hands, right?' he asked. 'Make it look like I'm your prisoner?'

Shavila nodded. 'You're a male. A Repseg wouldn't treat you kindly, would she?'

'Well, make it so I can slip my hands out,' said Jack with a scowl. ''cause I might need to.'

The guards on the gate grumbled, but didn't ask Shavila any questions. One of them gave Jack a hard stare as they passed through. At the inner fence, where some captives were being unloaded, they demanded to see Shavila's ID then wrote her name in a ledger. 'Half an hour,' said the woman. 'And no unauthorised sales,' she added, pointing at Jack with her pen.

But then they were through. As they advanced towards the auction pit – Shavila had told Jack to keep up a quick pace – he heard her muttering: 'No Guards. That's something.' He knew she meant, no inquisitive Repsegs.

They reached the pit to find an auction in full swing. Buyers were bidding for a muscular woman with fair hair and a square jaw, who stood head and shoulders above the security guards. Jack watched, fascinated, as a woman in the red coat called out the bids.

'Fifty boudicks – thank you madam, sixty. Sixty boudicks – any more? Come on, I'm robbing myself here, ladies! Just look at this fine specimen,' she added, slapping the slave's cheek in mock playfulness. 'She'll be an asset wherever she works. Look at these muscles! Am I bid seventy?'

She fetched eighty-five in the end. Jack's throat was tight. Is this what Clara had been through? How much had *she* been sold for? He tried to think of something else, but the slaves kept coming and the auctioneer kept shouting and the picture of Clara, head bowed, shackled, beaten, kept returning. Gradually, though, the auctioneer worked her way through the batch until only the thin and undernourished remained. Nobody was bidding for them.

'Come on,' said Shavila. 'Now, act like a prisoner.'

Jack swallowed. He told himself that he trusted Shavila, that she wasn't really going to try and sell him. He tried flexing his tied hands. The rope felt tight, but he had to admit there was a bit of wriggle-room. He might be able to work it loose, but it'd take time. Too late to worry about that now.

They pushed through a clump of buyers. 'I need to see the auctioneer,' Shavila was telling the security guard. 'There's a girl I'm looking for, a thief. She's been working with this one,' she added, giving Jack a shake.

The guard looked Shavila up and down. 'All right,' she said. 'She won't like it, though.' In a moment, they were in the auction pit. Shavila shoved Jack forward, and he tried to look dejected.

The auctioneer glanced up as they reached her. 'What's a Repseg doing here?' she asked with a scowl. 'I run a legal operation, y'know.'

'I'm looking for a girl,' explained Shavila. 'She's been on the run. The boy says she might have been brought here.'

The auctioneer took a pull from her whisky-flask and shook her head. 'We don't keep names or nothing. The ones that come here, they're just numbers, see. Know which lot she was in?'

'She'd have come from the west,' said Shavila. 'A few days ago.'

'More like a week,' said Jack.

The auctioneer glared at him. 'Hmm,' she said, running a finger down her clipboard. 'Well, the New Forest girls did bring couple of wagonloads in. A week ago today.'

'Who did they go to?' asked Shavila.

'Anywhere and everywhere,' said the auctioneer, showing her the clipboard. 'Dock building, chem works, domestics...what did she look like?'

'Bit shorter than me,' began Jack, but suddenly he felt Shavila dragging him to one side. She grabbed a fistful of his shirt. 'One more word from you,' she shouted, 'and I'll throw you in the nearest dock! You speak when you're spoken to! Bloody men,' she added, turning back to the auctioneer. 'Like he said with the height. Pale-skinned, light brown hair, slight build, pointed nose.'

The auctioneer looked down her list again. 'Hang on – did she have a scar on her left arm?'

Shavila prodded Jack. 'Well?' she growled.

Jack thought maybe she was playing her part a bit too enthusiastically. He nodded, hoping he looked frightened enough.

'Ah,' said the auctioneer, raising her eyebrows. 'That's this one here.' She pointed to the last entry. 'Coastforce.'

Jack thought that a shadow crossed Shavila's face. 'Coastforce?'

The auctioneer tapped the clipboard. 'Yep, they needed another deck hand. They get through 'em quick on the good ship *Scorpion*.'

Shavila nodded. 'The *Scorpion* does the East, doesn't it?' she asked. 'Dover Straits?'

'Nah,' said the auctioneer. 'That's the *Sarka*. *Scorpion* covers the West. She was a thief, then?'

'Like I say,' said Shavila. 'Working with this male.'

The auctioneer leaned close. 'D'you wanna sell him? I can offer you a good price.' She nodded at Jack. 'Plenty of demand for young lads. If you know what I mean.'

Shavila shook her head. 'Sorry. I need to take him in. Got to have something to show my superiors.'

Jack let himself relax a little.

'Ah, yeah,' the auctioneer was saying. 'Incorruptible Repsegs, and all that. Your loss.'

'And you're sure this girl went to Coastforce?'

'Sure as I can be,' grunted the auctioneer. 'You can tell your bosses she's got worse than prison where she's gone. Okay? Now get out of it, Repseg. I got slaves to sell.'

Before Shavila could march Jack away, the auctioneer began to chuckle. 'What's so funny?' she asked.

'I just remembered,' said the auctioneer with a grin. 'That girl. She volunteered.' The grin widened. 'She actually volunteered for Coastforce!'

They left her shaking her head as the next batch of slaves filed into the pit.

16 The Cerdic

Shavila hurried Jack through security and out through the great gates. Above, the clouds had thickened to form one grey mass, but the wind was still moderate and there was no rain. The main road was busy with pedestrians and horse-drawn traffic, so it wasn't until they'd covered another fifty yards that Shavila, with a glance over her shoulder, pulled Jack down a side-street.

'You're still my prisoner,' she said, undoing the rope from his wrists. 'I need to carry on being a Repseg for now.'

She was close, her breath warm on his neck. Once again Jack could smell her sharp, acidic sweat. 'There,' she said as the rope fell away.

'That's definitely Clara,' growled Jack, rubbing his wrists. 'Actually volunteering for things. Shit, that girl – if there's trouble going...' He trailed off. Then he said, 'What's Coastforce? It's bad, isn't it?'

Shavila nodded. 'It's bad.'

'Why?' Jack snapped. 'Tell me.' As he said it, he realised that an ex-Repseg was unlikely to have much idea about breaking things gently.

'Coastforce patrol the Channel,' said Shavila, 'to stop refugees from France and the Low Countries getting here.'

'People want to come to Anglia? Why?'

Shavila shrugged. 'Coastforce aren't government-run, but the Republic pays them. They run steamboats, and the Republic makes sure they're always supplied with coal, even though it's scarce. Come on, stay in front of me – remember, I'm watching you.'

'Which way?'

'Back to the road, then left. We need to find another ferry.'

'Great,' said Jack over his shoulder, 'more water.'

'Well,' said Shavila, 'you need to start enjoying it. Work it out: you want to find Clara. She's somewhere on the English Channel. Therefore...?'

Jack groaned again.

They had to swing north, towards Sandenise, to reach the ferry that would take them across the broad channel of the Itchen. The old jetties had been submerged long ago, and all that remained above the water were the ruins of old red-brick houses. This time the ferry turned out to be a pulley-hauled one that used the skeleton of the old road bridge, taking only four passengers at a time. The pulleys were worked by strong women winding the winches on either side. Jack felt sick. How, he asked himself, could he do anything for Clara when he was scared of falling in a little river? Or was it just that he always felt sick nowadays?

They crossed safely enough, and turned south. By the time they reached Bitterne, the short day was declining and a thin rain had started to fall. Shavila pointed ahead to another set of wooden gates. Lamps were glowing in the adjacent gatehouse. 'That's the Marine Guard Pound,' she said.

'What,' said Jack, 'you mean–'

Shavila nodded. 'The place where they were taking that fishing-boat this morning.'

Jack turned. 'Oh, great. We're going into the Channel – all those waves – all that wind – in a tiny fishing boat?'

'For pity's sake,' said Shavila, 'turn around, will you? Act like you're under arrest!' Hurriedly, she glanced up and down the street. For the moment it was deserted, apart from a single old woman trudging along ahead of them. 'Can you think of a better idea?' she said.

'Well, I–'

'Besides,' said Shavila, 'we're going to have to steal it first.'

'Great,' Jack snarled.

Jack stopped just outside the gatehouse in order to let Shavila pass, then followed her under the archway. A stout wooden gate barred their way; to their right was a low counter with a wooden shutter, fastened open. Behind it a stocky, bushy-haired woman in a faded grey jumper was drinking tea from an enamel mug while reading *The Republican Woman* by lamplight. She looked up with a frown.

'Republican Guard,' said Shavila, flashing her ID card. 'Security check,' she added, and pulled out a pocket-book.

The dock-keeper was eyeing Jack. 'Oh, yeah? Funny time o'day. And what's with him?' Her voice was a petulant whine.

Jack just had time to get worried before Shavila answered smoothly, 'The prisoner's here because I'm investigating a theft, and he's got information. Now,' she said, pointing, 'show me what you've got.'

The woman scowled, and took a long, deliberate pull at her tea. Then she made a show of searching for her keys, before grabbing a lantern and plodding out to unlock the gate.

'I'll want the log book,' said Shavila. She was rewarded with another scowl.

'Sixteen, at the minute,' said the woman, nodding towards the dock and thrusting a dog-eared ledger at Shavila.

While Shavila leafed through the pages, Jack looked around the dock. By now it was quite dark; all that remained of the day was a thin grey streak in the western sky. The rain was no longer bothering to fall, but there was a nip in the wind and a chill from the water that made Jack shiver. The dock had clearly been rebuilt since searise, for the concrete was of the modern hard, unfinished sort. The pound was closed in on three sides by tall stone walls, and to Jack's right, the dock gates stood open. Heavy chains led to a great winch with a long handle. Jack tried to imagine how hard it must be to wind the gates shut. At the far end of the dock, yellow light filtered from the windows of a squat blockhouse.

'You've got them all secure?' Shavila was asking the dock-keeper.

'As best I can,' sniffed the woman, thrusting a hand into her pocket and pulling out a squashed packet of cigarettes. She nodded towards the dock. 'They're secured one to another. Nice and tight, not too much room for 'em to move about in a storm. Ones at the edges are tied up to the dock bollards. As for criminal access – you can see for yourself.' She lit a cigarette.

'You've de-fuelled them?'

'Mostly.' She exhaled smoke through her nose. 'Haven't had time to do the last one,' she said, gesturing at the blue-hulled boat that Jack remembered seeing that morning. 'You can't hurry when you're siphoning.'

'The *Cerdic*,' read Shavila, glancing down the list. 'I'll need to inspect it.'

'Please yourself,' said the woman, and sauntered off with the lantern.

Shavila watched her go, then reached into her pack and pulled out a leather-sheathed knife. 'Here,' she said, handing it to Jack. 'You'll need this. I'm not sure she believed my story.'

Jack drew the knife and hefted it. In the dwindling light he couldn't see the edge, so he tested it lightly with his finger. He'd owned a knife once. He'd owned a sword once, too, a sharp one that had killed a woman. He shook himself. Already, his time with Hurn seemed an age ago.

'This way,' said Shavila. 'I'll find a gangplank.'

Peering through the gloom, Jack saw Shavila dragging a narrow board out of the shadows towards the dock edge. If only the dock-keeper hadn't taken the lantern...he looked in the direction that she'd gone and saw the lantern moving rapidly towards the blockhouse. The saunter had changed to a jog.

'Something's wrong,' he said.

Shavila looked up. She said nothing, but threw the board across the gap and ran over to the *Cerdic*. 'Cut the lines!' she cried. 'I'll get her started.'

There were shouts, and Jack turned to see three figures emerging from the blockhouse. One was the dock-keeper, but the two at the front had electric torches and they were moving fast. 'It's the Repsegs!' he cried. 'The ones who brought the boat in!'

On the deck, Shavila nodded and disappeared into the wheelhouse. The Repsegs were approaching rapidly, but at least with their torchlight Jack could now see better. He looked around for where the *Cerdic* was tied: one hawser ran to a dockside bollard, another to the adjacent boat. But the Repsegs, each wielding a baton, were getting closer. As he turned back, he saw that they'd split up. One was making for the winch – she was going to close the gates – but the other was coming straight for him. Thinking fast, he feigned to run – then at the last minute crouched down into a ball. He'd seen it done before; if you take them by surprise, then as they trip over you, you stand up, throwing them into the air. It buys you time.

But this time it didn't work. The Repseg simply dodged and carried on to the dockside before leaping down into the boat.

'Look out!' cried Jack, and Shavila emerged from the wheelhouse in time to plant the sole of her boot into the Repseg's face. Jack hurried to the bollard and began cutting the hawser. It was tough, and in the gloom he had to keep feeling the rope to make sure that the cut was true. Suddenly, a broad, muscular arm was around his neck and he was dragged backwards. The arm was thick and the wool was thick, so for the moment the arm wasn't reaching his windpipe. He'd forgotten the dock-keeper! She was sturdy and short, and Jack couldn't get a purchase as she dragged him backwards. He felt his jaw being pulled upwards; soon she'd have him.

But he still had the knife. He struck backwards, and the blade found something. Her grip loosened and he staggered away, leaving her groaning and holding her thigh. He made for the hawser again.

In the boat, a struggle was going on. The torch had fallen to the deck and all Jack could see was the silhouette of the two women wrestling. A squeak and a creak from his right told him that the dock-gates were closing. Desperately, he hacked through the remainder of the first hawser. The last strands twanged, the rope flicked backwards and the *Cerdic* began to drift away from the dockside. Now the gangplank shifted, twisting and tipping away from the wall. Jack started towards it – he needed to board the boat to help Shavila, who was still fighting the first Repseg. Then he'd have to cut the rope that held the *Cerdic* to the next boat. But the clanking of a rachet reminded him that the gates were closing. He turned to look, and that saved him. Limping out of the dark came the dock-keeper, who'd found a heavy, vicious-hooked gaff. With a yell she swung it, and Jack only just had time to duck before it passed an inch over his head. He threw himself into the woman's midriff, wrapping his arms around her so that she couldn't swing the weapon. They landed heavily and rolled, Jack clinging as hard as he could. The knife was still in his hand, but his arms were pinned beneath her and it was all he could do to keep his grip on it. The woman was breathing hard and swearing. She tried getting a purchase on the rough concrete with her heels; that propelled them towards the edge of the dock. Then she thrust Jack forward, so that his backbone thudded into a bollard and he was almost winded. He gripped harder, but now they'd reached the edge and he could feel them slipping over. The dock-keeper wailed and dropped the gaff, her hand reaching back into space; but Jack, groping behind him, found the remnant of the hawser, and grabbed it. Over the edge they fell, but, using the rope, Jack swung himself around and scrambled upwards. From behind him came a splash.

As Jack pulled himself onto the dockside, he heard another splash below. On the deck of the *Cerdic* he could make out one shadowy figure, who gripped the gunwale with both hands. The second figure was gone. 'Tori?' he cried.

There was no answer. The figure, back-lit by an electric torch that rolled on the deck, stood with her head bowed.

He hauled himself to his feet. 'Tori!' he called. 'You okay?'

Now the woman looked up. She lifted an acknowledging hand.

'Get the other rope,' Jack shouted. The figure waved again; below, he heard the dock-keeper cursing and splashing as she tried to scramble aboard another boat.

The gates! The second Repseg, turning the massive winch handle, had almost finished closing them. Beyond, the tide must be rising – sea-water was squirting into the dock through the remaining gap. That meant the Repseg had been working against the water pressure as well as the mass of the gates. Through the gloom he saw her, stooping, pulling, lifting, pushing. At each turn the ratchet clanked another notch.

SCORPION

Jack grimaced. This was a powerful woman, a gene-designed Repseg. How could he stop her? But now to his left he heard a chugging, hesitant at first, then steadier. Shavila had started the engine. Now, he thought – the Repseg won't see me – I can run up and knife her. Now! Come on, he told himself. You'll never be able to fight her. It's the only way.

'No,' he said out loud. It wouldn't do. He couldn't stab someone in the back, in the dark. *Coward again*, said a voice inside his head.

He looked around for something, a stick or a club, and almost tripped over the gaff, lying where the dock-keeper – who was now hauling herself aboard a boat – had dropped it. It was still a nasty weapon, with its barbed hook, but it would have to do.

Then things moved fast. The gates thudded shut, and the Repseg stood straight. Grabbing her torch, she pointed it at the *Cerdic*, where Shavila was cutting the second hawser. In a moment the boat would be free, but now there was no escape from the dock. As Shavila worked, the *Cerdic* drifted back towards the dock wall; and Jack saw the Repseg stand ready to leap as soon as the boat got close. He glanced down at the gaff, then back at the Repseg. Crouching, he scuttled towards her, still unseen and unheard. As the Repseg braced herself, poised to leap, he crept up and hooked the gaff around her left leg.

She jumped; the force of her leap pulled the gaff from Jack's hand and sent it flying into the dock. But it had also spoiled her jump, spinning her to the left and making her crash onto the prow of an adjacent boat. Jack ran for the winch and, with a heave, unlocked the ratchet. At first the gates didn't move, then, slowly at first, they began to swing open as the sea poured in and the winch-teeth clattered over the unravelling chain. Water rushed into the dock and Shavila had to fire up the engine to keep the *Cerdic* still. Jack yelled and waved; Shavila couldn't see him. The Repseg's torch lay on the ground. He grabbed it and waved it over his head. Then Shavila must have seen him, because she brought the boat close to the dockside. Jack leapt. The deck rushed up to meet him; the shock buckled his knees; the engine roared. The *Cerdic* surged through the gates and out into the channel.

17 The Solent at Night

The *Cerdic* rolled gently on the swell, its engine pulsing through the boat's ancient timbers. Jack sat with his back to the hard wood of the mid-deck locker and his backside in a puddle of seawater, while his breathing returned to normal. He looked up. Save for a few lights on the shore, all around was dark. They'd done it.

But, he wondered, what was it they'd done? They'd got a boat. How on earth were they going to find Clara? Always assuming the Repsegs didn't come after them, of course...

'Jack?' Shavila came out of the wheelhouse, clutching her arm. 'Good,' she said, seeing him get to his feet. 'You'll have to steer.'

'What?' said Jack. 'Me?'

'You ever driven a motor van?'

'No,' said Jack. 'When would I have done that?'

'What about boats?'

'Like I say, I've rowed. On a river...'

'Good. It's the same idea, but with a wheel.' Shavila slumped down onto a locker. 'Before you do, fetch me the first-aid kit, would you?'

'You're hurt?'

'My arm,' she said, sucking in her breath and holding her wrist to her chest.

Jack fetched the first-aid box from the wheelhouse.

'Thanks. Now get in there,' said Shavila, taking it from him. 'Just ease us out into the channel for now. Not too fast.'

In the wheelhouse, a lantern burned low. By its light Jack could just make out the throttle control; push it forward if you want to go faster, said the panel. In the centre of the console was a worn red wheel. He grabbed it and experimented with steering left, then right. In the dark he could hardly tell if the boat was responding.

'How do I know where I'm going?' he called to Shavila.

'Keep away from the shore lights,' she answered. 'Give me a minute, I'll get the charts out.'

Jack swallowed, and edged the *Cerdic* forward as slowly as he could. There was a steady swell, and rain spattered on the windows. Hard though he peered, he could only just make out the lights on the nearer, eastern, shore. Soon his eyes were throbbing.

'Here,' said Shavila, hauling herself back into the wheelhouse. 'Help me spread these out.'

He saw that she'd tied her right arm into a rough sling. 'What happened?' he said, taking the charts. 'Did the Repseg do that?'

Shavila nodded. 'It's broken,' she said, pivoting her elbow out.

'Broken? For a moment Jack wondered how they were going to manage, if Shavila was crippled. But then he remembered. 'It'll get better, right? Repsegs mend fast, don't they? Clara told me something about your teeth.'

'Yes, it'll mend,' said Shavila with a frown. 'But these days it's taking longer. I'm getting old, Jack. Past my expiry date.'

'I'm sorry,' said Jack. Once more, there was that surge of recognition – Tori Shavila was as real a person as he was. 'How long, d'you reckon?

Shavila looked away. 'I don't know,' she said. 'Now, let's have a look.' She turned up the lantern then, with Jack's help, unfolded the charts.

'I've just thought,' said Jack. 'Have we got any food?'

Shavila laughed. 'I didn't have time to think of that,' she said. 'Did you?'

'What about water?'

Shavila shook her head.

'Great,' said Jack.

It took them nearly an hour to round Calshot Point and turn west into the heavier waters of the Solent. Shavila told Jack to steer closer to the northern shore, then, working the sounding-line despite her injured arm, she called out the depths as they approached.

'That's three fathoms,' she said. 'Stop the engines. Can you see the anchor control?'

By the lamplight, Jack scanned the panel. 'Yep,' he called. 'We're anchoring here?'

'Yes,' said Shavila. 'We daren't go any further in the dark,' she went on, as Jack pressed the button and the rattling anchor-chain sent shivers through the deck. 'We've left the main channel, and if we keep our lights out, no-one will see us.'

'D'you think they'll have followed us?'

Shavila joined him in the wheelhouse. 'No, not after dark. But we'll need to use all the daylight hours to get away from here. I don't think they'll bother with an all-out search, but the patrols will be out in the morning.'

'So we wait.'

'We wait. You should get some sleep.'

'So should you.' Jack peered out at the deck, where a mizzle was now soaking everything. The deck was short, maybe fifty feet aft of the wheelhouse, and there were lockers full of ropes and nets. 'Where can we bunk down?' he asked.

'In here, if you can curl up in the corner. Fairly dry there. There's some oilskins here,' she added, taking one off a hook. 'I'll take first watch.'

As Jack squatted down beside the control panel, Shavila slipped the oilskin over her shoulders before seating herself on the wheelhouse step. Jack turned the lamp to its lowest.

'Tell me more about this *Scorpion* thing,' he said.

Shavila half-turned her head. 'Like I say,' she said, 'there's a constant stream of people trying to get to Anglia from across the Channel. Coastforce's job is to stop them. As far as I can make out, they get a bounty for every boat they "nullify". That means either ramming them or blowing them out of the water.'

'Who'd wanna cross the Channel?' said Jack. 'Don't they talk about "a wreck a day", with the wind and the waves and that?'

'Desperate people would. The further south you go, the more there's war, and starvation, and disease.'

'Seems to me,' said Jack, 'Coastforce don't have much to do. The Channel does most of it for 'em.'

Shavila winced as she flexed her arm. 'Coastforce also go raiding,' she said. 'They raid the towns along the Wessex coast. Or the French, if the weather's good enough.'

'Nice girls, are they?'

'That's how we can find them, I think,' said Shavila. 'If we ask at every likely place along the coast, we can find out where the *Scorpion*'s been raiding.'

'And after that,' said Jack, 'it gets easy.'

Shavila chuckled. 'Now shut up and get some sleep,' she said. 'I'll wake you in five hours.'

It felt like a lot less than five hours, and a lot less sleep than that, when Jack felt a touch on his shoulder.

'Here,' said Shavila. 'Water.'

Blinking, Jack felt a leather bottle pressed into his hands. 'Mm?' he mumbled. 'Where'd you get this?'

'It's rainwater,' said Shavila. 'I made a basin in some tarp.'

'Still raining then?' said Jack, groaning as he eased himself into a sitting position. He swigged at the water. 'That's good,' he said. 'Thanks.'

'It's – it's a pleasure,' said Shavila. She eased herself out of the oilskin and hung it in a corner of the cramped wheelhouse. 'Y'know,' she said, 'this might sound silly, but it's little things like that – just giving you water, for instance – it's those things that have made the difference.'

Jack waited for her to go on.

'Being a Repseg, it was all about orders, and duty, and efficiency. Fighting, and beating people up – that came under "efficiency". You didn't use force any more than you had to, but you *did* have to use enough...but, giving things to each other, giving them when you didn't have to...well, it never crossed our minds.' She lay down near the control panel.

The boat creaked, the anchor-chain clanked, and the rain spat on the windows. 'And now?' prompted Jack, handing her the water-bottle.

'I enjoy it,' said Shavila, settling herself down. 'I enjoy it, and I enjoy it more when someone says "thank you". I've got a lot to thank your Clara for. A lot. She gave me freedom. She didn't have to tell me that Repsegs were all Geemos, but she did. Wake me before dawn, will you?'

'Yeah,' said Jack. 'She's like that. Gets inside your head. Justice. Fairness.' He reached for a dry oilskin. 'Total nutter, she is. But you can't ignore her for long.' He gave a rueful chuckle. 'There's got to be some reason why I'm chasing her all over the place.'

Shavila didn't reply. She was already asleep.

When is "before dawn"? Jack didn't know. An hour came when he wondered if there was the suggestion of pallor in what he thought was the eastern sky, so maybe now was the time. Besides, he was cold to the core.

Shavila was curled up behind the skipper's chair. Holding the lantern closer, Jack studied her face: the high cheekbones, the heavy eyelids, the untidy strand of hair falling over her cheek. Gently, he brushed it away. Next second her eyes opened, and Jack found himself staring into them.

He cleared his throat. 'Er. I – I think it's morning. Well, nearly...'

She sat up. 'Any more water?' she croaked.

'Yeah,' said Jack, 'I got some. It didn't stop raining till half an hour ago, so I filled the bottle again and we've still got some more and–' He stopped. Why was he so absurdly proud of himself?

Shavila drank thirstily. 'Thanks,' she said, peering up at him.

Gulls wailed overhead. Jack caught a pale glimpse as one of them dived into the waves.

'Should we...get moving?' he asked.

As Shavila pulled herself to her feet, the boat pitched and she toppled forward. Jack caught her. 'Thanks,' she said again.

Jack nodded. 'It's okay.' His stomach was clenching. Seasickness? Hunger?

'I'll get the engine started,' said Shavila. 'Then you'd better steer again. And see if you can find some binoculars. I lost mine in the fight.'

Jack exhaled deeply. 'What's the plan?' he asked.

'All we've got to do,' said Shavila, reaching into the engine, 'is keep a course through the Needles Channel without hitting anything. And avoid the patrol boats.' The engine coughed, and failed. 'And,' she added, pulling at the handle again then stepping back and closing the hatch as the engine grumbled into life, 'find somewhere to get fuel.'

Jack looked at the gauge and grimaced. 'Quarter of a tank,' he said. 'How far's that going to get us?'

The view eased from a dark, iron grey sky to a paler mix of grey sea, grey clouds and grey shores. The *Cerdic* pitched and waves washed over the wheelhouse. Jack was still hungry, but he wasn't sure whether, if he ate anything, he'd be able to keep it down. Shavila, who'd been standing at the stern and watching the receding straits through the binoculars, weaved her way forward to the wheelhouse. Leaning against a bulkhead, she eased her arm from its sling.

'See anything?' asked Jack, peering through the salt-stained window at the shoreline, about a mile distant. Just here, it was marked by the remains of a drowned village.

'I'm pretty sure,' said Shavila, moving her forearm experimentally, 'that I saw a patrol just now.'

'Shit,' said Jack. 'Should we go faster? Can we outrun them?'

'No,' said Shavila, although Jack wasn't sure which question she was answering. 'I don't think they've seen us. They paint those boats yellow, which is okay if you want people to know that the law's after them. But not so good for camouflage.' She came and stood next to Jack.

'How's the arm?' he asked.

'Still sore,' she answered. 'Not long ago, it would've mended by now. Like I say,' she went on, 'I should've retired already. Did Clara tell you she found my spec?'

'Umm ...?'

'The specification for all the Shavila batches. The one that Geneco used for me.'

'Yeah. I think she said something about it.' It was a long time since Jack had had a chat with Clara, as opposed to an argument, or an apology, or a plea.

'It said, decommission after thirty years.'

'And that goes for you? Is that another reason you're not a Repseg any more?'

Shavila turned towards the stern and raised her glasses again. 'No,' she murmured, 'can't see them any more...nothing.'

'I'll keep at this speed, then?'

'Yes,' said Shavila, 'and you can edge a bit closer to the shore.' Then she went on, 'Remember I told you I got hold of some personnel records?'

'Yeah?'

'I found one of the Guards who used to work for me – Sonia, her name was – before she "retired". She was living in Essex, beyond Grays. It was like some kind of hostel, but with thick fences and high security. Called *The Meadows* or something. It'd be suspicious if I walked up and demanded to be let in, so I climbed a tree and stayed there for two days, watching through binoculars. In the end, I think I saw Sonia. Of course, all clones look the same, and Geemos more so, so I can't be sure. But I think it was her. She was white-haired already, and she had a stoop, and she needed a walking-frame. She'd left the Guards only two years before, in full health.' She paused again, scanning the horizon. 'No sign of that patrol,' she said.

'She'd aged quickly, then?' asked Jack.

Shavila nodded. 'It was scary. Another thing I'd seen was the supply carts coming in and out. One evening at dusk, I followed a driver who'd done her deliveries, and grabbed her. Said I was working undercover, that we'd heard rumours that the place was being run badly.

'She said she didn't know about that, but she did know that nobody who went in ever came out, even though more women were arriving every week. All the girls in there had single rooms – so that was one good thing – but she said every room had a supply of high-power sleeping pills. She'd heard that most of them decided to take an overdose rather than face their bodies falling apart.

'I badly wanted to know more, but I didn't dare break in to find Sonia. Besides, I had to get back to my unit. On the way I tried to work out how old I was, and how long it'd be before I got sent to *The Meadows* myself. I needn't have worried – there was a letter waiting for me when I got back. It said I was retiring immediately, and to report to the commanding officer at once. I told the girls what I'd got, and said I was going to report – then I left the barracks, stole a motor-van and headed west.'

'Shit,' said Jack. 'Was it for real?'

'Might've been. Or, they could have got suspicious about what I was up to. Anyhow, that's why I was a bit nervous back in Southampton.'

Jack nodded, then a wave crashed over the prow and pounded on the wheelhouse windows.

'I don't like the look of that sky,' said Shavila.

18 Charis Clark

Clara was sore all over. Not only did she have to shovel the coal that Riss was pushing to the front of the heap, but she also had to contend with the violent pitching as the *Scorpion* butted its way through the heavy seas. On Crudger's instructions, Clara and Xavi had stoked the furnaces until they could be heard even over the rumble of the engines and the pounding of the waves. Smoke escaped into the boiler-room and stung their eyes, and all the time, the sweat rolled down their dusty faces and stuck their sodden clothes to their bodies. Outside, it was raining hard. Water poured off anyone who came down the companionway, and for the last twenty minutes Wilson had been keeping as close to the furnace as the rolling of the ship would allow. Eventually she retired to her station, cursing.

Clara stole a glance at Xavi. His brow glistened in the amber light, and his arm-muscles rippled as he moved. But there was pain in that face, and every time he put weight on his bad leg, he winced. As she filled her shovel once again, Clara wondered. There was an ache in her heart, a tugging in her guts and a tingle up her neck. Was this what love felt like? But how could she and Xavi ever be together? He'd have to go back to France, to look for what was left of his family, while she needed to get back to Sophia and James. She'd promised, hadn't she?

Xavi limped over to check the pressure gauges again. He tapped them and nodded, and when he came back she asked, 'Xavi, what will you do when we escape?'

He smiled sadly and Clara felt their eyes lock. He reached out and placed his palm on her cheek. She pressed herself into his touch, then took his hand in hers and kissed his fingers. 'I want to come with you,' she said.

Then the hatch banged open, and although the wind and rain swirled into the boiler room, the pale light told them that the weather was beginning to clear. Boots clanged on the companionway and down came Crudger, followed by Captain Suggs. Crudger's grey hair was dripping and she carried an electric torch, which she shone at them. Clara swallowed. What now?

'She's up there, Captain,' said Crudger.

She shone the beam at Riss, who was already clambering off the coal-heap. 'She been working all right?' Suggs asked. 'Even with the wound?'

'She's mostly on the stack,' replied Crudger. 'But yeah, she works okay. Come here, girl,' she added to Riss.

Xavi touched Clara on the arm. 'Wilson watches,' he said in a low voice. They resumed work, but Clara kept glancing back to see what was going on. It looked like Suggs was inspecting the dressing on Riss's arm. 'Get it cleaned and changed,' she told Crudger.

Then she shone the torch at Riss's face, making her blink, and studied her for a full minute. 'Blue hair,' she said. 'Catches the eye. Then you don't notice the face so much...'

'Ma'am?' said Crudger.

Suggs looked Riss in the eye. 'I bought a copy of *The Republican Woman* in Southampton,' she said. 'I've just got round to reading it.'

Riss returned her gaze, but said nothing.

'Captain!' The first mate was calling down the companionway. 'Captain, there's a sighting!'

'On my way,' Suggs called back. She grinned at Riss. 'Talk later, shall we?' she said.

'Bloody woman,' said Riss, watching Suggs as she and Crudger hurried up the steps, calling the customary warning to Twitcher as they went. 'I bet she knows.'

'Knows what?' asked Clara.

Riss glanced at Wilson, who was slumped on her stool, lighting a cigarette with trembling fingers. 'I got something to tell you,' she said. They felt the ship tilt to starboard as it turned. Riss spoke quickly. 'I'm wanted,' she said. 'Looks like the captain's rumbled me.'

Xavi had joined them, and for the moment they weren't working. They'd be in trouble if Wilson spotted them.

'My name's Clark,' said Riss. 'Riss to my friends, but my mother–' she snarled at the word '–calls me Charis.'

Clara's eyes widened. 'Those posters! *You're* General Clark's daughter?'

'Who is General Clark?' asked Xavi.

'Someone important,' said Clara. She put a hand on his arm. 'Head of the military council. And there are posters in Southampton saying that her daughter's missing.'

'I was trying to hide,' said Riss with a sigh. 'I hated what she was doing. I was with a friend, but we fell out and I went and I got smashed–'

'Drunk,' Clara told Xavi.

'–and now I'm here,' Riss finished. 'Look, don't tell anyone, hey? Although I'm sure Suggs has guessed. She'll want the reward.'

'But if she turns you in, at least you'll get out of here,' said Clara, gesturing around them.

'I'd rather stay put,' growled Riss.

The ship made another turn, and the engines roared. They knew what was coming, and before Wilson could yell at them, they were stoking the fires again. The deck shook beneath their feet, and coal clattered off the heap whenever the *Scorpion* lurched over another wave. Riss was cursing, Wilson was cursing and Xavi was wincing in pain. Five minutes passed, six, then the first shock, a minor one that didn't throw them off their feet. Then a crunching under the keel, and the *Scorpion* had moved on, turning sharply to port and surging forward again.

Clangs from above told them the gun was being readied. Clara stole a glance at Xavi. He was pale, but his jaw was set. Still the *Scorpion* surged on. More clangs came, then the sounds of running feet. Wilson pulled out a hip-flask, drank a great gulp of rum, and held on to a bulkhead. More shouts; the gun was fired. The concussion reverberated through the whole ship. Xavi looked up briefly, but carried on shovelling.

Then came a smashing and a creaking, a shock as the *Scorpion* recoiled, debris thumping against the hull. Through the open hatchway, screams reached them. Voices, foreign voices, terrified voices. Xavi threw down his shovel, and Clara could see that he was shaking. He began to limp towards the companionway, and she had to run and throw her arms around him.

'No!' she cried, pulling him to a halt. 'No, Xavi! Remember what happened to me.'

He tried to force her off. 'I no care,' he said. 'Is murder. I have to stop.'

Clara glanced at Wilson. It seemed that the guard wasn't her usual self – normally she'd have been after them with her shock-stick by now, but instead she was just swallowing more rum.

'You'll be killed,' Clara told Xavi, tugging at him. 'Come back and work, before *she* sees you. There's nothing we can do.'

Still he stared up at the open hatch. They heard more yells, and the sound of a rifle. Xavi flinched. 'Is better to die, than to help the killing.'

'Xavi, no,' moaned Clara. 'I want you to live.' She pressed a palm to his chest, and she could feel his heart pounding under his ribs. 'Please.'

He wouldn't move. Clara tried once more. 'We *will* stop them,' she said. 'Somehow. Somehow we'll get our revenge. We'll pay them back.'

He glanced down at her.

'Yes,' she went on, 'we'll make a plan. But don't run up there now. You'll be shot, and that won't help anyone.'

He bent his head and allowed himself to be led back to work. 'We pay them back,' was all he said.

As they worked, the sounds diminished. They heard something being hauled aboard, then all they heard were the wind and the waves. Wilson carried on drinking. Neither Suggs nor Crudger returned.

The January dusk came. Wilson had dragged herself up the companionway, lurching from one side to the other and swearing. The gauges were high, and the sea had calmed. Clara, Xavi and Riss sat at the bottom of the coal-heap, shovels in hand in case Wilson came back.

'I was one,' said Xavi, looking down at his hands. 'Like them. I was *refugiado*. We cross Viscaya, for France. No ships run us down.' He sighed. 'I was one.'

'Those voices we heard,' said Clara. 'Were they from Spain?'

He shook his head. 'No. I think Africa.'

'Africa!'

'*Sí*. Bad things, they happen everywhere.'

'I knew people were trying to cross the Channel,' said Riss. 'But don't they know they can never make it?'

'I saw bodies,' said Clara. 'The boatman said they were from Africa.' And she told them of the desperate trip she and Sophia had made, escaping from Wight with Khan's help, and of the mass of bodies, their skin bloated and rotting, that had blocked their way in Keyhaven lagoon, and how the dead seemed to pluck at their oars even as they rowed.

'Crossing the Channel!' said Riss. 'They must have been *so* desperate.'

The hatch opened, and they leapt to their feet. Crudger came halfway down the steps. 'Better sort yourselves out down there,' she called above the wind. 'There's a storm coming.' In confirmation, there was a white flicker in the night sky.

19 News

'Find anything?' Jack called. He peered through the sea-scarred windows and gripped the wheel tightly. The sea was heavy, and he was afraid that if he let go, he'd be sick again.

Shavila made her way back to the wheelhouse. 'Only what you'd expect,' she said, gesturing at the deck lockers. 'Spare nets – there's a big trawl one under the deck – ropes, tarps. Rubber life jackets–'

'Bloody hell,' said Jack. 'I hadn't thought of that.'

'Yes,' said Shavila. 'We might need those if we're going to mix it with the *Scorpion*.'

'Good to know,' he replied, although he shuddered at the thought of finishing up in the water, life jacket or not.

'There's a couple of mallets they use for killing fish,' went on Shavila, 'but otherwise this is all I found.' She showed him a large pistol. 'It's not even a proper weapon.'

'What is it?' asked Jack.

'A flare gun. Last time I saw one of these, Mater Hedera was using it on some rioters.' She tested the loading action. 'Like I say, it's not a proper gun, but fire this at them, and it'll make them think.' She came to stand beside Jack. Through the sea-haze away to their right, they could see the dark outlines of the Bournemouth waterfront.

'We're still heading west?' said Shavila, checking the charts.

'Yeah,' said Jack. 'Tell me again why we didn't dock in Bournemouth? We could've got fuel there all right, I reckon.'

'Well, you're right, the sputs outbreak should have cleared by now. But it wasn't very long ago, so we can't be sure. And we do know there's martial law. Nothing official, but the mayor's paying anyone who can hold a gun to enforce the quarantine.'

'Might get the wrong sort of welcome, then,' said Jack.

'Look,' said Shavila, pointing ahead. 'That's Swanage. Just go a touch to port – that's it. And the other thing is, we wouldn't get news of the *Scorpion*. I'm betting they'll have left Bournemouth alone.'

Forty minutes later they moored in Swanage. To Jack's relief, Shavila, her arm now mending, had offered to manoeuvre the *Cerdic* for the last few hundred yards, around the end of the floating jetty that was itself moored to the old, submerged quay, and into the harbour. Gulls scattered at their approach.

'See that?' said Shavila as she eased the throttle back. She pointed along the jetty to where two armed women were striding towards them. 'Security. Something's made them jumpy.'

They disembarked. 'Fuel?' said one of the women in answer to Shavila's question. 'You'll be lucky.'

'She'll let you have a little,' said the other. 'It'll cost yer.'

They promised not to stay any longer than necessary, and went to find the harbour manager. Having negotiated to buy a couple of gallons – the security woman had been right about the price – they made their way into the town. Searise had almost divided it in two, and they had to follow the road uphill for some distance before they found an inn. Jack staggered along, feeling as if the hard tarmac was deliberately smacking into his feet.

'Is it always like this?' said Jack.

'Sea-legs and land-legs,' said Shavila. 'You'll get used to it.'

Jack noticed Shavila was also dragging her feet. 'You all right?' he asked.

'I'm stiff and tired,' she said. 'I need rest.'

Jack peered at her. Her face, exposed as the wind whipped her ponytail out behind her, was pale. 'Look,' he said. 'I can't do this without you, Tori. I need you fit, and all that. So let's put up here for the night, and you can have a good kip. We both can.'

'Don't you want to catch the *Scorpion*?'

'We can't rescue Clara if we're falling asleep,' said Jack, hoping that rest was indeed all that Shavila needed. 'Besides,' he added, pointing up a the rapidly-darkening sky, 'I don't think we're going anywhere tonight.'

Shavila sighed and nodded. 'Let's get some rooms, then,' she said.

They reached the *Nightingale* inn, where they could already smell cooking. Shavila was peering into her pack. 'Now, where's my purse? Hope I haven't lost it...'

'Come on, I'll get you a room,' said Jack as he pulled out his own.

'What about you?' said Shavila.

'I'll see if they've got male quarters,' he replied. 'Even if it's only a hayloft, I reckon I'll sleep better than last night.'

Shavila gave a wry grin. Before going indoors, she glanced up at the sky. 'You're right, looks like a big one,' she said. 'I hope that jetty's secure. It'd be a shame to wake up in the morning and find no boat.'

They passed though the vestibule and into the inn, where they paid for Shavila's room and a place in an outhouse for Jack. As they withdrew, Jack pointed to a door leading to a tatty side-room. *Males Allowed*, read the notice. 'I'll meet you in there,' said Jack. 'Six o'clock?'

'I'll go and get cleaned up,' said Shavila.

'To be honest, Tori,' said Jack, 'it's about time. You stink. Have a good wash, hey?'

Shavila grimaced. 'It won't help,' she added, looking down. 'It's my suit you can smell.'

'Yeah, all that tight leather. Why d'you wear it? I'm guessing it's not to make you look good. I mean, don't get me wrong – that is, you do look good. I mean–' He broke off, blushing.

'It keeps my bones together,' said Shavila, and started up the stairs.

By the time Jack scampered in from the yard and joined Shavila in the side-room, the storm had arrived. Rain ran down the windows while the wind beat against the shutters, hammered at the doors and almost drowned out the thunder. Jack tried not to imagine how Clara was feeling, out in this weather on the *Scorpion*. If she was even still there.

When the landlady, a tall woman with thick spectacles, brought them their plates of herring, they asked about the armed guards at the harbour.

'Oh, yeah,' she said, wiping her hands on her apron, 'there was a raid two nights ago. Bloody pirates.'

'That'd be the eighteenth?' said Shavila.

'Yeah. Middle of the night. Those girls knew what they was about – they went for the bank, and a few shops. Took some provisions, but otherwise it was mostly valuables, stuff they could sell. They're armed too. A few of our girls heard the break-in and went after them, but the robbers had guns. All it took was a couple of shots.'

'Anyone hurt?'

'No, but we gave up after that. You can't chase armed robbers in the dark.'

'You been raided before?' asked Jack.

'Well you're a forward one, ain't you,' said the landlady, 'for a male? Yeah,' she said, addressing Shavila. 'About six months ago. Set fire to one of the storehouses then.'

When they'd finished their meal, Shavila went to get more drinks. Jack had managed one beer to Shavila's three whiskies, yet she wasn't even merry (although he did wonder if Repsegs *ever* got merry). She'd only been gone for a moment when she put her head around the door and beckoned him into the crowded bar.

'Listen to this,' she said, pointing at two women who'd just entered. 'They say Bournemouth *was* raided, after all.'

'...four nights ago,' one of the women was saying as she hung her dripping oilskin on a hook. 'So I heard.'

'Thought they'd sealed the place off?' somebody asked. 'With the plague, and all.'

The second newcomer joined her companion. 'Yeah, but the roadblocks, and all that, they're on the landward side,' she said. 'They wasn't takin' no notice of the shore.'

'Anyhow,' the first one said, 'they went for jewels and cash. They came by night, and they was leavin' in their boats before anyone caught up with 'em. Set fire to a few houses, and all.'

'They never done that here,' said someone.

'Well, you got off light then.'

There was a rumble of thunder. Rain came down the chimney and hissed on the fire. The two travellers turned their attention to ordering food, and Shavila motioned Jack to follow her back to their table.

'They're moving west,' said Shavila.

Jack nodded. 'Listen,' he said. 'This *Scorpion* thing, it's big, right? Steel-built? It's got guns?'

'That's right.'

'Well, how the bloody hell are we going to tackle it? They'll just run us down, or blow us out of the water. We're too slow to catch it, even if can we find it in the first place.'

Shavila raised an eyebrow. 'What,' she said, 'd'you want to give up?'

'No,' said Jack. 'O' course not.'

'Well, then,' said Shavila.

Jack stared at the rain on the window-panes. Bloody Clara, he thought. Bloody, bloody Clara.

20 Desperation

The storm had gone. On the *Scorpion*, many hours had passed and full night had fallen. Their meagre food had arrived, and, despite the heavy seas, Clara had managed to keep hers down. They'd drunk, too, although in the heat and the dust there never seemed to be enough water in the stoup. Finally, they'd had their ration of grog and Xavi had limped off to make his bed in the coal. His leg didn't seem to be getting any better.

For the moment, the work was light. The *Scorpion* was making slow ahead, and the engines were uncharacteristically quiet. The steam pressure seemed to be staying up of its own accord, and Clara and Riss were spending half the time leaning on their shovels. Riss's arm had been re-dressed, and Clara was just about to ask if she could have a look at it when there was a gurgle and Wilson, who was on watch, slithered off her stool and landed in a heap on the floor.

'Whatchoo lookin' at?' she demanded as she dragged herself to her feet. She peered at them, trying to focus. 'I've 'ad enough of this fucking ship,' she said. Hauling herself to the foot of the steps she called up, 'Oi, Twitcher. I'm comin' up, and if you mess me about, I'm shovin' that rifle where the sun don't shine. All the fuckin' way! Savvy?'

Clara and Riss looked at each other. No work, no guard, said their glance. They flopped down onto the coal-heap while Wilson staggered up the companionway.

'She's going to get herself in trouble,' said Clara.

'I think she's losing it,' replied Riss, tapping her head. 'Nothing to do all day except watch us shovelling.'

'Yes, at least we don't have that problem. At least we keep busy, hey?'

Riss swore and dug her in the ribs. Above them, they heard the derricks swinging and the boats being lowered into the water.

'Another raid,' said Riss. 'I wonder where we are?'

'We've no way of telling,' said Clara. 'We could be off Dorset, we could be into Wessex. We could even be off France.'

They sat for a few minutes. Then Clara broke the silence. 'So,' she said. 'Go on, then. How come General Clark's daughter's been pressganged by Coastforce?'

'You know I'm not making it up, right?' said Riss.

'When they shipped us to the slave market, the truck stopped right beside one of the posters. You're famous, you know. "Have you seen this woman?" and all that.'

Riss sighed. 'Bloody Mother,' she grunted.

'It was a good picture,' said Clara. 'Once you told us, I remembered it.'

Although there was no-one but the sleeping Xavi in the boiler room, Riss looked all around and lowered her voice. 'Mother made the mistake of sending me to a decent school,' she said. 'There was a teacher there – well, she taught us to always ask questions. Mostly to ask *why*.'

'Ooh. Dangerous.'

'Exactly. Then, to make things worse, Mother sent me to work in the munitions place in Rochester. So there I was, helping to make bullets and guns when they keep telling us there's no steel left, and when half the poor sods who live in the town are starving.' Riss shook her head. 'I couldn't stand it. I left.'

Clara glanced at her. 'That was brave,' she said.

'Brave, maybe. Stupid, definitely. Then I fell out with my girlfriend, moved out, drifted for a while. I wound up in Southampton – don't ask me how – getting totally out of my skull. Next thing I remember, I'm in a rowing-boat, trussed up like a pig, heading for the *Scorpion*.' Now it was her turn to look at Clara. 'What about you?'

Behind them, Xavi groaned.

'Ooh,' said Clara. 'Long story. *Long* story.'

'Summarise. In less than a thousand words.'

Clara chuckled. 'I'm a Natural, but somehow my mother got me into the Academy.'

'Oh, yeah – the posh place in London? Anna went there.'

'Anna?'

Riss shook her head. 'Girlfriend. Go on.'

'Well, after I left there, I was a Truth Sister. But then I got found out, and I've been running ever since, more or less.'

'On your own?'

'Not all the time,' said Clara. She sighed and tried not to think of Jack, and Sophia and James. Then she said, 'Did you ever hear about something called Aquaster?'

Riss pulled a face. 'Can't say that I have.'

'The Republic puts it in the water supplies. It takes away sexual desire and makes people docile.'

'Ha!' said Riss. 'D'you know, I've got absolutely no difficulty believing that.'

'I've tried to avoid tap water ever since. Even when I worked at the smithy, I'd store rainwater when I could.'

Riss nodded. 'So. *Your* sexual desire's all right then.'

Clara felt herself blushing. In the darkness, and under the coal-dust that covered her face, Riss wouldn't notice, but still...

'I've seen you,' said Riss. 'You and him,' she added, glancing over her shoulder to where Xavi lay. 'You fancy him, yeah?'

Clara bowed her head. 'What does it matter?' she said. 'Yes, I do "fancy" him.' A groan and a clatter told them that Xavi was waking up. 'Whenever I'm near him it's like – it's like...' she trailed off. 'But we're never going to get out of here, are we? So what's the use?'

'I've been thinking about that,' said Riss.

'How do you mean?'

'It comes to this.' Riss's jaw was set. 'Do you want to die here? And *that* won't be very long in coming, will it? Or – or do you want to risk everything, for a chance to live?'

Xavi joined them. 'Where is Wilson?' he asked, easing himself down next to Clara.

She was aware of his backside next to hers, their bodies pressing against each other. She swallowed. 'She's gone up on deck. We don't know why.'

'We were talking about escaping,' Riss told him.

'*Sí*,' said Xavi. 'I hear you. You think is possible?'

Riss inclined her head. 'Like I was saying.' She made the points on her fingers. 'We can die here, worn out by the work. Or, we can die trying to escape. Or, we might make it.'

Clara put a hand on Riss's arm. 'But you've got an easy way out. Suggs is going to send you back to your mother and claim the reward. What's wrong with that?'

She shook her head. 'No. D'you know, Clara, I think I'd *rather* die.'

'What are you thinking?' asked Xavi.

There was a commotion on deck, but as yet no-one came down the companionway. Riss spoke quickly. 'The other thing is, we might not all make it. But there won't be time to stop and help each other. So if anyone falls, we got to keep going.'

Xavi shook his head, but said nothing.

'These raids,' went on Riss. 'They've got to bring the *Scorpion* close in to the shore, right?'

'Right...?' said Clara.

'No more than a mile, I'd say. So, we get off the ship, and we swim.'

Clara and Xavi digested that for a moment. At last Clara said, 'I can see some problems with that.'

Riss nodded. 'Of course. We wait till the boats have gone out on the next raid, wait till it's quiet. We overpower Wilson, grab her stick and shock her. Easier said than done, I know. We call up to Twitcher, as if we're Wilson. Then we charge her, all together.'

'She will shoot,' said Xavi.

'She won't get all of us,' said Riss. 'We could even use Wilson as a shield, if we can a manage her.'

Clara gave a long exhale and shook her head. 'I'll go first, then. I–'

'We'll come to that,' put in Riss before Xavi could object.

'To get into water, we have to climb up steep side,' said Xavi. 'Is difficult. It take much time.'

'Maybe we can get Twitcher's gun,' said Riss.

'And,' put in Clara, 'once we do get into the water, there's the little matter of the waves. And the currents – we could be washed out to sea.'

'Yep,' said Riss. 'All that.'

There was the sound of chains, and voices at the hatchway. They jumped up and pretended to work.

'Are we going for it?' asked Riss, as the first footsteps were heard on the stairs.

'Yes,' said Xavi.

Clara couldn't bring herself to say it. It was bound to fail. They might all die. And if she was the one who made it, and the others died, how could she live with herself? But they'd each be facing the same dilemma, wouldn't they? In the end, she nodded.

'Not tonight,' said Riss. 'Next time.'

It was Crudger who came down the steps. She already wore a scowl. 'How are we doing?' she said, checking the gauges. She adjusted one of the regulators. 'Get stoking,' she said. 'We're getting steam up soon.'

There were shouts on deck. Chains rattled, pulleys squealed and the bumping on the hull told them the boats had returned.

Later, when it was her turn to sleep on the coaldust bed, Clara pictured flinging herself at Twitcher, taking the bullet and heroically saving both the general's daughter and the man she loved. Xavi would be without her, but he'd be free to go and find his family. Then she thought about Jack. He wouldn't think much of their plan. Mad, he'd call it. And last, before sleep took her, she thought of Hashim. Poor Hashim, who lived here and died here. Was Riss right, then? Was it better to die sooner, trying to escape? Or later, when you're too exhausted to live?

21 Lulworth

Clara had told Jack, once – or probably more than once, he decided – that just because the world had warmed and the ice had melted, it didn't mean it'd never be cold. And she was bloody well right, he thought. Last month it had snowed, the first time he'd ever known it, but it had only lain for a few days. Although it wasn't snowing today, it was bloody freezing again. The wheelhouse was supposed to get heat from the engine, but the hot air stank of diesel and smoke, and Jack had closed the vents early in the voyage. Now, with his shoulders hunched, he held the wheel with one hand while keeping the other in his coat pocket. Of course, he thought, those ten minutes he'd spent trying to clean the windows, so that he could actually see out, and the soaking he'd got while he was at it, wouldn't have helped.

It was early afternoon. The grey clouds were high, the wind had dropped to a stiff breeze, and to his right he could hear the squawks of the gulls and gannets as they dived for food. The morning's sailing had been uneventful: Shavila had sighted a large vessel far away to the south, but had pronounced it to be a fuel tanker. 'They're getting rarer,' she'd said, pointing. 'One day we'll run out of oil altogether.'

Jack had asked if that was because there was none left in the world.

'I don't think so,' Shavila had said. 'But it's risky to extract and expensive to ship, and when hardly anyone can use it nowadays, it's not worthwhile.'

Now he glanced behind him to where Shavila slept, slumped on a crate that she'd wedged into a corner of the wheelhouse. She looked pale. Although he didn't like to wake her, he gave her a gentle shake. 'Tori,' he said, 'I think we're there. Lulworth. And there's smoke.'

Shavila blinked twice then got to her feet, leaning forward on the bulkhead. 'You're right about the smoke,' she said, raising her binoculars and yawning. 'Looks like it's over that hill.'

Jack glanced at the chart. 'That's where the village is. You reckon it could've been the *Scorpion*?'

'Every second night,' mused Shavila. 'We're on the trail, Jack.' She turned to stare at the grey swell, the drifting flecks of froth and spume. 'Sometimes,' she said, 'I'd really like a swim. We didn't do recreation when I was a Repseg.'

Jack glanced at her. 'What did you do, then? When you was off duty?'

Shavila continued watching the waves. 'We just rested,' she said. 'We ate, and we rested. Didn't need so much then. Rest, I mean.'

'Well, don't go for a swim yet,' said Jack.

Shavila shook herself. Then she frowned. 'Hang on,' she said. 'What's that?'

Jack glanced over his shoulder. Ten yards off the starboard side, something white was bobbing in the grey waves. At first he thought it might be a large fish, or a dolphin or something. He turned back quickly. Got to watch my course, he told himself.

'It's a body,' said Shavila.

Jack looked again. 'Dead?' He could see arms now, and a black-haired head, nodding in time to the waves.

'Definitely,' said Shavila, peering after the object as it fell behind.

Fighting down an urge to be sick, Jack made himself slow the *Cerdic* to a few knots and ease between the sea-ravaged cliffs that protected the cove. Before them opened an almost-circular inlet a quarter of a mile across, walled in by chalk cliffs on the landward side. Immediately the water became calmer, and Jack steered between several sailing-boats at anchor, then gently on towards the western shore. On their right a conical heap against the cliffs told of a recent collapse, and nearby, three more boats wallowed in the shallows. Of these one had been dragged onto the beach, and they could see ragged splintering around a fresh row of holes on its hull. The other two were partially submerged, with their superstructures burnt and blackened. There was an acrid tang in the air.

On Shavila's direction, Jack ran the *Cerdic*'s nose into the shingle while she loosed the anchor. They jumped into the shallows, sending a handful of crabs scurrying, and waded ashore. Then from further up the beach they heard a shout. At the head of the slipway, a woman was emerging from a wooden hut. She was aiming a crossbow.

'Raise your hands,' said Shavila.

Jack did. Even at this distance he could see the woman's hands were trembling.

'Oi!' the woman cried. "Oo are yer? State yer business!'

'We want to buy fuel,' answered Shavila.

'And food,' added Jack.

The woman swore, and peered over their heads towards the entrance to the cove. After a minute she appeared to be satisfied. 'Stay where you are,' she told them. 'Mungo, you little shit,' she called, 'get yerself 'ere!'

A small boy peered around the door of the hut, then hurried up to the sentry. He was thin and pale, and wore a threadbare jumper and ragged trousers. For a moment Jack felt as if he was looking at his younger self, left all alone after his mother died; and when the sentry gave the boy a cuff across the head for not being quick enough, he could almost feel the blow himself.

'Hey!' he called, as the boy ran off on his errand. 'There's no need for that, he's doing his best!'

'Leave it,' said Shavila. 'We need these people to help us. Don't annoy them.'

Jack shook his head.

The sentry was approaching, bow still raised. She glared at Jack. 'What's it to you, *boy*?' she sneered, and spat at his feet. Only now did Jack notice a great black bruise on the woman's temple.

Shavila still had hold of Jack. 'You've had trouble here,' she told the woman.

The sentry frowned. 'How d'you know that?'

'Well,' said Shavila, 'two of your boats have been burnt and another one's holed. That's a bit of a clue. And the smoke,' she added, nodding inland to where the pall, though now thinner, still rose. 'What happened?

'You'll have to talk to Fenny,' said the woman.

'Fenny?'

'She's the harbourmistress. You wait here.'

Jack and Shavila sat on the edge of the concrete slipway, their feet dangling over the edge. Ten minutes went by, while the sentry watched from her hut.

'I feel warmer already,' said Jack, 'out of the wind.'

Shavila nodded.

'Sorry about before,' Jack went on, looking at his feet. 'I've always just, you know, accepted it. Men are inferior, end of story. It was us that caused all the trouble with the climate, and the sea, and the energy running out. So we can't be trusted, and all that. But Clara–'

Shavila chuckled. 'Her again,' she said.

'Yeah,' said Jack, 'her again. She told me, it used to be women that was inferior. Second-class. And then, for a good few years, people was sort of equal. And now,' he finished, 'this.'

'I'm afraid I can't help,' said Shavila. 'Repseg Geemo. Can't even trust my own memories.'

Jack looked at her. What must it be like, to have grown so quickly, to have been so strong, so invincible? And now, to doubt everything, even as you feel your strength ebbing? He patted her shoulder, and Shavila stared at where his hand had lain.

Footsteps sounded from the top of the slipway. The messenger was returning with a tall, narrow-waisted woman in a close-fitting brown tunic, and an even taller, fair-haired and muscular man. Jack and Shavila stood.

The woman nodded to the sentry. 'All right, Fifi,' she said. 'I'll take it from here.'

Jack watched as the sentry retreated into her shed, followed by the boy. 'She's got a crossbow and she's called *Fifi*?' he muttered to Shavila.

She shrugged. 'Does it matter what she's called?'

The woman came up to Shavila and extended a hand. They shook, then to Jack's surprise she offered her hand to him too. 'My name's Fenny,' she said, her voice deep and smooth. 'I'm the harbourmistress here. Who are you, and what do you want?' She was polite, but there was steel in her tone.

Jack caught the man's eye. He nodded, but said nothing.

'I'm Tori,' said Shavila, 'and this is Jack. We're short on fuel.'

Fenny folded her arms across her chest. 'It's a bit strange, you turning up now – the day after a pirate raid.'

'So,' said Jack, 'it *was* last night.'

'And,' said Fenny, 'you're asking questions.'

Shavila glanced at Jack. 'We can tell them,' she said.

'Well,' said Jack, 'it's true, we do need fuel. We've less than a quarter-tank left.' He looked into Fenny's face. Could he trust her? 'But those pirates,' he went on, 'they've got – they've got, er, a friend of mine.'

Fenny grimaced. 'Pressganged?'

'Slave market,' said Jack.

'And you're chasing them? In that thing?' Fenny pointed at the *Cerdic*, settling lower on the shingle as the tide ebbed. 'You're mad.' She thought for a minute. 'What else do you know?' she asked.

SCORPION

'Ship's called the *Scorpion*,' said Jack. 'It's the Republic's – Anglia's – Coastforce. They're supposed to be keeping seas clear, but all it means is sinking refugee boats.'

'And this,' added Shavila, pointing at the burned-out boats, 'is unofficial pirating. The Republic denies all knowledge.'

'They've raided Swanage–' said Jack.

'–and Bournemouth before that,' put in Shavila.

'Yes,' said Fenny, 'we'd heard about Swanage. But Bournemouth too? Even with the plague?'

'So we heard.'

It began to rain. Fenny looked up. 'You'd better come up to the village,' she said. 'Well, you're right,' she continued. 'They hit us last night. They got all the way up to the village. But we had a watch, and a few of us chased them. Two dead, one missing, I'm afraid.'

Jack glanced at Shavila, who shook her head. The body they'd seen would be miles away by now. So he just said, 'I'm sorry.'

Fenny scratched at her cheek. 'Yeah. Good friends.'

'Did they have guns?' asked Shavila.

'That's right,' said Fenny. 'Once they started shooting people, they knew we'd have to stop and help. We gave up the chase, but they still set fire to the old lodge – took half the village to put the fire out. Bastards! Then they did these boats in. The *Jennilee*, they holed her in the shallows, and left her in the way of any other boats getting out. We dragged her up with ropes. That makes three of our diesels gone.'

Jack glanced behind. The man was following them, and the boy Mungo had joined him. 'We think,' he said to Fenny, 'they're raiding every second night.'

'Moving west,' added Shavila. 'They hit Bournemouth on the sixteenth, Swanage on the eighteenth, and here last night.'

'Any idea where they'd go next?' asked Jack.

'Good question,' said Fenny. 'Portland, I'd say. The other places are small, not worth bothering with. Portland's well defended, but I guess they can come at them from the Chesil side.' She thought for a moment, her brows drawn. Then she called the boy over. 'Mungo,' she said, 'go and find Shima Carter. Tell her to take a message to Portland. Tell 'em what's happened, and to be on guard.'

The boy ran off. 'Shima's got a good horse,' Fenny explained. 'Fastest way to get a message to them.'

They reached a stone-built building with a low, tiled roof and a smoking chimney. Fenny beckoned them inside. 'My office,' she said. 'Come and warm yourselves for a bit. I need to think.'

Jack lingered. Thirty yards off, where the road forked before winding away into the winter-grey hills beyond, a knot of people had gathered around a black, horse-drawn coach. He could see that one of the women was bent forward, her face thrust into a white handkerchief; he could hear her sobs. Another woman had an arm around her, her gaze firmly fixed across the fields as if she needed that distance in order to stay strong. Other people carried bunches of flowers.

'They're off to the pits.' Fenny was at his shoulder. 'My sister's the tall one, there,' she added, pointing. 'Her partner, Amina. Shot in the head. At least it was quick.'

'Uh, the pits?' asked Jack.

Now Shavila joined them. 'The old plague pits, I guess?' she said.

Fenny raised an eyebrow at her.

'Oh,' said Shavila, 'I've seen it before. I've worked in Hampshire, and Surrey. Lots of places, Jack, dug plague pits when Nile Flu came. Or even before that, 'cause they'd already had some killer epidemics.'

'Yeah,' said Fenny, looking back at the mourners, who were now clambering into the cart. 'This one's been here all my lifetime.'

'Brockenhurst's got one,' added Shavila. 'They filled the pit in, years ago – but it's still where they do their burying.'

Fenny shook herself. 'The killing,' she said, 'has got to stop.'

22 Portland

Inside the roughly-plastered room, Fenny pulled a chair up to the battered oak desk and pushed some papers aside. The man, who still hadn't said anything, followed them in and stood by the doorway. Was he guarding them?

Jack shivered, and went to join Shavila beside the tiny stove. He'd almost forgotten how cold he was. Holding his hands out to the heat, he said, 'How long will it take us to get to Portland?'

Fenny gave a wry grin. 'You want to get to Portland tonight, so you can be ready for them tomorrow?'

'That's right,' said Jack. 'We–'

'And what will you do then?' Fenny asked. 'Sail out and fight them? They're armed, aren't they?' She leaned forward. 'You need a plan. Have you got one?'

Jack and Shavila looked at each other.

'Thought not,' said Fenny. Abstractedly, she rubbed thumb against fingers. 'If only we had more boats...wait!' she said, looking up. 'Have you got winding gear?'

'Yes,' said Shavila. 'We haven't used it, of course. But it looks okay. And some nets.'

Jack looked at Fenny. 'You're not asking that 'cause you're planning a fishing trip, are you?'

Fenny stood and walked to the map that hung on the wall. 'After the last raids, I had a chat with Georgia,' she said, peering at the map. 'She's harbourmistress down in Portland. Georgia and me, we've got an idea.' She turned to face them. 'Thanks to you,' she went on, 'we know when they might attack next. But with them burning our boats, we can't stop them. Unless you can help.'

'To stop the *Scorpion*? said Jack.

'Stop it for good. *Can* you help us?'

Jack glanced at Shavila, who nodded. 'Of course,' he said. 'Count us in. I want to get my friend off that thing.'

Fenny nodded, and turned to the man. 'Tay,' she said, 'go round the village. Tell Kirry, and Lexi, and the others – tell them it's on, and to get to Portland this afternoon.'

The man nodded. 'Right,' he said. His voice was high-pitched and rough. 'Will I get Serena to bring them some fuel?' he went on, nodding at Jack and Shavila.

'Yeah,' said Fenny. 'Good idea. We can spare them, say, a couple of canisters.'

'What's the plan?' said Jack as Tay disappeared.

'I'll tell you,' said Fenny, 'but you'd better come and get some food. You look famished.'

They sat at a beer-stained table in a dingy bar-room. A couple of farmhands were drinking at the bar, but otherwise the place was empty. Fenny ran a hand through her close-cropped hair. 'Georgia,' she said, 'knows some girls who work in quarrying.'

'Quarrying?' said Jack.

'Portland stone. They're still digging the stuff out, even after all these years. Anyhow, the point is, they got explosives.'

'No!' said Jack. 'I don't want Clara blown up.'

SCORPION

They fell silent while the landlady brought their dishes of shepherd's pie. 'Tuck in,' said Fenny when she'd gone. 'The potato's underdone, there's too much onion and hardly any meat, but bloody hell, Sara's food always fills you up.'

Jack pulled a face and looked at Shavila, who had been staring abstractedly into space, but who now had her face almost in the dish as she wolfed down the pie.

'About your friend,' Fenny went on. 'We got to talk to Georgia. We'll see what we can do. How's the *Scorpion*'s armed?'

Shavila looked up. There was a drop of gravy on her chin. 'Small arms, and a narrow-bore cannon,' she said, swallowing.

'Oh, great,' said Fenny. 'All we've got between us is a couple of guns. So it'll be really, really dangerous. Some of us are gonna die.' She sighed and ran a hand through her hair again. 'But we *have* to stop them, and now we've got a chance to do it. Once and for all.'

Jack had been frowning. 'You need us,' he said. 'Right?'

'We need your boat.'

'Condition, then. We'll help you, but you've got to give me a chance to get Clara off. I don't wanna help you kill her.'

'Jack,' said Shavila, wiping her mouth. '*We're* more likely to be the ones getting killed.'

Jack looked at Fenny. 'Even so,' he said. 'I've got to try.'

Fenny stared at him for a minute. 'All right,' she said. 'So long as Georgia agrees. Ten minutes is all we can give you, though.'

Shavila gulped down some beer. 'The *Scorpion*'s a steelhull, you know. You'd better have a lot of explosive.'

'I wouldn't worry about that,' said Fenny.

An hour later, the now-refuelled *Cerdic* had passed out of the harbour, heading west. Shavila was steering and she seemed, to Jack's relief, to have revived a little. He was glad she was there. She'd not only been a help, she'd been company, and he realised he'd grown used to her. She was clearly still struggling with her life as an ex-Repseg, and she'd shown worrying signs of physical weakness. But right now she seemed happy enough.

'See that stack?' she called over her shoulder. She pointed to their right, where a thick, jagged-topped column of limestone rose out of the sea.

Jack joined her in the wheelhouse. 'Yeah?'

'That used to be connected to those cliffs there. A great big arch, apparently. I've seen pictures.'

'Must've been impressive,' said Jack.

'I heard that people used to come from miles around to see it.'

Jack shook his head. 'Mad,' he said. 'It's only rocks.' He looked back over the stern. A quarter of a mile behind, another boat was following them. The *Pelican* was a little larger than the *Cerdic*, but still nowhere near the reputed size of the *Scorpion*. What chance did they have?

'At least the sea's calmer,' said Shavila.

'You're not fancyin' a swim again, are ya?' asked Jack.

'I do, as a matter of fact,' she said. 'Looks lovely and cool.'

'Freezing, you mean,' said Jack.

SCORPION

Shavila steered a little more to the south-west. 'No swimming for now, anyway,' she said. 'Job to do.'

'Yeah.' Jack gazed out at the sluggish waves. 'I hope it stays like this. How are we gonna find the *Scorpion* if the sea gets big? You said it was painted black, and sat low in the water.' He shook his head.

'Do you think the weather's going to change, then?'

Jack watched as a gull landed on the prow. It eyed them for a minute, then flew off. 'It always does.'

'You say that like you know.'

Jack held on to a bulwark as the *Cerdic* heaved to port. 'I grew up by the sea. Till I was about twelve.'

'Oh. But you're not a good sailor?'

'Nah, Mam'd never let me. Said I wasn't old enough. We was poachers and smugglers. Whole village was pretty much in on it. Then the Repsegs came...oh, sorry...'

Shavila shrugged. 'What did the Repsegs do?'

Jack told her about how they'd raided the village, confiscated the contraband and any weapons they'd found, arrested the village leaders, and murdered his uncle. Shavila went quiet.

'Sorry,' said Jack. 'I mean–'

'No, it's okay,' said Shavila with a sigh. 'It's what we did. Looking back now, it feels wrong.'

Jack listened.

'But I wonder,' went on Shavila, 'if that's because I know I'm getting old...'

Dusk was falling as they sighted Portland, looming dark above the waves like the head of a monstrous serpent, with its snout pointing to the open sea. Following Fenny's directions, they navigated around the Bill and beached the *Cerdic* in Chesil Cove. Another fishing-boat was already there, rocking on the swell, blood-red in the setting sun. From their left came the hollow groan of disturbed shingle, where the remains of Chesil Beach lurked under the waves.

By the time Jack and Shavila had leapt out, made fast the *Cerdic* and scrambled up the shingle, the *Pelican* was arriving. 'Let's find Georgia,' panted Fenny as she joined them.

They climbed the hill then turned left. The harbourmistress's office, perched above the castle, looked down on the old harbour. In the houses below, a few lamps had already been lit against the winter dusk.

Georgia was a round woman with a red face, and was dressed in a thick off-white sweater and heavy wellingtons. 'Come in, come in,' she said, shaking their hands. 'So you're the ones who are going to help us do something about these raiders?'

'Well,' said Jack, glancing at Shavila for reassurance, 'we think they strike every second night. We've followed them, so we can see the pattern. I guess it depends on the weather...'

'Bournemouth, Swanage, Lulworth,' put in Fenny. 'It's got to be Portland next.'

Georgia nodded. 'We're big enough, for sure.' She scratched an ear. 'And it'll be tomorrow night?'

'If the pattern holds,' said Fenny.

'Any idea of size?' asked Georgia. 'How big's this thing?'

SCORPION

'We didn't actually see the *Scorpion*,' said Shavila. 'I'm no sailor, but it's got to be three times the size of one of your fishing-boats. Steam engine, coal-fired. The prow's reinforced, for ramming.'

'When they raided us,' said Fenny, 'they came in two rowing boats – a good dozen of them in the raiding party, so the rowing-boats alone must be pretty big...'

'We did see her anchorage in Southampton Water,' said Shavila. 'She can't have been huge.'

'Yeah,' said Fenny, 'but huge enough.' She looked at Georgia. 'It'll be hard.'

Georgia pulled a face. 'We've got to try. Just so long as everyone knows what the risk is. Governor's called a meeting in the morning, in the old hall.'

'My friend's on the Scorpion,' said Jack. 'A slave. I've got to get her off.'

Fenny said, 'I promised him ten minutes.'

Georgia blew out her cheeks. 'You say the Scorpion's armed? And a steelhull?'

'Shallow draught,' put in Shavila. 'Built like a longship, with curved-in sides.'

'For the high seas,' said Fenny, nodding. 'You're going to have your work cut out, Jacko.'

'Shallow draught, you say?' said Georgia. 'That's something.'

'Fits with your idea,' said Fenny.

'What's this "idea" then?' said Jack.

'Need to work on it,' said Georgia. 'Tell you tomorrow. Fenny, take them to the hall, they can sleep there tonight. Get 'em some food, too.'

As they closed the door behind them, Georgia was already scribbling on a large piece of paper.

They walked past the eastern harbour, where work had begun on new walls in stone and concrete. Tall yellow-brick buildings looked down on it, their feet in the water and their windows smashed. There were no reclamation gangs here. Following Fenny up a steep, narrow street, they reached a solid stone building.

'The Hall,' she told them. 'You can kip here for the night. Be up by nine, though – this is where the Governor's meeting is.'

23 The Plan

The buttered bread felt like glue in Jack's mouth. He had to help it down with swigs of tea. While he and Shavila breakfasted in the musty hall, women were arriving and setting out benches and chairs around a broad table at the far end. A few were already settled, sitting forward, or leaning over the backs of chairs as they debated the business before them.

Jack felt queasy. Having slept fitfully on a thin mattress, he'd woken early and gone down the high street to look at the sea, but he'd left his coat behind and the keen air had cut through him. Had he been hoping that the sea would be heavier today, that maybe a storm was coming? Because that would delay the raid, and if the raid was delayed, tonight wouldn't be the night when Clara died. But the breezes were light and the sea quiet. There was no hope there.

After all, he believed her: she *had* gone back for him. True, she'd left him alone that night in the empty cottage; but she'd left to get him food. Then she'd got caught, which was why she couldn't return. By the time she'd escaped and got back to the cottage, Jack had moved on, and they'd lost each other. After everything he'd thought about her, after all his cursing and despair, it turned out that she hadn't let him down after all. But now, what? These people from Portland and Lulworth were going to try and destroy the *Scorpion*, with Clara aboard. He pictured an exploding ship, he saw Clara's body flung into the air and sinking under the waves, and he thought about never talking with her again, never laughing, never getting another chance to be her friend. He whimpered.

He joined a hugely-yawning Shavila on a bench and leant his back against the wall. More people were arriving. There were maybe two dozen women: by their clothes, some were quarriers, others fisherwomen, others farmers and labourers. Georgia was among them, in animated conversation with the only one who was wearing a suit: a slim, fair-haired woman whom Jack guessed to be the Governor. There were a few men, too, and Jack recognised the tall and silent Tay, leaning against a pillar, arms folded across his chest. The conversation in the room was getting louder as each group strove to make itself heard. Jack and Shavila exchanged glances.

'How'd ya sleep?' asked Jack.

'Not too well,' said Shavila, rubbing her arms. 'It's weird, all this. I kept thinking about how to stop the *Scorpion*.' She lowered her voice. 'Before,' she said, 'you know, when I was–'

'In your first job,' suggested Jack.

She nodded. 'I'd always know what to do. I could think, I could be decisive, I could plan. But then, I had orders. Now it's different.'

The chatter subsided, and when Jack looked up, the Governor was standing behind the table. She held up a hand and then, in a high, clear voice, began to speak. She spoke about the raids they'd suffered before, about the women who'd been killed and the property they'd lost, how it had been going on for many years, and how it had to stop. They'd never forgive themselves, she told them, if they let this chance slip. Up till now, the raiders had always taken them by surprise. 'But this time,' she said, gesturing towards Jack and Shavila, 'thanks to our friends, we know when they're coming. We know when they're coming,' she repeated, 'and we're going to be ready. We'll lay a trap. My friends, there are no two ways about this: it will be *very* dangerous. This is no rag-tag band of pirates, but an Anglian Coastforce ship. It's armed. Those of us who go on this mission – well, we might not come back.'

A dozen of the audience began talking at once. 'It's impossible!' said one. 'How are we even going to find them?' cried another. 'It's suicide!' But others were shouting back, 'It's the one chance we're gonna get,' or, 'We've got to do *something*!'

Jack watched intently as the Governor gradually managed to calm them down. 'Hear what Georgia's got to say,' she said. 'Wait till you know what the plan is. And give her quiet, all right?'

The harbourmistress came to the table carrying, helped by Fenny, an old flip-chart. She had an ink pen that was already staining her fingers.

'This,' she said, starting to sketch a map of the island, 'is a plan we've had for some time. Since the last raid, in fact. But we never knew exactly when we'd need it.'

Shavila leaned forward, peering attentively at Georgia's drawing. Jack thought he could see some of the old efficient Repseg there, and once again he was glad she was on his side.

'We've got some old pair-trawl nets,' went on Georgia. She added some outlines, a little way out from the island. 'They haven't been used for years, on account of bad seas, and probably never will be. What we'll do is, we'll play them out between three boats, like this.' She drew some lines. 'We weight them so that they float a few feet below the keel-line. Then when the *Scorpion* sails across them–'

'They'll foul on her screws?' said someone in the front row.

Georgia nodded. 'Exactly.'

'Then what?' called someone else.

'We've got some Readyblast from the quarry,' said Georgia. 'We'll have to get close enough to throw it – we're told the *Scorpion* has high sides and a deep deck-well. The explosives'll be in small packs, all right?'

'No questions yet!' cried the Governor as voices rose again. 'Please wait till she's finished!'

Fenny came forward. 'There'll be three of our boats, with the nets strung out over half a mile. The *Scorpion* will need to anchor close enough to shore for the raiding boats to cover the distance – we reckon no more than a few hundred yards. We'll need to be a little further out.' She pointed to where Georgia was indicating on her sketch. 'The *Scorpion* puts out to the open sea between raids, so they'll come in from the south, and probably towards the Chesil side. We expect them in the early hours – after midnight – so the tide'll be too low for them to get over the old harbour ruins.'

'The weather's set fair,' added Georgia. 'That'll suit them for a raid, and it'll suit us too. Once we stall her, we'll cut the nets then get close enough to lob the charges.'

Jack stood. 'I've got to get my friend off!' he said. 'You said you'd give me ten minutes!'

Faces turned to him. Heads shook. 'You're *friends* with one of them?' somebody asked.

SCORPION

'She's a slave,' said Shavila. 'They crew the boiler room with slaves.'

Georgia shook her head. 'There's no other way of doing this. You say they're armed – what if they kill your friend as soon as we attack? And then kill us? We've got to use the surprise, we've no choice. It's the only chance we'll get.'

'But you promised!' shouted Jack, and he started towards Georgia.

Shavila hauled him back. 'They're right,' she said.

'We'll be killing her!' moaned Jack.

Shavila shook her head. 'They're right about it being the only chance,' she said in a low voice, 'but the chances of it working are tiny. If it doesn't, and the *Scorpion* turns on us, we're done for. She's a steelhull, too, remember? Ten to one, Clara's going to be safe.'

Jack, his jaw set, turned on his heel and made to leave the hall. Again, Shavila stopped him. 'Jack,' she said. '*If* the trap works, *if* we don't get blown out of the water, and *if* she escapes, we'll need to be there. We can't help her if we're not.'

Jack wiped his eyes. 'We're going to kill her,' he said.

'No,' said Shavila. 'We're doing our best for her. And you've got a Repseg on your side, remember?'

Jack sniffed, and nodded.

It was late afternoon. There were clouds on the western horizon as Jack, cuffs pulled over his knuckles, scrambled down the beach. He felt the salt air chilling his lungs. Ahead of him the *Pelican*, secured to a dockside post by a long lanyard, had settled deep into the shingle as the tide ebbed.

She now listed slightly to starboard. From the deck came the sound of hammering. Jack grabbed the rope ladder and hauled himself up.

'Tori?' he called, in a lull in the hammering.

'Down here,' came a voice.

Jack gained the deck and peered into the hold. The *Pelican* was nearly twice the size of the *Cerdic*, and she would be lead boat in the ambush. 'They said I'd find you here,' he said. 'Whatcha doing?'

Shavila looked up. 'Wiring,' she said. 'I thought you were having a rest?'

'Couldn't sleep,' said Jack. 'You the same?'

Shavila nodded. She frowned as she screwed a connector into place. 'I asked them what lights they had. They hadn't thought about it. There'll be a moon, they said. I pointed out that the *Scorpion* will have at least one searchlight, maybe more.'

The deck rocked under their feet as the waves washed the hull.

'That's a generator?' said Jack, looking at the bulky object that Shavila was sitting on.

'Quite a good one,' she said. 'Should be able to run a couple of strong lamps off this. Here, hold these, will you?'

'How d'you know where all these wires go?'

'We learned it. We did electrical engineering at Fortis College.' She held out her hand. 'Thanks. We learnt all the electrical stuff in two days. Of course, we learnt other things, like unquestioning obedience. "Unquestioning" was the theme, really. Facts, facts, facts. You could ask what, who, where and how, but never why. Why was right out.'

'Wow.'

'Hang on, let's see...this one goes in there...' She waved the screwdriver. 'You've got to hand it to them, it was great technology. The Geemo labs, I mean. However they produced us, it worked. The learning programmes worked. The whole system worked. It's just that it all depended on getting the right materials, the right bio supplies, the right equipment.'

'And nowadays? Want me to hold that still for ya?'

'Thanks. Nowadays, well – first, there's no fuel. I believe they actually used to *fly* stuff in. Now, even if you had a plane, you'd have to wait months for good weather, and,' she added, waving to her right, 'you can't take things by sea any more.'

'So we've run out.'

'Yeah. But that's a good thing. We – us Geemos – we're not natural.'

'I bet it's the same with the cloning labs, then.'

Shavila wiped her hands. 'Now,' she said, reaching down. 'Let's see!'

She pressed a button. The generator coughed then gave a deafening roar. Jack recoiled as a blast of bitter diesel fumes hit him. Shavila scrambled out and shut the hatch. The noise diminished.

'There,' she said, pointing at the electric lamps that now glowed either side of the wheelhouse. 'We'll be able to see what we're doing tonight.'

'I thought we were leaving all the lights off?'

'Yes, until we engage. And then, it'll be a fight. That's when you'll have to get across to the *Scorpion*.'

Jack felt his throat tighten. 'I've never swum in the sea – only ever been in a river – I won't last.'

'We'll put a rope around your waist – don't stay in the water any longer than you need to. Anyway, it'll have to be you.' Shavila opened the hatch, reached in and turned the generator off. 'I can't do it.'

Jack looked at her. 'You can't?'

'My – my bones won't hold. They're brittle.'

'Is that why you wear the leather?'

'Yep. Helps to hold me together. Literally.'

'Seriously?' said Jack. 'I mean, what happens? Have you actually broken anything?'

Shavila nodded and lifted her right arm. 'My bones are ageing faster than my muscles. Eighteen months ago I cracked both bones in my forearm, just lifting a heavy box. I lifted it easily enough – until my arm went floppy. Then, a few months later I banged my shin; that took a month to heal. This leather – if I keep it tight–' she pointed at some straps '–then I'm fine. I just wouldn't want to risk it too much, though...'

Jack looked out over the shingle, to the western harbour and the mainland cliffs beyond. 'Look, Tori,' he said. 'Thanks for all you've done. You didn't need to come with me; you didn't need to leave everything behind.'

'I'm sorry I can't do more. Besides, I–'

'What?'

'Oh, nothing. It's been good working with you, Jack.'

He tried to catch her gaze, but she looked away. He could never really tell what she was thinking. He wished he could. 'Yeah,' he said. 'It's been good. So,' he added as he led the way down the ladder, 'you don't wish you were back on the Bewley ferry?'

And Shavila laughed. Till he'd met her, Jack wasn't sure he'd ever heard a Repseg laugh. Had to be a good sign, right?

24 Waiting for the Scorpion

The gibbous moon hung high among the pale stars, silvering the fast-moving clouds and glinting on the spume-topped waves. Jack gripped the handrail as, under his feet, the *Cerdic*'s deck gently rolled and pitched, and it felt for a moment as if he was spinning in space, as if he'd soon be able to reach out and touch those clouds. If this was to be his last night on Earth, at least it was a beautiful one.

There was a tremor in the boards, too, for the *Cerdic*'s engine was thrusting gently to hold her position against the current and to support the weight of the net. The diesel fumes whirled around Jack before drifting out to sea. He looked ahead to the wheelhouse, where Fenny monitored the controls, then aft, to where Tay was busy with coils of rope and sacks of something that Jack didn't want to think about. Shavila, at the starboard rail, was watching through binoculars. A quarter of a mile off, Georgia, in the *Pelican*, held her station. Jack knew that further away the *Marytavy* held the end of the second net.

Why? Thought Jack. Why am I doing this? Why didn't I just walk away? He could have walked away from Hurn's camp, couldn't he, when he woke and found that Clara had drugged him and taken his place among the prisoners? He could have ignored the note she left, asking him to see her parents safely into Wessex. But for some reason, he'd done as she'd asked. And then, as if that wasn't enough, he'd promised Sophia and James that he'd go and find her. Why?

He passed a hand over his eyes and went to join Fenny in the wheelhouse. Anything for a distraction.

'Nothing?' she asked, looking up.

Jack shook his head. 'I can't see much. I'm looking for something black, in the black waves.'

'At least there's a moon. And they might have lights on,' said Fenny.

'Maybe. But if there's anything to be seen, Tori'll see it before me.'

'Hmm,' went on Fenny, peering through the wheelhouse window, 'the sea's getting heavier. Did you see those clouds in the west?'

'No...?'

'Heading this way. The weather's changing. This is our only chance, Jack.' She curled her lip. 'We've *got* to stop them.'

Jack wanted to say, it can't be so important that you can't spare me ten minutes to try and get Clara. But he heard the anguish in Fenny's voice, and all he said was, 'How many times have they raided?'

She glanced at him. 'Last few years, maybe twice a year. But they're coming more often now. They're getting bolder. That'll be the war.'

'The war? Has it started, then?'

Fenny tapped one of the dials, then eased the throttle back a little. 'It's coming, anyone can see that.'

'Anglia and Wessex,' said Jack. It was a statement. He knew it in his bones.

'Wessex,' said Fenny, 'have just occupied all the mainland behind us. Portland's supposed to be part of Wessex now.'

'So?' said Jack.

'This,' she said, 'with Coastforce – it's provocation. Here,' she said, handing Jack a flask. 'Brandy. Keep you awake. Give some to the others, will you?'

Jack went to Tay first, partly to get a look at the sacks of explosive he was preparing. Behind him in the stern was the winding-gear, from which the two net-lines, taut as bowstrings, disappeared into the waves. In front of him, stacked in a locker, were what looked like a dozen large bags of flour with string tied around them. 'They're safe,' said Tay. 'Don't worry.' He grinned. 'Although if you fancy putting a match to them, you could fly home. In pieces.'

Jack didn't laugh, but went off to find Shavila. In the lanternless dark he had only the moonlight to guide him, so it wasn't till he got near that he saw she was slumped forward over the handrail, binoculars dangling unheeded from her neck.

'Tori!' he cried, grabbing her arm and pulling her back.

She blinked. 'Jack,' she said. 'Hi.'

The deck heaved, and she pitched forward into Jack's arms. 'Are you okay?' he asked, helping her to stand upright. He could still smell her stale sweat.

'Y-yes,' she said, as if wasn't sure. 'Yes, I'm all right.'

'Tired?' said Jack, holding out the flask.

She nodded and took a long pull at the brandy. 'Didn't sleep much. The sea looks – inviting, don't you think?'

Jack steered the conversation away. 'Seen anything?' he said, nodding at the binoculars.

Shavila inclined her head. 'The nets are a lying bit high in the water for my liking,' she said. 'But these people know best, I suppose. They've fished all their lives. Oh!' she said, turning to a locker behind her and raising the lid. 'You'd better take this.' She held out something that looked like a sleeveless shirt, white-striped and heavily padded.

'A life jacket,' said Jack, taking it. It felt heavy, yet squashy. 'This'll help me float?'

'More than that, Jack – it'll *make* you float. Wear that, and you won't sink. And look here – the rope goes through these loops and round your waist.' She picked a heavy coil out of the locker. 'I'll have the other end,' she said, 'to haul you in.'

'And the white stripes? Is that paint?'

'So that I can see you better in the water.' Then she stood straighter, alert. 'Quick!' she said. 'Tell Fenny to turn off the engines.'

Jack ran, and in a moment both he and Fenny were back at Shavila's side.

'Listen!' said Shavila. 'Hear that?'

Jack did: a deep throb, a growl of powerful engines. Coming from the south, from out at sea. His guts clenched.

In the *Scorpion*'s boiler-room, it was almost peaceful. Maybe, thought Clara, it was because they hadn't murdered any refugees for a few days. All day yesterday the ship had sailed the Channel, making turn after turn, as if searching. But the only thing that had happened was the change in the weather, with the wind easing and the swell diminishing. Now, she and Xavi were working as easily as it was possible to do in that pit of heat. Crudger had told them to keep the pressure up, but for the moment the engines were quiet, and all it needed was couple of shovelfuls every few minutes. The coal-heap was diminishing again, but Riss had found somewhere in the corner furthest from the toilet, which was stinking badly, and had slept soundly since dusk.

Wilson was back at her post, but was dozing, her shock-stick dangling from her wrist. Under her stool rolled several empty bottles. Carefully, Clara put down her shovel and stepped up to Xavi.

'Where do you think she gets all that rum?' she said, placing a hand on his chest.

He gave a quick smile and bent his face towards hers. Then the ship lurched; he sucked in his breath and winced.

'Is it your leg?' she whispered.

He nodded. 'Is hurting much. Is not getting better. I do not know what is problem. Bones do not join.'

Voices came from the head of the companionway: voices, and hurrying footsteps. Looking into Xavi's eyes, greatly daring, she gave him a quick kiss on the cheek. She realised she was breathing hard.

'Another raid,' he said. From the deck they heard the rattling of chains and the creaking of ropes.

Wilson must have heard it too, because she gave a start and slipped off the stool, landing among the coal with a clatter. She blinked three times then leapt up. 'Bashtards,' she said.

At that moment Crudger came down the steps. 'How's that pressure?' she called.

But before Xavi could answer, Wilson lurched forward and grabbed a fistful of Crudger's tunic, thrusting her face forward. 'You said I could go on this one,' she snarled. 'You said I could get off this bloody coffin!'

Crudger pushed her off. 'You're drunk!' she said. 'And don't you *dare* touch me. Understood?'

Wilson swayed and licked her lips. 'Just a few hours!' she said between her teeth. 'That's all I'm askin', all right?'

'In that state?' Crudger waved a finger in Wilson's face. 'Look at you! You're so pissed you can't even stand! What use would you be, hey?' She gave her a shove. 'I'm reporting you to the Captain for this, so help me!'

Clara knew something was going to happen, by the way Wilson's lip curled and her eyes narrowed. And it did: Wilson leapt forward and landed a powerful punch, square on Crudger's jaw. 'You bitch!' she screamed as Crudger fell back against the steam pipes.

Scalded, Crudger yelled in pain and pitched forward into Xavi, who caught her before her momentum carried them both to the floor. The ship rolled.

Wilson glared, then with a yell, ran up the steps.

'No!' cried Xavi. 'She will–'

Wilson had almost reached the top when the shot rang out. Twitcher was still alert. Clara was convinced the shot had missed, for she clearly heard the bullet ricocheting from the ironwork, but she was wrong. There was something about the heavy way Wilson slithered down the steps that told Clara she was dead. The bullet had passed right through her.

Clara cried out. In the corner, Riss was struggling to her feet and swearing. Crudger was swearing too, and, crawling to the foot of the companionway she yelled, 'Twitcher! Twitcher! Get your ass down here! You've shot Wilson!'

In a moment Twitcher had joined her, and between them they began to carry Wilson's body up the steps.

'What's going on?' said Riss, joining them.

'You lot,' called Crudger as she struggled with Wilson's legs. 'Get the fuck stoking!'

They hadn't even time to get coal on their shovels when from the engines there came a scream, like a slaughtered animal, and the *Scorpion* pitched steeply to stern. Crudger and Twitcher tumbled back down the steps along with Wilson's corpse, and Clara and the others were thrown onto the coal.

25 In the Nets

'There it is!' said Shavila. From the deck of the *Cerdic* Jack could descry, cutting through the waves two hundred yards to starboard, a low, dark shape. At that distance, the *Scorpion* must be passing close to the *Pelican*, and Jack thought he could make out the boat's outline, lurching in the *Scorpion*'s wake.

'Has she caught?' said Fenny. 'Has she caught?' Then, when nothing happened, she turned to Shavila. 'Quick!' she said. 'You take the wheel. We'll have to follow!'

But then they felt it. The *Cerdic* yawed heavily prow-to-starboard, and the stern, plunging low into the waves, took on water. Shavila scrambled up to the wheelhouse as the engines laboured.

'Loose the nets, loose the nets!' cried Fenny. 'Or we'll be dragged under!'

Tay was in the stern already, struggling with the release lever. Jack pulled out his knife and, bracing himself against a bulwark just a few feet above the hungry, licking waves, he began to saw at one of the two warp-lines. Soon he was wiping sea-water from his eyes. Frantically he sawed and sawed as, strand by reluctant strand, the rope began to give way. To his right, Tay was having difficulty keeping his footing on the slippery deck as he wrestled with the waist-high lever. Jack could hear him cursing. Lights began to appear to port, where the *Scorpion* was flailing in the swell.

The *Cerdic's* deck was pitching more steeply now. Hanging on to a rail, Fenny yelled to Shavila, 'Give it as much as you've got!'

'Nearly – through,' gasped Jack, 'nearly – through!' Then with a crack, all the remaining strands snapped. The free end smacked into Jack's face and, with a yell, he slid into the water. His knife flew into the waves, but his left hand still clutched the frayed end of the rope. He grabbed onto it and began to haul himself out; then with a clang the lever sprang back. Tay leapt out of the way as the second rope spun from the reel and vanished into the waves. Now Jack held on desperately as the stern, no longer pulled downward, recoiled. As soon as the tilt was in his favour, he dragged himself further onto the deck, grasping the cold railings to pull himself along.

Fenny hurried up and held out a hand. Jack took it, but as he got to his feet, they heard gunfire. Fenny swore. 'Shit,' she cried. 'Look!'

The *Scorpion* had switched on its searchlights. It lay a hundred yards off, lurking wave-low like a sea-monster; but immediately beyond it they could make out the *Pelican*, dragged close as the nets tangled, illuminated stark and white in the searchlight. On the *Scorpion's* upper deck, they could see figures firing rifles in the direction of the *Pelican*. Amidships, something smooth and cylindrical was moving.

Shavila ran up. 'Another searchlight!' she said. 'It'll be on us soon. Have we got any guns?'

'Er,' said Fenny, raising her voice above the waves, 'I think they're in that locker. But they're not loaded!'

'Not loaded?' said Shavila. 'Fantastic!'

'We can't get any ammunition these days,' said Fenny. 'All we've got is the Readyblast. Now let me help Tay. We're going to give them bastards a shock all right.' She turned and made her way aft.

Shavila thought. 'Hold on a minute,' she said, and returned to the wheelhouse. Jack saw that the swell was bringing the *Scorpion* closer. The searchlight passed over their heads and began another sweep – any minute, they'd be seen. Then Shavila came back, brandishing something. 'This'll have to do,' she said, and once more Jack saw Shavila-the-Repseg as she braced herself, legs apart, arms straight ahead, eyes fixed on the *Scorpion*. Just as he realised what she was holding, she fired. With a great screech a flare shot across the waves and crashed into the searchlight, where it erupted in a blaze of white light then died away. The searchlight was knocked out.

'They know we're here now,' said Shavila. 'Take off your clothes.'

'What?' said Jack.

'Your coat, and trousers. And your boots, they'll drag you down. Leave your shirt on, or the rope will chafe.'

Jack let Shavila help. While he wriggled out of his coat, she pulled off first one boot, then the other, then helped him off with his trousers. He swallowed. Her hands were cold against his legs.

'Up,' she said, and Jack stood. Then, before he knew what she was doing, she'd taken the long coil of rope and passed it three times around his waist. 'Get the float jacket,' she ordered, as she tied the rope off. 'I can't see enough of her shape,' she went on, nodding at the *Scorpion*, 'but you're going to have your work cut out getting aboard that thing. There should be a ladder up the side – look out for rungs.'

Jack shrugged into the float jacket. As Shavila helped him secure it, he glanced to his right. Fenny and Tay were readying the sacks of explosive. Things were moving too quickly.

'Right, go!' snapped Shavila, and she practically wrestled him over the railing. As he stood on the edge of the bulwark, poised to leap into the sea, there came a loud *boom* and a flash from the *Scorpion*. The *Pelican* had started throwing explosives.

In the *Scorpion's* boiler room, Crudger swore as she and Twitcher tried to disentangle themselves from Wilson's corpse which, to Clara, looked as if it was fighting back.

'What's going on?' Crudger shouted above the squealing engines and juddering pipework. 'Have we hit something?'

Twitcher was already leaping up the steps. 'Nah,' she called back. 'Something else. Come on, quick!'

This time they made it up the companionway, although the ship still rolled and strained. They left Wilson's corpse face-down among the coal, limbs crumpled under its torso. Clara stared. It was so easy, she thought, for life to vanish.

'What *is* going on?' said Riss, creeping to the foot of the steps and peering upwards.

'Careful!' cried Clara. 'Twitcher will–'

'Twitcher's not there!' said Riss. 'People are running. There are lights! They've got the searchlights on.' A rifle fired, and she flinched before shrinking back from the companionway.

'Is up on deck,' said Xavi, hobbling towards the steps and peering up as more shots rang out. '*Sí*, is up on deck. Twitcher, she is not watching.'

Clara gasped. 'We're under attack,' she said. 'We must be!'

Xavi and Riss looked at each other.

'We were getting ready for a raid,' Clara went on. 'We can't be far from shore.'

The deck gave another lurch as the engines screeched louder. 'And *that* must be something to do with it,' said Riss.

Xavi nodded. 'We have to get off the ship,' he said. 'If we sink–'

'And we're close to the shore,' said Clara, taking his hand. 'We might make it.'

'It's dark!' said Riss, just at the moment when a bright white light flashed above. 'It'll be dark in the sea – we won't know which way to go.'

Then came an ear-pummelling concussion and another flash of light. The whole ship recoiled and Clara fell to her knees. As Xavi helped her up he said, 'We go, now. I go first.' And, hauling his sore leg behind him, he limped up the companionway.

Clara beckoned to Riss then followed him. As she stepped over Wilson's corpse she noticed the shock-stick, still attached to its wrist.

On the *Cerdic*, Shavila ran back to the wheelhouse. 'Hold on!' she shouted to Jack. 'I'll try and get closer.'

The swell was growing now, and as Jack clung on to the rail, the *Cerdic*'s rolling plunged him towards the waves, soaking his face and bare legs, before lifting him back again. His arms were trembling from the cold, and from the effort of holding on. As the *Scorpion*'s dark bulk edged closer, he risked a glance. The high, curved hull was a deep night-black, but within the deck-well there were lights – and a fire! Something was burning, but before he could make out more, the ship's rolling obscured it from view.

Shavila appeared at the rail next to him. 'I daren't bring her any closer,' she said. 'Ready?'

Jack glanced at her, swallowed, and tried to nod.

She put a hand on his shoulder. 'Once you've got her, you'll have to haul yourself in. I'll have to keep steering.' She peered at him. 'You'll be okay, Jack. And that's a Repseg telling you.'

Jack took a breath and relaxed his grip. Not yet – the sea was too far. Now? The dark water heaved up to meet him. Now? Then he felt Shavila's hand on his back and, crying out, he fell. He began to gasp, but there came a punishing shock as the water hit him, slapping him in the face and wicking straight through his shirt. The cold penetrated his flesh, and he sank deep, then deeper. His eyes were shut tight and his lungs felt like they were about to burst, but then he felt the float jacket tugging at his armpits, lifting him up, up, until he bobbed to the surface. He gasped a breath in then yelled, a formless, animal shout, to show himself he was still alive. It was like the flood, when Acker had thrown him in the Thames before the great wave hurtled up the river and washed him away. He cried out again as the next wave bore down and he was submerged again, but this time he surfaced at once.

The memory came, the sight, the sound, the stench: on the Thames, that huge wave. Clara had been with him then. Clara...cursing to himself, he set his jaw and began to swim. Something huge was rolling in the black water ahead, but although it seemed only a few yards off, he wasn't getting any closer. He tried harder, fighting the cold that numbed his limbs. To his right there was a bright light – a searchlight – the *Cerdic*? Tori must have started the generator. Now he could see the *Scorpion*'s hull, black and smooth and curved. Where was the ladder? There must be one somewhere. He let the waves take him for a moment, while he paused for breath. But now they were pushing him further away...what if she wasn't there? What if ...?

26 Death at Sea

Clara wrestled the corpse's wrist out of the hand-loop and made for the companionway. Xavi had already reached the deck. Gunshots rang out, and a second later the cannon fired, and the whole vessel recoiled.

'Xavi! Clara screamed, flying up the steps. As she reached the top, one of the deck-hands, staggering across her path, grabbed at her. Before Clara could do more than pull herself aside, Riss emerged and, hauling on the woman's legs, flung her down the steps.

For the first time since they'd disposed of Hashim's corpse, Clara felt cold air in her lungs. She started forward, but another of the crew appeared from her left and grappled with her. 'Prisoners!' she cried. 'Prisoners escap –'

She fell to the deck, stunned. Clara looked in wonder at the shock-stick in her hand. Then a pale object, like a small sack of flour, flew over her head and skidded into the bilges. She just had time to see that its tail was glowing before there was a deafening explosion and she was flung ten feet through the air. She crashed into a bulkhead and, stunned, rolled face-down onto the iron deck. She shook herself and tried to rise, but her right arm and her ribs were cramping in pain. She whimpered and fought for breath. There were lights, there was fire, there were screams. There were also rifle shots. Deck-hands were scurrying to and fro; one stumbled over Clara's outstretched leg. She dragged herself out of the way and propped herself against a bulkhead. More gunfire came, but at last her vision was beginning to clear. A few feet away lay one of the crew, her neck at an unnatural angle and a pool of blood spreading beneath her. A spotlight swept over the superstructure – from the other ship, realised Clara – and now to her horror she saw, in the *Scorpion*'s gun turret, Xavi. He was struggling with one of the crew – it might have been Twitcher – and there was a rifle between them. Then the spotlight moved on and darkness covered them. Clara still held the shock-stick. Forcing herself to her feet, she staggered in their direction.

'Clara!' Peering through the gloom, she saw Riss, who was likewise scrambling to her feet, her face bloody. Behind her another crew-woman lay, groaning. Riss beckoned. 'We got to get off here!'

Clara barely paused to nod. She had to save Xavi. The deck rolled; she staggered; she grabbed a handrail. A gun went off. Xavi had wrested the rifle from Twitcher, and now that she was within reach, Clara struck. There was a spark, then Twitcher gave a yell and fell to the deck, not twitching at all.

Xavi was grunting, holding his midriff. 'Go!' He shouted at Clara. 'Go!'

'I'm not going without–'

He waved a hand. 'Go!' he yelled. 'I follow! You must be safe!'

He loved her, didn't he? He wanted her to be safe. And he said he'd follow. Peering through the thick smoke, Clara saw that Riss had found some rungs and was scaling the hull wall. To port, something was burning. From the starboard, the spotlight swept again. How many attackers were there?

Ignoring the pain, she pulled herself up by the rungs. She reached the top of the gunwale and glanced back, then everything happened at once. She saw that Xavi had swung the cannon around to point straight down into the boiler-room. He looked up and their eyes locked – she saw a dark stain on his shirt – something struck the *Scorpion* on the port side – the deck lurched. Clara, arms flailing, was flung into the sea.

Jack surfaced again. He spat, and drew in a quivering breath. How cold the water was! He had to keep moving, or his limbs would seize up. The float-jacket was keeping him on the surface, tossed by the waves, but it was hindering his strokes. He felt for the rope; at least that was still secure. Away to his left, the sea was on fire. No, not the sea! A boat – one of the fishing-boats. The waves hid it from view, then brought it back again.

The searchlight played over the *Scorpion*, and Jack saw it was no more than twenty yards away, heaving up and down in the waves, smoke rising from its deck. Against the fiery glow, he saw a figure jumping from the ship. Another appeared, and he thought he knew its shape. Then the ship tilted and the figure disappeared into the waves.

It was Clara, it had to be her. He beat the water with his arms, battered at it with his legs. Then there was a great concussion and the waves seemed to pause; the sound pummelled Jack's ears, his head, his whole body. *Doom*, said the *Scorpion*. He shouted for Clara, but his voice was carried away by the wind.

Clara thought she knew the how cold the waves would be. But still she cried out as she hit the water and plunged into the maelstrom, flinching at a chill that ate into her flesh while the sea dragged her down then flung her back up again. She clenched her jaw. For some minutes she sank and rose, rose and sank, and all she could do was wonder where the next breath was coming from. At last, she broke surface on a rising wave and snatched air into her screaming lungs. She spotted Riss, picked out by a sweeping spotlight, not far away. She called, and tried to swim to her.

Xavi! What had happened? Where was he? Had he escaped? She tried to shut out that last image of him: the dark stain on his shirt, the gun, the look in his eyes. Then, as the freezing water dragged her down again, there was a great noise, a physical blow that shook her bones and rang through her head like a deep bell, then a violent pulse in the sea that hurled her away.

She surfaced again, deafened, spluttering. Now there was smoke, a hot, lung-scouring reek, and she cried out for Xavi again. Riss was clawing her way closer through the froth and the waves, and now Clara could hear Xavi. Clara, he was calling, Clara!

Maybe she was dying. It must be Xavi, but it sounded like Jack Pike, the little boy who once stole a loaf and climbed some gates. 'Xavi!' she cried. 'Where are you? Xavi! Xavi!' Yellow flames leapt above the *Scorpion*'s gunwale.

Riss reached her, and still Clara screamed Xavi's name.

'Clara! Grab hold of me!' came that other voice. 'I've got a rope!'

'Get off me!' shrieked Clara. 'Xavi! Oh, Xavi!'

Salt! So much salt. Riss's voice, and the one that couldn't be Jack's but wasn't Xavi's. They're telling me to leave him, she thought, and she kicked and thrashed and punched until someone grabbed her head in both hands and yelled at her, and she thought it was Riss, something about a stupid cow trying to drown them all, but Xavi still wasn't there.

'He fired the gun,' she thought Riss was saying.

They were leaving him behind! She couldn't let them take her away, she *couldn't*. But her bones were numb and her arms wouldn't move and her throat was caked with salt. Those hands gripped her about the midriff. Then water, water, water.

Dark, except for the bright searchlight. She fought as they dragged her out of the water. How dare they? Then someone was thumping her back, hard, and she couldn't fight any longer. They were beating her up and there was liquid in her mouth and it must be blood but it was so salty...

She woke, shivering violently. A damp blanket was around her shoulders. She was on a boat. Others were there, huddled on hard wooden boards. Riss was among them, shivering too, and someone was being hauled out of the water as the engine throbbed and the boat rolled up and down. The wind blew and the rain came, and the sky was an impenetrable black.

'Xavi?' she said.

She stood, bracing herself against the lurching of the deck. She tripped over someone, but the handrail wasn't far and she could jump into the sea and look for him. She reached it, and began to climb over, but then hands pulled her back and she was sobbing. Then she gave a long, high wail, that slid all the way down the scale and ended in despair.

27 Survivors

The wind had risen, and the hiss of the shingle had become a roar. On Fenny's orders the boats had made their way to the east of Portland where, at this hour, the tide was high enough for them to sail clear over the drowned harbour. 'There's a force twelve coming,' she'd explained. 'If we moor on Chesil Bank, the boats'll be matchwood by morning. They'll be safer here.' Now the *Cerdic* was slowing for its approach to the quayside.

Jack, perched on one of the lockers, tried to suppress his shivering. The blanket they'd given him had helped at first, but now the water from his clothes had soaked through and the wind was chilling him afresh. His ears ached, and his salt-crusted hair stuck to his forehead. Peering over the gunwale, he could see a dozen cowled lanterns flickering on the rough concrete quay. To port, he could see the lamps on the *Marytavy* and, at the end of the tow-rope, the silhouette of the *Pelican*, its hull intact but its superstructure gone, except for a few skeletal struts. The boat had taken a direct hit from the *Scorpion*'s cannon, and now all across the decks of the other vessels lay the injured, the dying and the dead. Jack could hear the groans, the whimpers, the words of encouragement from their comrades, the false reassurances. He glanced at the three prisoners, crewwomen of the Scorpion, who lay bound hand and foot beside one of the lockers. They had a lot to answer for.

He looked down. Clara, the girl he'd come all this way to find, lay curled in a ball at his feet. Her blanket flapped in the wind. Here she is, he thought. He'd never really believed he'd get this far, never believed he'd see her again. It did his heart good to feel her so close. But what next for her? What next for him?

The *Cerdic* turned and edged in towards the quay. Sailors shouted and threw ropes; women on the dockside worked them around the bollards and hauled the boat closer, before dropping the gangplanks across. The boat was hauled closer and the gangplanks dropped in place. There was a strong smell of fish.

Gingerly, Jack touched his bruised nose. At least the fight had gone out of her now. Only when the flaming remains of the *Scorpion* had been lost in the black swell had she stopped struggling and fallen to the deck in a fit of sobbing. Now that, too, was spent.

Beside her sat the other girl, the one who'd helped, the one who'd got Clara to see sense. Her head rested on her drawn-up knees, a blanket pulled tightly around her shoulders. Exhausted, thought Jack. We all are.

He hauled himself to his feet. He could see, by the activity on the quayside, that word had spread. Townsfolk were hurrying through the alleys and down the streets, and when the boats tied up, many hands were there to help with the casualties. Relatives wept; exhausted sailors stumbled from the boats and flung themselves into the arms of loved ones. Someone yelled in pain. 'Careful, careful!' a voice called. 'Give us a hand here,' said another. Soon a few shivering survivors, draped in blankets, their heads bowed, were being led away from the dockside.

Jack tapped Riss on the shoulder. 'Can you help her off the boat?' he asked, pointing at Clara. 'Follow those people there, see? You both need to get warm. Hey, uh, what's your name?'

'Riss,' she said. 'What were you doing down in the water? Were you really looking for her? Is all this–' she waved a hand in the direction of the sea '–your doing?'

'Nah, not mine,' said Jack. 'Long story. I'll tell you later. I'm Jack.' He held out a hand and helped her up. 'Get warm,' he said, wagging a finger.

He left her bending over Clara and went to help Tay. The man had a bandage on his head and another on his thigh, the trouser leg ripped away. He nodded as Jack arrived. Their task was lifting the dead onto boards, stretchers, old canvases, anything they could find, then passing them down to the helpers on the quayside. Jack reckoned he might as well help with the dead: he'd handled casualties before, whereas most people here probably hadn't. An image from his days with Hurn came to him: Tallah's body, piled in a cart with Pedro and the others. He set his jaw.

Why hadn't he gone with Clara and Riss, to make sure they were all right? Maybe she needed space, he told himself. What was up with her anyway? He touched his nose again, then peered at his fingers: as far as he could tell by lamplight, the bleeding had stopped. From Clara's words, it sounded like there'd been someone left behind, this Zavvy person, but how could that matter so very much? She'd escaped, hadn't she? Maybe being cooped up on a privateer for so long could send you crazy. 'cause that's what she'd been: crazy. Thrashing about in the waves, trying to get back to the *Scorpion* when, if they'd stayed in the water much longer, they'd all have drowned, or died of cold.

The first corpse was a plump woman with a barrel-neck and chest. Blow to the head, a great gash above her right ear. 'Ready?' said Tay. 'One – two – three...there, that's it.' Together they tied her onto the pallet, then manoeuvred it over the gunwale into the hands of two women on the quay.

The next was a small woman with half her shoulder missing: maybe bled to death. Then another, and another. The body of a man, wearing a surprised expression even without its eyes. A bony girl with a long wound in her midriff. It went on. Another wail of grief went up as someone recognised one of the corpses.

By now Shavila was on the quayside, helping with the wounded, but Jack could see that she was moving slowly and stiffly. 'Tori!' he called. 'You all right?'

She turned and waved, but Jack didn't think she meant it. He sniffed, and wiped his eyes.

Next there was a trek up the steep, winding streets, where the villagers were fastening their shutters against the coming storm. This time, Jack and Tay were carrying the wounded up to the hall where they'd held the meeting the night before. Jack held the lighter, front end of the stretcher, but it was still hard work, and the poor woman whimpered at every step they took. By the time they arrived, he was panting heavily. They manoeuvred the stretcher though the doors, out of the chill wind and into the large, warm space of the hall. Here lanterns hung from the beams, the wooden floor had been cleared, and a bright fire burned in the grate. Behind them, some women pushed through the doorway with bedding and blankets. There was a smell of onions and frying eggs, and Jack's stomach knotted.

Fenny, pale and drawn, came up to them. 'They've only a small clinic,' she said. 'The urgent ones we're treating there, but these others'll have to wait here. Put her down over there.' She pointed to where a lone nurse was strapping a splint onto a woman's arm. Behind her, a dark-skinned woman was moaning as she was transferred onto a mattress. 'All of us from Lulworth,' went on Fenny, 'we'll have to bed down with them in here, for tonight.' She passed a hand down her face.

'You all right?' asked Jack.

Fenny shook her head and swallowed. 'Ten dead. Four lost.'

'Is the other woman about? The harbourmistress?'

'Georgia?' said Fenny. 'She's down in the clinic.' She shook her head. 'She was on the *Pelican* when they blasted it.'

'I'm sorry,' said Jack.

'She'll make it,' said Fenny. She looked around. 'You find your friend?'

'Oh, uh, yeah. Someone's with her. She'll be up here soon, I guess.'

'That's something, at least. She okay?'

Jack frowned. 'Physically, yeah. I think so. But not so good up here,' he added, tapping his head.

'Yeah,' said Fenny. 'Join the club.'

It took two hours to bring the remaining casualties up to the hall. With heavy rain arriving on the gale, it became harder and harder for the stretcher-bearers to climb the slippery streets. By the time they'd finished, all Jack could do was slump down in a corner, clutching the mug of soup that somebody had thrust into his chafed hands. Somebody else gave him a dry blanket, so, first struggling out of his sopping tunic, he wrapped it around his bare shoulders, feeling its roughness on his skin. He let his gaze wander over the room, pretending to himself that he wasn't looking for her. The injured lay scattered across the floor on mattresses, on piles of blankets or on doubled-up rugs. Was she here? Ah, yes – there, huddled next to Riss on a bench near the fire. At least she was sitting up; at least she was getting warm.

A bottle of beer appeared before his eyes. He looked up. 'Ta,' he said.

'They've just brought a couple of crates in,' said Shavila, dropping down beside him and taking a swig from her own bottle. Her leather jacket was torn and stained, her face streaked with grime, her hair matted.

'Never seen you look so tired,' he said.

'Getting old,' said Shavila. 'Still, *young* Jack,' she added, holding up her bottle, 'we did it.'

Jack clinked his against hers. Outside, the storm skeltered though the narrow streets and hammered at the shutters. The roof-timbers creaked, and in the grate the fire leapt and spat. Then the door burst open, admitting a blast of cold air. A woman, her oilskin dripping, forced it shut behind her. 'Renu!' she cried, breathlessly. 'Renu! Is she here?'

From the far corner, voices answered. The woman gave a yelp and ran to one of casualties who lay on a straw mattress, then sobbed as she clasped her. 'You're alive!' she kept saying. 'You're alive!'

Jack blinked. Ten dead, four missing, more dying in the clinic. But, he told himself, Clara was alive. He swallowed the last of his soup, took a pull of his beer, and stood. He felt queasy. 'I'll go and see how she is,' he said, but when he looked down, he saw that Shavila had fallen asleep where she sat, her beer hardly touched. He fetched another blanket and covered her, before picking his way among the forms on the floor. Some were already asleep on the hard boards.

'All right?' said Jack to Tay, who sat on a low stool, his bandaged leg stretched out before him. Tay nodded. 'Knackered,' he said, and returned to his soup.

Someone began to put out the lanterns, and Jack wondered what the time was. The early hours, certainly, but whether two o'clock, or three, or five, he didn't have a clue. He reached Clara and Riss, their backs to him, and for a moment he stopped. Then Riss looked over her shoulder.

'Here,' she said, her voice low. 'She's not eating. See if you can do anything.'

Jack nodded. On the bench beside Clara was an untouched mug of soup. He moved around them, his back now turned to the warm fire, and crouched so that his face was level with Clara's. He saw that Riss was holding one of her hands, dark skin interlocking with pale. Like Jack, Clara had a blanket around her shoulders. She was wearing something underneath, but the blanket hung loosely and he could see her smooth collarbones, the hollow of her white neck, her soft throat. He made himself look at her face. 'Clara?' he said. He meant to be gentle, but his throat was raw and the words rasped.

She looked back at him, but it was as if her gaze didn't stop. It passed clean through him, through the wall and out into the storm. He shifted to look more closely into her eyes. They were pale blue – how had he never noticed that before? – but red-rimmed. Her jaw was set, her bottom lip puckered upward, and her hair was long and lank. Tears had left grimy lines down her face.

Gingerly, he reached for her shoulder, and tugged the blanket more closely around her. 'Clara?' he said again.

She shook her head, and swallowed. 'You're not Xavi,' she said, her voice flat and hard.

He glanced at Riss, who pulled a face. 'Nurse has just given her some valerian,' she said. 'To help her sleep.'

Jack turned back to Clara. 'No,' he said, 'I'm not Zavvy.' Something was catching in his throat. 'But you need to eat, all right? You'll – you'll get ill. Please, Clara.' He held the mug out to her.

She shook her head, and again she was staring over his right shoulder. She rose, and tried to push past him, but her legs gave way and he caught her. 'Leave me alone,' she said, but she let him help her to a thick rug, where she sank down and curled in a ball.

Jack knew he shouldn't feel happy that he'd held her in his arms. It was just, he told himself, that he'd got her safe, like her parents had wanted. He looked up at Riss. 'What happened?'

Riss sighed and sat down again. Jack sat next to her, watching Clara. 'There were three of us in the boiler-room,' Riss said, 'under guard. They made us work, pretty much all the time. Xavi–'

'He was a man, right?'

She nodded. 'From Spain. The *Scorpion's* job was smashing up refugee boats.'

'Yeah, I heard.'

'I think it got to him. It could easily have been him, you see, 'cause he was a refugee too. Anyhow, during the fight, he got to the cannon.'

'It was him that nearly sank the *Pelican*?'

'No, it was after that. He fired it down into the ship.'

Jack thought for a minute. 'Oh! So *that* was the big explosion. I thought maybe we'd hit an ammo store or something. And you two had jumped into the sea, just before that?'

Clara wriggled on the rug and pulled the blanket tighter.

Jack lowered his voice. 'He died, then?'

Riss lowered hers too. 'Must've done. There'd be no surviving that. Did you see what happened to the *Scorpion*? Did it sink?

'No. At least, I saw it was on fire, but it didn't look like it was going down. Lost sight of it after that. Waves was too big.'

'Better not tell Clara,' whispered Riss. 'She might want to go looking for him.'

Jack frowned. 'Er, thanks for helping,' he said. 'With Clara. She was – well, if you hadn't yelled at her...'

Riss looked at him. 'How's the face?

'Bit sore. She's got a strong punch.'

'I'm sorry,' she said, looking away.

'Wasn't your fault,' Jack began. But then he realised that's not what Riss meant, because now it was her turn to cry. He put an arm around her shoulders.

28 Aftermath

Clara sat on the floor close to the fireplace and rested her back against the wall. She could feel the warmth on her legs, on her bruised hands. Maybe there was a bit of life coming back into them, because they were hurting.

She looked around the hall. Ancient oak wainscoting, stained by the years, ran along the walls. There were old radiators here, too, that no-one had got around to removing. She'd heard about these things, about how hot water used to be pumped through them to make the room warm, back in the days before the coal and the oil ran low, back in the days when it got properly cold in the winter.

There were a couple of dozen other women in the hall: some crouched on chairs and benches, talking in low voices, others sitting on the floor like Clara, stunned, waiting for their thoughts to untangle. One was asleep under a blanket, and two were carrying a corpse out on an old door. Clara watched as they negotiated the inner doorway then fought their way out into the storm, into the wind and lashing rain. The door slammed, and Clara flinched, because it reminded her of the doom that had overtaken Xavi, the explosion that had deafened her. Even now her ears rang.

'Tea?' A woman bearing a tray stopped in front of her and held out a steaming mug.

Clara reached up and took it, trying to stop her hand from shaking. 'Thanks,' she said, and she wasn't sure if she'd said it too loudly, because she couldn't hear properly. 'What time is it?'

'Two o'clock,' said the woman, looking down on her. She was slim, and her hair was long and greying. 'In the afternoon,' she added, reading Clara's expression. 'You did a lot of sleeping there. Do you good.' And she went on with her round.

Clara set the tea down while it cooled. Better not hold it, she thought, while I'm shaking. Yes, I'm shaking, she thought, because Xavi's dead, isn't he?

She knew. Of course she knew; he'd told her, hadn't he? He'd told her with that look, that piercing glance he'd given as the blood oozed through his shirt, as he swivelled the cannon down into the *Scorpion*'s guts, while Clara teetered on the edge of the hull. He'd told her that he was going to die, but that he'd be avenged on the *Scorpion* for all the refugees it had killed, for his own family, for everything. But Clara had been pierced too, right through the heart, for that same glance had told her that he loved her. And she remembered his tender eyes, his tight muscular chest, his lovely dark hair, his gentle hands...

She bowed her head and shut her eyes. Nothing happened. It didn't seem like she could cry any more. Not yet. She picked up the mug and held it in both hands. The china was hot against her skin, the steam warm on her face. Then she frowned. Something about that woman, the one who'd given her the tea, was familiar. The voice? Not the hair...

It didn't feel like she'd dozed, but she must have done, for when she opened her eyes the light had changed again and the rain, for the moment, had eased. At the fireplace, a woman was talking loudly. '...last of the wood,' she was saying. 'After that's gone, no more fires till the storm's over and we can get back to the mainland...'

Then came the sound of people struggling in through the main door: the wind, the thud as they fought it closed behind them, the stamping of boots. The inner door was opened, and there stood Riss, with Jack Pike.

Clara frowned. Two people who came from different parts of her life, people who didn't know each other, had just arrived together. Why? She shook her head. Something was in there, wasn't it? She felt that she knew why Jack was there, and why she, Clara, didn't feel shocked. Something had happened, hadn't it? Something in the water. It had happened when Xavi died.

Ah! *There* it was. *That* was where the tears had been hiding. She let them run down her face, let them drip off her nose while her shoulders shook, because nothing mattered now. People sat down beside her. Riss on one side, putting an arm around her. Jack on the other.

'You're in shock,' whispered Riss. 'You're ill, as well – you were on that ship a long time. They never fed us properly, did they?'

More people were coming into the hall now. It sounded like glasses and mugs were being given out, drinks poured.

'Jack?' said Clara, turning to him. He was gazing at her, and she knew him well enough to see he was troubled. For a moment she was too overcome to speak, but then she said, 'Jack, how come you're here?'

He looked down at her hand, and she could see that he was thinking about holding it. 'You don't know?' he asked gently.

Clara wiped her eyes and shook her head. 'Where are we?'

'I told you, love,' said Riss. 'Isle of Portland.'

'Xavi's dead, isn't he?'

Riss nodded. 'I'm sorry,' she said. 'I know that you two–'

'There was a fight...' said Clara.

There was a regular throng in the hall now. Through the crowd, Clara could see the grey-haired woman coming towards them. She definitely recognised her now. But where from?

'They're going to raise a toast,' said the woman, holding out a hand. 'Come and get a drink.'

Clara stared at the hand. Then, taking it, she hauled herself up. She could feel Riss's hand under her elbow. Jack stood close.

'How do I know you?' she asked the woman.

'Clara,' said Jack, 'don't you remember her?'

Clara winced.

'It's Tori,' he went on. 'Tori Shavila. She saved your life last night.'

'Getting to be a habit,' said Shavila, with a wry smile. 'Pulling you two out of the water.'

Clara put a hand to her head. Riss with Jack, and now Jack with this Tori Shavila. 'Um,' she hazarded, 'saved my life?'

'Yes,' put in Riss. 'You'd swallowed half the Channel. You were choking.'

'I remember,' said Clara, frowning. Someone had been hitting her on the back, hadn't they? 'That was you?' she went on. 'Wait!' She peered into Shavila's face. 'You're – you're–'

Shavila was nodding; Jack was nodding.

'–*Sergeant* Shavila? What are you doing here? I mean, your hair – and–'

'I don't go by that name any more,' said Shavila. She grimaced as she eased herself down into a chair. 'I don't move so well, either.'

Somebody rapped a spoon on the table at the far end of the hall. 'That's the Governor,' said Jack, pointing to the fair-haired woman.

The Governor, this time dressed in an unbuttoned tweed coat, climbed on a chair. 'Everyone,' she said, 'I just want to say a few words. Last night we lost fourteen of our friends and relatives. It's a hell of a sacrifice, I know. And I know that some of our lives will never be the same.'

Clara frowned. It was all about them, wasn't it? What about Xavi? He'd been lost, too.

'In a minute,' the Governor was saying, 'we'll drink a toast. To them all.'

'What about Xavi?' murmured Clara. No-one heard, not even Jack, standing beside her.

'But for now,' went on the Governor, 'let's all realise what a great victory we've won. For too many years, we've been the victims. Times were hard already, and when these raids came, well, they got even harder. Food stolen, goods stolen, families starving. Hard-working women injured and even killed.'

Clara saw a number of the audience nodding. 'What about Xavi?' Now she said it out loud.

Jack turned and frowned at her. So did Riss. Clara glared back.

The Governor slipped off her coat, and it made her look smaller, diminished. 'Along this coast,' she said, 'we've always worked together, we've always looked out for each other.'

Clara looked at her fingertips. She could feel Xavi's warm skin beneath them, feel his muscles, his bones. She thought she could feel him pressing against her, his face stooping down to hers. She groaned aloud.

'But this,' said the Governor, her voice rising, 'is far, far beyond anything we've done before. We've taken on the enemy, and we've destroyed them! Armed only with what we had to hand, against their guns and their cannons–'

'What about Xavi?' This time Clara shouted it.

The Governor stopped, peering through the audience to see where the disturbance was coming from.

Clara could feel someone tugging at her sleeve, but now she felt herself striding forward, pushing her way through the crowd. She felt hot, too. 'You're so bloody smug, aren't you?' She shouted. 'You think killing is great? What about us? Hey? Down in the belly of that ship, starved, and – and – tortured! And made to work till we dropped! We could all have drowned, and you didn't care! And–' her voice was trembling now '–Xavi died! He *died*!' She could feel fifty pairs of eyes on her, feel the shock and the anger. Someone took a step towards her. She could hear Jack calling her name. 'Get off me!' she shrieked, before turning and running for the door.

29 Apologies

I hate them, she thought as she threw one door open. I hate them, she thought as she pushed the next and found herself outside in the wind and the hammering rain. I hate them.

Beyond the black clouds that drove overhead, the last of the daylight was failing. Clara turned to her right and strode down the steep hill, the cobbles under her feet running with water as the gutters overflowed. She slipped once or twice, but staggered on, jaw set. 'Aaargh!' she cried, punching a brick wall as she passed.

There was a voice far away behind her, but she didn't care. Now the houses on her left melted away as the road bent to her right. More exposed here, Clara stopped and braced herself against the gusts, blinking into the rain and feeling the chill through her sodden clothes. Below lay the harbour, with its swaying storm-lanterns; and over there, she could see the ruins of Chesil bank and the sea-drowned Fleet. In the west the clouds were tinged with red.

'Clara!'

She turned to see a man bearing down on her, his eyes wild, his beard dripping. She blinked again.

'What the hell d'you think you're doing?' he yelled, smacking his palms into her shoulders, so that she staggered backwards.

'Jack?' The word blew away on the wind.

'You–' he pushed her again; again she staggered. 'You just insulted them! They saved your bloody life, you mad–' another shove '–bitch!'

Clara swallowed. The rain was running down her back, and her lips dripped as she spoke. 'Jack, I–'

'*They* had people die, too. You're not the only one, for pity's sake.' He was panting now. 'People died in Lulworth. Those bastards in the *Scorpion* killed 'em. These people here–' he waved an arm back up the hill '–they risked everything, and now their families'll never see them again. And you *insult* them? You – you–' He wiped rain from his eyes. 'I know you don't mean it, Clara. I know you don't. Tell me you don't...'

'What are you doing here, Jack?' she snapped. 'Can't you stop following me around?'

'No, I bloody can't,' he snarled. He looked away. 'And it's not 'cause I haven't tried, believe me.'

Clara stared. She wouldn't cry, she wouldn't.

'It's not a coincidence, Clara. I came after you.'

She swept the water from her eyes. 'You...? Of course you did.'

'I did like you said. Your parents are safe. And after that, I came to find you. *You*, Clara. You stupid, stupid...'

'You came after me.' She bowed her head. She supposed that she herself was crying now, although it was difficult to tell.

'Your knuckles are bleeding,' he said, his voice still raised against the wind.

Clara looked at the angry red grazes on her knuckles. Then she felt Jack's hands on her shoulders again, but this time they just rested there.

SCORPION

She shrugged him off. 'Get out of my way,' she snarled, and pushed him aside before struggling back up the hill, her knees aching, her thighs aching, her head aching.

Jack watched her go. He couldn't chase her any more. He didn't want to. What had it all come to? He sniffed and wiped his eyes with a sleeve. He'd promised Sophia and James that he'd bring her back to them, but he hadn't really known what he was letting himself in for. He'd come so, *so* far, and here she was. But would she want to go back to her parents? And, with the way she was behaving, would they even want her?

He shivered. He didn't want to face her again, to face the embarrassment of whatever madness she was up to now, whatever insults she was dishing out. But he couldn't stay out here in the cold. He needed to dry out. Swearing, head down, he trudged back up the hill past the shuttered houses and under the overflowing gutters. It was nearly dark. How long was this bloody storm going to last? Pace after pace, splash after splash. He pushed wet hair out of his eyes.

When he reached the hall, he turned away and sheltered in a doorway opposite. He still didn't want to go in. But after a minute he realised he couldn't stay there, either. It had to be done, he supposed. He'd have to put up with her for a bit longer. Because there was nowhere else to go, nothing else he could do.

Eventually he crossed the road and, grasping the door firmly so that the wind didn't snatch it out of his hands, made his way inside. In the hallway he stood dripping, and listening. To kill time, he struggled out of his tunic and wrung it out yet again. Well, from what he could hear, no-one was yelling, so that was something. Had she sneaked in, quietly, hoping no-one would notice? That'd be better than making even more of a fool of herself. *And making a fool of me*, said a voice inside his head.

He pushed the inner door open, and the first thing he heard was a single voice. Nothing else, just the voice. It was Clara's.

'...no excuse,' she was saying. 'Yes, the boy – the man – I loved, died.' Jack noticed how one or two of the women flinched when Clara said that she loved a man. It wouldn't have been allowed, back in Anglia, in the great women's republic. But here? He didn't know.

'But,' Clara continued, 'I know you've all lost people, too, and I – I was wrong to speak the way I did. It was cruel of me. I don't know how to make amends–' she looked around at the group of women who stared back at her '–but I want to try. I – I'm sorry.' She bowed her head.

Jack saw that the Governor had got down from her chair and was now standing in front of Clara. Two women, he thought, looking nearly the same. Similar height, both slightly-built, faces drawn. Then he frowned. He supposed Clara *was* a grown woman now. If only she'd act like one.

'Well,' said the Governor, '–what did you say your name was?'

'Clara,' said Clara. 'Clara Perdue. Apparently–' she looked at her feet, where a puddle of rainwater had formed '–apparently it means "lost".'

The Governor nodded. 'Well, Clara, I can't deny that you upset us. But thank you for your apology. I guess we'll accept it. And we'll also accept your offer – there's lots to do, once the storm passes. But right now, go and dry out, then get some rest. You're exhausted.'

Jack watched for a minute then, shaking his head, followed Clara to the fireside. Some of the women were still scowling at her.

'What were you playing at?' Riss was saying, as Jack came up and joined them.

'You lost it a bit, I reckon,' said Jack.

'It's like the Governor says,' said Riss. 'You're knackered. We all are.'

Clara stood as close to the fire as she could, and steam began to rise from her trousers. She looked at Jack. 'I saw you come in,' she said, nodding towards the doorway.

'Yeah?' he said. 'Shove over a bit, I got to dry out too.'

She peered into his face. 'I'm sorry, Jack. I'm sorry for everything. I'm always apologising to you, aren't I?' She was breathing fast.

'Here,' said Riss. 'What is it with you two? And why,' she said to Jack, 'were you in the sea, with a rope?'

Jack glanced at Clara. 'Like I say,' he said, 'it's a long story. We've known each other for – well, on and off – what is it?'

Clara was about to speak, but Jack went on: 'Couple of years, I guess. Feels like all my life. Oh,' he added, colouring, 'that is...well, the main thing is, Clara's parents – oh! Uh...'

'Riss knows I'm a Natural,' put in Clara, but she was still watching Jack.

'Um, they're in Devon. Communal farm. Sophia said it was best, see. And – and they wanted me to get Clara back.'

'Oh, they did, did they?' said Clara.

Jack licked his lips. 'Well. They tried to stop me from going...'

'Wait,' said Riss. 'They wanted you to fetch her back, but they tried to stop you going?'

'Sort of. Um, see, she took my place. I was the one who should've been sent to the slave market.'

Riss shook her head and sighed. 'No, I don't see. But let it go, hey?'

Jack looked around. 'Where's Tori?'

'There's a little storeroom up those stairs,' said Riss, pointing. 'She's gone for a kip.'

'I hope this party doesn't wake her up, then,' said Jack. Behind them, tables were being moved and chairs set out. Someone had brought more bottles.

'Oh, yes!' said Clara. 'How come *she's* here, Jack?'

'Ah,' he said, 'now that *was* coincidence. Found her running a ferry, in Bewley.'

Riss raised her eyes to heaven. 'I'll get some beers,' she said.

After she'd gone, Jack turned to Clara. 'You very sad?' he asked.

She nodded. 'But I guess you know how I feel, don't you? That girl, the one you said you'd – you know – with her.'

'Tallah, you mean?' said Jack. 'Yeah, a bit.'

They stood in silence for a minute then, together, turned their backs to the fire.

'Jack?' said Clara.

SCORPION

'Mm?'

'I – I'm sorry. Again.'

30 Another Plan

The weather worsened. The wind blew gustier and stronger, sometimes pretending to abate before returning more fiercely. The rain fell heavily for hours at a stretch. Tiles were ripped from rooftops, dustbins rolled down the hill, and outhouses lost their roofs or were flattened completely. For two whole days the storm rattled the windows and beat upon the doors of the meeting-hall, and anyone peering out of the rain-lashed windows could hardly see across the street.

Clara and the others continued lodging there, along with those Lulworth villagers who'd survived the attack on the *Scorpion*; but at night the men – Jack, Tay and two others – were segregated, trudging up the hill to sleep in a cottage. The cottage was empty, they heard, because its owner had been lost overboard when the *Pelican* was hit.

Clara spent most of the first two days lying on her mattress, staring into space, feeling her bruises and trying not to think of Xavi. Whenever she woke from a doze, it took her a moment to remember where she was: the roaring of the storm, the breaking of the waves, and the shuddering of the hall, all made her feel like she was still on the *Scorpion*. The only things missing were the rumble of the engines, the heat of the furnaces, and Xavi.

Jack had been coming over every couple of hours to check she was all right, but this annoyed her, and she'd snapped at him. So he stopped bothering her at all, instead spending most of his time with Tay and the other men;

although several times she noticed him staring at her across the hall. That annoyed her still more.

Tori Shavila was best at dealing with the ceaseless tedium. She seemed able to switch herself off and sleep for hours on end, waking refreshed and helping around the hall whenever it was needed. Clara reckoned she must be sleeping fifteen hours a day. Riss, on the other hand, spent her time pacing up and down, glaring at the rain or playing cards with some of the other women. Whenever she came to sit with Clara she'd look out at the dark sky and begin with, 'I wish this bloody rain'd stop.'

Also, the hall was cold and the diet frugal. With no contact with the mainland, they were rationing the wood, and the fire was lit only for a few hours in the evening. At least there were plenty of blankets, but having to wear them all the time added to the dreariness, as did the food. There was little bread, owing to the lack of fuel for the ovens, and most of the time they ate cold pickled herring or tinned vegetables. The novelty wore off quickly.

Late on the second day, Clara was staring through the rain-spattered windows, watching the charcoal clouds as they hurtled eastwards.

'Real tree-ripper, ain't it?' came a voice from behind her. She turned.

Jack was holding out a mug of tea. 'They got a fire going,' he said. It was the first time he'd spoken to her all day.

Clara didn't know what to say. In these days of weather extremes, "tree-ripper" was a common enough phrase, and Jack had probably used it automatically. But straight away she remembered the incident, on the day of the Great Flood of London, when Jack had thrown her to the ground, giving her a bloody nose but saving her from being struck by an uprooted tree. And as she looked in his eyes, she saw that he'd remembered it, too.

She took the mug. 'Thanks,' she said.

They stood for a few minutes, sipping their tea while they listened to the storm and watched the raindrops scurry down the window panes. Jack remained at her shoulder, but he didn't say anything, which was good.

'I'll be all right, you know,' said Clara. She turned her head. 'I'll be all right.'

He nodded.

One of the women had observed, dolefully, that she remembered one storm that had lasted a whole week. That hadn't cheered anyone up. But on the third day, there seemed to be a little less wind, a little less rain, and a little more light in the sky. In the hall the mood lifted somewhat, and there was a rumour that a gig would set off for the mainland that afternoon, if the weather didn't worsen, to get supplies.

Riss seemed the most affected by the improvement. She was positively cheery, chatting animatedly with Jack and Tay, and holding a long conversation with Fenny about how they managed to fish in seas as rough as these. Clara wasn't surprised when, after working her way around most of the hall, Riss came and plumped herself down on the floor next to her. 'Phew!' she said. 'Thank the Teacher we'll get out of here soon.'

'Mm,' said Clara.

Riss looked sidelong at her.

Clara sighed. 'I'll be all right,' she said. 'I told Jack the same.'

'Just give it time, eh?'

'Just give it time.'

'It's always good,' said Riss, turning to look around the hall, 'to keep busy. If you're sad, I mean. Don't do what I did and spend your time getting out of your head.' She frowned.

'Yes,' said Clara, 'but I can't exactly do anything when I'm shut up in this place.'

'Aw, you've been resting. You were half-dead, Clara. But, anyhow, I mean, like a project. Something long-term. Give you focus.'

'You sound like one of my old teachers.'

Riss chuckled.

'Well,' said Clara slowly, 'Xavi wanted peace. He told me that's what we should have, instead of fighting each other. And he's right.'

Riss nodded. 'That's what Anna thought, too.'

Clara turned to look at her. 'Oh?' she said. She'd wanted to know more about Riss's ex, but had never had the courage to ask.

'It's how we fell out,' said Riss. She looked down at her hands. 'Anna was always – I don't know – *moral* about things. I'm not saying it was always black and white with her, but if there was something that had to be done, she'd do it, and not ask questions. Someone starving outside your door? Feed them. Thief being beaten up by Repsegs? Stop 'em.' She glanced at Clara. 'Yeah, they happened. I was with her. Really embarrassing.' She chuckled. 'And then, of course, the war came up. Anna said I should go and have it out with Ma, tell her to make it stop.'

'How would that help?'

Riss sighed. 'Ma always had a soft spot for me. Anything I wanted, any clothes, any money, whatever I wanted, I could have. Maybe it was love. Maybe I was a bit spoiled. Anyhow, Anna knew – she could see it, I didn't have to tell her. She thought Ma would take notice of me.'

'So what did you say?'

'What did I say? I laughed in her face. She said, if I didn't try, it'd always be on my conscience. And I said – well, you know what I'm like, Clara. Can't keep my mouth under control. I said things I shouldn't.' She shook her head. 'I really miss her.'

Clara saw tears starting in the corners of Riss's eyes. 'Where is she now?' she asked gently.

'Ach, she won't want to see me. Up at her ma's old place, I think.'

'Well,' said Clara, 'you could still go and plead with your mother. Do what Anna wanted. Would that make things better between you?'

Riss bent and ran her finger across the floorboards.

'It could be a project for you,' said Clara.

Riss sat up. 'You could come too.'

'Me?'

The doors banged open, and two women came into the hall, shaking out their rain-capes. 'Definitely clearing,' announced one. 'Harbour's a bit of a mess, but the boats are all okay. Any tea going?'

As they hurried off to the kitchen, Riss went on: 'You're a Truth Sister – or you used to be – and you've seen everything I have. And more. You could back me up.'

Clara chewed the inside of her lip. 'For Xavi...'

'And Anna.'

'I promised Jack, though. I promised Jack I'd go back with him, back to my parents.'

Riss shrugged. 'You could go afterwards. After we've seen Ma.'

'He won't like it,' said Clara, still chewing. 'He won't like it at all.'

'You backing out, then?'

Clara shook her head quickly. 'No. I'll come. I have to. But I can't face Jack yet.'

'Well,' said Riss, looking up at the window, 'if the weather's clearing, you haven't got long. Want me to tell him?'

Clara pictured Jack's reaction if he heard it from Riss. She'd hate him to think that she, Clara, didn't have the guts to face him. 'No,' she said firmly. 'I should. I'll tell him tonight.'

Riss glanced around the hall. 'Where is he, anyway?'

'He went to help with the unloading, when the supplies come back.' Clara looked up at the clock. 'Should be soon.' She stood up.

'Where are you going?' asked Riss.

'I'd better go and see what Tori thinks. Let her know what we're planning, anyway.'

'She went down to the smithy, didn't she?'

Clara nodded. 'I'll find her. And leave Jack to me, all right?'

It was the first time in three days that Clara had set foot outside the hall. The storm might have eased, but the rain was still falling and a stiff wind was blowing from the west. She kept close to the housefronts as she made her way down the steep hill, hugging her cloak tighter as she picked her way around the rubble: smashed tiles fallen from roofs, and broken glass; sticks, stones and dirt that had been washed into miniature riverbanks as the storm water had run down the street. One house, she saw as she reached the exposed harbour and turned right, had lost its chimney.

By the time she reached the smithy, her nose twitching at the familiar smells, she was looking forward to warming herself by the forge. She'd half-expected to find Shavila dozing again, but as she turned into the alley, she saw the ex-Repseg leaning against the doorpost.

Shavila raised a hand in greeting. 'I like watching the sea,' she said.

Clara nodded, and peered at her. 'How are you today? Did you sleep all right?'

'Oh, yeah,' said Shavila, glancing up as a party of gulls swept overhead. 'But it's not lack of sleep that's making me tired, Clara.'

Clara didn't know what to say to that, so she just followed Shavila back into the shop. Just now the opposite doors were closed, to prevent a cross-draught that would cool the iron too quickly, but Clara could see that in the heat of summer, three sides of the shop could be opened to the air. Two anvils dominated the middle of the floor, with a bellows-driven forge set in a stout brick chimney at one end. Hammers, tongs and drifts hung in timber racks, and a stack of iron ingots stood in one corner. On one of the forges lay the heavy bracket that Shavila had been working on and, donning a mitten, Clara picked it up.

'You made this?' she said.

Shavila nodded. 'The engine's held in place with eight of these. One of them had sheared off.'

'And it's better to make a new one than fix the old.' Clara turned the bracket over. 'Good job.'

'You know forgework?'

Clara nodded. 'I worked in a smithy for a while, trying to save some money. Jack and I had got separated, you see. Did he, er, tell you about that?'

'No,' said Shavila. She gave a quick grin. 'But, like I told him, you've both got a talent for getting into trouble. I guess I wouldn't be surprised at anything.'

'Jack said you were a great help to him. You needn't have left Bewley.'

Shavila shrugged, but said nothing.

'Look,' said Clara, 'I haven't thanked you for getting me out of the water.'

'It was Jack's idea.'

Clara turned to her. 'Yes,' she said, 'but then you got the water out of me. You saved my life again.'

'You saved mine once, if you remember. The time the rioters started shooting at us...'

'We go back a long way, don't we?'

Shavila nodded. 'I guess we're friends, then. Of course, Repsegs don't need friendship or anything, but, uh...' She trailed off. '*Are* we friends?'

'Definitely,' said Clara, patting her on the shoulder.

They stood in silence for a moment, watching the rain. Then Shavila took the bracket. 'This is cool enough now. Help me close up?'

Clara nodded. 'By the way,' she said as she fastened one of the shutters, 'where's the smith? How come you had to do this yourself?'

'She's in the mortuary,' said Shavila.

Clara swore. Another reason, she thought, that the fighting had to stop. Innocent people were dying.

'You coming back up to the hall?' asked Clara.

'Yes,' said Shavila. 'I'll leave it till the morning to fit this. Then if the weather's better, we can leave.'

'And what then? What will you do next?'

'Oh. I hadn't thought. To tell you the truth, I wasn't expecting to still be alive. I thought we'd never stop the *Scorpion*. Rational analysis of the risks, and all that.' She shrugged. 'I suppose I could go back to Bewley...it'll seem a bit dull, though.'

'Look,' said Clara, thrusting a bolt home. 'Riss and I have got a plan. We wondered if you could help...'

31 Breaking it to Jack

'So, Tori,' said Jack, tearing off another piece of bread, 'what time are you setting off tomorrow?'

It was evening, and they were sitting at a table with Clara and Riss. Shavila had already finished her food and was sitting back, fingering her glass of small ale. 'If I can get that bracket fitted,' she said, 'we should be away by late morning.'

The supply-boat had returned, and more trips were planned for the next day. The improvement wasn't huge – tonight the pickled herrings had only been augmented with bread and beans – but the prospect of a return to normal had lifted everyone's spirits. At one of the other tables the Governor, and a few others from the town, had joined Fenny for what they expected to be a farewell meal. There was laughter amid the animated conversation.

'How many are going back to Lulworth with you?' asked Jack.

Shavila was looking at Clara, who was chewing her lip. 'Six or seven,' she said.

'And you're going, too?' said Jack, turning to Riss.

Riss and Clara looked at each other.

'What?' said Jack. 'Oh,' he said to Riss, 'd'you wanna come with Clara and me? That'd be fine, y'know–'

'Jack,' began Clara, then stopped as someone from another table squeezed by. 'Jack, I...' She looked up, hesitant.

'Wait a minute,' said Jack, frowning. 'What are you saying?'

Riss started to speak, but Clara held up a hand. 'Riss and I are going to London, Jack.'

Jack's mouth fell open, and Clara was sure she could see his shoulders droop. 'What?' was all he could manage.

'We're going to see General Clark,' Clara went on, trying to keep her voice steady, 'to demand that she stops the war.'

Jack inclined his head. 'Nah,' he said, 'nah. You're having me on, right?'

Clara tried to look him in the eye. She swallowed. 'No, Jack.'

Across the hall, somebody had struck up a song. No-one at the table took any notice.

'That's just stupid,' said Jack. 'Stopp messin' me about, Clara. You can't walk up to a bloody general and tell her what to do. They'd stop you getting near her in the first place! It's mad.'

'She can,' put in Riss, lowering her voice, 'if she's returning the general's missing daughter.'

Jack looked at Clara, who nodded.

'My real name's Charis Clark,' Riss went on. 'General Clark's my mother. They'll let me through, and anyone who's with me.'

Jack stared. 'You? You're the one on them posters?' he said.

'And if she won't listen,' went on Riss, glancing at Clara, 'I can threaten to tell the press about the virus weapons that the Republic claims it doesn't have. *The Republican Woman* is no friend of the army.'

'No,' said Jack, shaking his head, 'no. Supposin' all this is true, supposin' she's who she says she is – the bloody general's never gonna listen, is she? Call off a war just 'cause her daughter says so? You're havin' a laugh.'

'We've got to try,' said Riss, while Clara fidgeted. 'I've got to do it for Anna, and...'

'And I've got to do it,' said Clara quickly, 'for Xavi.'

Jack's brows were knotted. 'And what about your parents, Clara? They want you back. Or had you forgotten?'

'I'll go back to them afterwards,' said Clara, frowning. 'Of course I will.'

'Oh yeah?' said Jack. 'And what if you get killed? Or maybe,' he went on, waving a hand at her, 'maybe you'll change your bloody mind again! Maybe you'll think of something else to do first!'

'Jack, I–'

'And what about *me*, Clara?' asked Jack, pushing a fist into his chest. 'I promised them I'd bring you back, if I could. I jumped in the bloody sea to get yer. And now – and now...' He trailed off, and Clara saw tears in his eyes.

Riss leaned forward. 'You can't do anything about it, Jack. We're going, and that's that.'

'Riss, wait–' began Clara.

'You're leaving me behind?' said Jack, swallowing.

Clara shook her head. 'No, Jack, no. Come with us.' To her right, she was aware of Riss looking up to heaven. 'Please?'

Jack sat for a minute staring at his plate. Then he stood, and pushed his chair back.

Clara put a hand on his arm. 'Jack, please...'

He snatched it away. 'Nice to know what you really think,' he said with a sneer. Then he stomped out of the hall.

'Jack!' Clara called after him.

'Ah, leave him,' said Riss as the door slammed. 'He's a man, what d'you expect?'

Clara glared at her.

Jack turned left, into the wind and into the drizzle, feeling the cold air in his lungs and wishing it could clear his brain too. He strode on, up the hill, until the road bent left and the houses fell behind. The night sky was black with cloud, but below lay the lights of the town and, further to his left, bright pinpoints that marked the dwellings along the shores of Lyme Bay. In the dark he couldn't even see the sea, but he knew that across that bay, not fifty miles off, lay the mouth of the Exe. If you followed that river upstream for a few miles, you came to the community farm where Sophia and James were waiting. Waiting for him to bring Clara back to them.

He swore. Clara hadn't seen them, had she? She hadn't seen them when they read the note that she'd left in Jack's pocket, after she'd drugged them all and taken his place among the prisoners. *She* hadn't seen their faces when they realised she'd left them.

The wind was tugging at Jack's hair, and the drizzle was slowly soaking him, but he didn't notice. He was hearing Sophia's screams, he was watching James as he stumbled then fell then began to cry. He was trying to calm Sophia, helping James up, trying to still his own heart. He'd got them together, found a cart, and driven them away from Blandford. He'd driven westward, like Clara had said, and all the time her parents were crying, wanting to turn back.

SCORPION

He could hear their pleas now; he could see Sophia when she jumped from the moving cart and ran back the way they'd come, screaming Clara's name. He'd stopped the cart, hurried after her, and coaxed her back, and she and James had held each other while the miles rolled by.

Two hours had passed by the time Clara managed to disengage herself from Riss, who had drunk several beers and become tearful about Anna. The fire was sinking into embers. Most of the other people in the hall had settled down for the night, and the remaining few were doing so. With a sigh, Clara flung herself onto her thin mattress, pulling the blanket over her whole body, including her head. She used to do that when she was a little girl, she thought, but she'd never wondered why. She couldn't have been hiding from anything, not at that age, surely?

After a few minutes, she uncovered her face and listened to the wind. *Bloody* Jack, she thought. No, that wasn't fair. He'd done his best, but he'd never understand. He'd never understand how important this was for her: to stop all of the fighting, to stop it for Xavi, to stop it because people were going to have enough of a struggle just to stay alive, without killing each other. And she was going to go with Riss, because she had to, even though it might be futile in the end.

She frowned. Jack needn't come, if he didn't want to. But of course, she told herself, he would. Definitely, he would. Now, if she'd hit him and scratched his face, like she'd done before, then that might have been enough to turn him away. This time, though, it was just that he was being stubborn.

If he didn't come, she supposed she'd miss him. It wasn't as if she'd seen much of him since that day a couple of months ago when he brought them food in their cell at Hurn's camp; and before that, it had been over a year since they'd parted. She'd got used to him not being around. But then, he *had* followed her all the way back to Southampton, and then along the Channel; and then he'd swum out to rescue her, with a little rope around his waist...

Next morning she woke with a stiff neck, and in a bad mood. She'd dreamed that Jack had gone to live with her parents, and that when she herself had turned up, months later, they didn't want her. Stupid dreams, she told herself.

After she'd splashed cold water over her face, she went to look out of the door. The wind had dropped, the sea was much calmer and there were even breaks in in the cloud canopy. They'd get away today, for sure. Jack would have to make his mind up soon.

Someone had baked bread again, and Clara found Fenny tucking into a still-warm slice spread with butter. It smelt good. Alongside her, Riss was nursing a mug of tea and a hangover.

'Good weather,' said Clara, sitting down and pouring herself some.

Fenny, who was looking less haggard than she'd done a few days ago, swallowed and took a sip. 'I make it a rule never to trust the weather,' she said with a wry smile. 'But yes, if Tori can get the *Cerdic* going, we should make it to Lulworth. I hear you're coming, too.'

'Yes,' said Clara. 'Have you seen Jack?' she asked, looking around the room.

'Him and Tori are fixing that bracket,' said Riss, peering over the rim of her mug.

'We won't get away much before noon,' said Fenny, 'so it'll be late when we get to Lulworth. You'd better stay over – although I should say, it won't be much fun.'

'Of course!' said Clara. 'They don't know what's happened yet, do they?'

Fenny shook her head. 'There's bad news that I'm going to have to break.'

'If there's anything we can do to help...' Clara looked at Riss for confirmation, and received a curt nod in answer.

'Thanks,' said Fenny, 'but I guess it'll be better coming from people they know. Where are you heading after Lulworth?'

Clara frowned. She hadn't even thought about their route. What would Jack say if he knew that?

But at Fenny's question, Riss looked up. 'We'll go around Wight to the south. I was talking to Tori,' she explained. 'She and Jack stole the *Cerdic* from Southampton, so they want to avoid the Solent. Then Portsea's full of soldiers, so we'll go further on, and beach in Hayling Marshes.'

'Well, I hope the weather holds,' said Fenny. 'Look,' she added, rising from the table, 'I've got a few things to sort out. Give me a shout when you're ready to sail, will you? I'm all packed, I'll only need twenty minutes. See you later.'

Clara and Riss sat in silence for a minute. Then Clara said, 'So, you talked to Tori?'

Riss shrugged. 'She asked what our plans were.'

'Ah,' said Clara, nodding. The people at the next table were pushing their chairs back. 'I guess Jack and Tori had their breakfast earlier,' she said.

'I suppose so,' said Riss. 'Looks like he's going to come with us, then.'

'Mm,' said Clara. 'Two questions,' she went on. 'One: if we get ashore at Hayling–'

'Emsworth's the nearest place.'

'–at Emsworth, maybe we could go and find your Anna on the way up to London?'

Riss shook her head. 'No, no,' she said quickly. 'Anyhow, Basingstoke's out of our way.'

Clara raised an eyebrow.

'What's question two?' said Riss.

'Question two?' said Clara. 'Have we got any money?'

Jack and Shavila didn't get back till late morning. Tay, it turned out, had been helping too, and Jack pointedly remained deep in conversation with him while they washed their hands and grabbed something to eat.

Shavila, however, ambled up to Clara, drying her hands on a thin towel. 'All ready to go,' she said. 'I'm a bit worried about one of the bearings, but it should be okay for a few miles.'

Clara nodded. 'Riss was saying you're happy to come with us, to Hayling Marshes?'

'Yes,' said Shavila, shrugging. 'I – I'm not sure what I want to do. If I want to get back to Bewley, I'd be better off going across country. But I'd like to see a bit more of the sea...it's not a big deal...'

About two in the afternoon, they went down to the harbour. There were ten of them in all, including Fenny and five villagers from Lulworth. Jack was still ignoring Clara, but she noticed that he glanced her way once or twice. Debris – mostly smashed wood and washed-up seaweed – had been collected and piled along the quayside, and there was a strong smell of salt. The *Cerdic* bobbed safely at anchor in the harbour, and they made their way out in a small rowing-boat, in two relays. Clara saw that Jack held tightly to the gunwale, his knuckles white.

32 Back to Lulworth

Jack spent most of the voyage to Lulworth in the wheelhouse, steering while Shavila navigated. He felt safer in here, away from the waves. Shavila guided them north-east at first, then along the coast, to avoid Lulworth Banks. He noticed that when she wasn't looking at the map, she was gazing out at the waters. All right, there wasn't much else to look at, apart from the clouds and the gulls, but it felt like there was a sad kind of hunger in her face. He told himself this wasn't a good time to ask about it. For now, it'd be better to say nothing.

Which, he thought, was what he and Clara had been doing since she dropped that bloody bombshell: saying nothing. He swore under his breath. Well, it was all her fault, wasn't it? So she could bloody well make the first move – he wasn't going to. It just didn't help, he thought as he glanced over his shoulder to where she sat with one of the Lulworth women, that whenever he saw her, he wanted to grab her, put her in a cart and drive her back to Wessex. Back to her parents, where she belonged.

'Hey.'

Jack blinked. 'Tori. What's up? Am I steering wrong?'

Shavila had turned from the window and was holding out a small leather bag, fastened with a thong. 'Would you look after this for me?'

'Your purse?' he said, frowning. 'Why?'

She smiled, and Jack thought she was getting better at it. 'I'm always losing it. You'll keep it safe for me, won't you?'

'Sure,' he said, putting a hand on her arm. 'Are you okay?'

She nodded, and the smile got broader. 'I am,' she said. 'Thank you, Jack. Now,' she added, turning to the chart, 'let's see where we are...'

There was still an hour of daylight left by the time they beached once more in the cove. Clara saw that the recent storm had bitten a huge chunk out of the cliff, exposing the virgin sandstone beneath, while seaweed mingled with long-forgotten flotsam in great heaps above the high-water tide line. In the cove itself a solitary boat rode at anchor. Gulls perched on its swaying mast, but otherwise the harbour, including the watchwoman's hut, was deserted.

They jumped into the shallows, the chill sending a shiver up Clara's legs, and splashed their way up to the causeway. She looked back to see Jack bringing up the rear, chatting to Shavila as they shook water from their boots. She frowned. He'd hardly said a word to her since their argument – so why did she need to keep checking where he was, and what he was doing?

'This way,' said Fenny, and she led the way up to the village, Clara following behind with Riss. The wind had risen a little, but the clouds were high and white, and Clara hoped the good sailing weather would hold. She looked around with interest. They passed the remains of some twentieth-century huts whose purpose Clara could only guess at, before reaching a short row of cottages. All was quiet here, and she was beginning to think that the villagers must all have fled, when they heard the sound of hammering from a large house on their right. The hammering ceased, and a stout woman emerged around the side of the house, carrying a ladder. One of their own party gave a cry and ran past, calling out to the woman, who turned and embraced her. At this, the rest of the party broke up, hurrying back to their homes, eager to see their families. Of the locals, only Fenny and Tay now remained.

'Right,' said Fenny, and her voice shook. 'Better get on with seeing the victims' families. Tay will take you to my cottage, you can stay there tonight.' She put a hand to her eyes.

Clara realised that Jack was standing close behind. Then she heard herself saying to Fenny, 'Do you want me to come with you?'

'Oh – ah, okay,' said Fenny. 'That would be kind.'

Clara turned and, for a moment, looked Jack in the eye. He gave the slightest of nods.

She and Fenny visited three houses in the lower village, breaking the news of two bereavements and one serious injury, and leaving the women and families distraught. Then, as dusk fell, they made their way uphill, past the inn. On the open ground opposite, a dozen campfires were burning.

'Hello,' said Fenny. 'What's going on here?' She crossed the road and peered over the hedge.

Clara followed. 'It's like a camp of soldiers,' she said. 'There are carts, look. And I can smell horses.'

'No,' said Fenny, 'it's not the military. See,' she added, pointing through the gloom, 'there are children.'

As Clara's eyes adjusted, she could see makeshift tents beside each of the fires; and now, she could smell cooking. 'Who are they?'

'Come on,' said Fenny, turning on her heel and striding towards the inn. 'Let's ask Sara,' she called over her shoulder.

The bar was quiet, apart from a couple of women lounging by the fire. The landlady, a tall, wide-waisted woman in a brown headscarf, explained. 'They're getting away from the fighting,' she said, hanging up the glass she'd been drying. 'Oh, it's miles away yet, and some are saying there's hasn't actually been a battle, or anything. But they reckon the Wessex army have been moving down the Stour from Blandford.'

Clara pulled a face. This wasn't news to her – Hurn's camp, the place where she'd changed places with Jack, was at Blandford, and the Wessexers had taken it over weeks ago. Out loud she said, 'That's a long way off. Why have they come here?'

'She's with me,' said Fenny, in answer to Sara's quizzical look. 'She's been a great help.'

Sara shrugged. 'Maybe they think it's safe here.'

'Anyhow,' said Fenny, 'we've got more bad news to break.' She glanced at the clock, then turned to Clara. 'Look,' she said, 'I'm thirsty. Shall we have a drink?'

With a start, Clara realised that neither she nor Fenny had drunk anything since leaving Portland. And there were still more victims' relatives to be visited. 'All right,' she said, nodding.

SCORPION

Half a mile away, Jack sat astride a heavy wooden beam fifteen feet above the ground, trying to hold a sheet of corrugated metal steady against the wind. A thick rope, tied around his chest and noosed back onto the beam, was supposed to hold him if he fell; but to be fair, he told himself, it wasn't a big drop to that pile of grain-sacks, which would make for a softish landing. The sheet was a replacement for one that had blown off the barn in the storm, and eight feet away, Tay sat fixing the other end into place. Below, Riss had joined two other women in shifting the sacks to a drier corner of the barn: the damage had happened late on in the storm, and most of the grain had been saved.

Jack was pleased with himself. Considering how scared the sea made him, the job of climbing a ladder in a windy field, just as dusk fell, had gone pretty well. And maybe, he admitted to himself, he was a tiny bit pleased with Clara for offering to help Fenny in breaking the bad news. He himself would have run a mile to avoid a job like that. Maybe she wasn't such a callous, hard-hearted, selfish bitch after all.

A gust of wind came and the iron sheet lifted. 'Hey!' cried Tay, in his high voice.

'Sorry!' Jack answered. 'Took me by surprise.'

No, of course Clara wasn't any of those things, not most of the time anyway. Why, then, was he, Jack, acting as if she was? He leant his weight a little more forward. Maybe it was because if she carried on being herself, and doing one crazy thing after another, then one day she'd get hurt. Or killed. The thought unsettled him.

'How much longer you gonna be?' he called.

It had been dark for an hour when Clara and Fenny returned to her quarters, by the light of a borrowed lantern. The wind had turned cold, and they hurried indoors, to find that Tay had just got a fire going.

'We haven't been back long,' he said. He stood, stretching his back, and explained about the barn repairs. He nodded towards the kitchen. 'Jack and Riss are just getting cleaned up.'

'What about Tori?' asked Clara.

'Sleeping,' he said, with a shrug.

Again? Thought Clara. She wondered if Jack was as worried about Shavila as she was. He probably is, she thought. He probably is.

Next morning the sky remained grey, with the breeze and sea-swell both moderate. Clara and Riss sat on the quayside watching white horses as the waves broke at the entrance to the cove. From the *Cerdic*, anchored twenty yards away, came the sound of hammering.

'It'll be a rough ride when we get going,' said Clara, shading her eyes.

Riss pulled a face. '*If* we get going,' she said.

'Tori's a magician when it comes to machinery,' said Clara. 'She's always got it fixed before.'

'Yeah, if she doesn't fall asleep.'

Clara peered at the *Cerdic*. She could see Jack sitting on one of the rear lockers. He'd gone on the pretext of helping

Shavila, but from here, he didn't seem to be doing much. Still, if he was up on deck, then it was Shavila who was doing the hammering, and therefore she wasn't asleep.

'Now,' said Riss. 'Important thing: is there any blue left in my hair? At all?'

Clara chuckled. 'Not one bit, I'm afraid. You got covered in coal dust as soon as you came down into the pit with–' she blinked '–with us.'

Riss nodded. 'You miss him,' she said. 'Xavi, I mean.'

Now Clara had to look away. 'Well,' she said, sniffing, 'I suppose I hadn't known him very long. He told me his story. I felt sorry for him.'

Riss waited. 'And?'

'And I...' Clara swallowed. 'He was beautiful.'

Riss turned the corners of her mouth down and nodded. 'Yeah, he had a good body. Though he *was* getting thin.'

'I – I *wanted* him, Riss.'

'Yeah,' said Riss quietly, 'I could see that.'

For a moment they said nothing, watching while a gull plunged into the waves and emerged again, fishless. Then they heard a rattle, a splutter, and a roar as the *Cerdic*'s engine started. They could see Jack shouting something down to Shavila. Then he turned and gave them the thumbs-up.

'Ah!' came a voice from behind them. They turned to see Fenny striding down the roadway, carrying two cloth bags. 'You've got it going.'

'Looks like we'll be off soon,' said Riss.

'Thanks again for your help last night, Clara,' said Fenny, a little breathless, as she came up. She put the bags down.

'I didn't do anything,' said Clara.

'No, but you were with me. It meant a lot. Really.' She patted Clara's shoulder. 'Look,' she added, indicating the bags, 'I brought a few supplies. Just bread, and cheese, and some dried fruit. Didn't know if you had a stove...'

'Oh, thanks,' said Clara. 'I hadn't thought about that...'

'Any more about those refugees?' said Riss, getting to her feet.

'Yes,' said Fenny. 'I went to talk to them this morning.'

'So, what's the trouble?' asked Clara. She was watching Jack climb gingerly into the small skiff that they'd had to use to cross to the *Cerdic*, the tide being in, while Shavila held it steady.

'They tell me it's not so much the Wessexers,' replied Fenny, 'it's that there's no law any more. People are panicking about what'll happen over the next few months – so there are gangs going round, stealing food, livestock, anything they can lay their hands on. There've been killings, too, and there's a rumour that they've burnt down houses.'

Jack and Shavila climbed out onto the harbourside. 'All right?' Jack said.

It took Clara a moment to realise he was talking to her. 'Er, yes,' she squeaked.

'We'll just go and get cleaned up,' he said, and together he and Shavila went back up the hill. Clara watched them go. Shavila walked heavily, and she noticed that Jack touched her arm every now and again, as if encouraging her.

She realised Fenny was talking. 'I'll take my leave,' she was saying. 'You'll want to get your supplies aboard, and – well, I've still lots to do. We're arranging sea burials for our friends, and that means a lot of people will want to get to Portland. On the other hand, with all these incomers...'

'No problem,' Riss said. 'Thanks for putting us up.'

Clara was wondering what she could add, when Fenny hugged her. 'Thanks again,' she murmured. As she released her she added, 'And any time you, or Jack, or Tori want to visit, you know you'll be welcome. Well,' she added with a wry grin, 'maybe not for a week or two. After that, we might be in a better state to take guests!'

As she, too, disappeared up the road, Riss said: 'It's begun. All these refugees – this is just the start. We've got to get to Mother.'

'Let's hope she listens,' said Clara grimly.

33 The Waters of the Sea

By late morning they were able to set sail, once again hugging the coastline except when the charts warned otherwise. Jack was huddled in the *Cerdic's* wheelhouse with Riss, showing her how to pilot the boat. They'd agreed that Shavila should rest, and she was slouched against one of the stern bulkheads, wrapped in a blanket.

They reached Albana's Head, a towering block of limestone that jutted into the sea like a giant's boot. Recent rockfalls had left great gashes across its face. To clear the headland, Jack was forced to push further out to sea, where the swell was worse, and soon everyone felt queasy. But after twenty minutes they were able to turn north into the sheltered waters of Poole Bay, where the swell slackened. The Bournemouth shoreline loomed through the sea-haze, then gradually fell behind as they approached Hengistbury Head.

Clara thought she'd better check how Shavila was, and made her way astern. The ex-Repseg was slouching back with her cap pulled over her brows. That face! How familiar it was. The features were lined, the hair was long and grey, the skin slack and pale. Underneath, it was the woman Clara knew: genetically designed, strong, agile, but with a built-in lifespan – a lifespan that Shavila had now exceeded. It was so sad, Clara thought. Just when she should be looking forward to half a lifetime of freedom, she was ageing even as Clara watched.

'Have you ever thought,' murmured Shavila without opening her eyes, 'about going for a swim?'

'In the Channel?' said Clara, glancing up at the grey waves. 'No, not really.'

'I read somewhere,' Shavila went on languidly, 'that people used to swim all the way to France. Just because they could.'

'The Channel's full of bodies now,' said Clara with a grimace. 'Little boats, trying to make it across. And the ones that the waves don't get, Coastforce runs them down.'

'Hmm,' said Shavila. 'Swim,' she murmured to herself.

Next moment, there came a *boom* from the engine compartment. Immediately, the screw wound down and the *Cerdic* began to drift.

Shavila sighed and heaved herself up. 'I'll look,' she said, and dragged herself towards the ladder. Clara followed her down. They both grabbed torches, but when they shone their beams through the cage, Clara couldn't see anything wrong.

'It's that bearing again,' said Shavila. 'No more I can do.' And she hauled herself back up the steps.

'Hey!' Clara heard Jack saying. 'Tori! What shall we do?'

'Nothing,' said Shavila.

Clara scrambled back up to the deck. Riss was still in the wheelhouse; Shavila had retreated to the stern and was covering herself in a blanket again. Jack had followed and was trying to rouse her.

'Jack!' Clara called, beckoning.

He turned. 'What? She's got to fix it.'

Clara shook her head. 'It's no good,' she said. 'She says there's no more she can do, and I believe her. Besides,' she added with a shake of the head, 'she's exhausted.'

Riss had joined them. 'Well, what we gonna do?' she asked.

Clara chewed her lip. 'Look,' she said, pointing, 'we're not too far from the shore.'

'That's no good if we've got no engine,' snapped Jack.

'Uh,' said Clara, 'what's the tide doing?'

'How d'you mean?' asked Riss.

'Look in the tables,' said Clara. 'Is it going in, or coming out?'

'What are you thinking?' asked Jack.

Riss had run back into the wheelhouse. 'We're just past low tide,' she called, waving a dog-eared booklet.

'We'll drift in,' said Clara. 'On the rising tide.'

'How do you know that'll work?' said Jack.

'Have you got a better idea?'

'Let me try running the engine again,' he said. 'Even if we can only make a bit of headway, that'll be something.'

'Yes,' said Clara, following him back to the wheelhouse, 'and if the tide's helping...where are we now?'

'Well,' said Riss, scanning the chart, there's a harbour behind the headland.'

'We're too far out,' said Jack. 'I'm gonna have to steer close in.'

The next forty minutes were anxious ones. The wind was rising and the swell increasing, but gradually they edged around the headland, and the seaway to Crichurch harbour came into view. Jack kept starting the engine, and although it soon stopped, each time they made a little landward progress.

'We're gonna overshoot,' he said. 'The current's pushing us east.'

Riss ran to the prow. 'There's drowned buildings there,' she cried, pointing.

Clara shook her head. 'We've no choice. We've got to get ashore.' As she joined Riss, she cast a glance at the stern, where Shavila seemed to be fast asleep.

For another ten minutes the *Cerdic* edged towards the shore, drifting, as Jack had feared, beyond the harbour channel. Clara and Riss stood in the prow, willing the strand to come closer, willing the waves to drive them forward, at the same time watching for signs of sunken ruins.

Then Jack called, 'It's overheating! There's a warning light come on.'

'Keep trying!' called Clara.

He was shaking his head as she joined him. 'We'd better let it cool for a bit. The tide might carry us closer.'

'Give it another five minutes, then.' Clara turned to him. 'Are you all right?'

He shook his head. 'If there's sunken buildings under the water – look, see those breakers there? – we'll have to swim the last bit. See if there's any more life vests.'

'But you – the water?'

'Look, I'd rather drown trying to swim than drown going down with the ship,' he said, gripping the wheel tighter. His face was ashen. 'Now go and find them!'

Riss helped Clara to look. There didn't seem to be any method to the way things were stowed, because they found one vest, like the one Jack had worn during the sea-fight, in a locker alongside coils of rope, and another under some tarpaulin. Jack tried the engine again. This time it fired and kept going for two minutes before, with another loud bang, it died.

'Nearly there,' cried Clara. 'Can't be more than three hundred yards...'

Now there were more thuds, but this time they came from underneath the hull. Riss leaned over the rail. 'Ruins!' she cried. 'Just here!'

Just then Jack fired the engine again. The *Cerdic* drove forward, but within a few yards the keel smashed into something hard, throwing Clara and Riss onto the deck. There came a tearing, splintering groan from beneath their feet.

'What was that?' shouted Riss, grabbing the handrail.

'Into the life-vests!' said Clara. 'Riss, you take this one.' She turned to Jack as he came hurrying up. 'Jack, you put the other one on.'

'What about you?' said Jack.

'I can swim, a bit,' said Clara. 'I'll hold on to you. Tori can go with Riss.'

Jack nodded. 'Clara–'

'Just take it. Quick!'

He grabbed it. 'I'll get Tori.'

Clara joined Riss at the rail. The *Cerdic* had recoiled from its collision and had drifted closer to the shoreline, where crumbling walls and fractured roadways sloped out of the waves. Beyond, they could see a row of abandoned houses, waiting for their turn to be swallowed. But there was something odd about the boat's attitude. 'We're listing,' said Riss, bracing herself as she tied the life-vest. 'Look, that side's coming up out of the water–' she staggered as there was another impact under the hull. 'We'd better get off, now.'

Then they heard Jack calling. There was a shrill edge to his voice. 'Clara! Riss!'

They ran round the wheelhouse and aft, to the spot where Shavila had been resting. Now there was just a blanket, abandoned on the deck. Jack turned to them with wide eyes. 'She's gone!' he wailed. 'She's not here!'

'I'll look in the engine room,' said Riss, leaving Clara and Jack to stare.

'She's jumped,' said Jack. He climbed up on the bench and leaned out over the stern. 'Tori!' he shouted, but his voice was lost. The swell was big, and the sky and the waves were merging into one grey wall.

'She wanted a swim,' said Clara. She could feel her own heart beating faster.

'Tori!' screamed Jack, over the waves. 'Tori! Can yer hear me? Tori! Tori!'

Riss returned. 'No,' she said. 'She's not there.'

Then there was another shock and the *Cerdic*'s deck trembled under their feet. Jack was thrown off the bench, landing on his back, while Clara and Riss held onto the wheelhouse walls. There was a grinding sound and the boat's prow began to sink.

'We've got to go,' cried Clara. 'Jack, get your vest on! Jack, please!'

She had to drag him away from the wheelhouse and down the tilting deck to where the water was now creeping over it. Riss had already jumped.

'Over the side!' Clara cried. 'Together!'

34 Flotsam

Clara gasped as she plunged under the water, once again feeling the warmth sucked from her. Her feet found some drowned stonework and she used it to kick upward, spitting seawater as she surfaced. She gulped in a breath, beating the water to stay afloat. Compared to the swell out at sea, she'd expected it to be calmer here. But she found herself pummelled forward and hurled back, and in her ears there was a great roaring. And it was so cold! She had to keep moving, had to keep kicking, before her muscles froze.

A wave crashed over her, and she tried to get her bearings. Jack! Where was Jack? There! A few yards away, a striped float jacket thrown up and down, a pale face among the waves. She kicked, and yelled, her lungs straining. And Riss? But no, she couldn't worry about her. Riss would have to shift for herself. Nearly there! Jack was shouting, spitting, waving. From the corner of her eye she saw, looming through the spray, a row of houses, maybe a hundred yards to her left. That was the direction to go. She stabbed a finger, and went under again.

When she surfaced, Jack was there. She grabbed his arm; he yelled, and dipped below the surface. Another wave came. He tried to tell her something, but he was shivering so much she couldn't make out the words. Flung up on a wave, she saw the stern of the *Cerdic* tilted above the waves as its prow sank.

She threw an arm around Jack's back and slipped it down to his waist, gripping tight. 'Swim!' she gasped. 'Kick!' Jack was cold, she was cold, the waves buffeted them and beat them. Again they rose, again they fell as the wave passed; but when the next one came they were a little closer to shore. Clasped together as they were, their legs often connected as they kicked, slowing their progress.

'Watch out,' she gasped. 'Watch for walls! Down there.'

He nodded, and they fought on. Sure enough, their feet began to strike obstacles, sharp and rough; and they were sometimes flung against them by the waves, so that they had to spend precious strength pushing themselves away. Jack cried out, and stopped swimming. Clara held on to him.

'What is it?' she shouted.

He swore. 'Knee,' he called. 'Hit something.'

'Keep going!'

A few yards off, they could see the top of a wall that lay across their path. 'Careful!' shouted Clara. Her lungs were weary, her legs were heavy. She couldn't go on. The wall was so huge.

A wave lifted them up, and if seemed as if it was pausing, holding them in its grip. Clara yelled; she heard Jack shout, and they were flung down at the wall. She lost hold of him. Her midriff thumped into the wall, and she felt herself rolling head-over-heels in the water. For a moment all she could feel was the pain in her belly and the bursting in her lungs, then she broke the surface, and Jack was grabbing her collar. A minute passed, and now she tried kicking. She realised she wasn't being thrown about so much. Jack was shouting something.

'We're over it!' He was shaking her. 'Put your feet down!'

SCORPION

She swung her legs downward, and her feet meet something broken and slippery. Jack's hand was there, helping her to turn. They grunted and gasped, and cried out when they tripped, but yes, there was firm ground under them. Now they were half-swimming, now they were wading, now they were splashing through the shallows...

They collapsed and lay on their backs, shivering and panting. They were on a broken tarmac roadway. To their left stood some abandoned houses, their windows smashed and their roofs damaged, while to their right the sea had encroached further, making an inlet some twenty yards wide, along the course of an old river. Clara realised one of her legs was lying on top of Jack's, but it felt too heavy for her to move. She also realised she was clasping his arm tightly, but she didn't let go. Jack was grunting, and she could feel his chest moving up and down, even as her own did.

'You...all...right?' She managed.

'We made it,' he croaked, still panting. A wave washed over them, making them shiver, and Jack wrestled himself out of the float jacket, before starting to ease himself up. 'Hey,' he said, 'you're hurt!'

Clara glanced down. Over her belly, her tunic was stained dark red. 'It's nothing,' she heard herself say.

'I'm gonna look,' he told her.

She nodded, but then she didn't watch what he was doing, she watched his face instead. Water was dripping from that wispy beard, and his skin was blotchy. He was shivering. She felt him gently peeling the wet tunic up, and suddenly she was conscious of her midriff, exposed under his gaze. But then she saw him relax.

'It's a nasty cut,' he said, nodding, 'but it's not deep. Looks sore.'

'Can't feel anything,' she said. Their eyes met. 'I'm cold.'

He nodded. Wincing, he got to his feet, then gave her a hand up. She staggered, and he caught her. She looked in his face again. 'Thanks,' she said. She could feel his cold body through their wet clothes, and for an instant they regarded each other.

'Oi!' came a voice. 'Remember me?'

They turned, to see Riss standing some fifteen yards away, safe on the other side of the inlet. Clara managed to wave.

Riss pointed. 'Go upstream!' she shouted.

They trudged up the road, their sodden clothes clinging and their feet squelching in their boots. Clara, her legs ready to give way at any moment, was still holding on to Jack, who was limping heavily. They passed through what must once have been a rich residential area, where abandoned houses stood among wildernesses of weeds. When they met Riss, about half a mile on, she made them wring out their clothes. 'We didn't drown, but we don't want to die of cold,' she said. 'Jack, go and hide in those bushes while you do it. We'd rather not watch.'

They did so, and felt a little warmer for it. Then they pressed on, past houses that had lost parts of their roofs, and one where an oak tree, toppled by the recent storm, had demolished the entire gable end. Then, as the day declined, the wind rose and the rain returned, and soon they were shivering once more. When they reached the main road, they were surprised to see a train of people trekking east, in the direction of the New Forest, and Clara remembered travelling that road in the days when she and Sophia had to work felling timber, a few short months ago. There were horse-carts and carriages, women with hand-barrows, and hundreds of people on foot, laden with bundles, bags and packs. Clara and the others joined the throng until, after another half-mile, they came to a large inn. Here, forty or fifty travellers had gathered in the courtyard.

'What's going on?' she asked a grey-haired woman who was weaving her way back through the crowd.

The woman swore. 'They won't let us in,' she said. 'Bloody woman's only gone and doubled the prices. I mean, look at us!' She waved a hand behind her. 'We only want a roof over our heads for the night. Says she's "got no room,"' she added in a mocking tone. 'I mean, what are we gonna do?'

Clara's heart sank. Of course, none of them had any money. How could they get shelter?

'Where have you all come from?' Riss asked.

'Where d'you bloody think?' the woman snapped.

Clara and Riss looked at each other and shrugged. Then Jack, who'd been standing behind them, said, 'has the fighting started?'

'Has the fighting started?' said the woman with a sneer. 'Yeah, the fighting *has* bloody well started. Where've you all been? The moon? Or,' she added, taking in their clothing, 'have you swum here?'

They were jostled as another group of disappointed travellers made their way back to the road.

'Where *is* the fighting?' asked Clara. 'Is it close?'

The woman sighed. 'Up near Ferndown. Our girls decided to get at the Wessexers before they could reach Ringwood. That's where we're mostly from. Battle happened yesterday, and we heard it hadn't gone well, so we got out. It's taken us all day to get here, and that bitch,' she said, pointing, 'won't let us in.'

'They've evacuated Ringwood?' asked Riss.

'Nah,' said the woman hunching her shoulders as the rain began to fall more heavily. 'A lot of people stayed. Fools, if you ask me.' She turned to Jack and looked him up and down. 'He's yours, I suppose,' she said. 'Nice work if you can get it.' She glanced up at the darkening sky, swore, and hurried away.

'What did she mean, "nice work if you can get it"?' said Clara, turning to Jack.

But Jack wasn't listening. He'd pulled something from his pocket and was cupping it in one of his hands. The other was pressed to his eyes. 'Tori,' he said, with a sniff. 'It's her purse.'

Quickly, they moved into the light that spilled from one of the inn's windows. Jack undid the thong, coaxed the sodden leather open and pulled out a roll of notes. 'Hundred boudicks...two, three...' he counted, then began to cry. 'There's nine hundred here!'

35 No Papers

It didn't take many of those nine hundred to convince the landlady, a thin woman with her hair in a tight bun and her face in a surprised grimace, to let them have a room. The higher price was, she said, 'not 'cause I'm trying to make a quick profit – it's just, with people like that, you don't know who you might be letting in, do you? I don't want to wake up in the morning with my takings all gone, or my throat slit.'

Their room was poky, and the window rattled, but it was a lot better than nothing. It turned out that the landlady had already let out all of the haylofts and outhouses – she wasn't as choosy about her clientele as she'd claimed – so that Jack would have to sleep in the same room with them. It would be the floor for him. But none of them expected to care where they slept.

Before turning in, they had to eat. The bar room was rammed full, but they managed to squeeze around a tiny table, not too far from the fire. They sat with bare feet, having added their boots to the heap of other people's that were steaming and stinking around the grate. Thin soup and hard bread were all they could order, but again, it was better than nothing.

'It's my fault,' said Jack, his eyes red. He wiped his face with the end of his sleeve.

'What is?' Clara asked.

'Tori.' He sniffed again. 'She was minding her own business, back in Bewley. Making a living, ferrying folk across a little river, and getting drunk at night. But I had to go and drag her away, didn't I? I dragged her away, and now she's dead.'

'I thought you said she invited herself along?' said Clara.

Riss tutted. 'Pull yourself together, Jack. If she's–' she looked around and lowered her voice '–an ex-Repseg, she was going to die anyway, wasn't she?'

'You knew?' said Jack.

Riss nodded. 'She told me. Said I might as well know.'

'She's done like she said,' went on Jack with a sigh. 'She kept saying she fancied a swim.'

'She was telling me that people used to swim across the Channel,' put in Clara. 'Just because they could.'

'I reckon she knew her body was giving up,' said Jack. 'So she–' He shook his head and sniffed again. 'That's why she gave me her purse...'

Riss held up a finger. She'd been distracted by a conversation at the next table, and had half-turned in her chair. Clara and Jack tried to listen, too.

'...a thousand of our girls,' a woman in a brown smock was saying. 'Seems like the Wessexers didn't expect 'em to have crossed the river already, and they took 'em by surprise.'

'Many dead?' asked a red-cheeked woman.

'Hundreds,' said the first. 'But the Wessexers pretended to retreat, then got round the flanks. Sounds like nobody won, not this time anyhow.'

'How d'you know all this?' asked another.

'Heard it off a woman from Ringwood. Said she'd got the hell out of there, before they come blowin' her house up?'

'They got artillery then?'

'I wouldn't be surprised,' said the smock woman.

'Well,' said the red-cheeked one, '*I* heard they're puttin' roadblocks everywhere. London's practically locked down, you can't get in without papers...'

Riss turned to Clara and Jack. 'Papers!' she said, aghast. 'We haven't got papers!'

'Of course!' said Clara. 'I'd forgotten. What can we do?'

Jack sniffed again, shrugged his shoulders, and returned to staring at the table.

Clara knotted her brows. 'Hey,' she said, lowering her voice, 'could we get hold of some false papers? They'd be expensive, but we can afford it now...'

Jack looked up. 'How would you find someone to do it?' he said, his voice hoarse. 'You'd need to know someone.'

'What about...?' Clara looked at Riss. 'What about Anna? Could she help?'

Riss set her jaw, but didn't answer.

'I think Basingstoke's on our route, isn't it?' Clara went on.

Jack stirred. 'Yeah, pretty much. What's this about?'

Clara caught his eye and, almost imperceptibly, shook her head. Turning to Riss she said, 'You told me you want to do this for Anna. She wanted you to talk to your mother, didn't she?'

Riss looked at her fingers; she looked around the room; she pursed her lips.

Clara touched her on the arm. 'She must be missing you,' she said gently.

'All right!' snarled Riss. 'All right! We'll go and see her. Just – just come with me, hey? Both of you.'

'Of course,' said Clara. 'That is, Jack, are you–'

'Yeah,' he said. 'Limpet, that's me, remember. Who's Anna?'

'Riss's partner,' said Clara, again catching his eye.

Jack nodded. 'Will she be able to help us?' he asked.

Clara felt herself relaxing a little, although she didn't know if it was because she was beginning to dry out, or because she'd managed to get Riss to look for Anna. Or, was it because the conversation had distracted Jack? He'd taken the loss of Tori very hard.

'Probably,' Riss was saying. 'She's a bit like Clara here. Went to the Academy – she's a little older than you – but she stopped believing in all that stuff. And she doesn't normally let little things like obstacles stop her.' She gave a wry smile.

'Still got to get to Basingstoke without papers,' said Jack.

Their food arrived, and nobody said anything for a good ten minutes. As she ate, Clara found herself watching Jack. For a moment she saw once more the little boy who'd told her how his mother pined away after his dad walked out, who'd then looked away to hide his tears.

Then she said, 'Shall I go and get some more drinks? Shall we raise a toast to Tori?'

Jack looked at her and nodded. 'Yeah,' he said. 'That'd be good.'

They turned in, leaving their still-damp outer clothes by the bar-room fire. Riss fell straight asleep, and began to snore loudly, making the walls of the little room resonate. Clara, shivering under a scratchy blanket in the opposite bed, sighed.

'You awake?' Jack whispered. He was squeezed into the space between the end of Clara's bed and the wall, to keep out of the draughts.

'She s-sounds l-like a motor-engine,' Clara whispered back.

'You cold?'

'Of course I'm bloody cold.' It had occurred to Clara that she could get into bed with Riss for a bit of warmth, or she could even invite Jack into hers. But a moment's thought told her what a bad idea that'd be. So she'd just have to shiver.

'What're you thinking about?'

Clara frowned. Why was he asking that? 'The last time I was in Crichurch,' she answered. She waited, but it sounded like he was waiting too. 'Mother and I were working,' she went on, keeping her voice low, and pausing when Riss's snores drowned her out. 'We had to make some money. We were timber rustling, in the woods outside town.'

'Timber rustling?'

'Unlicensed felling. Anyway, Mother got ill, and the forewoman put us in her cart and drove us round the inlet, to a hospital. She was so ill – Mother was – I thought I was going to lose her. Are you listening?'

'Yep. 'fraid so.'

'I thought I was going to be alone. I'd lost James, I'd lost you, and now I was going to lose mother...' She frowned. Had she just mentioned Jack in the same breath as her parents? And had he spotted that?

Riss gave an especially loud snore, and turned over, making the bed creak.

Keen to change the subject, Clara asked, 'What about you? What were you thinking about?'

'Yeah,' said Jack. 'Tori. I miss her, y'know.'

'I know,' she said gently. She heard him swallow.

'I thought we was friends,' he said. 'Me and Tori, I mean. All that stuff we went through. And she said she was grateful to me, and to you, Clara. But...'

'But what?'

'She sneaked off. She must've got to the stern, and jumped, and swum out to sea. And she never said goodbye.'

'We wouldn't have let her go, Jack.'

'I suppose not. It hurts, though.'

'Yes, it must. But you have to admit, she didn't do badly for a Repseg...I mean, turning normal.'

'Almost Natural.'

Clara chuckled. 'Jack?' she said.

'What?'

'Shut up and go to sleep.'

The next morning was bright and clear, with white clouds racing on a strong, chilly wind. They were forced to set off on foot because every cart, coach or carriage had already been taken. Jack was yawning widely, Clara was sneezing and Riss couldn't understand why she had a sore throat. At least they were warmer today, although their clothes had a salty crust and the fabric was gritty under their fingers, while their boots were cracked and stiff.

SCORPION

Their route to Basingstoke would take them away from the fighting and across the New Forest. Access to the forest was usually restricted, but the landlady had assured them that the army was letting refugees pass unhindered, and Riss suggested they make for Lyndhurst, towards the northern edge. It was only fifteen miles, but they knew that in their exhausted state they'd make only slow progress. Besides this, they'd been unable to find any food to buy, and all they had to sustain themselves was one bottle of water.

At the edge of town a few women crouched under a makeshift shelter, begging for food. When Clara offered one of them a few boudicks, she sneered. 'What use is that?' she said. 'Can't eat money.' But she took the coins all the same. As they pushed on north-eastwards, they found groups of other travellers trudging in their direction: backs stooped, voices subdued, eyes never lifting from the road. Clara felt queasy and weak, but for all that, and slow though they were, she, Jack and Riss found themselves going quicker than many of the travellers. About two hours into the trek, they overtook a long caravan of people with backpacks, handcarts and barrows.

After a rest stop, they continued, into a denser part of the forest where a mature plantation of straight oaks pressed close against the old roadway. In places, trees had fallen across the road, their trunks splintered and gashed open by the recent storm. In others, great banks of mud had spread across their path. For an hour, all they could hear was the wind and their own footfalls, but then they caught the sounds of heavy hoof-falls and rattling wheels. Drawing aside, they watched as a large box-cart, pulled by a pair of steaming horses, came into view. As it rattled past, the driver acknowledged them with a wave of her whip. A large red cross was painted on the side.

'Casualties,' said Clara.

As the afternoon drew on, the sky began to fill with grey clouds. 'Could do without another soaking,' remarked Jack, eyeing them doubtfully.

But he was destined to get his feet wet, at least. They came to quarter-mile stretch where streams had once run in neat culverts under the road, but where now the road had fallen and the streams had swollen. There was nothing for it but to wade through.

Then, emerging from the trees not twenty yards ahead, came a troop of a dozen soldiers dressed in military fatigues and toting bulky packs. They made as if to cross the road, but on seeing Clara and the others, halted.

'Stop,' said Jack, holding out an arm.

One of the soldiers peeled away from the head of the column and walked a few paces towards them. Then Clara saw, to her horror, that two of the others had unslung rifles and were pointing them in their direction. 'Jack?' she whispered.

'Wait,' he said.

Now the first soldier spoke. 'Stay where you are,' she said, in a high, clear voice. 'Put your hands in the air. Good. Move now, and you're dead. Understood?'

'Clara, you answer,' whispered Jack.

Clara took a moment before she called back, 'Er, yes. Understood.'

'Where have you come from?' said the soldier. 'And where are you heading?'

'We've come from Crichurch,' Clara called back. 'We want to get away from the fighting. Is it far to Lyndhurst?'

'I'm asking the questions!' snarled the soldier. She beckoned to another, and sent her jogging towards them. 'You're gonna keep really still,' she said. 'Or we shoot.'

The soldier came running up. 'Turn around, slowly.' She looked them up and down, then patted Clara's and Riss's pockets. Then she stood, considering Jack. 'D'you want the man?' she called back over her shoulder.

'No,' replied the captain. 'Need to get a move on.'

'Nothing here, then,' said the other. She trotted back to the captain, who shook her head, gave an order to the riflewomen, and led the column off into the trees.

'I think I'm gonna faint,' said Riss.

She didn't, but the three of them sat on a fallen log while they recovered. 'Deserters, I reckon,' said Jack at last.

'I thought they were gonna shoot us,' said Riss. 'That'd be ironic. My own mother's troops killing me. I could've tried telling them who I was,' she said with a nervous chuckle, 'but they'd have laughed.'

'Why deserters, Jack?' asked Clara, hunching her shoulders and hugging herself.

'They're going away from the fighting,' said Jack, 'which I suppose might have been okay, but they're not using the proper roads. And there's only a few of them.'

'And they weren't Geemos,' said Clara, realising now that the soldiers hadn't been identical, in the way that regular soldiers were. 'They're ordinary women who've been conscripted.'

'Well,' said Riss, 'whoever they were, I shat myself.'

'We'd better get going,' said Jack, 'in case any more turn up.' Turning to Riss he said, 'We was all right 'cause we didn't have nothing to steal. And if we had,' he went on, 'we'd still have been okay if we'd handed it over. They'd only have shot us if we'd tried to fight them, or given them lip.'

'Why,' said Riss, 'are they fair-minded or something?'

'No,' said Jack, 'but I bet they haven't got much ammo.'

'Hey,' said Clara, 'what about Tori's purse? Why didn't she find it?'

Jack shrugged. 'She didn't look,' he said.

'See,' said Riss, nodding at Jack, 'he's got his uses. They probably thought we wouldn't trust a man to carry the money.'

'Hooray,' said Jack. 'I'm useful.'

36 The Boy-Grabbers

They reached Lyndhurst at dusk, just as the congealed clouds dropped their cargo of rain. To Clara's amazement and relief, they found room at the third inn they tried, and even the male quarters weren't full. Exhausted, it was all they could do to take some food, dry out their boots and drag themselves to bed while, outside, the deluge continued.

Next morning, they were cheered by the news that half a dozen coaches had come in from the neighbouring towns to take the many refugees away from the front. By paying well over the going rate they secured places on the coach for Andover, having decided to avoid the garrisons around Winchester. Before the coach left, they had time to buy travel-capes from a second-hand shop. Today, they thought, the travelling would at least be warmer.

Early in the afternoon their coach stopped at Romsey to change horses. The *Georgia* was a vast, rambling inn with a broad central block and long wings that sheltered the three sides of a courtyard littered with straw, horse-droppings, water-troughs, piles of luggage and great sacks of feed. Passengers loitered in twos and threes, stamping their feet and blowing on their hands.

Riss alighted first, stretching her neck and rolling her shoulders. As Clara followed, Jack climbed down from the box, where he'd been riding with another male, and rubbed his back. 'How long we stopping for?' he asked. 'Have I got time for a pee?'

'Ten minutes or so,' said Clara, glancing up at the clock mounted on the inn's roof. 'Don't be long.'

Jack nodded, and hurried through a low archway to the back of the stables. Then Clara and Riss decided to go too. When they'd finished, and washed their hands in icy water, they hurried back to the coach. The fresh horses were being harnessed, but there was no sign of Jack.

'Thought you 'ad a boy wiv yer?' said the coachwoman. 'He'd better get a move on.'

Clara shook her head. 'He went to the toilet. I'll see if he's out.' She dodged among the waiting travellers, went through the arched passage and found herself in a long, concreted yard with a colonnaded walkway on the near side. Opposite were more stables. At first she couldn't see anyone, but then she heard a grunt and a scuffle. She turned, just in time to see three women rounding the far corner of the building. They were carrying something that struggled.

'Hey!' she yelled. 'Leave him alone!' She sprinted down the colonnade, her feet thumping on the boards. 'Leave him!' she shouted again. In answer, there came a muffled cry from Jack. At the same time, Clara heard running feet behind her. At last she rounded the end of the building. On a patch of scrubby grass not ten yards away, the three women had hold of Jack, who was wriggling and twisting in their grip. One had a hand under his jaw, trying to keep him quiet. As Clara appeared, the biggest woman – broad-chested and muscular, with a short ponytail and a scar over one eye – turned to face her. She brandished a rough wooden club.

'Get off him!' cried Clara as she halted, keeping out of range of the club. 'He's mine!' Part of her registered Riss's voice from behind her.

The big woman grinned. 'Go on,' she snarled. 'Come and take 'im, then!'

'I'll – I'll get the Repsegs on you!' cried Clara.

The woman laughed. 'Hear that?' she chortled, and half-turned to her companions, but now Clara took her off guard and launched herself at the woman's midriff. The woman's club smashed across the back of her thigh, but she threw her arms around her and held on as they tumbled to the ground. The woman grunted and swore, then punched Clara in the ribs with her free hand. Crying out in pain, Clara switched her grip to the woman's club-arm, pinning it to the ground and throwing her weight on top before working at the woman's fingers. Distantly, she was aware that Riss had set upon one of the other attackers.

With a roar, the woman rolled herself on top of Clara, but now the club was free and Clara grabbed it, jabbing the handle backwards into the woman's face. She cried out and held her cheek, giving Clara time to roll from under her. The woman grabbed her leg, and Clara was thrown to the ground, but she managed to swing the club so that it connected with the woman's kneecap, making her stumble.

Clara glanced up: Jack was on his feet, but he was bleeding freely from a cut beneath his eye. There was a growl, and the woman was coming at her again, and Clara still held the club, and she swung it, swung it two-handed, swung it *so* hard, for Jack, for Tori, for Xavi. There was a hollow *thwock* as the club hit the woman's skull. She crashed to the ground and lay still. Clara stared, horrified.

'Come on,' cried Riss. 'Let's go! Now!'

Between them, Jack and Riss had got the better of the other two attackers, who were both on the ground, dazed. Riss grabbed Clara's arm and urged her away. Jack was limping as they scurried across the yard. Clara realised she was still holding the club, and flung it to the ground. There was blood on it. As they turned into the alley, she glanced behind. The attackers weren't following. The big woman was lying prone, and the other two were trying to rouse her.

'We'd better be on that coach,' said Riss. 'We don't want to be around if the Repsegs turn up. I'll go and hold it,' she added, running ahead.

Jack swore and held a hand to his temple. 'What did they want me for?' He peered at the blood on his hand, then pulled out a stained kerchief.

Clara's thigh was screaming in pain, and she found herself shaking. No, not just shaking. Crying. Weeping uncontrollably. Jack, even after what he'd been through, coaxed her onward.

She realised they'd made it to the coach. As they came within earshot, she heard the coachwoman saying to Riss: 'The boy-grabbers, was it?' She shook her head and tutted. 'If 'e's yours, you wanna look after 'im. Now get in!'

The other man, already seated on the box, gave a still-shaking Jack a hand up. Then Riss shoved Clara inside, the driver flicked her whip and the coach drove away.

SCORPION

The coach was full, and smelt of wet leather and damp wool. Besides Clara and Riss there were two women who wore heavy travel-coats and spent the whole of the journey complaining about the fighting, and how it was bad for business, and a woman who tried to keep two young girls quiet. Squeezed into a corner, Clara wiped the condensation from the window with her sleeve and peered out at the sodden fields, where green cereal shoots lay battered and drowned.

The rain returned and the wind rose. With a sigh, Clara turned away from the window and held on as the cart rattled and bounced over the uneven road. She tried to put that fight from her mind: her anger at them trying to take Jack and her horror at what she'd done to that woman. Then her attention was taken by a line of people trekking south, capes over their heads against the rain. The driver reined in the horses and called down to the travellers. Riss pulled down the window so that they could hear.

'It's been looking groggy for the last week,' a tall, fair woman was saying. 'We're getting out of there before it goes.'

'Nah,' said the coachwoman, 'I been past it every day. Looks all right to me.'

'Please yourself,' said the fair woman, gesturing at the coach. 'Don't blame us if you all get drowned.'

As they started off again, Clara stuck her head out of the window, blinking as the rain got in her eyes. 'Driver?' she called. 'What were they talking about?'

The driver didn't answer, but then Clara saw Jack's hooded head appearing around the rear of the coach. 'The dam,' he called. 'They're on about a dam. They think it's gonna go.'

A few minutes later the road bent to the right and ran along a straight causeway. The surrounding fields were flooded, the water rippled by the wind and broken by occasional tufts of sedge, and as they crossed the bridge over the Test, the horses had to splash fetlock-deep through the flood. Clara swallowed. Maybe those travellers had been right to worry.

Then she realised that these roads were familiar. A couple of months ago, when she and James were hurrying back to Blandford in a stolen cart, they'd crossed the river just north of here. She remembered the dam, although she hadn't paid it much attention at the time. She wondered how much water it held back.

Now the road began to rise a little, curving right again, and Clara began to breathe more easily. The mother and her two girls were peering out of the opposite window, no doubt trying to catch sight of the dam further up the valley, but as the road climbed it entered some woods, obscuring their view. The coach, Clara noticed, was swaying more than usual, and she realised the coachwoman was driving the horses faster. Worse, the road began to dip downwards again.

Then one of the girls gasped. 'Mummy!' she cried. 'What's that?'

The mother leaned forward, and so did the other passengers. 'What's going on?' she said. 'What's happening?'

Riss was on her feet, craning over the other passengers and swearing; but, whatever it was, the driver had seen it too. Her whip cracked, and suddenly their pace doubled, the coach rocking violently and throwing Riss to the floor. As Clara held on, she thought she heard Jack shouting something, and the coachwoman shouting something back. Then at last they were climbing again, but the coach was jolting over a broken surface, making the windows rattle and hurling the passengers into the air at each bump. The mother was holding her daughters, having to raise her voice to reassure them. One started crying.

Then Riss managed to get the window down again, and looked out. 'The road!' she cried. 'It's breaking up!'

Clara elbowed her aside and stuck her head out into the rain. Sure enough, as she looked behind, she could see that the downhill side of the road had sunk by a foot, causing the old tarmac to buckle and break. From somewhere nearby there came a rushing, roaring sound, as if every trunk in the forest was beating, all but drowning out the coachwoman's shouts. As the road bent once more, Clara could have sworn that one of the trees toppled out of sight. She ducked back inside. The coach began to slew to the left, but now the ground was rising more steeply. At long last the pace slackened, and she heard the driver soothing the horses.

She stuck her head out into the rain once more. 'Jack!' she called. 'Jack, are you all right?'

There was no answer.

'Jack!' she cried. 'Jack! Jack!'

At last, his head appeared. 'Still 'ere,' he called. 'My mate here's got a bloody nose, though. Hey, driver–'

He didn't get a chance to finish his question, because with a loud crack the coach sank lower and canted to the right. Clara could immediately see what had happened. 'The wheel!' she called. 'The wheel's broken!'

Slowly, the coachwoman climbed down from the driver's seat, her face like whey. She grimaced at the rear wheel, splayed out at a grotesque angle, then, with a shrug, pulled a flask from her pocket and took a swig. 'The dam,' she croaked. 'Did you hear it?'

Clara was the first to climb out. 'It burst?' she asked.

The coachwoman nodded, and drank again. 'That noise,' she said. 'Never heard nothing like it. And the road–' she swallowed, and gestured back down the road '–there was a landslip.'

Riss and the other passengers had gathered around, and Clara saw Jack helping the other man, who held a rag to his nose, down from the box.

'Thanks for getting us through,' Riss was saying to the coachwoman.

The coachwoman took a third pull before stoppering her flask. There was more colour in her cheeks now. 'Well, all right,' she said. 'Never should've set out. Anyhows,' she went on, pointing at the damage, 'can't get you no further. Axle's gone.'

'Where are we?' said one of the other passengers.

'Not far from Somborne,' said the coachwoman. 'Mile or two up the road. Better grab your luggage.' She reached up and pulled her own pack from underneath the driver's seat, then went to unhitch the horses.

Jack had come up beside Clara, and she turned to him. 'Somborne,' she said in a low voice. 'Last time I was there, I stole a cart.'

SCORPION

Jack gave a quick laugh. 'I won't even ask,' he said.

37 Anna

'Where is everyone?' said Clara. It was late afternoon. They'd followed the road into the village, past tidy houses with smoking chimneys, then down into the valley. They'd now reached a wide crossroads. On Clara's right a narrow road led down from the wooded hill where she and James had discovered Dora Thorn's dog-savaged remains, and had fled for their lives. Only now did it occur to her that the dog-pack could still be marauding – she should have warned her fellow-travellers. Well, they'd made it here all right...

'How d'you mean?' asked Riss, tramping along beside her. Behind, Jack was conversing with the coachwoman, who was leading one of the horses. She'd let the two girls ride. The other travellers brought up the rear, carrying their luggage.

'I'm not sure,' said Clara. 'I thought there'd be lots of refugees. You know, with the fighting. And we saw people getting away from the dam...ah, here's the inn.'

The *Jenny Gaunt*, half-timbered and red-roofed, stood back a little from the road, and to their left was a row of stables, and a coach-house. The other travellers started eagerly forward, but Clara beckoned to Jack and Riss. 'Can we go last?' she said. 'I might get recognised.'

'You said you stole a cart?' said Jack.

'I was with James. He's my father,' she added, to Riss, 'and he's only got one leg, so they'd be more likely to remember him than me. But still...'

'You stole a cart?' said Riss.

'Shh! Keep your voice down. It was a man that served us. If he's around, I'll need to hide.'

By the time they'd been given rooms – Clara and Riss sharing, Jack in a males' room above the stables – the bar-room was full, and Clara felt more reassured. There were a few refugees, besides their own party, but it looked as if most of the villagers had turned up as well, to hear the news about the dam. It had collapsed completely, and twenty thousand tons of water had scoured their way down the valley. There were no villages in the way, they said, but there were a couple of farms gone, and the low-lying parts of Romsey would have been inundated.

Clara and the others found a quiet corner and slumped into their chairs while they waited for their food. The place was warm and dry, and they were exhausted. For a long time, none of them could be bothered to make themselves heard over the sea of voices. Then Riss shifted in her chair and said, 'We're lucky to be alive, aren't we?'

Clara looked blankly at her. 'I suppose so,' she said.

'I mean, we could have gone down with the *Cerdic.*' She rubbed at her arm. 'Ow,' she said. 'Those girls meant business, didn't they?'

Clara didn't need to ask which girls. She hadn't seen much of Riss's part in the fight at Romsey, but she couldn't have escaped unscathed.

'And,' Riss went on, 'if we'd left Romsey ten minutes later, we'd have been washed away when the dam went.'

'They really wanted to take me away,' put in Jack. 'Didn't they?'

Clara nodded, and put a hand to her eyes. *Thwock*. The hollow skull. The shock, travelling through the club and back up her arm...

'Brothel, probably,' Riss was saying. 'They'd get a good price for you. Then you'd have to have sex for a living.'

Jack went red. 'I – uh–'

'You'd hate it,' put in Clara. 'Dora Thorn and I finished up at a brothel–'

'Oh you did, did you?' said Riss. 'You're a dark horse.'

'I didn't *know* it was a brothel!' said Clara quickly, blushing in her turn. 'But I saw what they do with the – with the "boys". They give them endurance drugs, so they can work all night long. And I saw one man having snow stuffed up his backside. Anyway,' she finished, 'I hope I didn't kill that woman.'

'Here's the food,' said Riss. 'Hush now.'

Clara glanced up. To her relief, it was a young girl, and not the man she'd seen last time, who brought their pies. She exhaled slowly. Why did life have to be so complicated?

Jack touched her arm. 'You okay?' he asked.

Clara looked into his face, and burst into tears.

It was ten minutes before she felt like eating, and when she did, she wondered if her fork was doing to the pie what her club had done to that woman's skull. 'I killed her,' she said. 'I know I did.'

'For pity's sake,' said Riss, 'keep it down.'

'Look,' said Jack, 'it was her or me, right? You prob'ly saved my life, 'cause it sounds like the work would've killed me sooner or later.'

Clara played with her food. 'I suppose...'

'Well. I'm glad it was me.' He gave her arm a squeeze.

'I think,' said Riss, 'he's trying to say "thank you". You're welcome.'

Jack winced. 'Yeah, of course, Riss. Thank you, too. Thank you both.'

Riss tapped her finger on the table. 'And bloody well eat up, Clara. I'm not *carrying* you to London.'

Clara shrugged, but began to eat.

As Riss watched, she said: 'She'd better listen, or I'll kill her. Mother, that is. I mean, look at what's happening!'

'There's a lot of crap goin' on,' agreed Jack.

The people at the next table got up to leave, so the three of them picked up their plates and took the chance to move closer to the fire.

'First,' went on Riss, counting on her fingers, 'the *Scorpion*. I guess raiding Wessex is what you do if there's a war, but sinking refugee boats, that stinks. Then, look at what we've seen since then. They're nearly starving at Portland. They'll be starving in Crichurch soon. Soldiers are deserting – we saw them, right? And dams are falling down because nobody can be bothered to maintain them.'

'Crops,' added Clara, swallowing a mouthful of her pie. 'Crops are failing. If we don't stop fighting, and pay more attention to what really matters, more people will starve.'

'Blimey,' said Jack after a minute. 'You've got me convinced, anyway.'

'It's not funny, Jack,' said Clara.

'No,' he said, 'I mean it. I'm not takin' the piss. It's just – well, it's not me you'll be talking to, is it? It's a bloody general.'

'And before that,' said Riss, frowning, 'I've got to find Anna.'

The male quarters were surprisingly cosy. There were no bedsteads, the mattresses lying on the bare boards, but the blankets were clean and, once the stair hatch was closed, there were no draughts. About half the mattresses were occupied, and in the corner someone was snoring. But that wasn't why Jack was awake. He lay staring into the dark night, listening to the breathing around him and the snorts of the horses below, and trying not to move too much. Tired and sore as he was, he couldn't stop thinking about his near-kidnapping, the hard faces of those women, their iron grip, the way they laughed at him. What sort of world was he in? It was bad enough, back in his days with the Scrapers, when men were detested and shunned. But at least they were left alone, most of the time. Now, though, things had changed. Now he was going to have to be careful.

And Clara. Bloody Clara! She'd only gone and saved him again. He should be grateful, he told himself. And he *was* grateful, he was. But she was always doing one more stupid, stupid thing, like she was addicted to danger. She was going to get herself killed one of these days, and Jack didn't want to be around when it happened. He sighed.

Riss's girlfriend Anna, it turned out, didn't live in Basingstoke itself, but in a village a little way to the east, off the old London Road, which meant that it took most of the next day to get there. For ten boudicks a carter took them from *The Jenny Gaunt* up to Micheldever. After a wait of two hours in the wind and the drizzle, they were able to take a post coach along the weathered twentieth-century roadways, past collapsed warehouses and vegetation-covered tower blocks on the outskirts of Basingstoke, and into the inhabited centre of the town. Finally, they hired a cab to take them the remaining couple of miles. Passing through a stretch of arable farmland, they arrived, late in the afternoon, in a tidy village that looked as if part of the town had wandered away, to hold itself aloof from the bustle and decay.

The cab set them down in front of a row of terraced houses with brightly-painted doors and shutters, and empty window-boxes waiting for the spring. While the cab turned and rolled back to town, Riss stared at the houses and licked her lips. 'The green door,' she said. 'It's that one...'

Clara put a hand to her head, then blinked. 'Well?' she said. 'Come on, let's knock.'

'Uh,' said Riss, swallowing, 'she might be out. She'll be at work.' She nodded. 'Yeah, let's come back later.'

Jack had been looking at Clara. 'You all right?' he asked.

'Just a headache,' she said. 'I'll be okay.'

'Riss,' said Jack, 'she needs a rest. Can't we just try?'

Riss sighed. Then, looking up to heaven, she stomped up the garden path. Clara and Jack followed, and waited while Riss tapped tentatively on the knocker. 'If she's not in–' she began, but the door opened.

A tall, slim woman stood there, olive-skinned and statuesque, with large brown eyes and long dark hair that tumbled down in braids. She wore a pale lilac woollen jumper and dark trousers, her feet thrust into heavy work-boots. She stared.

'Riss?' she managed eventually.

Riss unstuck her tongue. 'Hi,' she said. They regarded each other for a moment. 'I – I'm sorry for what I said,' she went on. 'And you were right, what you said about Mother. And everything.'

Anna was still staring, her brows knotted.

Riss glanced at Clara, and for the first time Anna seemed to register that Riss wasn't alone. 'Hi,' she said to Clara. She nodded to Jack.

'Well, um,' said Riss, 'I wanted to come back, but–' She broke off, because Anna had slapped her across the cheek.

Clara gasped, and Jack took a step forward. Riss held a hand to the cheek. 'Right,' she said, 'I guess I'll–' This time she broke off because Anna had given a little yelp and thrown her arms around her. They hugged, and kissed, and began to cry.

Jack turned to Clara. 'Wow,' he whispered, as they followed the others into the house. 'Some welcome.'

'Don't worry,' said Clara. 'I won't do that to you.' Then she frowned. Why had she said that?

38 Sorry Again

The terrace's water supply was a shared standpipe, and Anna had rigged up a bucket-shower in the old bathroom, so at long last they were all able to get clean. Riss's room had been left untouched since she'd left ('Don't get sentimental,' Anna said, 'I just never got round to clearing it out'), so some of her own clothes were still there. Clara, and even Jack, were provided with some of Anna's spare clothes while their own were laundered. They didn't fit properly, and Jack swore he'd never normally be seen in bright yellow, but they were clean, and dry, and warm.

The house had a tiny living-room and an equally tiny kitchen, where Riss and Anna were now occupied preparing vegetables. When she'd finished cleaning herself up, Clara found it easier to join Jack, dozing by the fire in the living-room. From the kitchen, she heard, among the clatter of knives and dishes, Riss and Anna conversing loudly and quickly, as if they wanted to cover all their missing ground at once. Once or twice there was a silence, when Clara thought it was probably a good thing she wasn't in there with them. She lay back and closed her eyes, trying to follow Jack's example, but her head ached and she felt queasy. A bit of food was what she needed.

They squeezed around a tiny table. Anna and Riss had cooked peppers and pilchards, with a few tomatoes and some flatbread. At first Clara ate with a will, ravenous after the long day she'd had, but halfway through, she began to feel light-headed and had to slow down.

'So, Clara,' said Riss, putting her fork down. 'We've got a problem.'

Clara made herself look up. 'Sorry?' she mumbled.

'About the papers?' asked Jack.

'I can't help,' said Anna. Her voice was breathy and musical. 'If you'd arrived a month ago, we could have got you papers. Good ones,' she added.

'Who's "we"?'

Riss leaned forward. 'This is confidential, all right? Anna's friends run – well, *ran* it until last week – a kind of newspaper.'

'An underground newsletter,' said Anna. 'Exposing government lies, campaigning against the war. Rights for men, too,' she added, nodding at Jack. 'They had a printing press, and I know they've forged papers for people a few times. All the right fonts, the paper thickness, the watermarks, everything. I used to help out when I could.' She twined one of her braids around a finger. 'The Wednesday before last, I had a hell of a headache when I got in from work, so I didn't go. Next day, I heard the Repsegs had been in, arrested everyone, and smashed the place up.'

Riss put a hand over Anna's. 'I'll help you, love,' she said. 'I'll help you get back at them.'

Clara, who'd made herself finish her food, clattered her fork into the dish and shuffled to an armchair. 'Is there anywhere else we can try?' she asked.

Anna shook her head. 'Not that I know of. Yasmin – she's one of the girls who got arrested – she had contacts everywhere. She'd have known.'

Clara shivered and tried to focus. Her stomach was hurting. 'We couldn't steal any, I suppose?'

'That'd be really tricky,' said Anna. 'I can't think where we'd steal them from. People don't wave them around in public, not unless there's a checkpoint or something. And what if we got caught?'

Jack had been watching Clara. 'Here,' he said. 'What's up?'

Clara shook her head, hauled herself up and hurried to the toilet. For a moment they listened to her throwing up, then Anna sighed and said, 'I'll go and see if she needs any help.'

'We won't be going anywhere for a while, then,' said Riss with a frown.

'You could've caught it anywhere,' Jack was saying. It was late the next evening. After a night of being sick, Clara had spent all the cold day swaddled in blankets in the spare bed. She'd got up half an hour ago and managed to eat a morsel of bread, and now she and Jack were in the living-room, close to the crackling fire.

'I suppose,' mumbled Clara. 'All those crowded coaches. You're breathing other people's germs all the time. I never thought it'd be healthier to ride on the box.'

Jack snorted. 'Good to hear you complaining again. You warm enough?'

Clara nodded. Then she said, 'Have you been indoors all day?'

Nah,' he said, shaking his head. 'Went out shoppin' again, with them two. Couldn't go on me own. Riss said I had to have an escort.' He gave a rueful laugh. 'Seems like all I'm good for is carryin' shopping.'

'Maybe,' said Clara, peering at him, 'we can get you somewhere safer soon.' She looked around. 'Where are the others?'

'Upstairs. Talking.'

'Uh, where are you sleeping? There's only two bedrooms.'

'In here,' said Jack, with a wry smile. 'Floor's a bit hard, but it's warm enough.'

'Did they have any ideas about papers?'

'Not that they've told me.'

In the night, Jack woke from a nagging dream in which Leroy, his captain in Hurn's militia, was yelling at him, and prodding him in the small of the back. His eyes opened on near-darkness: moonlight filtered around the edges of the heavy curtains, but otherwise all was black. Cursing, he shifted – it was a fold in the rug that had been prodding him, so he smoothed it down and covered it with a cushion. Then, as he pulled the blankets around himself again, he heard a whimper. He listened, and in a moment there came another, and a sniff.

He stood, and wrapping a blanket over his shoulders, groped his way across the cold floor to the stairs. He crept up as quietly as he could. From one bedroom came a low throb: Riss snoring again. Anna must be a really heavy sleeper, he thought. But the crying was coming from the Clara's room. He heard it stop and transform into a cough, then the sound of water being slurped, thirstily.

He raised a knuckle to knock on the door. Should he go in? Wouldn't it just make things worse? But while he stood undecided, he found that he'd knocked anyway. From behind the door he heard a faint 'Who is it?'

He pushed the door open, but remained on the threshold. 'It's me,' he said, just loud enough for her to hear. 'I heard yer...'

She blew her nose. 'Sorry I disturbed you.'

'No,' said Jack, 'you didn't.' He realised he was tensing his shoulders and neck. Must be the cold. 'I just – er, can I get you anything?'

'Oh. Thanks. Could you get me some more water? I've drunk it all. Cup's on the side there.'

Jack's eyes were beginning to get used to the darkness in the room, and he could make out the outline of the window and its curtains. But he still managed to stub his toes twice on the way to the bedside dresser. The room smelt of disinfectant. Saying nothing, he took the cup and groped his way out.

His bare feet were thoroughly chilled by the time he returned. As he opened the door, he interrupted Clara mid-snore. 'Sorry,' he said softly. 'Here's your water.' This time he'd brought a night-lantern with him, so he could see her pale arm outstretched in the gloom, and the oval of her face beyond. He pressed the cup into her hand, and their fingers touched. 'I, uh, hope you get back to sleep,' he added.

He'd reached the door when Clara said, 'Jack?'

He stopped and turned. 'Yeah?'

It was a moment before she spoke. 'I'm sorry,' she said. 'Thanks for the water.'

He closed the door softly. Riss, in the other room, had gone quiet. With a shiver, he hurried back to the living-room, eased himself onto the rug and flung the blankets over himself. Which particular thing, he wondered, was Clara apologising for this time?

Clara, meanwhile, huddled her own blankets around her and curled up, making the bed creak. After the brief lanternlight, all was dark again. She still felt weak, and staying warm kept the shivers and the queasiness away. If only she could sleep, and get herself better, maybe she could find a way to get those identity papers. Yes, yes – she had to get papers. Or maybe they could try getting into London without them? It was so long since she'd been there, though. And of course, it was the army in charge now. She pictured road-blocks and checkpoints on every road, sentries in the streets, bodies by the roadsides. Was she dreaming, or awake? She opened her eyes: awake, then.

And then she noticed that she was smiling, just a little, and that for some minutes she'd been rubbing her thumb across her fingertips, where Jack had touched them. She frowned. Why was she doing that? No reason, she told herself. Just the difference between warm and cold. It was kind of him to check up on her, that was all. And then she thought, what if she and Riss *hadn't* rescued him from the boy-catchers at Romsey? If those girls had managed to drag him round the corner of the inn, out of sight, she'd have wasted precious minutes looking for him, and they'd have got away. If that had happened, then she would really have lost Jack, and lost him for good. Maybe it would be safer to get him away from Anglia, at once.

No, no, no. She simply had to stop the war, to face down Riss's mother, to tell her that they couldn't afford to fight, because – because Xavi had wanted peace. Because she, Clara, wanted peace. Bodies by the roadside, bodies in the water. Refugees, deserters. Black waves in a black sea...

To try to fall asleep, she made herself think of Xavi, of the hard muscles on his sweat-slicked chest, his warm, coal-dusted lips, his gentle touch on her bare waist. It didn't work.

39 Sneaking Off

The next day dawned grey and damp. Riss, who'd looked in on Clara, reported that she was sleeping soundly, and Jack joined her and Anna around the table for a breakfast of scrambled egg.

'Smells great,' he said, pulling his chair in. 'This might wake her up.'

They started eating, but neither of the others seemed to want to say anything. Jack put his fork down. 'What is it?' he said. 'What's up?'

Riss looked at Anna and nodded.

'I went out this morning,' said Anna. 'There's been another battle, near Wimborne. Seems the army advanced a good few miles into Wessex. But it came down to hand-to-hand, and they were basically fighting in mud. Heavy losses on both sides.'

'If it carries on,' said Riss, 'both sides will want revenge, one thing will lead to another, and we'll never be able to stop it. We need to see Mother *now*. We can't waste a day.'

Anna nodded. 'She might not listen, but a slim chance is better than none. And Riss is right. We can't waste any more time.'

Jack leant back in his chair and frowned. 'So what are you saying?'

'We're setting off today,' said Anna. 'As soon as we can. We can't wait for Clara to get better. We can't wait for her to get papers. And...'

'And there's you,' put in Riss.

'You mean,' said Jack, 'more snatch gangs? I'll be a liability?'

'Uh-huh.'

Jack blew out his cheeks and shook his head. No,' he said. 'No. I'm not going along with this.'

'What?' snapped Riss. She glanced in the direction of the stairs. Then, lowering her voice, she went on, 'You were against Clara coming in the first place. What's changed?'

'Look,' he said. 'I can't stop yer, right? I can't stop yer walking out of here and grabbing the next coach to London. And I'm not gonna try. But she was in this with you, right? And you're leaving her, without a word. It ain't fair.'

'But you said yourself, you wanted her to go back to her parents.'

'Yeah, I'm not denyin' it.'

'She's got no papers,' said Anna, 'and it's impossible to get any. It doesn't matter that she's a Truth Sister. The general knows *me* already.'

'All I'm saying is,' said Jack, 'tell her.'

'No,' said Riss, looking at Anna. 'We don't want any arguments. We're all packed, and we're off now.'

Jack shook his head again.

'And don't you go waking her up, just to tell her,' said Riss.

'Not my place to,' said Jack.

'You're as bad as us,' snapped Anna. 'Look,' she added more gently, 'you can both stay on here, until she's well enough to travel. Okay? Now, I'm getting my pack.'

Jack watched her disappearing up the stairs, then turned to Riss. 'When we do go,' he said, 'I'll put the key back through the door.'

Riss was frowning. 'You can get her away to Devon, Jack. It's what you've wanted to do, isn't it?'

He shook his head again. 'What will Clara think, when she wakes up and finds you've run? No,' he said, holding up a hand, 'don't bother, all right? You got your reasons, I guess. Just promise me, Riss – promise you'll make it count. When you do see your mam, convince her. Do whatever it takes, and if she won't listen, keep trying. Keep trying, and never give up. 'cause that's what Clara does.'

Riss fell silent.

'You got food?' said Jack.

'All ready,' said Riss, taking a package from the shelf and pushing it into her pack. They heard Anna coming down the stairs.

'Promise,' Jack said again.

Riss nodded. 'I promise.' She handed Anna her pack, and shouldered her own.

'Right,' Anna said. 'Let's go.'

'Hey, Anna,' said Jack. 'You *have* got your own papers, right?'

She gave him a glare and opened the front door.

'Go on, then,' said Jack. 'Bloody well get to London and see the general. We'll leave here as soon as we can. Like I said to Riss, we'll put your keys back through.'

On the threshold, Riss paused and looked back.

'Nice knowin' ya,' said Jack.

The door closed. They were gone, and Jack put his head in his hands. What, oh what, was he going to tell Clara? He had to hand it to them, they'd been decisive. No messing about. And, looked at from the point of view of speed, they were probably right.

Suddenly he felt very weary. Nothing was easy; everything was hard. Might as well let her sleep on, he thought. She'll hear the bad news soon enough. Dishes, he thought. I'll do the dishes. Then maybe I'll think of the right words.

As he hauled himself to his feet, he heard a creak. His chair scraped on the wooden floor as he pushed it back and hurried to the foot of the stairs. Clara was standing halfway down, a blanket around her shoulders, looking paler than he'd ever seen her. He swallowed. 'You heard?' he said.

She nodded, and the light caught the tears glistening on her cheeks. Jack took a step towards her, spreading his arms, but then stopped. 'Want some tea?' he said.

'They've gone,' said Clara, her voice flat. 'Haven't they?'

Jack nodded. 'Yeah,' he said with a sigh. 'Just now.'

Clara curled her lip, and sat down on the stair. For a moment she said nothing, breathing hard. 'Was it your idea?'

'What?' said Jack. 'No! Didn't you hear us talking?'

'Oh, so you were planning it, were you? Behind my back?' She put a hand to her forehead.

'No – Clara – you know I wouldn't! We had a deal, remember?'

She nodded. He'd promised, hadn't he, to go to London, if she then came to Devon with him? And then he'd leave her.

Jack spread his hands. 'I told them they should go and tell you, but they wouldn't listen.'

She stood, pulling the blanket tighter, and made her way down the remaining stairs. 'Why didn't you stop them?'

'Argh, for pity's sake, Clara!' said Jack, glaring. 'What d'you expect me to do? Lock the door on them? Stand in their way and not let them past?'

Clara poured herself some water and started back up the stairs. 'Well,' she said. 'You got what you wanted.'

Jack swore under his breath.

An hour later, he sat staring out of the window. She must have gone back to sleep, because there'd been no sign of her. They needed food, and he ought to go shopping soon. But he should let her know first. And when he did, she'd think he was going to walk out on her, too. Which he wasn't going to do, obviously, he thought, but maybe it'd bloody well do her good to think so.

He sighed, and drummed his fingers on the chair. What should he do, once he'd got Clara back to her parents? Did they have boy-snatchers in Devon? Would he finish up in a brothel? Maybe he should volunteer for one – that would have some compensations, he thought wryly. But then the hours would be long, and the pay, if any, lousy. And there'd be all those drugs... Or maybe he could find manual work, maybe in Exeter. But there wasn't much he was good at, he thought, except stealing.

Then he thought, maybe I don't need to worry about getting a break from Clara and her mad schemes. To get her back to her parents, we're about to cross a war zone. As schemes go, this one's madder than most. And it's my own.

Clara wasn't asleep. She lay on her back, the bedclothes rumpled all around her and tangled up with the blanket, a handkerchief on the floor beside her. She hadn't cried for long, because she didn't want Jack to hear. Riss! Bloody Riss, who'd been down in that boiler room with her, who'd shared in her despair and her pain, who'd slaved and laboured in the fire and the heat. Riss, who'd battled the seas alongside her, and who wanted to stop the war just as much as she did. She'd been a ray of hope. She'd been – she'd been her last link with Xavi. And now she'd left her, and ruined Clara's chance to make a difference, without so much as a goodbye.

She heaved herself up and shuffled to the top of the stairs. 'Jack?' she called, and started down.

She heard him sigh. 'What?' he said. 'D'you want us to follow them, or something?'

'No,' she said as she reached the bottom. 'No, it's too late. We'll – we should go to Devon.'

He raised his eyebrows. 'Seriously?'

'Seriously. I've failed again, Jack. So I may as well give up.'

'Don't be stupid, Clara–'

'Can we start now? Right away?'

And Jack actually laughed. 'I've said it before,' he said, grinning. 'You're crazy.'

'What d'you mean?'

'The way you change your mind. You don't mess about, do yer? No umm-ing and ah-ing for you.' He was still smiling. 'But you've hardly eaten anything for a couple of days, so let me go and buy us some food. Besides, we can't get back to town, for a coach, until first thing tomorrow.'

'Tomorrow, then. I can't stay here a moment longer.'

40 On Foot

The following evening saw them twenty-five miles further west, with no incidents along the way. They'd ridden in a small delivery cart back into Basingstoke, then joined a crowded post coach for the rest of the journey. At Andover there was a vast inn that, according to the ostler, was famed for its antiquity. But Clara couldn't see much of it in the February dusk.

'How're you feeling?' said Jack, cutting into his potato. It was the first proper chance they'd had to talk all day: as usual, he'd been riding on the box seat while Clara, still fragile, had ridden inside, wrapped in a blanket. Now they were seated, with twenty other people – this was a staging post for seven routes – at a long table in a spacious hall lit by flaring candles. It was noisy, but the faded hangings around the walls helped to deaden the sound.

'Oh, don't fuss,' said Clara. 'You've been watching me all evening, like I might faint any second. I'm all right. Tummy still feels like I've been kicked, but I'm all right.' She played with the cheese on her plate; she didn't think it should be glistening like that. 'I wanted to see the general, I really did. I wanted to change things...'

'You'll be better soon,' he said. 'And if it's any consolation, about the general, I mean, she's never gonna listen, is she? Think about it. She's got thousands of troops all set and ready to fight, so she can hardly change her mind. People'd think she'd gone loopy, then someone else'd take over and carry on anyway.'

'Great,' said Clara. She stabbed at the cheese. 'Great. You couldn't have said something earlier, I suppose?'

'I did,' growled Jack. 'You didn't listen to me then, and you wouldn't have listened if I'd brought it up again.'

Clara sighed. 'Let's not argue. It's all too late now, anyway,' she went on, raising her voice over the laughter that rose from further along the table. 'You know, at the Academy, they taught us that women wouldn't make the mistakes that men made. It was men who'd done so many bad things. You know: men had oppressed women, they'd caused climate change and made the seas rise – and especially, they'd caused war. Wars were all men's fault. They said women were too wise for that.'

'But wars've been going on for years, ain't they? I mean, we was fighting Milland before. And now it's Wessex. Anyhow,' he said, softening his voice, 'you had the right idea.'

Clara blinked, and chewed her lip.

'What's up?' said Jack, peering at her.

'Who said there's anything up?'

Jack pulled a face, shrugged, and wiped the last bit of butter from his plate.

Clara shifted in her seat. 'It's that woman,' she said. 'The one I hit.'

'That's what's really bothering you, isn't it?'

She nodded. 'I've got too much time to think, Jack.'

'No point in tellin' you to forget it, is there?'

'No.'

'Or remindin' you that you saved me life?'

She gave him a flicker of a smile. 'No.'

He glanced around at the people sitting next to them. 'Wanna go outside?' he said. 'Get some air?'

They pushed their plates away, drained their cups and left the dining-hall, emerging into a broad courtyard that led to the main dormitories. Under the veranda roof, a few lanterns swung in the wind, casting wavering shadows over the cobblestones.

'So,' said Jack, looking out into the night, 'd'you wanna talk about it? Or just change the subject?'

'I don't know, Jack. I'm tired.'

Jack turned, as if he was going to lay hand on her arm, but he stopped. 'Look,' he said, 'it's like I say. You had a choice, didn't ya? Let them kidnap me, or try and stop them. And if you're going to stop them, you can't spend time wonderin' how to do it. You've got to get on with it. No time ter think...'

'I suppose so...'

'Anyhow, like I say. If it was them or me, I'm glad you chose me.'

'I was angry, Jack. I was really, really, angry. It was like, it wasn't me in this body. It was like I wasn't in control any more...' She broke off. More people were coming out of the hall and hurrying on to the dormitories, turning up their collars against the wind.

'We should turn in,' he said. 'Try and forget about it, hey?' And this time he did pat her on the arm, before turning in the direction of the men's barn.

'At least we're keeping your promise now,' she called after him. 'It was – it's good of you to help my parents like this.'

He stopped. 'Better get some sleep,' he said. 'We're on foot from here, and it's a long way.'

Jack lay on his straw mattress and stared into the gloom. A cowled lantern glowed on a post outside, but otherwise all was dark. The straw rustled occasionally as a sleeper turned over, and there was a tang of dust in the air. One of the other men was mumbling in his sleep.

It's good of you to help my parents like this, Clara had said. But all along, every step of the way since he'd left the community farm, Jack had been ignoring a little voice inside his head. The voice had been getting more insistent just lately, and tonight it wouldn't leave him alone. You're kidding yourself, the voice was saying. You're not doing this for Clara's parents, are you?

He swore out loud.

Early next morning they laced up their boots, shouldered their backpacks and set off southwards, with a steady wind blowing in their faces and pale grey clouds rolling high overhead. They planned to pass well to the south of Salisbury, where the Wessexers were reinforcing their garrison, before swinging west. Jack reckoned that, if the weather stayed dry, they'd make Yeovil in four or five days, so they'd packed plenty of cheese and dry biscuits, and their packs were heavy. They spoke little, and kept their voices low when they did.

As far as they could, they kept to the hedged bridleways: the hedges to give them cover, the bridleways to allow quick progress without the chance of meeting too many soldiers. And there were plenty to avoid. Twice they saw infantry columns marching west, and in the early afternoon they had to take an hour's detour to avoid a troop camped outside a village. Veering south, they climbed a wooded hill and at dusk found themselves in a village where the roads were broken and overgrown, the houses crumbling and the gardens run to wilderness. Clara remembered her Academy lessons: before Nile Flu there'd been many other pandemics, and the result was that hardly one in three of the old villages was still occupied. The rest were like this, and suddenly she found herself imagining all the death, all the fear, and all the sorrow as these places slipped silently away. She wiped away a tear.

'Wonder where we are?' said Jack. 'Let's see...' A fallen, rusted signpost stuck out of some undergrowth, and he grabbed one side and lifted. 'What's it say?'

Clara peered through the gloom. 'Uh...it says, "Thank you for driving carefully through our village."'

Jack dropped the sign with a thump. 'What does that even mean?'

The next day they continued south-westward, the clouds still high and the breeze brisk. Clara found that she didn't know what to say to Jack: on the one hand, she didn't feel like talking to him about her parents; and on the other, if, after they'd arrived, he went off on his own – it was part of his "deal" – then she might as well start getting used to the idea. Besides, he kept looking at her as if he was scared. Was he scared that she'd change her mind again? Didn't he trust her? But as the morning went on, she found herself frowning a lot more.

Around noon, their route crossed one of the old tarmacked carriageways. It had once been wide and two-laned, but even now the central section was in good condition and a steady trickle of refugees were heading north-west, some in horse-drawn carts, some with hand-barrows, others bent under bulky packs. Most looked resigned, trudging doggedly along, but a few were belligerent, and Clara and Jack witnessed a couple of brawls breaking out. When they tried to find out what was going on, some shrugged and others simply glared.

Later that day, they discovered that the military had closed all the roads into Downton, and, turning south, they found an abandoned house on the road to Woodgreen. The house itself had no windows left, but behind it was an old woodshed where the doors were intact and the floor was dry. The night was cold and starless; in the small hours they woke to the pounding of hooves on the road.

In the morning – the second after Andover – they ate a frugal breakfast. Then they shouldered their lighter backpacks and set off again, crossing the Avon channels by two bridges, the first iron, the second stone, before striking out across country. Jack's idea was to head for Cranborne Chase, well to the north of Hurn's old headquarters, which the Wessex army had now occupied. Last they'd heard, the river had marked the front line between the two armies, and although there was no sign of fighting here, they hurried on.

They'd been tramping over rolling fields for an hour or so when a thought occurred to Clara. 'What do they do about men in Wessex?' she asked.

Jack had been scanning the hillside that lay half a mile to their right. 'How d'you mean?' he said.

'The Republic,' said Clara, jerking a thumb over her shoulder, 'wanted to do without men altogether, using cloning. They stopped women from squabbling over the men that were left, by putting Aquaster in the water supply.'

'That hormone thing? I thought they was running out of it.'

'Yes,' said Clara, with a grimace, 'and if they do, there'll be trouble. But what about Wessex? I don't suppose they ever had Aquaster. Do women fight over the men there?'

Jack shrugged. 'Didn't see none of that. But your mam said somethin' about men needin' to have a sponsor, or something. I wasn't there for long enough to work it out, but I think all the men have got to be registered as – it's not quite *belonging* to someone – it's more like, the woman promises she'll take responsibility.'

Clara shrugged. 'I don't see how that helps.'

'I guess it means, my sponsor can tell me what to do. An' if I don't, it's trouble.'

They thought about that for a minute.

'Shit,' said Jack.

'What?'

'They can rent us out, can't they? Like a farmer rents out a bull. Or they can put us in a brothel...' He trailed off. Clara didn't know what to say.

They passed through some bare woods and, with the wind in their faces, descended a gentle slope across deserted fields before reaching a road. Following the road for a mile and a half, they came to a stretch where low buildings huddled among dense woods.

'That's another thing to avoid, then,' said Jack.

'What's that?' said Clara.

'Shagging for a living. I mean, it sounds like I'd be like a slave, or something.'

'Shagging?'

Jack sniggered. 'Having sex, stupid. Didn't they teach you nothing at that school?' Then he frowned, and looked away quickly.

Clara saw he'd gone red. Maybe she should change the subject. 'What else have you got to avoid?'

'Oh.' He looked at his feet. 'Well. Going to sea. It still scares the shit out of me, and there's a lot of it around Wessex, ain't there? And getting conscripted. If this war goes on...'

'Jack, listen,' said Clara. She reached out and took his arm, but as he turned, she happened to glance back down the road.

'What?' Jack growled. 'You're not gonna–' But then he saw her staring. 'What is it?' he whispered.

Clara held up a hand. 'I thought I saw something.'

For a full minute they stood, calming their breathing, but all they could hear was the wind fretting in the branches.

SCORPION

'Probably nothing,' said Clara.

'We'd hear 'em,' said Jack, 'if it was soldiers.'

'Would we?' said Clara.

41 Caught in the Fighting

They found an old track running off to their left between bare hedgerows, and followed it for an hour. Above, the clouds were gathering, and the light began to fail. Then the track petered out and they had to trudge across muddy fields and wade through muddier ditches, and it was difficult to find their way.

'Afternoon's getting on,' began Jack. 'We should find somewhere–' but then he broke off. From away to their left came the unmistakeable sound of gunfire: a staccato fusillade, then another, and another. Fighting.

They listened for some minutes. Then Clara said, her voice hoarse, 'Jack, they're getting closer.'

'Make for those trees,' he said, pointing. They set off across a ploughed field that sloped down to their left, but the heavy, clayey soil stuck to their boots, slowing their progress. Clara could see that a summer crop had been sown here: tiny green shoots had struggled through the sodden clods. All the way, they kept glancing in the direction of the firing, and Clara felt her heart pounding.

'The Anglians,' panted Jack, and Clara could hear the quiver in his voice. 'They've come further than we thought.'

Then, as they reached the copse, the firing ceased. Though they listened hard, all they could hear was the wind hissing through the pines, and the bare oak branches creaking. Clara glanced at Jack, who nodded. 'Can't stay here,' he said. 'Got to keep moving. Besides,' he added, looking up, 'more rain's coming.'

They pressed on, between dark trees and through hogweed and brown nettles, the smell of decay in their nostrils. After a few hundred yards they emerged into a shaggy grassland, with a hollow to their left and a low hill to their right. Spots of rain flew on the wind. Before them, the land sloped up towards a long, scrubby thicket, but there was no sign of any track or path. 'Maybe we'll get a better view from up there,' said Jack. 'You okay?'

Clara wasn't. Her legs ached, her lungs were heaving, and she felt sick again. But she nodded.

They left the copse and started across the field, the thick, wet grass sucking at their feet, but they'd only covered twenty yards when, without warning, six riders cleared the rise and galloped towards them. Gasping, Clara looked around. 'Back to the trees!' she cried, but immediately she knew they weren't going to make it. The riders had seen them, were bearing down fast. 'Halt! Halt!' she heard one calling.

As they came under the trees Clara looked at Jack, who was panting. He shook his head. 'Better stop,' he said.

She swallowed. There was no way they could go any further. When, oh when, would this ever end? They turned their backs to the trees and faced the riders. Three of them dismounted and strode towards them. 'Anglians,' said Jack out of the corner of his mouth. 'Looks like they've got swords. Can't see no guns.'

'Stay where you are,' snarled the first rider, who seemed, by her uniform, to be the captain. 'Put your hands up, where I can see them.'

SCORPION

Jack had been wrong. The soldiers were indeed wearing swords, but one of them now produced a pistol and kept it trained on them, while a third came up and felt their clothing for concealed weapons, before searching through their packs. After interminable minutes, she stepped back. 'Nothing on 'em, Ma'am,' she said.

The captain came a step closer. Her face was pale and lined, her nose wide and flat. Her keen grey eyes searched Clara's face. 'You're either monumentally stupid,' she said, raising her voice against the wind, 'or you're spies.'

'We're no spies,' said Clara, trying to stop her voice from shaking. The rain began to fall in earnest.

'What's the boy for?' the captain asked, nodding at Jack, who stood close behind Clara.

'The boy can answer for himself, thanks very much–' began Jack, but Clara held up a hand.

'We're travellers,' said Clara, trying to steady her voice.

'Doesn't mean you're not spies,' sneered the captain.

'We're *not* spies!' cried Clara. 'We're not–' The captain slapped her across the face. She staggered, and turned her head away, reaching for a tree trunk to steady herself. Then things happened quickly.

'Leave her alone!' she heard Jack yelling. She didn't see whether he'd actually punched the captain, but as she turned back, she saw that he was now on the ground.

'Shoot them,' said the captain to the soldier next to her, 'both.'

'No!' screamed Clara, flinging herself towards the gun. The soldier knocked her away, there was a shot, and Jack, who'd been struggling to get up, was flung backwards into the nettles.

With a yell, Clara threw her arms around the soldier's waist, no longer caring what happened – this woman had shot Jack, and she was going to pay. But the soldier was strong, and somehow she managed an uppercut to Clara's face. Reeling, she felt her grip slackening. If the soldier got time to raise her gun–

There was another shot. But to her wonder, Clara felt the soldier go limp. As the pair of them tumbled to the ground there was more firing, and she heard the horses neighing and the captain screaming orders. There was blood on Clara's arm, and as she disentangled herself, she realised that the soldier now had a bullet-hole in the side of her head. Clara tried to stand, but her head was still throbbing from the punch. Jack, she had to get to Jack, he'd been shot! She blinked. There were more horses. An Anglian soldier galloped past her, then slid off her horse as another *crack* came from behind. Clara staggered on, desperately scanning the undergrowth. She was yelling now. 'Jack! Jack!' His legs – she could see his legs, there among the nettles. He wasn't moving. 'No!' she cried, but somebody else was yelling, and then came a blow on the back of her head that made her eyes leap from their sockets and her teeth drive into her tongue. She saw flashes of light before darkness took her.

It seemed like hours later that she woke. Her head throbbed as if it might burst, and she could taste vomit. She was swaying, and something was pushing into her belly. Her arms were at a funny angle. When she opened her eyes, the world was upside down, and dark. The rain was falling upwards, and the lanterns were hanging the wrong way. Those weren't her own feet; they were horse's hooves

Sobbing is difficult to do when you've been trussed up and thrown across a horse, with your head and feet dangling. But Clara managed it.

Some time later – how long, Clara neither knew nor cared – she was lifted roughly from the horse. The ropes around her ankles were cut, but because her feet were numb, they had to carry her. They were soldiers, of course – probably Wessexers, by their accents. They took her down some steps and laid her on a beaten earth floor in what felt like a cellar. At least it was dry.

'Exhausted,' said a voice.

'Me too,' said another.

'No, I mean *her*,' said the first.

'Oh, yeah. You,' the soldier went on, prodding Clara with her boot. 'You're a civvy, right?'

Clara said nothing, but tried to sit. She nodded.

'Let's leave it till the morning,' said the first soldier. 'I wanna get some sleep, plus we'll get more sense out of her then.'

'Okay. I'll get someone to bring food and water. Then,' she added to Clara, 'we'll be back in the morning. You got questions to answer.'

The food came, together with a blanket. A little light came through a gap at the top of the cellar door, so that she could just about see the bread and the enamel cup. The blanket she wrapped around her shoulders, but her own filthy clothes were still sodden and soon the water had soaked through. She reasoned that more layers ought to keep her warmer, even if they were soaking wet, but still she shivered.

It was definitely the Wessex army who'd captured her. Those dark uniforms were plainer and simpler than the Anglians'. It must have been these soldiers who'd attacked, just when the Anglians had found her and Jack. And at the thought of him, she began to cry.

Don't, she told herself. Don't. He's just another casualty, like Matty, like the priest, like Xavi, and Hashim, and Tori Shavila, and all the rest. Jack's gone. All you can do, she thought, remembering something Hashim had said, is to remember him in your heart. But that made her cry all the harder, pressing a hand to the middle of her chest. She pictured him: showing her how to steal, that first night with the Scrapers; comforting Matty when they'd argued; coming at her with a knife; trying to paddle her away from the weir; throwing her to the ground to save her from a flying tree in the storm; hiding a knife in her backpack; shivering in a cold yard after a battle; swimming out to the Scorpion, to save her again; and holding on to her as the *Cerdic* sank behind them. All those times they'd had, all those things they'd done, and for what? Gone, all gone.

I can't give up, she told herself between the sobbing and the gasping. I've got to do it right this time. He promised he'd get me back to my parents, and I'll make sure he does.

42 In the Storm

It was the thunder that woke him. Wincing, Jack opened his eyes upon complete darkness. His right shoulder was screaming in pain, and he couldn't move the arm. He was also soaked to the skin, and as he realised that, he began to shiver violently. There was wet vegetation all around him, under him, dripping and drooping over him. Lightning flashed in the sky to his left. Trees – he was under some trees that creaked and strained in the wind. He tried to move, and yelped. Something in that shoulder was in the wrong place, and it felt like a hot knife was being twisted in his sinews. He tried to listen, but all he could hear was the moaning of the wind and the spiteful screeching of the trees.

Clara was gone. The soldiers were gone. Everyone was gone.

He could just lie here and die, he thought. But that'd be a cold, wet, and probably drawn-out way to go. Or else, he could move. Swearing, whimpering and gasping, he used his good arm to push himself to his knees, then, gingerly, he stood. So long as the lightning kept coming, he could guess where he was going...uphill, that was an idea. Then he could see what to do next. *If* he could see.

He yelled as he tripped over a dead soldier, his shoulder piercing him with fresh spasms, her body cold and heavy under him. Again he struggled up and staggered into the rain, holding his arm to his side, and so drenched that his shirt sucked against his back and his trousers dragged on his legs. He had to keep blinking, and rain dripped from his chin.

The storm grew closer, the thunder now following immediately on the flashes. Jack was almost deafened, but he knew that if the lightning stopped, he'd never find shelter. He felt the ground levelling off, and then he was at the crest of the hill. He waited for the next flash.

There! Half a mile downhill, the angular outline of a steep, tiled roof. Tall chimneys. Solid brick buildings. Gasping, he scurried on, hobbling and slipping over the sodden grass. Lightning struck something close by, and Jack almost leapt in the air, feeling a stabbing pain as his shoulder twisted. Now the wind was so strong that when he came to a gate, he struggled to open it.

Still shivering, he trudged on, but he could no longer see where he was going. So near, he thought, but so far. If I stay out here, I'll die. Then, at last, another flash. A deserted farmyard, some stables. To his left, a large, open-sided barn where the bales of straw were shifting in the wind. Not sheltered enough. Then, beyond, an outhouse that had both a roof and a door.

Without hesitation he stumbled inside, panting, and pushed the door shut. Realising he'd plunged himself into complete darkness, he groped around with his good arm. He found something like a packing case that he could sit on, and something like sacking that he could cover himself with. But, overcome at last with the effort and the pain, he ignored both and slipped down to the floor. Gasping, he shoved the sacking around the bottom of the door to keep out the draught. The lightning flickered, the hard rain hammered on the door, and all Jack could do was shiver and try to keep his shoulder still. He'd no idea how much blood he'd lost. He knew he might die here, and he knew he'd lost Clara. They'd have taken her halfway back to Anglia by now, surely. If they hadn't killed her.

If they hadn't killed her? He swore. What if she'd been lying there, in those woods, just as he'd been? He pictured her corpse, cold and sodden among the brambles. Or maybe, just maybe, she was alive but had been left for dead, like him? He'd have to go back. He'd go and look, in the morning. He'd go and look...

He only realised he'd fallen asleep when he woke with a start, making his shoulder scream. All was dark. Where was he? The shot, the woods, the thunderstorm...oh, yes, the pain! Like a burning, like a hot coal jammed under his shoulder blade. The rest of him was freezing cold. Then he thought he heard, over the wind and the rain, the snort and stamp of a horse. He listened, but the sound wasn't repeated. He slipped back into disturbed dreams, telling himself that the shouts he heard were only the wind.

Clara hadn't slept. All night she'd shivered in the cellar, her clothes wet and her head aching, listening to the thumping of the wind and the storm. Now, as day broke, the door was unlocked and a couple of soldiers appeared at the top of the steps. With swollen eyes Clara blinked into the light.

'You've to come with us,' said one, a different soldier from the previous night. 'The captain wants to interrogate you, but she don't fancy comin' down here to do it.'

As she reached the top of the steps, Clara took in her surroundings. The rain had cleared ahead of a strong easterly, and the clouds were high and pale. She was in a wide farmyard, with stables down one side and a row of tall cypresses at the far end. One of these had fallen in the storm, and two soldiers were slicing up its trunk with a crosscut saw. In front of her stood the large, grey stone farmhouse with a vegetable garden in front, recently tended but now storm-draggled. One of the chimneys had fallen in, damaging the roof and breaking some of the windows, but the remainder of the house was intact, and the Wessexers were moving boxes and crates inside, turning it into a field headquarters.

Her captors pushed her in through the front door and along a hallway with coat-hooks, picture-frames and a rumpled carpet. The trappings of normal life, thought Clara. For those left alive! They led her to what must have been a large pantry, with a high, north-facing window and a tiled stone slab for keeping food cool. A rough table and a couple of chairs had been squeezed inside.

'Wait here,' they told her.

Pale light was creeping into the little outhouse by the time Jack peeled his eyes open. The rain had stopped, although he could still hear running water. There were other noises, too: voices, and the rumble of wheels.

SCORPION

He was still alive, then. The pain in his shoulder had dulled, but in a way it was more insistent, like a huge toothache. His arm was swollen inside its damp sleeve, and he felt as if he was going to vomit. Water – yes, he was burning with thirst, he needed water. The rainwater – that must have collected somewhere. Now he'd thought of it, his need to drink became desperate. Cursing, and wincing whenever he jarred his arm, he pulled away the sacking and wrenched the door open. The sky was dim and grey, but after the gloom, the brightness hit Jack like a physical blow, and he raised a hand to shield his eyes.

He spotted a puddle in a patch between the weeds, and cupped a few bitter mouthfuls from that. Then, as his eyes got used to the light, he saw the edge of a stone trough peeping from behind the outhouse. He hobbled to it and knelt, cupping mouthful after mouthful, feeling his throat easing, feeling his guts sinking back into place, and it wasn't until he'd been doing this for a full three minutes that he became aware of the smells of straw and horses, and he remembered the night-noises.

He frowned, and his gaze followed the stream of rainwater that ran from the trough, glinting as it went diagonally across a yard, with mud, sticks and dead leaves banked up around it. It was a wide farmyard, and he could see carts, several of them, and horses being groomed by women in uniforms. A lot of women in uniforms...

'Stop right there!' cried a voice, and Jack looked up to see a soldier running towards him. Was that a pistol she was holding?

Slowly, Jack sat on the edge of the trough. He raised his good arm, by way of surrender. 'I'm hurt,' he said, wincing as another wave of pain swept through him. Then he toppled back into the trough.

When his eyes opened again, someone was forcing brandy down his throat. It was a soldier – a woman with a white apron over her uniform, her face grimy and her brown hair cropped short under a cloth cap.

'Ah, there you are,' she said. 'Welcome back. I've put some spirits on the wound, but I've got nothing to put you out, and this is going to hurt.'

Jack stared at the ceiling. What was it, another outhouse? A kitchen? It needed painting, anyway. There was a big stain over there. A bit of white paint would fix that...he tried to focus on the soldier. Oh, there was another woman, and she was holding something that glinted. She had a mask on. 'Uh,' he managed to say, '*what's* gonna hurt?'

'Drink some more brandy,' said the first woman. 'We need you good and pissed.'

Clara waited. Not that she had much choice. Half an hour passed, an hour passed, and still no-one came. It was cold in the pantry, and she was shivering again, so she banged on the door. 'Hey!' she called. 'I'm still here! I thought you were going to interrogate me! And,' she added, 'I'm thirsty!' She banged again and again. After a minute the door was pulled open, and she found herself staring at the point of a knife.

'Shut,' said the soldier, 'your face. Captain knows you're here, she's just been busy. She—' She broke off.

An agonised yell had echoed across the farmyard, and Clara's guts lurched.

The soldier's eyes were wide, and she swallowed. 'Er, like I say,' she resumed. 'Captain's got a lot on her mind, so just shut up, all right? Or else, she'll find the interrogation a bit one-sided!' She turned to close the door.

'What was that noise?' said Clara. 'Who was it?'

'Field hospital,' the soldier replied with a shrug. 'Patchin' someone up.' She slammed the door.

Clara sat down again, and put a hand to her throat. That cry! Why had it shaken her so much?

43 Daisy, Daisy

Half an hour later, the soldier returned with some water, bread and – to Clara's surprise – a chunk of cheese.

'Thanks,' said Clara. She swigged at the water. 'Did you, er, find out who it was?'

The soldier frowned. 'Who what was?'

'The person who screamed.' *Person*, she'd said. Did she think it wasn't a woman, then?

'No idea,' snapped the soldier. 'We've got twenty casualties out there. Could've been any of 'em. Now, no more questions!'

Clara sat, and chewed, and thought. It must, she decided, have been the sheer pain in that cry that had unnerved her. After so much death, maybe it was beginning to get to her... The food was tasteless, but that didn't matter. She ate hungrily. But she'd hardly finished before the soldier was back, this time with a short, stocky woman with an old scar on her forehead.

'Right,' said the scarred one. 'Bring her. I'll interrogate her while I'm eating. Then send Mbakwe over, to take notes. See what the spy's got to say for herself.'

Clara shook her head, but stood up and followed. 'How can I prove I'm not a spy?' she said, shrugging as the soldier gripped her arm.

'The captain's the one askin' the questions,' the soldier said between her teeth. 'Shut up.'

Well, thought Clara, I've been in worse places. Maybe I'll be lucky again. I've got to be. I've got to keep Jack's promise... Her lip trembled.

They left the main house and crossed the yard, making for a single-storey block with low shrubs in pots outside. To her right Clara could see a row of hastily-erected tents, with an ambulance cart standing in front. A soldier emerged, carrying rolled-up canvas stretchers; another unloaded a clinking crate of bottles from the cart. Then from behind her, she heard singing.

'*Daishy, daishy*,' the words came, '*give me your anshwer do...*'

She stopped and turned. Two soldiers were carrying a stretcher, and it seemed to be the casualty, wrapped tightly in a blanket, who was doing the singing.

'Oi,' the casualty said, 'careful where you're goin'. I'm fucking sore, all right? *...you'd look shweet upon the seat...*'

Clara squealed, wrested her arm from her captor's grip, and ran. 'Jack?' she said. 'Jack?' She got closer, and the casualty had straw-coloured hair, and she knew his voice, even singing that silly, stupid, beautiful song. 'Oh,' she squealed, 'it's Jack!' and now she was weeping, and her throat was too tight, and she was smiling, and she reached the stretcher, and reached out for him, and that was his face, his dear face, and his silly grin.

He stopped singing, and frowned. 'ello, Clara,' he said. 'Whatchoo doin' here? I've gorra really shore shoulder, y'know. Woo! Look at them clouds...'

The bearers had stopped, confused, and now the soldier had caught up with Clara, and had pinioned her arms behind her back. But Clara felt as if she was floating.

'Night, night, Clara,' said Jack. '*On a bishycle made for two...*'

The captain was asking Clara something about spying, and who the boy was, when there was a sound of hooves, and half a dozen riders cantered into the courtyard, their clothes and faces spattered in mud. Soldiers hurried to grab their bridles and help them dismount.

'Hold her,' the captain snapped, and ran up to the new arrivals. She saluted a thick-set officer, speaking quick and low. Another soldier ran up and handed a towel to the officer, who pulled off her cap and wiped her face. Then, with a nod to the captain, she and the other arrivals strode towards the farmhouse. As they passed Clara, Jack and the stretcher-bearers, she gave them a brief glance.

She'd gone another ten paces before the officer stopped and held up a hand. Then she turned, marched back to Clara, and stared at her. 'I don't believe this,' she said. 'Please,' she went on with a sigh, 'tell me it's not you again.'

Clara frowned. Then she stared, and for a moment her mouth wouldn't work.

The captain saluted. 'General, Ma'am,' she said, 'this one was with some Anglians. The one on the stretcher, we found him in the yard this morning. Thought they might be spies. Need to question them, Ma'am.'

'G-general Callington!' interrupted Clara. The stretcher-bearers stood irresolute. Jack stopped singing, and frowned at the clouds.

Callington it was: the soldier who'd once interrogated Clara and Sophia on the road, and who'd led the force that defeated Hurn. Now she turned to the captain, indicating Clara's bruised cheek. 'What happened to her face? And,' she added, pointing to Jack, 'how did he get injured?'

Clara spoke up. 'It was the Anglians,' she said. 'They did this to us. We haven't been harmed here.'

'Uh, yes, Ma'am,' the captain said, glancing at Clara and nodding. 'Are the prisoners known to us, Ma'am?'

Clara felt Callington's gaze boring into her. She tried to return it.

'Well, this one is,' sneered Callington. 'D'you know what she wants? She wants *peace*.' She nodded, and poked a gloved finger at Clara. 'She wants us to not fight back, wants us to lie down, and let Anglia walk all over us.'

Clara opened her mouth to speak, then thought better of it. She saw the other officers looking at each other and frowning.

'We lost *four hundred* soldiers yesterday, Clara Perdue,' said Callington, jabbing a finger southward, 'not ten miles from here.' She was so close that Clara could smell her stale breath. 'Four hundred good women and men!' Her jaw was tight, and her voice quivered. 'All dead.' She sliced a hand through the air. 'They'll never go home again, never see their daughters. And you'd have us ignore that, pretend it never happened? Hey?'

Clara swallowed. She looked at Jack, and thought of everything she'd seen, and everyone she'd lost. 'Look at the fields,' she said. 'Look at those crops, washed away by the rain. Look at the towns sinking under the sea. While you and

Anglia fight, people are starving. It's like–' she saw the image of a small girl and boy, in a little boat on the Thames '–it's like we're going over a weir. We've got to stop fighting, and all paddle in the same direction.'

Behind her, the captain suppressed a snort. Callington grimaced, then cuffed Clara across the face with the back of her hand, almost knocking her over.

'Oi!' said Jack.

'Take them,' Callington told the captain, 'and put them on the next cart that's going to Exeter. Yes,' she snapped before the captain could protest, 'I *do* know the rules. But she's no threat,' she sneered, looking Clara in the eye. 'She's just a lunatic. Come,' she said, beckoning to her aides.

'*Talk* to them!' Clara called after her. 'Talk to General Clark!'

'Shut up,' snarled the captain, her lip curling, 'or I might forget I'm supposed to let you go.'

It was mid-afternoon before they were put, along with a load of empty crates and boxes, into a tarpaulin-roofed cart. Clara had to give Jack a leg up so that he sat on the edge, then he rolled over and wriggled himself further in. The smells told Clara that the crates had been used to pack food, and maybe clothing, but also ammunition. Now they were, she guessed, being taken back to a depot to be refilled.

Jack was pale. His arm was in a sling and his shoulder was heavily strapped, but the brandy and spirits had worn off and he was clearly in great pain. For now, he was afraid to talk. 'Feel like I'm gonna throw up,' he croaked.

Only when the cart set off were they were given a couple of stale rolls and a water-bottle to share. As the convoy rolled out of the farmyard, Clara could hear gunfire again. Although it sounded far off, she was glad that there was a soldier riding inside with them, watching the road behind. The soldier chain-smoked and said little.

They sat with their backs to a crate, their sides pressing against each other. Clara took Jack's hand, interlacing their fingers, and squeezed it tightly. 'I thought you were dead,' she said. 'I couldn't stay with you – the Wessexers must have killed the Anglians – they knocked me out...'

He lifted their hands a little. 'And I thought,' he said, his breath still coming in gasps, 'I thought I'd lost you.'

Clara wiped her eyes on a sleeve. 'How did you find the farm? In the storm, I mean.'

'Got lucky,' said Jack, wincing as the cart lurched. 'Thunder woke me up...'

'Does it hurt much?'

He glanced at her. 'Yeah. It fucking hurts.'

She grimaced, and squeezed his hand again.

'The medic said the bone's pretty smashed up. But they got the bullet out.' He shut his eyes.

Clara swallowed. 'You should rest.'

He tried to smile. 'I am doing.' Then he said, 'What happened to your face?'

'I got punched.'

'Pair of us, eh?'

SCORPION

After a couple of hours dusk was falling, and they camped for the night outside a small village. By now the sounds of fighting had been left behind, but Clara could tell that the guard was still alert, even when she climbed out and stretched her limbs.

The soldiers gave Clara a fresh dressing to put on Jack's wound, but there wasn't enough light and she had to leave it till the morning. Even then she wasn't allowed much time, so she had to hurry it. The wound was deep, like a purple crater, and she grimaced as she dabbed some spirit on it, making him flinch. Fleetingly, she thought that the last time she'd touched a man's bare chest it had been Xavi's. Jack sucked in his breath.

'Sorry,' she said.

'Your hands are cold, is all,' said Jack, trying to smile.

Whatever she'd done, it seemed to help. After the convoy set off, Jack slept the morning away.

The rest of the trip passed in long hours jolting in the wagon, brief rest stops, little food, and cold nights. But by the third morning, they were within twelve miles of Exeter. The weather had been variable, wind and showers alternating with colder, drier spells; this morning, a fine drizzle was blowing on a stiff breeze from the south. Jack, who'd been by turns taciturn and sleepy, seemed a bit more like himself this morning.

'You got any money?' he asked Clara.

She shifted her position, leaning against one of the larger crates. 'No, it was in my pack. Are you wondering how to get to the farm?'

Jack nodded. 'I guess they'll just drop us in Exeter and leave us to fend for ourselves.' He sighed. 'Wouldn't mind a bit of food, too.

'We'll think of something,' said Clara. 'We usually do.'

'Yeah,' said Jack. 'We usually do.' He grimaced, and shifted his arm. Then he said, 'We're actually gonna make it, aren't we? We're gonna get back to your parents.'

Clara nodded. 'Yes,' she said. 'We are.' Her throat felt dry.

'I'm sorry you didn't get to London,' he said.

Clara sat up straighter. 'I just hope Riss and Anna can talk to the general. Then at least we've tried.'

With a thud, the cart jolted into a deep pothole. Jack yelped, and swore.

Drizzle continued to fall as they left behind a pine wood and entered a compact village with red-tiled roofs and once-tidy vegetable patches, now muddied by the rain.

'What will you do?' asked Clara. 'When we get there?'

In the gloom, she could see that Jack was peering at her. 'Depends,' he said. 'I mean, if it's all right, can I stay for a bit?'

'Of course.' Clara wondered if she'd said that a little too quickly.

'Just while me shoulder mends, y'know. Though, that could be a while. Thanks for bandagin' me, by the way.'

Clara stared out through the back of the cart, where the guard was lighting yet another cigarette. It was easy to see where they'd been, but she couldn't see where they were going. 'What will you do after that?' she said, without changing her gaze.

'I'll find something. There's not many things I'm good at. Burgling's not gonna be much use, I guess. They'll be looking for labourers, though. Like I say, maybe in Exeter. Or maybe in – um, what's that place further on?'

'Plymouth?'

'There.'

'If it's like Anglia,' said Clara, 'there'll be press-gangs.' She found herself frowning. What next for her, she wondered? Living with her parents, she supposed – except this time, she'd know that James wasn't just a servant. It'd be weird. Lots of things, she decided, stealing a glance at Jack, would be weird.

'Jack,' said Clara, 'I been thinking.'

'Oh, shit,' said Jack.

She chuckled. 'I've been doing a lot of thinking. About – about everything.'

'That's what I like about you,' he said. 'Never do things by halves, do ya?'

'Shut up, you. I mean everything I've done – since I left the Academy. Well, since before that.' She looked at her fingers. 'All the trouble I've caused – no, Jack, I *have* – and all the stupid things I've done. I think I know why it was.'

The cart bounced across some ruts, and Jack swore. 'Go on,' he said, gasping.

'It was Amy. Amy Martin.'

Jack turned to look at her. He was silhouetted against the sky through the back of the cart, and she couldn't make out his expression. 'Go on,' he said.

'You know what I did to her. I betrayed her, and I ruined her life. She might be dead. Jack, I've hated myself ever since.'

'You shouldn't,' he said.

'I've been trying to atone, to make up for it. All the things I've done – you'd call them crazy things – well, that's why. You said it was always about me, didn't you?'

'Well, I–'

'You know me better than I know myself, Jack.' She nudged him gently. 'And that's a bit scary.'

The cart rolled on.

44 Home

The soldiers dropped them at a military camp on the outskirts of Exeter. The sergeant who'd been in charge of the convoy pointed them in the direction of a large inn. 'Can't take you no further,' she said, 'but you can put up there for the night. Oh, and the general says she's given your names to the local police, so make sure that's the last they ever hear of you.'

Clara nodded. 'Don't worry,' she said. 'We'll keep out of trouble.'

At the inn they were given the remains of the evening's stew, and a night in the hayloft, in exchange for some chores, Clara doing the heavy ones because Jack couldn't use his right arm. They both slept badly, but by mid-morning the next day they'd trekked into town and cadged a lift with a carter who was heading up the Clyst valley. When she dropped them off, there only remained a couple of miles to cover on foot. Following her directions, they eventually came upon a stretch of land that Jack recognised, where the road descended into a wide valley before crossing the river at a narrow stone bridge. Jack's shoulder was painful, and he was having to walk slowly. Then, as the road rose to meet a mixed wood that covered the western slope, they came upon a painted signboard that read *Community Farm – 1 mile*.

They passed among solid, stone-built houses with strong overhanging roofs; barns, also of stone, built halfway down the valley sides; vegetable plots, protected by thick hedges; deep drainage ditches, ponds, and a water-mill with a rapid-running race. Jack pointed out the excavations for a planned underground reservoir, which would supply the farm during droughts. Then the road wound on through groves of coppiced hazel into a wide yard, with a large house, cottages, stables and barns. Two closed carts, laden with produce, were making ready to set off for town. A woman stopped them and asked where they were going, but at Jack's answer she just nodded, pointed up the valley and wished them good day. It made a change from being accused of spying, or getting beaten up.

The path, thick-hedged and tree-lined, wound between fields grazed by Highland cattle and hardy Herdwick sheep, then continued up the hill towards the head of the valley. Clara found her heart racing. She was about to face her parents, whom she'd abandoned the day she'd taken Jack's place all those weeks ago. After everything she'd been through, she was here by good luck; but what if, she wondered, that luck had deserted her along the way? What if she'd never returned? She pictured Sophia and James, thinking about her day after day, their hopes gradually dwindling and their lives becoming sadder and sadder. She was thoroughly ashamed of herself.

'Jack?' she said.

'It's all right,' he panted, 'it's not far now.'

'Jack, stay with me, would you? When I meet my – my parents, I mean. I'm scared.'

'Scared? Why?'

'Because I've been running from them, and I've hurt them, and...' They reached the track that led up to the house. She took his hand. 'Please?' she said.

He nodded. 'Sure,' he said.

Sure, thought Clara. Not *it'd better if you faced them yourself*, not *it's your problem*, not even *I'd rather not*. Just *sure*.

'Anyhow,' he added. 'I'm a bit scared too.'

Of course, there was no problem. When they reached the house, a small affair dug back into the hillside, Sophia and James were overjoyed to see Clara again. There were tears, and smiles, and laughter, and more tears. They hugged her and cried over her, and danced around her, and James even managed to hop, on his one leg and his sturdy crutch. They offered them tea, and food, and then forgot to make anything. Jack's role was limited to being congratulated and slapped on the back – which made him groan – and being kissed almost as much as Clara. And even later, when the sun went down behind the clouds and the rain returned, and the four of them sat around the small, smoky fire, and Clara told of her adventures, nobody asked her the question, why did you do it? Not yet, at any rate. The time would come for them to ask, and the time would come for her to answer, but it wasn't tonight.

After a heartier meal than either Clara or Jack had eaten in weeks, Jack dozed off in a chair and Clara, to her surprise, found herself falling asleep too. What the future held, she didn't know, but it was good to think that when she woke in the morning, she'd still be safe.

A week later Sophia took Jack to see a doctor in Exeter, to check his shoulder, and together with some business she had to transact, that meant them staying overnight. Meanwhile, Clara had settled herself into farming life, recalling the things that Sophia and James had taught her at Briar Farm to such good effect that she was able to help James with the lambing. The sheep were in one of their winter folds, protected by thick dry-stone walls. By now, in February, the grass had been grazed almost to nothing, and the sheep were living off the stores of hay and oats. Despite the muddy ground, James managed well on his crutch, and was attending to a multiple birth in the far corner of the fold. Clara herself was helping a ewe whose lamb had got her leg reversed. James had shown her what to do many times before, but it was still tricky and needed a lot of concentration, and she didn't notice when two heads appeared over the wall.

'Wow, Clara,' said Jack. 'Never thought I'd see you with your hand inside a sheep.'

Clara started. Sophia sniggered.

'Not a good time, Jack Pike,' snapped Clara. 'I nearly lost hold of it!'

'Want a hand?' asked Sophia.

'No,' said Clara, 'I think I've got her straight now. Come on, girl...nearly there. Ah...here she comes!'

The lamb slid out. Clara cleared its nostrils, rubbed it down with straw, and presented it to the mother, who began to lick it clean. Clara stood and stretched her back, while Sophia and Jack applauded. James, whose ewe had also given birth safely, came lumbering carefully through the mud.

'You got back all right?' he said, smiling. 'How's the shoulder?'

'Getting better,' said Sophia, looking at Jack, 'but he's got to be careful.'

'I've got *exercises* to do,' said Jack, holding up his arm, still in its sling, and looking up to heaven.

Clara caught his eye and smiled.

'Did you get the oil?' asked James.

'No,' said Sophia, shaking her head. 'That is, we did get flax oil, enough for the lamps. We dropped most of it off at the stores,' she said, gesturing down the valley, 'and we've got a small can in the cart. But there's no kerosene. They say the refineries have run out. There's no crude, and they think Anglia's run out too. There've been no tankers for months.'

James whistled. 'We'll just have to make do, I suppose. Anyhow,' he said, forcing a smile, 'I've done us some pork for dinner. Got to feed Jack up.' And with a nod, he set off up the hill to the house. Sophia followed, leaving Jack with Clara, who was frowning.

'They said it'd come,' she said.

'Who?' said Jack. 'What'd come?'

'At school. They said there'd be a time when there was no more oil, and no more coal.'

'Thought there was a bit of coal left.'

Clara nodded. 'Yes, they used to run the *Scorpion* on it. But that's running out, too.'

'We can manage, though, right?'

'Yes,' said Clara. 'We've come a long way. A place like this–' she gestured around the valley '–is set up to be self-sufficient.' She gave a brief laugh. 'It's not all that long since they were handing out licences to generate electricity in London. Well, they won't have to worry about that any more.' She looked at her bloodied, sticky hands. 'Got to wash this off,' she said. 'Come to the stream with me?'

Jack followed, rummaging in his rucksack as he went. 'I got you something,' he said. 'Well, your mam did, but it was my idea.'

'A news-sheet,' said Clara, turning round. 'What does it say?'

'Well, there's two things,' said Jack.

Clara arrived at the swift-flowing stream and stooped to rinse her arms. 'Eooch!' she shrieked. 'It's freezing!'

'Clara, there's a truce,' said Jack.

'What?' said Clara, turning quickly and nearly stepping into the stream.

'It's true,' said Jack. 'The fighting's stopped. Here, read it for yerself.'

Clara pulled up a tuft of long grass and wiped her arms. Then, grabbing the news-sheet, she sat on a fallen log and scanned the page. Jack settled himself beside her.

'There's a ceasefire,' said Clara. ' "Anglia has agreed to peace talks". That's great!'

'Read on,' said Jack.

' "In a joint statement, President Lanyon and General Clark said there was an urgent need to focus on securing food supplies, improving weather protection and keeping order. An immediate ceasefire has been agreed, and formal negotiations will begin in three weeks." '

'Next line.'

' " 'The boat is about to go over the weir,' said General Clark. 'Right now we all need to be paddling in the same direction.' " '

Clara's mouth fell open. She let the paper fall to her lap. 'Riss!' she said. 'And Anna! They must have seen her.'

'And those are your words, Clara,' said Jack. 'You said that to Callington, didn't ya? She must've been in on this.'

But Clara sat blinking, saying nothing.

'I used ter think you was stuck-up,' said Jack, ''cause you thought you was special. And I used to say you wasn't, you was just ordinary. Well,' he said, tapping the paper, 'looks like you *was* special, all along.'

Now Clara looked at him. 'No, no,' she said. 'This can't be because of me. Riss and Anna did it. It's just – well, it's common sense. Coincidence. They'd have realised it, without me, sooner or later.'

'Well,' said Jack with a quick smile, '*I* reckon you're special.'

Clara's stomach gave a lurch. 'W–what's the other thing?' she asked, peering at the paper so as not to look at him.

'Down there,' said Jack, pointing at a short article in the bottom corner.

' "Salvage",' read Clara. It says there's a wreck, on Orcombe Rocks – where's that?'

'Your mam says they're not far from Exeter. Says we could get there an' back in a day.'

' "...a steelhull...unusual shape...might be French..." ' Clara frowned.

'*Unusual shape*,' said Jack.

Clara read on. ' "...must have ridden low in the water...two hundred feet long..." Oh!' She put a hand to her mouth.

'Sounds like the *Scorpion*,' said Jack. 'And,' he added, tapping the paper again, 'they want help breaking it up before the sea takes it back.' He looked at Clara. 'Your mam says we could go down tomorrow. Take a cart. D'you wanna go?'

Clara nodded. 'Yes,' she said. 'I – I don't know why, but I think it'll do me good.'

'Me too,' said Jack. 'Not that I'll be much help.'

'Nothing wrong with your other arm.'

They lapsed into silence. The wind blew colder, and Clara shivered. 'You really think I could have changed their minds?'

Jack grinned. 'O special one!' he said.

She poked him in the arm, only remembering after she'd done it that, to her relief, it was his good one. 'You and I used to argue a lot,' she said.

'Yeah,' said Jack, 'we did. At least you never tried to kill me, though.'

'No,' she said, 'but I did beat you up and scratch your face.'

'I deserved it, though.'

Clara shook her head. 'No, you didn't.'

Again they were silent, watching the starlings wheeling above the hill. From down the valley came the lowing of cattle.

'I – I wish you wouldn't go,' said Clara.

'What's that?' said Jack.

'I wish you wouldn't go away. You could stay here. For good, I mean.'

Jack looked at his feet. 'Well, I–'

'Jack,' she said, taking his arm, 'I want to ask–' she swallowed '–that night, in the cottage, when you kissed me while I was asleep–'

'Clara, not *that* again,' said Jack, his head down. 'I've said I'm sorry.'

'No – it's okay, really it is – but I mean, why?'

Jack frowned, but said nothing.

'I'd just like to know, that's all. What was in your mind? I mean–'

Jack was shaking his head. He sighed. 'The moon was lighting up your face,' he said. 'You was all silver. And I was thinkin', I was lucky you was with me.' He blew out his cheeks and looked away, before turning to her again. 'And you – you looked beautiful, Clara. And I thought I'd never get another chance...'

Clara shut her eyes. There seemed to be a swelling in her chest, and something was pressing behind her eyes. 'Gmumh,' she said.

'Sorry,' said Jack, wearily, and Clara felt the log shift as he got up.

She sniffed, and wiped her eyes. Jack was trudging back up the hill. 'Jack Pike!' she shouted. 'You come back here this minute!' She pointed to the log.

Frowning, he walked slowly back and sat down. 'Never meant to make you cry,' he began. But he stopped because Clara had taken his hand and kissed it.

She looked in his face. A small smile was playing about his lips. 'I don't want you to go, Jack,' she said. 'You're my best friend.'

He squeezed her hand. ''course I'll stay. It was just, I didn't know how you felt.' He blinked quickly, then looked her in the eyes. 'You're my best friend, too, Clara. My *only* friend. And if you can put up with me–'

She pulled him into a hug, being careful not to hurt his shoulder. 'Don't say that, Jack. I'm the one who's been crazy, I'm the one who needs putting up with.'

'Maybe,' he whispered, his chin resting on her shoulder, 'we could put up with each other.'

She felt his voice tickle her ear. There was nothing for it, she decided, and she gave him a kiss on the cheek.

'Cla-ara! Ja-ack!' James's voice came from the direction of the house. 'Dinner's up! Oh!'

They looked up, to see James hopping hastily back into the house.

'I think he saw us,' whispered Clara, her voice trembling as she tried to speak while smiling.

'I can stay, then?' said Jack, as they stood.

She chuckled, sniffed, and wiped away a tear.

45 The Scorpion Returns

'Just see if there's anything that might be useful,' Sophia told Clara the next morning. She handed her fifty Wessex pounds. 'And nothing too heavy, either. The roads are bad, and we don't want that cart damaged. And,' she added to Jack, who was already sitting in the cart, 'you watch your arm, young man.'

Clara nodded, and climbed up. They took a route well to the east of Exeter, because, according to Sophia, the western road, from Exmouth to the Point, had been washed away some years ago. Low clouds rolled overhead, but there was a smell of spring in the hedgerows. Sometimes they looked at each other and smiled. By late morning they were passing through the dense woodland on Budleigh Common, where the thick-lying leaves and needles deadened the horse's footfalls. They caught their first scent of the sea.

'I was gonna ask a favour,' said Jack.

'Yeah?' said Clara, gently flicking at the reins.

'I should tell you,' he said. 'I – well, I can't write.'

'You can't *write*?' said Clara.

'Not much, anyway,' said Jack, blushing. 'I can read, an' that, but there was no school in our village. Never even saw a pen-and-ink till I was with the Scrapers. So, I was hopin' – when me shoulder gets better...'

'You want me to teach you?'

He nodded, raising his eyebrows in a question.

'All right. Exclusive lessons, just for you, Jack. I hope that's not the only reason you want to stay, though.'

He chuckled.

'Anyhow,' went on Clara, 'it'll take a while. It's going to be hard work on the farm, really hard. And at this time of year, we'll spend all the daylight hours working.'

'Yeah,' said Jack. 'Need to learn it, though. It'll be, like, useful.'

Clara was quiet for a minute. Then she said, '*Everything's* going to get harder, you know. Without fossil oil, it'll all change again. Goodness knows what's happening in the rest of the world.' She thought of all those countries, near and far: deserts spreading, seas rising, crops failing, rivers drying. Starvation, war, refugees...

'Uh, half a mile to the next turn,' said Jack, peering at the map. 'We're never gonna know about the rest of the world,' he went on, 'if the weather's always so bad that you can't even cross the Channel. How would we find out?'

'Yes. But here, we're lucky. We might pull through. If they're really going to stop fighting, we could have a chance. Big farms like ours, they're a good idea. And we haven't lost all the old skills yet...'

'So we won't be wearing animal skins any time soon?'

Clara laughed. That was something, she realised, she'd been doing more of lately.

As they came through Littleham, they found themselves following another cart down a hedge-lined lane, then out onto some stony ground on the headland. Here the once-tall cliffs had crumbled away to leave a gradual slope, of red earth and rocks, that led down to the shoreline. At the head of the track a few women were supervising the passage of carts up and down, and Clara and Jack had to wait while a large, high-sided wagon toiled up the slope, its wheels often slipping in the mud.

'Another reason not to get too much stuff,' said Jack, watching the horses snorting and steaming.

They looked out to sea, where shafts of sunlight broke through the canopy and played on the spindrift that the wind was whipping off the waves.

'I've been thinking,' said Clara.

'Again?' said Jack.

She ignored him. 'You know I said it was all because of Amy,' she said. 'What I did?'

'Yeah?'

'It was really the Republic's fault, wasn't it? They made me what I was. I try to tell myself that.' She pouted. 'Time I moved on, I think.'

He squeezed her arm.

The wagon had finally managed to reach the top of the slope, and as it rolled on towards the road Clara urged their own horse forward. Making a wide turn, she managed to get the cart onto the track, then safely down onto the low bank just above the wreck. From a distance, there was little resemblance to the sleek black vessel she'd first seen in Southampton Water. But as they got closer, Clara began to recognise the *Scorpion*, and she found herself awestruck. There was a curved outline that was certainly part of a hull, but it had been snapped off, leaving jagged edges; and it was all of a ruddy hue, like the sandstone on which it perched. It was up-ended so that the stern was below the tideline and the exposed, shattered midship was twenty feet in the air. The prow was missing.

They hobbled the horse and scrambled down the remaining slope to where the salvage gang were dragging things they'd salvaged: wood, fittings, pipes, cables, chains, even a large bulkhead door.

'Interested in anything?' said a woman in a thick sweater and sea-cap who carried a leather money-pouch over her shoulder. 'I'm Dwina. I'm the receiver here. Have a look, bring it over, and I'll offer you a price.'

Jack nodded to Clara and walked down onto the foreshore. Clara, meanwhile, stood with folded arms, watching the gang scrambling and climbing over the wreck. 'The power of the sea,' she murmured.

'Ah,' said Dwina, nodding. 'Many a ship's come to grief here. Used to be as you could see the rocks at low tide. Nowadays, the sea's that much higher, but them rocks are still there.' She nodded. 'This 'un must've ridden low in the water when she was afloat. Mind, she'd been abandoned long afore she hit the rocks.'

Clara looked at her. Better, she thought, not to mention that she knew the wreck's history. 'Sad, isn't it?' she said.

'Aye, it's always sad when a ship goes down. Pity she's so well built, though,' she added. 'The innards we can take out, but them plates is thick, and they're riveted solid. If the sea breaks her up some more, we could salvage some of the steel, but we haven't the tools to break it up by ourselves. Lot of good metal there.'

A couple of women staggered up the beach carrying armfuls of piping, and Clara took the opportunity to leave Dwina to it. She found that Jack had selected some usable wooden planks and beams, together with a couple of small, slightly bent, iron doors. Then together they made their way closer to the wreck, their feet sinking into the sand. A little rain began to fall. The sound of the breakers resounded through the hollow hull, producing a metallic ringing that somehow added to the melancholy scene.

'There's the boilers,' said Clara, pointing to a pair of broad cylinders, each ten feet long, with a mass of pipework exposed. 'And there, Jack, see? Up there – that's the furnace room.' The floor where she, Xavi and Hashim had once stood was suspended high above them, visible through the *Scorpion's* ripped-open carcass. Where the toilet cubicle should have been, where she and Xavi had hidden when the coal was loaded, there was a gaping hole.

'I told the receiver it was sad,' she went on, 'to see it like this.'

'But that's where they beat you up. It's where they gave you the shock-stick.'

'Yes,' said Clara, shivering at the memory. 'But it's where I lived, for a while...' She trailed off. 'Hashim said we should remember the dead,' she added.

'Yeah,' said Jack.

'So many,' said Clara, blinking.

'Matty,' said Jack, shaking his head. 'Shouldn't have happened to her...'

Clara nodded. Xavi, Hashim, Tori Shavila. Old Catwall. The list went on and on.

She felt Jack's hand on her shoulder.

They haggled for a good price, got some help in loading their haul onto the cart, and took their place in the queue before driving back up the slope. Here Clara turned the horse aside and reined in. 'One last look,' she said. 'We'll still get home in the light.' *Home*, she thought. She'd only been there a week, but already she was calling the farm "home". She thought she knew why.

'I don't know if I said it, Jack,' she said, wrapping her cloak around her as the rain strengthened, 'but thank you.' She took his hand. 'For coming back for me,' she said, looking again at the sorry remains of the Scorpion. 'You went back to Southampton, and you followed me all the way. You got me out of the water.'

Jack shrugged. 'Couldn't have done it without Tori's help. Besides–'

'Oh,' she said, 'I know you said you were doing it for my parents. But that wasn't all, was it?'

Jack twice started to speak before he said, 'I wanted to get something right, you know? I'd never done nothing much. I wanted to prove that I could get a job done.'

'Was that all?'

He sighed, and shifted closer. 'Nah,' he admitted. 'It was you. I reckon you got inside my head the first time we met.'

'When you found me in the barn? With the Scrapers?'

'No,' he said, glancing at his fingers. 'When you let me get away with that loaf.'

Clara smiled. 'Then? At the Academy, when I caught you stealing?'

'And you let me go,' he said. 'I'd have starved without that bread. Made a bit of an impression, you know?'

'And that's why you came and fished me out of the water,' she said, looking again at the wreck. 'I'd have died, if you hadn't.'

'You wanted to go back to the ship,' said Jack.

Clara stared again at the remains of the furnace-room. 'I knew what Xavi was going to do. I *knew* he was going to try and sink it. It drove me crazy, I think.'

The wind was blowing Clara's hair out behind her, and rippling both of their cloaks.

'You was in love with him,' said Jack.

Clara turned. 'Yes, I was. I wanted his body, Jack. So much.' She noticed Jack was going red. 'But there was something else. He seemed – he seemed so lost. I suppose he *was* lost, really. I felt like I wanted to protect him.' She sighed. 'He's gone now,' she went on, 'and I'm sad about it. But I think – I think he always knew he wasn't going to make it off the Scorpion. And when it came to it, he wanted revenge more than he wanted life.'

'Yeah, maybe,' said Jack, studying her face.

'But, Jack,' she said, 'do you know what's better than being in love?'

Jack frowned. 'No. What?'

She pulled him close and kissed him on the lips, not minding the spots of rain spattering her cheeks. 'Being in love with a friend,' she said. 'And,' she added, 'that's the truth.'

Also by Phil Gilvin

Truth Sister
Truth Sister
Blackwolf
Scorpion

Watch for more at https://philgilvin.com/.

About the Author

Phil Gilvin lives with his wife in Swindon, UK, nestling in the rolling downland of Wiltshire amid neolithic barrows, ancient droveways and stone circles – and the M4 motorway. When his children grew too old to have stories read to them he turned to writing, going to lots of workshops and winning a number of short story prizes. His short stories have regularly been shortlisted in magazine competitions and have featured in local anthologies. *Truth Sister* is his first published novel (his first two, unpublished, got consigned to the "that's how you learn" pile). Phil is a retired physicist, and he now enjoys walking in aforesaid downland as well as listening to classical music and prog rock, and murdering folk songs.

Read more at https://philgilvin.com/.

Milton Keynes UK
Ingram Content Group UK Ltd.
UKHW011309180224
438033UK00004B/17